Meander
Master Mariner

by
Captain S Baxter

DEDICATION

Although written by Grandpa with no indication of the dedications he would have made for his stories, I feel the duty and honour falls upon me.

Therefore, I dedicate these stories to his wife, children and grandchildren who have enjoyed, and occasionally groaned, at his great and sometimes long-winded stories of any and every imaginable subject.

I wish you were here to see your stories finally published Gramps. Love and miss you very much.

CONTENTS

INTRODUCTION

When looking for plain paper in Grandpa's office one day, I came across a notebook of his and glanced through it to remind me of his handwriting. On opening it up, I tried to read what it said and saw that it seemed to start mid-sentence. I read a bit more and it sounded story-like and, on the front, had the letters, 'T.W.M'. I dug deeper in the drawer I was looking in but could find nothing more to solve the mystery of this hardback notebook. I took it to my room, living with Gran at the time, determined to decipher the handwriting of Gramps (the teacher in me, I think) and promised myself I would ask Gran as soon as she was home.

Gran could vaguely remember the "story" but could tell me no more. No idea where any more notebooks could be found nor what it was about.

The mystery remained unsolved for months. I had moved out at this point and was, again, looking for something in Grandpa's usual storage spaces – this time for tools in the garage. I opened a drawer hoping to find a metal file and found a notebook matching the first. Excited, I examined it and found it to be part of the same subject as the first! A bit more rummaging, and more emerged, followed by brown envelopes filled with papers written using a type writer. I took some of the pages out and teared up when I realised I had found the whole story and eight more! I quickly piled them up in a sturdy bag and took them home for a better look (I asked Gran first, obviously).

It was obvious from the letters that accompanied the stories that Grandpa was trying to get them published and I was wary at first to read them in case my teacher head got too critical of my wonderful Grandpa. The first story I read was "The Birthday Present". I was fully prepared for a long-winded story of complication and excessive detail as was his usual story-telling practice – which I always enjoyed listening to despite this. I was even more pleased when I saw that Grandpa's story-telling ability came alive on the page and, from then on, I was determined to share these treasures with the rest of the family and, finally, getting Grandpa's dream of having them published, accomplished.

So here it is. Started in late Spring 2017. Typing and proofreading finished early December. And hopefully delivered to you soon after.

183,307 words

598 pages

149 hours to type

27 hours to proofread

10 hours to design front cover

9 stories

1 book

1 Gramps

1 THE MAN FROM DOWN UNDER

It had been a quiet Saturday afternoon, the silence only occasionally punctured by the sound of a car passing in the sunlit square outside. Quiet that is until the telephone suddenly commenced ringing. It was snatched up before the third ring and a brief conversation ensued.

"What is he like?"

Katherine fired the question at her twin sister the moment that young lady had returned the telephone to its rest.

"Blond, tall and gangling, wearing a wide-brimmed hat with corks dangling from it and holding a can of beer – typical Australian in fact," Then seriously, "How would I know? I've only spoken to him on the phone."

"Well what did he sound like you idiot?"

Katherine and Penelope were nineteen years old and were interested in tennis, modern 'music', and men. Particularly men.

"His voice sounded nice enough, not much of an Australian accent, in fact it had quite an educated tone."

"He could be interesting Pen. When did he say he would visit us?

Which afternoon? I did not quite catch what was said."

"This afternoon. He is settling in at his hotel and will come out afterwards, he could not say exactly what time."

"Today! He might have given us a little warning."

"Why? He only intends to drop in and see us whilst he is in the country, it will hardly be a social call. No doubt he is under instructions from his Mother to make contact."

"Awful bore for him, having to visit relations he has never seen. I wonder what he knows about us Pen?"

"About as much as we know of him I should imagine, very, very little. I could not even place the name, you probably heard me repeat it when he said who he was."

"'Jim Kelly'. He must be a very distant relation, I've never heard of any other Kellys in the family," said Katherine, "However a good, honest Australian name no doubt."

"Somewhat more believable than that character in Jane's new novel anyway."

The twins both laughed.

"'Paul Carrington' wasn't it? No, of course he was the one with the blond hair and dark eyebrows in her Cornish story," said Katherine.

Jane, the twins' elder sister, spent much of her spare time writing romantic novels and short stories which she sent at regular intervals to various publishers. Sad to relate the publishers, after the usual decent interval, sent them back with equal regularity.

"'Nigel Carlton' it was." Penelope laughed again, "Of all the absurd names for a New Zealand sheep farmer. Jane could surely have thought up a better name than that. She must have a penchant for men's names beginning with the letter 'C'."

"I wonder when she is going to let us see the new novel? Generally she is keen enough to let us read what she has written."

"You have already read it Kath!"

"So have you but 'officially' I mean. A sneak preview is not the same thing. I am dying to comment on it, some if it is quite good but that name will have to go for a start."

"I wonder what Jane would say if she found out that we had already read the thing?" mused Penelope.

"If she did not want it read she would not have left it lying about."

"In the bottom of a drawer beneath her underwear is hardly 'lying about' Kath!"

"I was looking for a pair of tights, she often borrows my things," Katherine replied defensively, "Anyway you had no scruples in reading it with me."

"It certainly was quite a story. A bit torrid even for one of Jane's yarns."

"I wonder why she wrote it in diary form Pen?"

"No doubt because she has tried everything else, third person, first person, even," Penelope continued in sepulchral tones, "'from beyond the grave' – you remember that macabre thing about the murdered doctor's wife?"

"Yes, that really was creepy, I did not like it at all. The sexy love stories she writes are much more my cup of tea."

"The new one for instance? Suggested Penelope, "it's about the hottest thing she has written so far. It will be a wonder if anyone dare publish it."

"No doubt a normal reaction of a frustrated spinster," decided Katherine.

"I loved that amorous scene in the hotel room," said Penelope, "It made me tingle from head to toe."

"When does one become a spinster?" Katherine continued her train of thought, "Jane is twenty-six. I wonder if she is still a virgin?"

"It certainly makes one wonder where she gets her ideas. There is little enough opportunity here to get in any fieldwork – although she never says much about what she does when she is away on holiday."

Katherine gave a little giggle, "Probably spends most of her time at the side of the hotel swimming pool polishing her nails and penning letters and post-cards. She certainly likes writing."

"Talking of her writing," Penelope said, "she will have to dream up a happier ending for that diary thing if she intends making it into a novel. I thought the ending was awful. After the great night of passion the girl was obviously getting too serious so the hero takes the classic way out – sends himself a telegram, 'Father seriously ill – hurry home'. Exit gallant lover. Dead corny!" She laughed, "In spite of that I would like to know where the hotel was supposed to be, it sounded quite a place to visit."

"It must have been somewhere pretty hot judging by the general lack of clothing," decided Katherine, "some tropical island or Australia or somewhere..... Australia! That Kelly fellow could be here at any moment and I am an absolute mess!" She leaped to her feet scattering the magazines from her lap, her pyjamas and kimono flapping as she searched for slippers under a chair. "I'll take a shower and get dressed....." she glanced at the light coat and handbag her sister had dropped onto a chair when she reached for the telephone a few minutes earlier and smiled sweetly, "whilst you are out doing that urgent shopping of yours."

Penelope turned, "This from my sister who but half an hour ago swore that nothing short of an earthquake would move her from her bean-bag and Hi-Hi before Mummy and Jane came home!" She glanced down at her old T-shirt and wrinkled jeans, "Race you to the bathroom!"

****

The front door bell rang an hour later. Penelope reached the door first and swung it open. If she had expected a gangling youth in a wide-brimmed hat lounging in the doorway swigging a can of beer her mind was immediately put at rest.

Standing four square on the steps in the afternoon sunshine was a broad-shouldered man in an immaculate suit. Short brown hair surmounted a tanned, clean cut face and a pair of blue eyes which caused Penelope's heart to do a loop. He was certainly the most attractive man she had ever seen. Parked in the road behind him was a bright red hired car but it might well have been a state coach or a pumpkin for all Penelope noticed of it. Her eyes were focused exclusively on the visitor himself.

After what seemed a matter of minutes to Penelope but was actually only seconds, the man spoke.

"Miss Ransome?" The voice was deep and strong.

Penelope tried desperately to keep her voice steady as she answered him.

"Yes, you have come to the right place."

"Have I the pleasure of addressing Katherine or Penelope?"

'He has certainly done his homework' thought the girl, 'I wish I had done so and knew a bit more about him. For a start he is older than I had anticipated, he must be thirty at least.'

"Penelope....."

"I'm Katherine."

The voice behind her made Penelope start, she had forgotten the existence of everyone except herself and this magnificent man.

"How nice to meet you both, I've heard so much about you. By the way my name is....."

"We know who you are," said both girls almost in unison- though Katherine at least would not have been surprised if he had announced himself as James Bond, "But please come in," she added.

Only generations of good breeding prevented the young ladies from grabbing an arm each and hauling the visitor into the house before any of the local girls caught sight of him.

When the man stepped into the doorway the girls realised how tall he was, inches over six feet. He was certainly a lot of man.

"I'm afraid Mother and Jane are out at the moment but they should be home in half an hour or so," said Katherine, "I am afraid you will just have to put up with us until then."

"I can't imagine anything more delightful," The accent was there alright, seeming to compliment the deep voice.

"Mother would certainly have stayed in if you had let us know beforehand that you were coming," saying this Penelope relieved the man of the large bunch of red roses, evidently intended for the lady of the house, and placed them on the hall table.

Entering the now tidy lounge Penelope indicated an arm-chair by the fireplace, "Please make yourself comfortable.

"Would you like a drink or a cup of tea?"

"A cup of tea would be fine thanks."

'Shaken, not stirred,' said Katherine to herself, then audibly, "I'll switch the kettle on."

The chair creaked in protest of the weight of the man as he settled into it.

'Everything in the room seems small and fragile in comparison to him', thought Penelope.

"is your hotel quite satisfactory James? – or should we call you 'Jim'?"

The visitor suddenly looked bewildered.

"'Jim'? What hotel? I've come straight from the airport!"

Something was wrong, very wrong. Suddenly everything about this wonderful man seemed to be falling apart. Was he a dream after all?

Katherine returned from the kitchen in time to hear the exchange of words.

"You are James Kelly?" Who else could he be?

"James Kelly? Never heard of him." The man started to raise himself from the chair.

Penelope took an involuntary step sideways as if to prevent the magnificent creature making a dash for the front door.

"I'm afraid there has been an awful misunderstanding," the deep voice continued, "I should have introduced myself properly – it seemed rather odd that you appeared to know who I was. Please allow me to rectify the matter. My name is Carlton, Nigel Carlton."

2 THE BRICK
(WHICH CHANGED THE COURSE OF HISTORY – ALMOST)

My Grandfather is very old and has been so for many, many years. I know as I can remember him from when I was a kid and I am nearly eleven now. He has a long white beard, he is _that_ old. My Grandmother is very old too of course.

I went to see them last week with Chalky my pal. We rode there on our new bikes. According to Chalky's milometer the journey was only seven miles each way but there must have been something wrong with it as it was obviously much further as it took hours. Of course we stopped once or twice to eat our sandwiches and to check on some ponds where Chalky had said there were newts last year although we did not find any.

It was a surprise visit, or at least it was meant to be. When we arrived I found Grandma talking to my Mother on the telephone so perhaps it was not.

Grandpa was gardening, or at least doing what he called gardening. He was sitting in his old basket chair in the back porch under the hanging flower basket. Actually it is not a basket at all but Grandpa's steel helmet which he used during the war, I am not sure which one. It was not an ordinary soldier's helmet as it was painted black although it is pretty rusty now. It has some letters painted on it and when I learned to read I made them out as 'A.R.P.', obviously the initials of some special organisation like the KGB or MI5. I have often wanted to ask Grandpa about it but probably he is not allowed to talk of it even now.

The house has two gardens, a large one at the back and a small one in the front of the house. The one at the back is something like a garden! Most of it is grass, too rough for cricket but ideal for most other games. There are bushes and trees all over the place for climbing and hiding in and at the end farthest from the house vegetable patches, a greenhouse and a couple of sheds. Also in this part of the garden are two old doors, a rusty plough, most of an old car, sheets of corrugated iron, planks of wood and all sorts of other interesting stuff.

The back garden is surrounded mainly by a fence of posts and wire half covered by blackberry bushes and partly by a wall. This wall runs from about half way up one side of the garden, past the house and out to the lane in the front. There are four strange apple trees flattened out on it and attached to the brickwork by nails and rusty wire. Grandpa has a special foreign name for these trees but I have forgotten it. The apples taste just like English apples. I can't see much point in flat apple trees, nor any reason for the wall either as there is nothing but fields all round the house. Perhaps the first owner intended building a wall all round the garden but ran out of bricks.

Grandma looked after the front garden. It was nothing much, just flowers and suchlike.

Chalky and I did all the usual things such as going over to Bryson's farm to look at the pigs, damming the stream at the bottom of the long field and exploring the old ruined mill at the top of the hill. By the time we had done all this we were getting rather hungry and Chalky asked what I thought we would be having for tea – and when we would be having it. It was his first visit.

Now Grandma's teas were really something special. There would be ham and tongue to start with, with lots of slices of hard-boiled egg in the salad. Neither Chalky or I were mad keen on salads but we would be allowed to pick out the slices of cucumber and leave them on the sides of our plates. After the salad there would be a trifle, jelly, two or three different kinds of cakes and as much jam and bread as we wanted. My mouth watered as I described the coming meal. We only have ordinary food at home, it's a wonder my Dad does not complain.

However there were a couple of snags. Grandma was much more strict than Grandpa, tea was at five o'clock – 'and not a minute sooner' and we had to get cleaned up for it. However having to wash one's hands was not much of a price to pay for such a meal. Another thing was that Chalky and I would have to drink tea. Both of us would have preferred milk, or better still orangeade or coke, but this was not allowed even at home. When visiting my Grandparents with my Mother I was always warned before our arrival not to ask for milk as they did not have much and if it was given to me by the glassful there would not be enough for their breakfast the following day.

It seemed odd to me to be short of milk in the middle of the country and even more strange that the daily bottle was delivered by an ordinary milkman rather than collecting as much as was required from the farm only a mile or so away. This gave Chalky and I the idea of obtaining some milk from one of the cows browsing only two fields away from the house. Then we would have as much milk as we liked for tea without leaving the old folks short.

We borrowed Grandma's bucket from the kitchen, (of course we would have asked her had she been there at the time), and took it over to the cow field. By the time we arrived at the gate all the big cows were strolling single file back to the farm for their evening meal or something but there were a good twenty or so smaller cows left in the next field. As Chalky said we only required half a bucket or so of milk so a small cow was all we needed. I secretly think he was a bit scared of the bigger animals.

The small cows obviously wanted to be milked for as soon as they saw us approaching they came right up and showed a great deal of interest in the bucket. They were rather frisky which made milking difficult, in fact we got no milk at all as one of the cows butted Chalky and knocked him off his feet. This was enough for him, he leaped up and headed back to the gate at great speed with a couple of the cows trotting behind him. Of course I laughed but as there was no hope of doing the milking by myself I had to join him. Somehow or other I forgot to bring the bucket but we got it back a little later when the cows moved away.

Unfortunately the cows had trampled on the bucket so as well as the mud and cow-muck on it it was split in one or two places. We took it back to Grandpa and asked if he had any glue to fix it with so Grandma would not notice but he considered it rather beyond repair. He said it did not matter much as it was only an old one and that he had intended buying Grandma a new bucket the next time he was in the village in any case. It did not look very old to me, (before we borrowed it of course,) but you can never tell with plastic buckets, they all look the same age.

Grandma was not too pleased when she saw her pail but smiled when Grandpa explained what had happened, in fact she laughed outright when Grandpa said the animals were Heffer's, (whoever he is, I thought the cows were Mr Bryson's). Although I could not see anything funny in what was said I decided not to ask any questions.

When the discussion was over and Grandma had gone back into the house there was still nearly half an hour before tea time. It was a pretty hot day so Chalky and I were enjoying the jug of lemonade Grandma had given us. Well not real lemonade, no fizz. It was mostly water with slices of lemon and lumps of ice in it but it tasted jolly good. Chalky and I had the jug between us as Grandpa does not drink much, only tea.

Now I had been swanking a bit about how good my Grandfather was at telling stories. Unlike most adults he knew everything about snakes and cowboys and pirates and suchlike. He also used to tell me about what life was like before space-rockets and jet aircraft, even about the really olden days before television. He could talk about anything. At least that is what I told Chalky and he took me up on it saying that he bet he could think of something Grandpa could not tell a story about. This had me a bit worried as even Grandpa must have his limitations. However I had to take him on.

Grandpa had been saying that some of the weeds in the garden were just about big enough to dig out, as if he had been sitting there all day waiting for them to grow to the correct size. He explained that it was no good digging weeds out when they were tiny- though Grandma disagreed with this- but to wait until the seeds were just about to fall when destroying them would not just kill one weed but wipe out the whole family. Although I was quite willing to allow Grandpa to pursue the subject Chalky was obviously not very interested in weeds and said to my Grandfather very politely, "Could you tell us a story please?"

Remembering our bet my heart sank but there was nothing I could do to rescue the situation.

"Certainly," replied Grandpa, "What would you like me to talk about?"

Without hesitation Chalky said, "That wall," and pointed to it.

I did not think this was fair. How could anyone tell a story about a wall? However Grandpa did not seem to take the request amiss.

"The garden wall Chalky?" he asked slowly, "All of it or just some particular part?"

"Oh." Replied Chalky welcoming the chance to make things even more difficult, "just part of it, in fact only one brick."

I could kiss goodbye to my Western Stock Knife which I had bet against Chalky's bicycle milometer.

To my amazement Grandpa became almost excited. He sat up in his chair.

"Which one boy? Which brick? Point it out to me!"

All the bricks appeared to be exactly the same but Chalky, slightly flustered, chose one."

"That one there, just to the left of the end tree with a big rusty nail in the mortar to the right of it."

Grandpa gripped the arms of his chair.

"Good heavens!" he exclaimed, "The boy must be psychic!"

Chalky and I did not know what to make of this so, of course asked Grandpa to explain. He told us what 'psychic' was – and how to spell it. Needless to say I wished I was a psychic too as Chalky was obviously going to swank about it but at least Grandpa was my grandfather so I did not feel too bad.

My Grandfather then explained what had so excited him.

"Do you know boys, that brick, that very brick, almost changed the destiny of mankind!"

For a moment there was silence then both Chalky and I asked at the same time how an ordinary brick could do such a thing.

"Ah," said Grandpa, "It is not an ordinary brick, in fact it is not even an English brick, it is a European brick. It was made many years ago in Bosnia or one of those other small countries which were lost in the changing of frontiers at the end of the First World War.

"Have you ever heard of a place called Sarajevo?"

Of course neither of us had. In fact when Grandpa started to tell the story we immediately began to wonder if there was such a place and that he was not making up the whole things.

I cannot remember Grandpa's exact word but the story was something like this.

Many, many years ago there was a bricklayer named Boris working in this place Sarajevo. He was one of a gang of men repairing the brickwork at the edge of the roof of a big building in the main street. It was his job to load a basket from a stack of bricks at the roadside. When the basket was full it was hauled up to the roof where his mates were working.

Boris was busy filling the basket when he heard shouting and saw a procession of cars going past. In one of the cars was the Archduke Ferdinand in a magnificent uniform including a plumed hat. (Chalky and I exchanged glances- this _was_ a fairy story we both decided). Being a nice warm June day the canvas hood of the car was folded flat.

As the cars passed there was a little cheering and booing with the odd egg and tomato thrown just like nowadays but there was no real violence until the Archduke's car was opposite Boris. It was then that a young man pushed his way through the bystanders and rushed towards the car. In his hand was a large revolver.

Boris shouted a warning but no-one took any notice. As he was too far off to tackle the man he did the next best thing and threw a brick at him. At least this was his intention but unfortunately his shouting had attracted the attention of a nearby policeman who thought he was trying to throw the brick at the Archduke so grabbed Boris by the arm and promptly arrested him. As the young man with the revolver succeeded in assassinating the Archduke a lot of other people were also arrested that day.

The brick was brought to the court as evidence when Boris' case was heard. Grandpa did not know what became of Boris but the brick itself was taken by one of the lawyers and for some years used by him as a door-stop.

The brick next changed hands at the end of the First World War when the lawyer sold it to a corporal in the Tank Corps for two tins of bully beef.

Now this corporal had been rescued from a burning tank earlier in the war by his officer so he reckoned he owed this officer a favour. As the war ended before he could return the compliment he presented his brick to him as a farewell present when they were demobbed.

The officer concerned was the Major Riley who had had built the house which was now Grandpa's. Not wishing the brick to become lost or stolen the major had it built into the garden wall where it remains to this day. He must have told Grandpa which brick it was when he sold the house, which was just as well as all the other bricks are very similar to it.

Grandpa had just finished the story when Grandma came out to tell us that tea was ready – we had been so interested listening to my Grandfather that we had forgotten all about tea- well almost anyway.

Chalky and I had to leave straight after tea in order to get home before dark. We talked about the brick as we rode along but neither of us was convinced the story was true.

We reached my house first, Chalky lived further down the road. My Dad was in the front garden when we arrived so I asked him if he had ever heard of a place called Sarajevo. He knows quite a lot of history even if he is not so hot on lizards or Formula One racing cars.

My Father said, and these are his exact words so far as I can remember, "Sarajevo? Yes, it is a town in Yugo Slavia. It's main claim to fame is that it was the place where Archduke Ferdinand was murdered in 1914. It is said that this was the initial cause of the First World War- and the fact that the world has never been right since. Anyway, why do you ask?"

"Oh," I replied, "Grandpa was speaking about it this afternoon."

So it was true! I wanted to tell Dad about the brick but it occurred to me that the fewer people who knew about it the better for if word leaked out someone might steal the brick or Grandpa might have to give it to a museum.

That evening whilst my folks were watching television I crept out to the telephone in the hall and called Grandpa. I knew he would not want the brick dug out of his wall at the present time as this would make a bit of a mess so I asked him if I could have it when he died. I suppose I could have waited until my next visit to ask him but as I said earlier Grandpa is very old so I did not want to take any chances.

Grandpa laughed a bit and said he had no intention of dying for a long time yet but he would certainly leave a note for whoever bought the house when that time came asking them to let me have the brick. What is more he said he would mark the brick with paint so they would be certain to give me the right one.

When I get the brick I want to keep it with me always. I will only sell it to a museum if I am very short of money later on.

It was a bit of a job getting the milometer off Chalky's bike and onto mine but now it is fixed properly it works perfectly. I will tell Grandpa how I won it the next time Chalky and I ride out that way.

3 SHOES

Shortly after my husband died I went to spend a few months with my sister Vanessa in Sussex, England. The weather had been excellent since the moment I arrived and there was every prospect of a record breaking summer so far as sunshine was concerned. They get all kinds there of course, as I well remember from my childhood.

One particular evening I had the house to myself for a while. Van was at a P.T.A. meeting, she always liked to know what was going on since the first of her three children had started at the school and over the years had become thoroughly involved.

Debbie was the youngest and it was she I was awaiting. As with many other girls of sixteen she had a passion for horses and her great ambition was to be a show-jumper. When her interest in ponies could no longer be denied her father insisted that she did the thing properly, Van's George was like that. The best equipment and the local riding school, even though it was the most expensive in the area. In return Debbie had to toe the line. No shirking if the weather was bad or some more exciting engagement was offered or anything like that. However this was no hardship for the girl, she lived and breathed horses. She took her riding very seriously indeed and this evening I knew was extremely important for her.

The fact of the matter was that the riding school's much loved and respected instructor was about to retire and this evening's gathering was in order for the students to meet his successor. Debbi's happiness depended a great deal on whether or not she liked him so I awaited her report with some trepidation.

The way the back door banged was a bad omen and when Debbie came into the room my worst fears were confirmed, the poor child was almost in tears. I wanted desperately to comfort her but knew that sympathy was not needed that moment.

"I hate him!" she cried as she flung herself down on a chair. Just to make herself perfectly clear she repeated, "I hate him! I hate him! I hate him!"

Pandering to her mood I said, "He sounds absolutely dreadful but what exactly makes you hate him so?" I could hardly imagine anyone deliberately engendering such strong emotions at a first meeting with people who would, indirectly, be paying his salary.

"He wants to change everything," replied Debbie, "Everything to be done to a time-table with periods of oral instruction – just like school. And dressage! Dressage! All I want to do is jump!"

"No doubt he has good reasons dear," I said as soothingly as possible. "From what I have heard he has a very good reputation."

"I don't care what his reasons are or what his reputation is, I hate him and I always will hate him!"

"Now steady on my girl," somewhat less soothingly, "You have only known him, how long? An hour at the most, that is hardly long enough to qualify for a life-long hate."

"You believe in love at first sight don't you?" Debbie, taking my assent for granted, immediately continued, "Well this is hate at first sight."

"Debbie, if you would be so kind as to listen to your old aunt for a few minutes I will tell you a little story. It is about a man I hated once, many years ago."

"I can't imagine you hating anyone Aunt Martha."

I laughed, "Of course I have darling," It was lovely to be able to use 'darling' after decades of 'honey' "you cannot get to my age without hating quite a few people. After a while you either forget why you hated them or forget them altogether. It is much more difficult to forget why you loved someone.

"However, this man I am going to tell you about I do remember very well indeed. I met him only briefly and I hated him for a relatively short time but I will never forget him."

This had Debbie's attention, as I thought it would. She had probably already decided that the man had besmirched my maidenly honour – and possibly been killed in a duel by some admirer shortly afterwards. I did not disillusion her.

"It concerned a hurricane," another attention getter, "Your Uncle Harry was always keen on yachts as you will know. Well it was only a few years after we were married that we were cruising up at Maine. The name of our boat at the time was 'Anastasia', Harry owned her before we were married and she was his pride and joy, in fact I must admit I was often a trifle jealous of her. Little did we know on the morning of the day I am going to tell you about that by evening she would be no more.

"We were berthed at a rickety wooden pier on an island with a long Indian name which I won't try to pronounce when we heard on the radio that the hurricane, which had passed New York safely and had therefore ceased to be 'news' had 'recurved' or something like that and was due in our area within hours. It had a name, although naming hurricanes after girls was a fairly new innovation as I remember, but Harry and I always called it 'Anastacia's Hurricane'. There were all sorts of conflicting reports on the radio, first it was going to blast us, then it was going south of our area, next it was curving out into the Atlantic again, we really did not know what to believe. However to be on the safe side Harry decided to ride it out at anchor in case it did come our way in any strength. We therefore shifted out to join half a dozen other boats and got 'snugged down' as Harry termed it. This took some time and it was well into the afternoon before we found time to look around. What we saw gave us quite a shock. Although we were sheltered by the high land across from the island and only experiencing a slight swell, only a mile away where the land ended abruptly the surf was bursting as high as a house on the rocks below the cliff. The sky was a horrible orange colour and it was rapidly getting dark.

"Harry did not say anything for quite a while. He looked at the sky, he looked at the bows of 'Anastasia' beginning to dip in the swell. He looked at the island and at the breakers. He looked at everything around him – except at me.

"I knew his quandary. He wanted to stay and help 'Anastasia' through what was obviously going to be a tough time but also he wanted me safe ashore. He could not very well dump me on the beach and come back to the yacht, I would have refused to be parted from him even if he had suggested it.

"The 'Anastasia' giving a particularly heavy thump on a swell seemed to decide him.

"'Martha,' he said, with a sickly kind of grin, 'it's time to go.' My heart bled for him.

"He went, and was I glad! Ours was the last yacht to be abandoned, everyone else was ashore. We left in such a hurry that we took nothing with us in the punt except the clothes we wearing and a few valuables. I suppose because it was so stiflingly hot we never thought of extra clothing although when we were nearly to the beach Harry stopped rowing and said, 'Hell! We should have brought our slickers in case it rains.' – Understatement of the year! 'Well it's too late now, let's just hope it doesn't come to much.'

"We sat on the beach in the clammy heat for nearly an hour. A few other people were in sight up and down the sand, mainly in twos and threes, watching their boats bobbing about in the swell and wondering if they would break adrift. There were no get-togethers until it was all over. We just sat in our individual worlds of worry and uncertainty.

"You have probably heard better descriptions of hurricanes than I can ever give so I will not go into details. However when that hurricane hit us it was absolutely unbelievable. We soon shifted up from the beach and tried to get some shelter in the tussocky grass nearer the top of the little island. At first we thought of seeking shelter in one of the few huts further along but it was just as well we did not as they were blown to pieces very early on. They were just flimsy hardboard and tar-paper affairs used in the summer by ice-cream and bait sellers. The owners would have packed off home some time before as the season was really over.

"Actually we were only on the edge of the hurricane, they say it hit the coast sixty miles north of us but it was certainly bad enough. We snuggled down as best we could but the wind and flying sand made things more than uncomfortable, downright terrifying in fact.

"A shriek came from down the beach aways and we thought at first that someone had been hurt. People were pointing and we saw that one of the yachts was adrift and rapidly being blown down towards the reef at the end of the island. The wind was still rising and although Harry said something about people not knowing how to anchor a boat properly I think it was then that he realised the same thing could happen to 'Anastasia'. Later it could have been scant satisfaction to him to see that his much loved yacht was the last to go, apart from the two which sank at their moorings.

"We watched 'Anastasia' go, slowly at first and then it seemed faster and faster as she neared the reef. She seemed so helpless...so...so deserted by us in her hour of need. What happiness she had brought us, so many memorable occasions. I cried as though a very dear friend was being tortured and killed before my eyes. What Harry's thoughts were I will never know. I just clung to him with all my strength.

"Then the rain came. Rain as I have never experienced before or since. Nothing could describe it, it seemed like solid water crashing down on us. And cold! Like ice after the hot, humid day. I have never been so cold, wet and frightened in my whole life. How we regretted not bringing extra clothes with us, particularly the oil skins. Harry tried to shield me as best he could but always part of me was getting battered by the icy rain even though Harry was a great husky man then and I was always a midget....."

"Aunt Martha please!" exclaimed Debbie in mock horror, "'Petite' is the word."

"Whatever you say dear, anyway I was young and healthy," I did not specify how young, twenty-nine to a sixteen year old was probably middle aged, "and I knew I would survive, but misery! I have never experienced anything to match it. My morale was very low indeed what with the weather conditions, the loss of the yacht, all my holiday clothes, camera, films we had taken, the lot.

"I offer this as a slight excuse for my behaviour in the next act of drama.

"When everything was about as terrible as could be a man came stumbling along the beach towards us. In the darkness and rain we could only make him out when he was but a few yards off. Harry saw him first as I was, I think, trying to burrow right into his chest in an effort to get warm. Harry said something, I don't know what, which caused me to raise my head and see the man standing right beside us. He looked a trifle startled when he saw my face, muttered something we did not catch, then with a silly sort of grin and a slight wave of his hand he went on his way just as if he had disturbed a couple of lovers on a park bench.

"What was he like?" asked Debbie.

"There was nothing exceptional about him apart from the fact he wore a black beard. This was when beards were not often seen, not on respectable men anyway. His age could have been anywhere between thirty and fifty, we could not see much of his face. He was large and gangling, his jeans were frayed at the hems, he wore a black shoe on one foot and a dirty white sneaker on the other – and no socks. And that is about as complete a description I can give of him. I never saw him again.

"Debbie, I hated that man with all my heart and soul!"

"But Aunt Martha! What did he do?"

"Nothing but what I have told you."

"But you can't hate a man just because he was scruffy or he thought you were a couple of lovers!"

"That was not why I hated him, I hated him because he was wearing a big warm, hooded coat. A great heavy-weather ex-services coat and I was very, very cold and wet."

"But you could hardly expect........"

"I know but it just did not seem right that I should be soaked and half frozen when a perfect stranger should be warm and reasonably dry.

"Harry did his best to console me but to little avail. He thought at the time incidentally that the man was probably a 'Loner' and had come in for shelter on the heavy, gaff-rigged yawl he could remember, and I very vaguely, approaching the anchorage as we were rowing to the beach."

I paused to let Debbie digest this. Bright girl as she is she saw a flaw.

"you say you never saw him again but at the beginning you said you hated him for a short time only. Why? Did you hear that he died or something?"

"He is still alive so far as I know although I've never heard of anyone meeting him after that day." I knew I was piling on the mystery but that was the way I wanted to tell the tale.

"Then it doesn't fit the theory that you forget the people you hate, or you forget why you hated them," said Debbie with a certain primness. Having settled that to her own satisfaction she continued, "About how long did you hate him then?"

"There is no 'about' in it," I replied, "I hated that man for exactly two years and eleven days, give or take an hour or two, I checked it out."

"Then you did meet him again."

"No dear, everything I have said is perfectly true."

"Then why? I mean, what happened?"

"Well Debbie, a couple of years after the events I have just told you about I was at a party of some sort, friend of Harry's rather than mine as I remember. I was introduced to a woman on the strength of the fact that her husband was also a yachting fanatic so we could therefore be able to commiserate with one another. We chatted for a few minutes about the things all yachting wives have to put up with and then discovered that not only had we been in the same hurricane but were actually on the same island! That really gave us something to talk about as you may well imagine. Neither of us could remember seeing the other there, she and her family were apparently at the opposite end of the island to us near to the footbridge linking it to the main island.

"I was horrified when she told me she had four small children with her. Recalling how cold, wet and terrified I had been at the time I said it was a wonder that they had survived.

"She smiled and said that had been her main concern. The children were half frozen in their light summer clothes and almost scared out of their wits. She and her husband had done their best to comfort and warm them but it was impossible to do much in the prevailing conditions. She said she was nearly hysterical with worry over the children, the youngest of whom was just getting over an illness.

"'I hardly thought any of us would live through that night,' she said, 'particularly the kids. Dan and I felt so helpless. There was no shelter and no one we could turn to for help as neither of us could leave the poor things – even if there was anywhere to go for assistance. As you will know the bridge was expected to be washed away at any moment and nobody would have ventured over that boiling water even if it were likely to hold. What people there were in sight were out of shouting distance and were in just as bad a way as ourselves in any case. Not that we really considered going for help anyway, I only wanted the kids to be warm. Their hair was plastered to their heads with the rain and they were blue with cold. They did not cry much but the way they looked at you, as if to say, 'We know it's not your fault but you, who have always loved and cared for us, why can't you do something for us now?' It tore your heart out.

"'Then something happened which I shall remember until my dying day.

"'A man appeared beside us in the torrential rain. I say 'appeared' as we did not know he was there until he spoke.

"'Over my shoulder he said to the children something like, 'Hey you kids, could you take care of this for me for a while?'

"'And do you know, he pulled off the great big coat he was wearing and sort of offered it to the kids. I grabbed it, I'm ashamed to say, I just grabbed it.

"'We had to lift the children off the sand they were so cold and helpless, in order to get them wrapped in the coat.

"'By the time Dan and I had them all snuggled into it, it was big enough but only just, the man was way down the beach. So far away that we could not even call out to thank him.

"'The sad thing about it all is that we never saw him again. There was no identification in the coat and Dan and I could not even remember what he looked like as we were so busy with the kids we hardly had time to spare him a glance. He must have been big because of the coat but apart from that and what we saw of his back in the rain at a distance, a light coloured sweatshirt and jeans, we have nothing to go on at all.'

"Was he wearing anything else that you remember?" I prompted.

"'No,' she said wonderingly. Then, 'Yes, shoes of course – and that was such a funny thing………'

"One shoe was black and the other a dirty white sneaker." I said quietly.

ENDS

4 THE BIRTHDAY PRESENT

The horse-shoe shaped ridge was picturesque but otherwise nothing more than an introduction to the mighty mountains beyond. Convenient of access it was well patronised by walkers and picnicking families in the summer months.

The full circuit of the ridge was a three or four hour tramp but there were a few well defined paths across the centre of the 'hoof' for those not wishing to make the full walk.

A little scrambling was required in a few places but otherwise it was all plain sailing, provided walkers did not stray away from the cairn-marked paths. Even then only a short section was particularly dangerous, a place where the side of the mountain had fallen away leaving a vertical cliff below an overhang of smooth granite.

The granite cap sloped down at about twenty degrees from the vertical for roughly eighty feet then sharply inwards to the cliff face. Twelve feet or so from the lower edge some freak of nature had caused a coffin-shaped piece of rock to pivot out from the face and point skywards. Although ignored by cartographers it was known to local walkers and climbers at 'The Coat Peg'.

The 'Coat Peg' had nothing to recommend it as a climbing

exercise. Ropes were required to get down to it and having been reached there was no where else to go except back up as below it was nothing but five hundred feet of fresh mountain air before the jagged scree in the valley below.

****

The first known person to reach the 'Coat Peg' without ropes was Anne-Marie Bennet.

Anne-Marie was not an experienced climber, in fact she was not a climber at all but walking, particularly among mountains, was one of her greatest pleasures.

Miss Smythe, a teacher at Anne-Marie's school, was also a keen walker so it was natural that the first sunny spring day would find them on the mountains. Initially the walk should have included several other girls but, having no heart for such exercise, they each found an admirable excuse to avoid the outing. This suited both Miss Smythe and Anne-Marie perfectly as they both preferred just the company of the other. Anne-Marie liked the way Miss Smythe treated her as an adult on these occasions and the teacher enjoyed the leggy teenager's chatter and constant questions.

'How wonderful to be that age', mused the teacher, even though there was scarcely a decade between their ages. She admired the girl's vivacity as she almost gambolled along the path, her new pale blue and white outfit contrasting vividly with her own well worn orange anorak and green trousers.

They had taken a bus out to the mountains that morning then walked round the base of the horseshoe for a few miles before stopping for the picnic lunch they had brought.

After the light meal they climbed up to the ridge, their laughter and conversation only interrupted by the occasional particularly steep parts of the well worn track when all breath was required for scrambling.

On reaching the crest several minutes were spent admiring the magnificent view, Miss Smythe indicating the various peaks to Anne-Marie and identifying them on her map. Then they were off again, striding along the ridge path and occasionally crunching through the patches of old snow, all that was left to remind them of the recent winter.

"At this rate we will be back to the road long before the bus is due", said the teacher after glancing at her watch.

Anne-Marie wanted to cry out "Isn't it wonderful!" but that would have been childish. She tried to think of something else to say and looked around for inspiration. She pointed ahead, "Look at that funny rock sticking to the side of the mountain. I wonder how it managed to get there, it is surprising it does not fall off."

Miss Smythe, familiar with the oddity, explained the structure of it and told the girl its colloquial name.

"We will be able to see it better when we get closer", said Anne-Marie.

"I doubt it," was the reply, "It is only really visible from here and a couple of places some way past it."

They knew when they had arrived directly above the 'Coat Peg' as the spot was marked by a length of very rusty angle iron set upright in cement which obviously once supported a warning notice. Miss Smythe was about to remark on this when a shadow spread on the rocks nearby. She stopped and glanced over her shoulder to see that the sun, which had shone brilliantly all day, was now obscured by a heavy black cloud. Although the cloud base was still some considerable distance away it gave a very good reason not to dawdle.

She turned to the girl beside her, "We will have to hurry...... Anne-

Marie!" The last two words came out almost as a shriek. The girl was not beside her but thirty feet away standing on a patch of snow at the very edge of the sharply sloping granite.

Anne-Marie laughed, "It is quite safe. I can just see the top of……"

The remainder of the sentence was replaced with an ear-splitting scream as Anne-Marie's feet slipped from beneath her and she disappeared from Miss Smythe's horrified gaze.

* * * * * * * * * * * *

Larry Potter had a great deal of experience of the mountains, too much he decided as he plodded down from the peak. There was no doubt about it, Doc. Gimbell was right, he was far too old for this sort of thing. Not that there was much wrong with his heart – so far at least, it was his lungs which were slowing him up. All right down hill but he was puffing like a grampus each time he reached the crest of a ridge. Yes it was high time he cut out these jaunts and confined his walking to the flat. He had no intention of sitting down all day as old wheelchair bound Joss was forced to.

Thinking of Joss caused him to wonder who's night it was to entertain. Yes, Joss' of course, so it would be a game of chess and a glass of port, there was still plenty of it left. Although their cottages adjoined the two old men avoided intruding on one another's privacy. The evening visit to one another once a week was another matter, that tradition had continued for years.

Less than an hour and he would reach his ancient car, a half hour's drive and he would be back at his cottage. His luncheon sandwiches had long since been consumed and Larry looked forward to his supper. The potatoes and carrots he had prepared the night before and the small pork chop was awaiting him in his refrigerator. After clearing away it would be next door for a game of chess and a chat.

As he clumped along in his tattered green coat and greasy pork-

35

pie hat Larry looked forward to the remainder of his day with pleasurable anticipation. Not really a very exciting prospect but then his life had contained little excitement anyway. Even during the war his experiences were similar to so many others in the forces he decided, a few hours of bowel-churning terror separated by months of sheer monotony. Apart from prisoners he had never seen an enemy soldier.

However Larry was content, he did not need excitement to get him through his days. His mountains and the ability to get around on them were sufficient for his happiness. Of course he would miss old Joss when he went and that could not be far in the future. Even if he remained above ground the interfering authorities would not let him stay at his cottage much longer. Yes, there would be a gap when Joss went --one way or the other.

Larry topped a crag and saw, as he expected, the piece of iron above the 'Coat Peg'. He often wondered if he was the only one left who remembered the notice board it once supported.

He saw something else, a man kneeling close to the edge. The kneeling figure suddenly observed him and leaped to its feet, waving and shouting. Larry was a little confused, the 'man' was apparently a slim young woman although he was not entirely convinced. 'Hardly tell them apart these days,' he muttered to himself.

A glance behind convinced the old man that the orange and green clad figure was certainly shouting to him. He quickened his pace, obviously something had happened but he could not decide what. The possibility of someone having fallen over the edge immediately occurred to him but, he cold-bloodedly decided, this was not indicated by the woman's movements. She dashed towards the edge twice as he approached. It must be apparent to a half-wit that anyone going over there would now be spread like jam over the rocks below, he mused.

Larry had difficulty in making out what the woman was shouting above the gasping of his breath and, he noted with alarm, the thudding of his heart. Even his legs were soon feeling the strain of the unaccustomed exertion but he could not stop now. Obviously he was faced with a serious emergency of some sort.

The woman dashed towards Larry when he was some thirty yards from the iron post and blurted out her terrifying story. She tried to drag the old man along with her but his legs by that time could carry him no further. He collapsed to his knees as the woman completed her account.

Above the heavy beating of his heart and gasping breath Larry Potter heard that the girl had fallen over half an hour before and was apparently still alive as she has called out a few times, the last occasion some ten minutes before his arrival. Weak cries, nothing intelligible.

The old man knew he could go no further without a rest and then not at any speed. It was therefore obvious that the woman would have to go for assistance.

It was fortunate that the young woman was familiar with the area so detailed instructions were not necessary before she was running as fast as she could along the ridge, determined to be back with her charge as soon as she possibly could.

****

Ten minutes after Miss Smythe had left him old Larry had his breathing under control and his heart back to its normal beat.

There was no further sound from the rock below but that meant little. Larry crawled on his stomach to the edge of the slope and was rewarded with only a view of the top of the 'Coat Peg' and one booted foot, exactly as described by the young woman. The remainder of the girl's body was obviously jammed between the protruding sliver of granite and the rock face.

Larry Potter had never felt so useless. Here he was on a gloomy mountain ridge with an injured fellow human being, just starting out in life, less than seventy feet away and there was nothing, absolutely nothing, he could do about it. He thought of lowering his small rucksack to the girl in the hope that something in it would be of use to her – if she were conscious. A second's thought dismissed that, he had no line and anyway nothing in the bag could be of much service. However in order to occupy his hands and mind Larry decided to check its contents.

Empty thermos flask, the wrappings from his lunch, compass, a pair of boot-laces, a small torch and whistle. Also, of course, a spare sweater. Larry was too old a hand to trust mountain weather.

The jersey might be useful to the girl but none of the other items, Larry thought.

'What was that?' Something splashed onto his hand, wet and icy cold.

'Oh God! What am I to do?' Larry almost shouted with frustration. Twenty years before in such a dire emergency he might have taken the risk of climbing down to the girl but he but a youngster then, still in his fifties.

A few more spots of ice-cold sleet spattered onto the rocks.

When would the rescue team arrive? Very shortly the rock face would be covered in ice and any cracks and hand-holds filled, making the young men's task even more hazardous.

Larry Potter sat on a rock with his head in his hands. How long was it since the woman had left him? How much time would be required to raise the alarm and assemble the rescue team? How long would they take to climb up from the road? Total two and a half hours at least, more likely three, the rescue station itself was fifteen miles away.

More heavy drops of sleet and the black, ragged clouds now racing over his head. Three hours! In twenty minutes the girl would be dead – if she was not dead already.

The old man felt an urgent desire to relieve himself and with this function in mind he modestly walked away from the skyline.

Miss Smythe reached the road and had only run a hundred yards along it when she heard a car approaching rapidly from behind. This she stopped by the simple expedient of standing in the middle of the narrow strip of tarmac and waving her arms frantically. She gasped out her story to the startled young driver and within seconds the vehicle was heading at a dangerous speed towards the nearest telephone.

It was not until she was in the car that Miss Smythe realised how dark it was rapidly becoming. Snow and sleet began to spatter on the windscreen and within minutes the wipers could only just cope with the accumulation of ice.

Miss Smythe's heart seemed as cold as the snow itself. 'Oh my God!.....Oh my God!.....Oh my God!' she repeated to herself, over and over again.

A farm afforded the telephone and within minutes the rescue was set in motion.

Although desperately wanting to return to Anne-Marie even Miss Smythe realised after a while the impracticility of such a prospect and was forced to submit to the ministrations of the farmer's wife.

*****

The weather deteriorated rapidly as the afternoon wore on to evening and by the time the rescue convoy was half way to its destination the sleet had turned to heavy snow, blinding the drivers and causing tyres to skid on the inches deep slush. In spite of the expert driving one of the landrovers spun round at a corner and came to a halt with two wheels in a ditch, completely blocking the road. Being the leading vehicle it held up the others. It took the efforts of the whole team ten valuable minutes to get it back on the road. Nearly an hour elapsed from leaving the post to the arrival of the vehicles at the end of the ridge.

The engines had hardly stopped before the men were striding up the steep track. Each knew what he had to carry in the way of equipment so words were few.

The climb up the ridge was a nightmare. The wind was in the men's faces most of the time and the light from the powerful lamps they carried did little more than illuminate the falling snow and were as much a hindrance as a help. However the main problem was underfoot, the loose, slippery snow making each step a hazard on the rocky path.

One of the team voiced the thoughts of all as the party neared the last ridge before the 'Coat Peg'.

"Not much hope for the poor kid Ted," he panted to the man beside him.

"No, not any kind of hope. If she was alive when this lot started she will be frozen stiff as a board by now. It's hard to realise that a matter of hours ago I thought Spring had at last arrived," rasped Ted.

"The weather report did say that this lot was coming over but I did not think it would be as bad as this," gasped the other man, "So far as the poor girl is concerned I reckon we are wasting our time."

Shouts from ahead attracted their attention. It was the team's leader, Lem, as usual well ahead, trying to attract the attention of anyone who happened to be alive in the vicinity of the 'Coat Peg'.

Ted and his mate Bob arrived ahead of the others to be greeted by Lem shouting "Where the Hell is old Larry Potter? He is supposed to be up here somewhere. I had a look behind those rocks," he indicated some boulders just off the track they had negotiated, "on the way up as I thought he might be sheltering there but no sign of him."

"You would think Lem had started out an hour before the rest of us Bob," said Ted.

"I suppose we will have to root around for the silly sod when we've got the girl sorted out," said Lem as the others joined him. "He must have dug himself a hole somewhere to await events."

"Be your age Lem!" commented Bob, "The old buffer has gone home long since. He knows the weather signs and after all he is damn nigh eighty."

"Not like him to push off under the circumstances," Lem hauled out his hand radio and contacted the man left with the vehicles.

"When you get a moment George nip along to the old quarry and see if Larry Potter's car is there – and let me know."

As he stuffed the radio back into his pocket Lem said, "Another worry but let us see what we can do about the girl first."

"Good God Lem! You are not thinking of going down in this stuff?" gasped Ted, "There is not the foggiest chance of her being alive so we may as well bivouac until the worst of it is over. No one could hold a rope in this ice."

Lem ignored the remark and commenced scraping away the snow in the vicinity of the iron post with his boot. Then, as two more of the team approached, "Here are the spikes and pitons. I want a good belay here," he stamped his foot on a crevice he had uncovered in the rock, "A good one young Ted, none of your couple of half turns round the old sign post." The nearest any of those present had heard in the way of a joke from the taciturn Lem. It proved how worried he was.

There was no question as to who was to go over on the rope so nothing was said in this connection as arrangements were made.

The stiff straps of Lem's harness gave a little trouble but in the event he was ready as soon as the ropes had been rigged.

41

Slowly Lem abseiled down the sharply sloping surface bracing his legs at each small step. Ted, lying on his stomach as near to the edge as he could get in safety, kept the remainder of the team informed of his progress.

Lem reached the lower end of the 'Coat Peg' and at first thought there was no one there, the clothing, encased in ice with its folds filled with snow closely resembled the surrounding rocks. He concentrated his gaze in the flickering light of the lamps swinging from lines above him and received a shock. His mittened hands clawed at the frozen clothing. Yes, it was true!

"On top!" Lem shouted up, unable to keep the surprise out of his voice, "They are both down here!"

A shocked silence, then Bob's voice, "Are they alive?"

Lem was already investigating this possibility but with old Larry having fallen right on top of the girl he considered the likelihood remote.

Ramming a gap between the bodies Lem whipped off a mitten and inserted his hand again. To his surprise there was a slight warmth, then, pressing his hand further, a faint pulsation.

"On top! There is a spark of life here!"

****

It was the day after Anne-Marie was removed from the life-support machine that her Mother arrived later than expected to visit her. Anne-Marie was about to reproach her when she was distracted by something unusual.

"Mummy, you are wearing a hat!" Her voice was still not much more than a whisper.

"I know dear, there was something I had to attend ..to," She hoped her daughter had not noticed the slight hesitation between the last two words and quickly changed the subject.

"Daddy had to go back to London today but he will be back at the weekend."

"Yes, you told me yesterday."

"Of course I did," then, "You look much brighter today dear, how do you feel?"

"Much better, thank you. My leg only tickles now." She glanced down at her plaster-covered limb.

For a moment Mrs. Bennet wondered what to say next but it was Anne-Marie who spoke first.

"Mummy, how much does a bottle of port cost?"

The odd question caught Mrs. Bennet by surprise. "I..I don't really know – but why do you ask?"

"I would like to buy Mr. Potter one."

"Why?" It was all her Mother could think of to say.

"Because of something he told me and the fact that he is a very wonderful old man."

"Do you really want to talk about it dear?" Mrs. Bennet was relieved to hear her daughter speaking lucidly after her whispered, jumbled utterances of previous days but she did not want her to recall the horrors she had recently undergone. She tried to think of some way of turning the conversation but Anne-Marie persisted.

"Yes Mummy, I want to tell you all about it, right from the moment I saw Mr. Potter's boots trying to find a hold just above my head. I was in great pain and kept passing out. Miss Smythe kept calling at first and I tried to shout back but that seemed a long time before Mr.

Potter arrived. I had hoped and prayed that someone would come and when he at last crouched over me I knew that everything would be alright. He wrapped a jersey around me but I was still very cold so he unfastened his coat and snuggled me up against his chest. He smelled awful – no not awful," Anne-Marie amended hurriedly, "but sort of doggish. He was lovely and warm."

"He told me all sorts of stories about himself, they were so interesting and funny that I often forgot the pain and even forgot to be frightened at times. Do you know he was in the army all through the war – which I could have thought was pretty serious but to hear him talk one would think it was all great fun."

"An old man named Joss lives in the next cottage to Mr. Potter, (he asked me to call him Larry but I always called him Mr. Potter," Anne-Marie explained in case her Mother had any doubts about her manners), "Although they don't see much of one another during the week they visit on alternate Sunday evenings. When at Joss' house they listen to the radio, play chess and have a glass of port – that is where the port comes in Mummy. Mr. Potter says they make quite a ceremony of it, 'Could I persuade you to take a glass of port Lawrence?' 'I'd be delighted Joshua, very kind of you.' It is 'Joss' and 'Larry' the rest of the time. At Mr. Potter's house it is much the same except that they watch television, at least Mr. Potter does and explains anything necessary to Joss as he is blind. They only have one small glass of port on each occasion to make it last and when it does run out they have coffee instead." Anne-Marie made a hopeless attempt to imitate a man's voice, 'A glass of port Joshua?' 'No thank you Lawrence,' replies Joss knowing there is none left, 'must not risk getting gout with all this good living. However I would love a cup of your excellent coffee.' The coffee is only ordinary instant of course. It is all so very funny the way he tells it.

"At Christmas they each buy the other an identical bottle of port and start all over again."

"Talking of presents Mummy, does Mr. Potter know where I am? I told him my birthday was on the eighteenth and he said he would remember it. I hope he sends me a card."

Mrs. Bennet felt her eyes flood with tears, she turned her head towards the window where, as if on cue, a pair of blackbirds could be seen winging their way across the daffodil-bejewelled lawn towards the trees on the far side of a lake as if nesting could not wait another minute.

"He has already given you his present dear," she murmured, "the greatest gift of all."

5 THE COMPLETE HISTORY OF WOMAN (FROM THE BEGINNING TO THE TWENTY-FIRST CENTURY)

The Chairman eased himself back on his seat and said, with something of a sigh of relief, "well that is about it then."

A subdued cough from about halfway down the table indicated his relief was premature.

"...apart from that additional project of yours, the 'super-model' or whatever it is you wish to bring to our attention," the Chairman added with a singular lack of enthusiasm "Let us hear about it if you insist."

"It is rather special," said the Chief Designer, "I am certain you will like it."

"As if there are not enough different designs already," muttered the junior member of the board.

"This is quite different," the C.D. was not to be put down, "Something entirely more complex than any of the others."

"Not *too* complex I hope?", offered someone, "You will remember the Camel? It is a wonder to me that it ever got past the committee stage."

"Get on with it," ordered the Chairman, "We have not got all day."

"Well briefly," the C.D. was glad to have the floor, "It would operate mainly by intelligence rather than by stealth or brute force."

"How big would it be?"…..”What would it look like?" The questions indicated that the committee was beginning to take an interest,

"I have got it on its side!" The junior member tried to turn the drawing through ninety degrees but the C.D. prevented him.

"No! That is the right way up."

"But it is standing on end!" exclaimed the junior member.

"That is what it is meant to do. If you will give me your attention for a few minutes I will explain why."

"Carry on," said the Chairman.

"Well the idea is that it will retain the standard four limbs but will balance and move on the two back ones only, leaving the front pair for other purposes."

"We have already done that." said someone.

"Ah! But not to the extent I envisage here. You will notice that more than half the head is above the eyes? This means a much larger brain-pan than anything else of relative size. The fore-limbs could be controlled to do more things than just holding food or digging holes in the ground."

"How big would it be?" the earlier question was repeated.

"I have not really decided on the exact size but imagine

somewhere between the size of a goat and a pony would be about right."

"What?" exploded the Chairman, "It would not last five minutes in tiger country! A succulent tiger's dinner if I ever saw one. It hasn't even horns or a long spiky tail with which to defend itself."

"That is where the superior intelligence comes in, it will be able to avoid tigers and the like," answered the C.D. defensively.

"Huh! I don't think much of it," said the Chairman, "Anyway is it really necessary, what use would it be?"

"It is nice to look at it," offered the junior member, "I particularly like the head-hair."

"I still don't think much of it," repeated the Chairman, "Anyway I suppose it would have to breed, have you thought of some kind of mate for it?"

"Quite honestly I haven't yet put much thought into its mate..."

"Well you had best put some thought into it or we will end up with just so many well fed tigers." The Chairman obviously becoming interested in the project, much to the C.D.'s satisfaction.

"It's mate will have to be bigger and even more ferocious than anything we have already," said the junior member logically.

"Oh No!", cried the Ancient Chronicler from the foot of the table, "We do not want to go back to dinosaurs, you will remember what a fiasco they turned out to be!"

"Of course not," replied the C.D. soothingly, "I have in mind something only slightly larger than 'proto-type'..."

"And nothing like so frothy and succulent?" interrupted the Chairman.

"Quite so," responded the C.D. "Something more hairy and...", he brought the palms of his hands slowly together as he searched his mind for a word to counter the Chairman's 'frothy'... altogether more dense."

"Would it not be likely to turn on 'proto'?" queried the Ancient Chronicler.

"Not if 'proto' uses the sense I've designed it with," replied the C.D.

"Have you settled on a colour? There is no indication on the drawing," queried someone.

"I envisage a basic brown but varying from almost milk-white to jet back with appropriate matching hair."

"Won't that look rather odd, flocks of them in assorted colours milling about?" said the junior member.

"I was not thinking of them being mixed up at first," replied the C.D., "but the various colours inhabiting different parts of the globe, white ones in one area, black in another, yellow somewhere else."

"It seems rather bare, will it not be cold?" was the next question.

"Not in hot climates, in cooler parts it would cover itself with the pelts of other animals," replied the C.D.

"And how," queried the Chairman with almost a sneer, "does one persuade an animal to give up its skin?"

"It's mate would be responsible for the strong-arm stuff, the killing and skinning and so forth," explained the C.D. somewhat glibly.

"Hardly looks capable of much to me," said the ancient C., "No fangs or claws or anything."

"Ha!" The C.D. was expecting this question, "That is all part of the complex design. The upright stance will allow him to wield weapons, throw rocks and the like and lack of size will be amply compensated with an above average amount of guile and a bellicose attitude to life."

"What about a name for it? We can't continue to call it 'proto'," said the Chairman, now completely hooked on the new design.

"I haven't got as far as a name for it yet," replied the C.D., "anyone with a suggestion?"

"Wait a minute!", cried the ancient C., "It is not as easy as that. There have been so many animals we are right near the end of the alphabet as it is." He scanned the lists in his massive ledger. "Hardly any room before the 'X's and 'Y's…. hold on though, there is a space between 'wolverine' and 'wombat' if you can use that."

Various suggestions were made ranging from a simple 'wommy' to an exotic 'womalitania' before a middle of the road compromise was selected.

"*Woman*", The chairman experimented with the sound of it. "It doesn't exactly roll off the tongue like 'crocodile' or 'anaconda' but I suppose it will do well enough."

"What about a name for its mate?" the junior m. chipped in.

"Does it *have* to have a different name?" groaned the ancient C., "There is hardly room for any more."

"Well it is usual," said the Chairman, "You know 'ducks and drakes', 'lions and lionesses' and so forth."

"'Womaness' sounds ridiculous," said someone, "Anyway it seems the wrong way round."

"Owing to the shortage of space in the lists how about using part of the 'proto's name?" suggested the ancient C.

"'Wom'", supplied the Chairman, "Can't say I like it, it would be different if 'proto' had a long name like 'hippopotamus' or 'rhinoceros'."

"What about the rear end of the word then, 'Man'?" suggested the A.C. "It is short and easy to spell, seems quite appropriate to me."

As they suited the other members of the committee the two names were adopted unanimously.

"Any further questions?" asked the Chairman.

"How would they communicate?" queried someone.

"The usual barks and grunts I suppose," offered the j.m.

"Oh No!" cried the C.D., "That would be sufficient for 'man' I suppose but my concept for 'proto' – 'woman' – sorry, is much superior, the design incorporates the ability to communicate continuously."

"Continuously! Ridiculous!" snorted the Chairman, "She would run out of breath."

"Not at all, it is allowed for in the design," replied the C.D. somewhat smugly, tapping the blue-print with his finger.

In general terms woman proved quite successful. She had her faults and failings of course but no more than other animals. She was, if nothing else, a survivor. In spite of her very many disasters, more often than not of her own making, she blundered on for generation after generation. It is interesting to speculate as to what would have happened if woman had existed on her own and managed to dodge the tiger and other perils but as it was she had her mate and was stuck with him.

Admittedly man did prove useful at times in digging caves, hunting for food and taking the can back when woman's devious plans came embarrassingly unstuck but when times were easy he soon adopted that pose peculiar to man, - but not to woman – of leaning one elbow on a flat rock or fallen tree-trunk and putting the world to rights over a horn or clay breaker or two of the current tipple. These discussions sometimes developed into arguments and occasionally into blows. Commencing as man-to-man contests they soon expanded into family feuds from whence it was but a step to tribal conflicts.

Eventually things got so out of hand woman decided to put her foot down and re-assert her authority. Alas! It was too late. Once man had developed a bad habit it stuck to him like a jam to a blanket. In no time at all village raids had progressed through full-scale battles to all-out wars.

Wars naturally resulted in a shortage of young men which meant that sometimes woman had to do without her personal hunter, or, perish the thought, *share* one thing that woman was not very good at. It also meant that woman, in order to compete, was forced to flatter man to gain his attention, which, of course, gave him ideas above his station.

This led to a slight tilting in the balance of power and after a while it occurred to woman that many of the rules governing her life, and certainly all of those concerning her morality, were dictated by man. Furthermore, whilst he was dashing all over the countryside creating mayhem and thoroughly enjoying himself she was left at home looking after the kids.

Enough was enough. Rather than accept life as it came and hope that in a future existence she would return as a man or a cat in a good home she decided to do something about rectifying the situation.

To achieve this end woman had first to get into 'Politics', a system whereby man, or a body of men, with sufficient clout could order others about to get things changed to their advantage without resorting to bloodshed. As woman had not been invited she gate-crashed the system, or at least she tried to. Unfortunately before the movement had got off the ground, man, either by accident or pure perversity, got himself involved in a war which by comparison made all previous conflicts resemble so many vicarage tea-parties.

The end result was once again a shortage of young men but this time woman was ready, she demanded and received the right to vote, not only to vote war entirely off the agenda but to vote for or against anything else she felt strongly about.

However, once again she was thwarted. Within a generation man was at it again with all his old enthusiasm.

Not for the first time woman wondered if man was really necessary and if the world would not be a sweeter, more comfortable place without him.

It was the resourcefulness of man which proved his salvation. Although most inventions were designed to make life easier for himself they often resulted in a lessening of woman's workload. For instance he nearly managed to contrive a private fire outside the cave, an unbelievable improvement on the previous system of searching a burnt-off hillside for a suitable Sunday roast. Damming and diverting a local stream provided 'running water' close to the abode – even if it was liable to flood the cave or wash away the mud walls of the hut in wet weather. Even man's propensity to homicide resulted in inventions which could be turned to woman's advantage; flying machines produced to rain death and destruction on the heads of perfect strangers at prodigious distances were modified to take woman to visit distant relatives or to sunny climes for holidays and a system of under-water swimming intended to facilitate attaching bombs under enemy battleships soon allowed her to explore the wonders of the deep.

Man also invented washing machines and refrigerators, electric irons and television.

He also invented the telephone. One could forgive him an awful lot for that.

In fact when it came to electronics man's inventiveness knew no bounds. One human activity after another, domestic and industrial, was taken over by the ubiquitous micro-chip until the human race was hardly necessary at all. Until, that is, the various viruses introduced accidentally or deliberately into electronic systems became too great to be sustained and the inevitable 'non-lethal bomb' wiped out the entire electrical world. Multi-millionaires became paupers overnight and those with a field of potatoes and a cow, rich beyond the dreams of avarice.

And woman, and man, came back into their own.

6 KNOTTY LOGS

Why, one may ask, use the term 'Log' when what is meant is a journal or diary?

Why a 'Knot' when a speed is the point at issue?

If you have ever wondered just sit back and I will tell you how it all came about.

Before we start I should mention that the nautical word 'log' is derived from the Middle English word 'logge' meaning, believe it or not, a roughly hewn piece of timber. The word 'knot' comes from the Old English word 'cnotta', meaning apparently, a knot such as often found in a piece of string.

A 'Dutch Log' is a very simple device for measuring the speed of a vessel through the water.

Although lost in the mists of time I should imagine it all started something like this:-

****

Old Captain Reuben was of a scientific turn of mind and for many years had the conviction that there was some connection between distance and time. For instance he knew that if he walked up and down his deck forty times at his customary pace between passing the town kerk and the first windmill his ship was making good progress but if he did sixty or seventy turns on the deck between these points the ship was doing badly – or the tide was against her or both.

Which was all very well when windmills or other landmarks were in sight but it was a different proposition at sea when only the odd sandbank and the like were to be seen. Of course when a tangle of seaweed or a piece of wreckage floated past a slight idea of the ship's speed was indicated but such convenient objects were never around when most needed.

Suddenly Captain Reuben stopped in his tracks and smote his forehead.

'Of course! Why did I not think of it before?' (Not his exact words of course as he only spoke very Low Dutch.)

"Jan!" he yelled at the ship's boy, "Take a log from the galley and when I tell you drop it in the sea from the bowsprit. The moment you have done that nip along aft and sing out when the log floats past the thunder-box on the taffrail."

The captain resumed his pacing but when Jan shouted that the piece of wood had passed the stern he stopped dead.

'Four and a half turns on the deck. Brilliant!' he said to himself. 'By the look of the sky the wind should freshen soon so I can further the experiment later.'

A log was dropped over the side an hour or so later and Captain Reuben counted the turns he made on deck before it floated past the stern. With the increases of wind he found that it came to just under four. The experiment was repeated several more times before it became too dark to observe the piece of wood on the surface of the water.

As soon as it was light enough the following morning another log was dropped. An hour later another and just before breakfast yet a further length of timber splashed into the sea. The experiment became an obsession with Captain Reuben. Hourly throughout the day a log was dropped overboard and the performance repeated until the cook was eyeing disconsolately his dwindling fuel supply and the crew had cold porridge for supper.

Something had to be done. The crew racked their brains for a few hours.

It was eventually the bosun, who's passion for economy had him known all along the coast as the meanest man alive, who hit on the solution.

"Why not bend a line to the log, pass it along the bulwarks and when the log has passed the stern haul it back on board and use it again?"

This mind-boggling suggestion was greeted with enthusiasm by the other members of the crew. It was the obvious answer to the problem.

However there was a snag.

"Who is going to tell him?" asked Piet, the ancient able seaman.

They all remembered the last time one of the crew had got above his station and suggested to the captain that he might be kind enough to consider the possibility of exchanging for a piece of meat the horse-shoe discovered in the foc'sle beef ration.

"It was the Bosun's idea," spoke up the brash young seaman Mikkel.

A minute or so later the bosun repeated himself as Mikkel disentangled himself from the windlass nursing his jaw.

"I was only joking Bose, honest!" said the latter plaintively.

"We need a volunteer," said Old Piet.

"Yes," replied the bosun, "but where is the little blighter? He was here a moment ago."

A sound such as a rabbit might make whilst trying to carve out a new life for itself in a sandy bank with a fox breathing down its neck issued from under and old sail in a corner of the deck.

The bosun pounced.

****

Jan approached the captain with considerable trepidation.

"Sir," he quavered, "The...the crew," (getting them all in at as quickly as possible in case of a lack of opportunity later), "...the crew thought humbly that it may please your honour...."

"For goodness sake get on with it boy," (free translation again – it sounded much better in Low Dutch), "Can't you see I am busy!" shouted the captain.

In actual fact his industry was not readily apparent as he was sitting on a coil of rope with his head in his hands – albeit cudgelling his brains trying to think of a way to overcome the obvious economic snag to his recent invention.

The trembling Jan got to the heart of the matter with more speed than diplomacy.

"Why not b-bend a line to the log and....."

"......carry it aft then heave it up and use it again!" continued the captain for him, "Brilliant!" (A favourite word of his.)

Captain Reuben was so pleased at this revelation of the solution to his problem that he so forgot himself as to thump Jan on the back and promote him to Able Seaman on the spot – which nearly meant promotion and demise for the lad at the same instant as he was but a light-weight and the captain of generous proportions even for a Dutch shipmaster.

The invention of the log-line brought an era of sweetness and light to the foc'sle. The cook had enough fuel to boil the garbage he called food so the crew had a hot dinner, which, as everyone knows, is much more palatable than cold garbage and the bosun, except in the captain's hearing, boasted of his magnificent bequest to navigators to anyone who cared to listen to him. Which was not many. The captain did exactly the same thing but more effectively as, of course, people had to listen to him.

In fact the only person who was not pleased at the outcome was Mikkel who, owing to Jan's promotion, was now junior member of the crew and was thus relegated to bailing out the bilges, washing the captain's socks and suchlike revolting duties.

****

Captain Reuben's invention came into its own among his peers at the inn by the harbour wherein many ships were laid up for the winter. Other shipmasters with a modern outlook took to the idea and the following season many adopted it.

One question which cropped up was a name for the new invention. Various suggestions were made and discarded until eventually someone said that if they did not decide on a name soon some foreigner, he gestured vaguely to the west, would do so and claim the credit. This remark prompted a master from Amsterdam to propose the name 'Dutch Log', adding that this would put the noses of the Venetians and those wild Viking boys thoroughly out of joint.

As almost the entire assembled company hailed from the Netherlands the name was agreed to the satisfactions of everyone – except perhaps Captain Reuben who had been trying to imagine what 'Captain Reuben's Ship Velocity Indicator' or somesuch would look like in print. Which was rather difficult as printing, even if it had been invented at the time, was not generally known.

****

Foreigners did get hold of the idea in time and improvements and modifications were made over the years. One of the most important innovations being that of allowing the log to drift astern on a long line which had knots in it at fixed intervals. With this arrangement obviously the more 'knots' that passed over the taffrail in a given time the faster the vessel was moving through the water.

It was but a few decades after the log's inception that an argument broke out in a certain harbour tavern concerning the speed claims of a particular vessel. The eventual conclusion of most of the company was that the knots in her log line must have been closer together than was the usual practice. However the discussion did cause an old Frankish shipmaster, (known as 'Henri the Navigator' ever since the time he was blown out of sight of land in a gale and actually got home again owing to a change in the wind), to suggest that a standard length between the knots in the line should be adopted on all ships. It was agreed that such a course had its merits but as the lengths of ship's decks and the speed at which individual masters pace up and down varied considerably it clearly did not solve all the problems involved.

The use of an hour glass had been investigated but an hour was found to be too great a period of time for practical purposes, except for particularly slow vessels, as the lines available were not long enough. In any case many ships did not carry an hour glass, their masters having no truck with such expensive aids to navigation. On these ships the mate rang 'eight bells' when he thought he had been on watch long enough – or the weather began to turn nasty. This was a bit tough on the second mate's watch who thus had little to look forward to except a long watch and a future prospect of promotion.

But I digress.

Attempts had been made to mark with paint half and even quarter hours on an hour glass but this proved highly inaccurate owing to the very shape of the thing. Even at that some of the masters claimed that a one hundred fathom line would not be long enough for a run of a quarter of an hour. This was not disputed to any great extent as no one present was able to work out this mathematical poser in his head – including those who made the claim.

"What we require is a glass which only runs for seconds," said the master of an English wine ship.

A Portuguese shipmaster with a nasty facial scar and a ring in one ear thought it was time he shoved his oar in, so, being reasonably certain that a second was a division of a minute considered himself on safe ground when he asked, "How many?"

"Yes, how many?" sneered Henri the Navigator. He did not like Englishmen generally and English tanker men in particular.

The English captain was nonplussed. He began to bluster when, to his infinite relief, a quiet voice from one of the four dark corners of the room said, without the slightest hesitation, "Fourteen."

All heads turned to where the voice had emanated. In the gloom, (it should be mentioned here that it was night time and the illumination from the two or three tallow dips in the room hardly gave off enough light to enable the customers to see what they were eating and drinking – which was probably the whole idea), they made out the hunched figure of Aaron the chandler.

"Fourteen?" queried one of the company.

"Fourteen," repeated Aaron with even more conviction.

Fourteen seconds was therefore adopted as Aaron's opinion carried considerable weight. This was partly due to his mysterious powers, the things he could manipulate in the way of lodestones, chemicals, columns of figures and the like was absolutely awe-inspiring. The main reason was because recently he had taken up as a sideline the supply of stores to ships, (which was an original thing for a candle maker to do at the time), so most of those present owed him money. The respect shown to him was however purely superficial as he was suspected of all kinds of nefarious practices, from short-changing to witchcraft and cross-bow running.

Having decided the time factor the next question was that of the distance between the knots in the log line. This led to quite a heated discussion so no one noticed Aaron quietly leaving for his shop.

On arriving at his establishment Aaron greeted his apprentice in his usual manner and said, "Go into the back room and dig out that case of fourteen second 'hour glasses' I was lumbered with a couple of years ago when they had that raw material shortage at the glass works, I want to change the price tags on them."

As the apprentice ran into the back room nursing his stinging ear

Aaron rubbed his hands together. No one was more adept than he at making a fast thaler.

＊＊＊＊＊＊＊＊＊＊＊＊＊＊＊＊

Meanwhile at the tavern the company had reached the conclusion that there must be some connection between fourteen seconds and the distance between the knots in the log line on the one hand and hours and miles on the other. However the sheer mathematics of the problem had them stymied. It was therefore eventually decided to take their difficulty to the local priest who was so well educated it was rumoured that not only could he read but write as well.

****

The deputation arrived at the priest's abode to be greeted by that worthy man at the door.

"The top of the marnin' to ye!" sang out the cheerful cleric, "And what can I be doing for you bhoys?" (Father Patrick came from some outlandish island in the Western Ocean which accounted for his strange mode of speech.)

The Mariners explained their problem which was listened to attentively by the priest.

"It's sorry I am my bhoys," he said when they had finished, "but it's not the figures I'm good at, it's university men you need for that kind of work."

He was asked to recommend a good university and, as if an afterthought, if he would be so good as to write the necessary letter for them, they muttering such excuses as, "It's so difficult to get hold of a decent piece of parchment these days," and, "I've just remembered that I'm out of ink," – which did not fool the good father for a moment.

****

Everything went according to plan, albeit rather slowly.

To start with Father Patrick could not change his writing style overnight and there were inevitable delays in procuring suitable red paint and gold leaf for the capital letters. The mariners' rambling explanations in seaman's terms had to be translated into Latin of course which also took time so the letter itself took a month or two to write.

65

Even then the whole process had to be repeated twice more as the original letter was used to light the supper fire of the band of brigands who had intercepted the mail in the first instance, (This was discovered when they made their confessions prior to being hung.) A second letter came to an even more prosaic end when the courier, having breakfasted on a surfeit of lampreys and old ale, found the motion of his horse and his stomach in disaccord.

The postal service was not up to much even in those days.

****

By the time the reply to the letter reached the tavern, (which in the interim had been rebuilt of brick as the original wooden structure had been reduced to ashes in the course of a previously unnamed winter festival which was thence-forward always referred to as 'Burns Night'), the original company had long met their destinies. The Portuguese had been hung for piracy, Aaron was the financial adviser of the Sultan of Egypt, the Englishmen had retired to Skegness and Henri the Navigator had been blown out of sight of land once too often. However their successors greeted the arrival of the missive from the university with great enthusiasm – once it had been translated from the Latin, a task Father Patrick gave to one of his minions as he by that time he was an Abbot and above such trivialities.

"Twenty-three and a half feet between knots," (Actually 23.644443 feet approximately if you like to work it out. Ed.) "Well at least we have got that settled," one of the new generation of mariners remarked, "It's a pity we got stuck with a fourteen second glass to start with though, I wonder whose idea that was?"

****

So, gentle reader, although it is incorrect to say 'Knots per hour' it is perfectly in order to quote 'Knots per fourteen seconds converted to nautical miles per hour'.

And much good it may do you.

****

The log line remained virtually unchanged for centuries, the only refinement being the marking of various 'knots', 5, 7, 10, etc, in a similar manner to a lead line for convenience in reading. The final version of the log itself, known as a 'Chip', consisted of a quarter circle of flat wood about nine inches across. Aided by a strip of lead let into the curved edge this floated vertically in the water and was attached to the log line by a three-legged bridle. One leg of the bridle served as a trip line being loosely connected to the chip by a peg plugged into it. After the log reading had been taken a jerk on the line would dislodge the peg allowing the chip to be hauled in edgeways thus lessening its resistance to the water.

A long time starting perhaps and Dutch Logs did not disappear overnight with the advent of 'patent logs' towards the end of last century. A 'chip' log was part of the original equipment of at least one ship in which the author sailed which was built well after the Second World War. It was, of course, just a reserve in case the more modern instruments failed.

The 'Log Book' acquired its name from the fact that one of the main entries was a record of the log readings which gave an indication of the distance run. Compass courses would also be entered followed by such weather information as the state of the sea and wind direction and other items of value or interest. Thermometer and barometer readings were added as these instruments came into general use. In spite of all these additions the book itself retained its original name.

7 LIFEBOAT

<u>Chapter 1</u>

Ben Travis glanced at the passenger in the seat beside him to ensure that he was not awake then slowly withdrew the silver medallion from his shirt pocket.

Most of the travellers were either asleep or quietly reading as the aircraft cruised on the long haul to Singapore so he felt happily isolated in a world of his own. Time to think of <u>her</u>. Not that he had thought of much else since they had parted.

How beautiful she was. It's a pity I am not a trifle more elegant he thought. The six feet one inch of him was satisfactory enough apart from being slightly overweight – 'must cut down on the beer a bit this trip.' The main disfigurement was his broken nose. Although some girls thought it attractive it repulsed most of the nicer ones – and all of the mothers. He had tried to explain that it was the result of a rugby football accident when he was a kid. The story did not improve with repetition and even Ben, although knowing it to be true, found it less convincing. Elizabeth had not mentioned it so he avoided the subject. He also wished that his reddish hair was of a slightly more dignified colour.

He allowed the thin silver chain to trickle through his fingers as he examined the disc itself. Engraved on it were her initials and the date of her eighteenth birthday surrounded by a floral design, roses by the look of them. A present from her parents, that much she had told him when he was ostensibly admiring it whilst trying to peep down the front of her dress. He wondered what her parents would say when they discovered that it was no longer in their daughter's possession.

Ben reminisced on those happy couple of weeks at the end of his leave. The first meeting at his dentist's surgery. Love at first sight? A hackneyed phrase but no doubt true. He had never seen her before as she had replaced the previous receptionist some time after his last check up. How he cursed himself for not arranging his appointment for as soon as he came on leave from his ship rather than leaving it until nearly the end. A second mate should have organised things much more efficiently he chided himself.

She was small, slim and dark haired. Her eyes the deep blue of tropic seas. When she smiled her whole person seemed to glow with vitality.

She smiled now, "Have you an appointment?" Her voice was music to Ben's ears.

"Yes" seemed to be the answer so he let it out.

"Your name please?" She glanced at the appointment book.

For a moment it eluded him. The pause was long enough to cause her to look up.

"Er, Travis, Ben Travis."

"Please take a seat Mr. Travis, I will let you know when the dentist is free."

Ben selected a chair in the waiting room which gave him a good view of the reception desk and picked up a magazine. Several minutes later he realised he was holding a lady's fashion journal so hastily swapped it for an ancient copy of 'Punch'.

Not a word of what the dentist said whilst in his surgery could Ben remember, his mind was entirely concentrated on the receptionist. On leaving the dentist's chair he returned to her to make a provisional appointment for his next periodic check up.

She smiled as she prepared to make the entry in the appointment book.

There was a pause as Ben struggled for words.

"What shall I put down?" she asked helpfully.

"Your telephone number," blurted Ben.

"What?" She appeared shocked.

"Your telephone number," he repeated, "I want to ask you out and we can hardly discuss arrangements here." As if it were the most reasonable thing in the world.

The girl was confused. "Please," she said, "a date for your next appointment."

"when I have your name and phone number"

"Why?"

Hell! Ben thought, I am making a mess of this. I should have had something specific to offer, theatre?, a week-end in the West Indies?, a trip to the moon?

However her 'Why?' gave him some hope.

"Can't tell you here," playing for time but covering this by gesturing to the waiting room behind him where the potential patients sat engrossed in their own private worlds of misery and boredom.

"But what of my boy-friend?"

Was this to put him off or was she interested? Either way he had nothing to lose. With more confidence than he felt he slid her scratch pad towards her.

"Give me his name and address and I will go and explain it to him." This was accompanied with a scowl of mock ferocity.

A master stroke! She smiled, than after a moment's hesitation, scribbled 'Elizabeth' and a number on the pad, tore off the sheet and handed it to him.

"Not before seven and now please let us arrange your next appointment, there are people coming in." The door opening on what appeared to be a whole family of sufferers confirmed this.

She was not in the office when Ben returned some five minutes later for his coat.

****

That first telephone call. It seemed to be forever waiting for seven o'clock. Keyed up, his patter all ready for when she lifted the receiver, he was sitting by the phone a good five minutes before he dialled.

A richly modulated voice repeated the number.

Oh Gawd! Her mother! Ben had not allowed for this.

"Could I speak to Elizabeth please?"

"Who is speaking?" – infinitely suspicious.

"Ben Travis," then, before she could hang up on him, "Are you her sister?"

"No, her mother."

"Oh, I do beg your pardon Ma'am, sounded younger…." He trailed off. Nothing like laying it on thick.

Voices in the background and the sound of hurried footsteps, then, thank goodness, Elizabeth's voice, slightly breathless, "I thought I said after seven o'clock?" almost cross.

"It was after seven, a good ten seconds after by my trusty wrist chronometer." Was that a slight giggle?

A rendezvous was arranged after the traditional amount of persuasion on Ben's part and reluctance on hers – feigned he hoped?

She had only given her phone number to avoid a scene.

If so then why not a false one?

Because it might have meant a worse scene the next day.

Damn right!

The first time they went out together. She shy but ravishing, he as clumsy as a teenager on his first date. Awkward silences then a collision of words as they both spoke at once.

After the initial nervousness however the sheer pleasure of her company. So full of life, always appearing to be vitally interested in everything he said – which was a surprise to him who would be the first to admit to being no great conversationalist.

****

All too quickly his leave drew to an end. The last few days were a rush, so many things to be done which he had intended to take his time over during the course of his leave. His ancient M.G. to lay up in the family garage, last minute shopping, his full discharge book to renew. Although these chores were carried out whilst Elizabeth was at work he begrudged every moment he was not either with or sitting thinking of her.

Eventually the sad day arrived. Elizabeth had arranged to take him to the air-port in her father's car. She turned up late and flustered at his home having been delayed by one thing and another. This left them just time to get to the air-port in comfortable time provided there were no traffic hold-ups. But then there was another delay.

Ben's luggage was in the car and he and Elizabeth about to climb into it when his mother gave a ladylike shriek and said, "The cake! You have forgotten the cake."

Every voyage since he first went to sea his mother had given him a large fruit cake to take away. On this occasion the cake had not been made until the previous day so had been left to cool overnight. In the excitement it had been forgotten.

Late as they were Ben's first reaction was to leave it but he quickly realised how hurt his mother would be if he did so. His conscience doubly pricked him in fact as on previous occasions he had made a point of making a great fuss about it intimating that he could join his ship without his sextant or his clothes but not without the cake. He knew well what pleasure this gave her.

There was nothing else for it but to remove a suitcase from the car and re-stow half of it to accommodate the rapidly wrapped cake.

Eventually they got away, by then very short of time. Ben took the wheel and the elderly Rover shrieked in protest at times as he drove it at a speed it had not achieved since the days of its pristine youth.

So far as conversation was concerned the journey was made mainly in silence, Elizabeth too full of thought for small talk and Ben concentrating on the driving of the unfamiliar car.

Nearing the airport Elizabeth suddenly ran her hand through

oddments on the parcel shelf before her, then glanced at the floor at her feet.

"Oh no!"

"Whatever is the matter?" asked Ben.

"Nothing really, just a book I was going to give you to read on the plane. I must have put it down on the hall table when I was searching for the car keys. Never mind, I'll post it to you." She was furious with herself. It was quite an expensive book which she had seen him take an interest in during a visit to the book shop.

"No, don't do that, it is certain to be lost in the post or held up by the customs somewhere. Keep it until I return, it will be something else to look forward to." He laughed, "We certainly can't go back for it now, here is the airport and it is still touch and go if I catch the plane."

He made it with minutes to spare. A mad rush, the car badly parked at the 'Departure' entrance, the luggage hauled out, the vehicle locked – luckily he remembered to hand Elizabeth the keys instead of automatically dropping them into his pocket – the gallop to the check in desk where he collected his ticket, fortunately there was no queue.

Elizabeth's tearful goodbye, obviously upset not only at the parting but also by the forgotten book as she mentioned this again. Even more upset when he slipped her a little package as a parting gift.

"But you have nothing from me!" Her eyes were filled with tears.

Then, "I know!" She reached behind her neck, unfastened the silver chain and slipped the pendant into Ben's shirt pocket.

"But I can't take this," he remonstrated, "It was from your folks."

Elizabeth realised this also.

"Bring it back to me."

A last embrace then a headlong rush to the gate for the shuttle service to London and the first leg of his journey.

"A close run thing" Ben quoted to himself.

Chapter 2

The voyage was similar to so many others, a mixture of dull and uncomfortable times soon forgotten and the happy occasions remembered.

The ship had spent an awful lot of time at sea even for a bulk carrier, Ben reminisced, Singapore to Port Kembla in ballast, from there to Saudi Arabia with steel, God! Did she not roll with all that weight in the bottom of her! All the way back to Wallaroo for grain – a very good time there – then the long haul to Nakhodka in Siberia and the long stay at anchor awaiting a berth. Now they were on their way to Seattle to load more grain for the Middle East.

But I won't see much of that! Thought Ben happily. Only the evening before a message from the company's head office had confirmed that he and a few others were to be relieved at the American port.

The high spots of the voyage for him had been the arrival of the mail. It arrived in bulk at infrequent intervals via the London office. There were generally a few letters for him from his mother but they now took second place to those from Elizabeth. She wrote frequently and well, always intimating that she was looking forward to his return.

'I should be home in a week', said Ben to himself as he hauled his uniform jersey out of the washing machine. It was the first time he could remember washing anything so large and woolly as both it and its predecessors usually survived until he went home. However, with considerable wear in Russia, Ben decided that the jersey was becoming slightly unsociable and, as it would most likely be required before he left the ship, the washing of it became necessary.

He was holding up the woollen by its shoulders and deciding that it somehow changed shape in the washing process and now resembled the hide of a newly skinned blue gorilla when the sound of hurried footsteps and the sudden appearance of the purser's head in the doorway interrupted his reverie.

"So there you are! The Old Man has been phoning all over the ship for you – wants you on the bridge right away."

"What's the flap about?"

"Don't really know, some ship in trouble I think."

By the time Ben reached the bridge the ship was already heading towards the casualty and the increase in vibration indicated that her speed was being built up to her maximum of just under sixteen knots.

The captain dropped the pencil he had been using onto the chart and said to Ben, "Just check that position and the course to it. – A ship on fire less than fifty miles away. When you have done that take over the watch from the third mate so that he can give the mate a hand preparing for survivors."

As the ship lessened the distance to the vessel in distress further details were received by radio. She was a tanker with an engine room fire which was now out of control. The last message sent from her was a brief one to the effect that the crew were taking to the life-boats. Then silence.

"I only hope they have enough sense to stay by the ship in the boats," said the captain. "It could be a job finding them in this otherwise." He gestured ahead where almost the entire horizon was obscured by rain.

"Not much wind thank goodness," he continued, "but that swell is going to make taking the people from the boats rather tricky. Should be able to find the ship herself alright though if the position sent was anything like accurate. If it were not for the rain we might be able to see the smoke by now."

"I wonder if she is loaded or in ballast?" Ben ventured.

"Just what I was thinking. Judging by the panic to get off it does not sound as if she is in ballast, unless she is not gas-free. If we knew which way she had been heading it might have given us a clue." Then to the third mate, now at the radar, "Any sign of her yet John? She should be under twenty miles off by now so you could pick her up at any moment."

The chief officer came on to the bridge to report that everything was as ready as he could make it. The long guest warp rigged close to the water-line, rope ladders, heaving lines, gantlines and life-buoys all ready to drop over the side at short notice.

"And the motor-boat is all set to go if it is needed," the mate added.

"I do hope it won't be required," replied the captain, "All being well I should be able to get close enough to the tanker's boats to get lines to them and......."

He was interrupted by a shout from the third mate.

"Echo ten degrees on the port bow...... seventeen and a half miles!"

"That should be him," the captain turned to the man now at the wheel, "Port ten degrees, steer oh four five....... I'm glad we have found her so soon, there is still well over four hours of daylight left."

Twenty minutes later black smoke was discerned in a gap between the bluish grey of the rain showers and shortly afterwards the vessel herself could be made out.

Approaching down the south-westerly wind the smoke from the burning tanker was blown away from the observers on the bridge of the advancing ship so as soon as a passing rain shower cleared away details became apparent. She was of modern design with bridge and all accommodation aft. The grey of her hull was in good condition but the paint on her tall, smoke belching funnel was already so scorched as to render its insignia unrecognisable, giving some idea of the intensity of the fire. Clouds of thick black oily smoke also billowed from various ventilators and other openings in the superstructure.

"Too deep in the water to be in ballast," commented the captain as he scanned her through his binoculars," but I don't think fully loaded. Probably a 'parcel' carrier but what would she be doing in the middle of the ocean only part loaded? I hope her pump-room proves a good enough barrier between her cargo and the fire anyway, no matter what she is carrying. Can anyone see any of her boats or life-rafts yet? They should……. Good God! Her port lifeboat is still housed – it must have jammed or been unapproachable owing to smoke……"

"There's the other boat sir," the third mate saw it first, "alongside still, right under her stern."

"They can't be all off yet then…." As the swell lifted the boat again it became apparent that it was in trouble. The captain continued, "They have the boat's painter round its propeller by the look of things and they are still attached to the ship. Damn! I can't pick them up that close to the tanker."

The boat, of the enclosed type, appeared to be covered in men, waving and gesticulating. The rope around its screw was too low to be reached from the deck of the boat and an effort was being made to cut it with a knife attached to the end of a boat-hook. Several attempts had been made with this contrivance, everyone on the boat apparently trying to help, when the inevitable happened, a particularly vicious lurch of the boat caused the man with the hook to slip and in grabbing hold to save himself the boat-hook fell into the water and bobbed away.

"Damnation" We haven't time for a repeat performance, now we will have to use our boat." The captain turned to the second mate, "Ben?"

"All ready to go sir!" Ben had been secretly hoping to take the boat away ever since the emergency commenced, something that rarely happened in a lifetime at sea. A little excitement to talk about in the years to come.

"How many men do you think you will require?"

"Fewer the better sir, I would suggest only the third mate and an engineer for the motor." Ben replied.

The third mate grinned happily, it was an opportunity that he would have hated to miss.

The captain nodded, "Yes, I'm inclined to agree. Leave us a bit thin up here though, it's a pity we have no cadets. However the purser can give a hand with the engine room telegraphs and maybe 'Sparks' will be available if he can get clear of the radio room for a few minutes." Then to the Mate and Ben, "Carry on then, get the boat swung out, I'll let you know when to lower away. Do not waste any time."

Ben dashed down to his room for extra clothes. It was mild enough on the bridge but he knew it would be much colder in an open boat – and wet. Oilskin jacket and jersey seemed the answer – then he remembered his soaking wet jersey in the laundry. "Damn! It will have to be the anorak then," he said to himself, "a bit bulky but it is fairly water-tight."

Having slipped on the coat and grabbed his life-jacket Ben

suddenly realised that with all the excitement he had not thought of Elizabeth for several minutes. 'This will be something to tell her!' he thought, then, in a flash of inspiration, 'Why not come with me?' Ben dropped the pendant into his pocket and dashed for the boat deck.

The motor life-boat was launched without a hitch.

"Any more for the 'Skylark'?" sang out the fourth engineer as the boast swung away from the ship's side.

Drawing just enough water aft to immerse the propeller and nothing forward the light glass-fibre boat was nearly blown over when she crested the first swell on leaving the lee of the ship.

"Steady the Buffs!" shouted Ben as he hauled on the tiller to bring the boat's stern into the wind, "I didn't realise there was so much breeze!"

"Didn't know there was so much swell either." The 'fourth' turned his head exaggeratedly as the boat dropped between the crests and both their own ship and the tanker momentarily disappeared from sight. "Are you sure you know where you are?"

"Completely lost." Returned Ben, and then to the third mate who was stumbling aft from the bows where he had just released the 'lazy' painter, "Can you see anything John?"

"Not a damn thing but water. By the way, I've had a change of heart about seafaring, turn the boat round I want to go home."

They kept up the banter to conceal their nervousness as they proceeded towards the stern of the disabled vessel.

It seemed to take an age to reach the survivors boat but eventually they arrived and the fouled painter cut with the third mate's trusty Bowie knife, the cook's knife, snatched from the galley as a reserve, was not required.

Before reaching the survivors John had transferred the boat's painter from the bow to the stern and this was put to use as a tow-rope.

At first the boats hardly moved but slowly way came on them and the distance from the stern of the burning tanker slowly increased. Being nearly beam on to the wind and sea they both rolled alarmingly but by judicious use of the helm Ben avoided a repetition of their earlier fright as they crested each swell.

They had reached a position about two hundred yards from the stricken tanker with their own ship easing into a position to pick them up when renewed shouting from the survivors attracted their attention. Several men were gesturing towards the smoking hulk and a moment later it was realised what they were pointing at. What at first appeared to be a bundle of rags attached to the main deck rail just forward of the accommodation revealed itself as the smoke-blackened figure of a man, waving feebly.

From being an exciting interlude in an otherwise rather dull voyage the affair suddenly took on an aspect of horror. To add to the drama a sudden 'whoof' from the tanker's superstructure heralded a great increase in smoke and for the first time flames were to be seen.

Ben rapidly weighed up the situation. Although not so far from the tanker as had been intended there was enough distance to allow their ship to pick up the survivors without danger of collision. But if he left them was he justified in risking the lives of three men in the hope of rescuing one? It was apparent that the tanker could explode at any moment. But what if it did not? Possibly she could burn for a week without blowing up, it had happened before. Much depended on what cargo she was carrying.

The squawking of the 'walkie-talkie' radio slung around his neck reminded Ben that he had means of communicating with the ship and that the captain was apparently trying to contact him.

It also gave him an idea.

He signalled the 'fourth' to stop the boat's engine then, to the third mate, "John, grab this radio and hop onto the other boat. Tell the Old Man the situation, he can pick up the boat here. You to Dave," to the fourth engineer, "this mob won't be much use," indicating the shocked survivors, "they will need all the help they can get to board the ship. Some of them are injured too by the look of things. I'll nip over and collect the other bloke, shouldn't be more than five minutes and I'll be back to give you a hand."

Both of the others commenced to remonstrate but Ben was adamant, "Come on, move! There is no time for arguments – look the boat is nearly alongside."

A heave on the painter brought the two boats into contact and the two officers reluctantly transferred, still trying to convince Ben that they would be of much more use where they were. As soon as they had crossed over Ben leaned forward and opened the throttle.

With the boat lighter than ever Ben took a large sweep up wind and then down towards the burning ship. It was not going to be easy getting close on the weatherside in the heavy swell, he thought, 'I only hope the fellow has enough strength and sense to jump as soon as I am alongside.'

****

Although not entirely unexpected the explosion of the aftermost cargo tank of the stricken vessel caught everyone by surprise.

A tremendous bang was accompanied by a blast of displaced air. Great fingers of burning liquid shot out of the ship like a gigantic firework display then resembled rivers of molten lava where they settled on the water, still burning in many cases. A large ball of fire leapt from the burst deck which quickly changed to a cloud of thick, black smoke.

Everyone on the bridge of the rescue ship was frozen with

horror at the spectacle. The vessel herself suffered no damage although one of the tentacles of oil streaked across the main deck, fortunately missing the members of the crew assembled there.

To a great extent the tall superstructure of the tanker protected the survivor's boat although a stream of burning oil splashed down either side of it.

The man on the deck of the burning vessel was incinerated instantly.

The rescue boat, cresting a swell at the moment of the explosion, caught the full blast.

****

After considerable effort the survivors were brought on board. All were in a state of shock and most had minor injuries. However two men were very severely burned and required expert medical treatment. It was these two who decided the captain to abandon all thought of searching for his own boat and to proceed at full speed to Victoria, B.C., the nearest port. With a last agonised gaze towards the smoke enveloped position where his boat was last seen he gave the necessary orders.

"There is no hope for him I am afraid," he said more to himself than to anyone who may have been within ear-shot, "God, what a way to go!"

Chapter 3

It was the sound that awoke him, a dreadful cacophony of noise which hammered at his brain until it felt as if it were about to burst. On the point of screaming in agony the sound diminished rapidly to a feint hum than faded altogether. However this did nothing to ease his splitting headache. The pain was so great he had difficulty in mustering his thoughts. 'Where am I? – What happened? – I must be still asleep. – What a nightmare! – Worst hangover I've ever had!'

Ben heard again the humming noise, slowly increasing in volume. Whatever it was seemed to be approaching like some demented fury. The noise became louder and louder and louder until it reached a crescendo apparently in the room with him. This time he did scream, a horrible bubbling scream. It appeared to do the trick, the hideous sound once again faded.

Ben desperately tried to think. What had he done to get into this mess? Slowly recollections filtered back into his brain. Disjointed at first, scenes of the ship. Smoke, yes lots of smoke. Dave the 'fourth' saying something about his being lost. But why? The scenes in his mind did not fit with the ship….. of course the boat! They were down a hole in the sea. Was he still there? …….. His thoughts were interrupted by the return of the diabolical noise to torture him once again.

As before the sound came and went. By gritting his teeth he survived it without screaming. More awake by this time, memories came flooding back. The burning tanker, the survivors. Then in a flash the man on the burning ship's deck. What after that? He could not remember.

Where was he now? That was the main thing. Now that his eyes had become used to the darkness he realised that there appeared to be a feint glimmer of light behind him. Perhaps that would reveal some kind of clue to his predicament?

Ben tried to turn but found that although being swayed and jolted he could not move. He panicked, struggling violently but although his legs seemed to move in slow motion and his hands seemed to function they found nothing to touch or grip. He moved his head but immediately his face came into contact with something flat, cold and wet. It came to him then that his whole body was wet and very, very cold.

The slight movement of his head however allowed him to see from the corner of one eye the source of light. A greenish watery gleam brightening and fading with the movement....... It came to him in a flash.

'The boat! I'm still in the boat! I'm trapped under the boat!!' He struggled with renewed vigour until the dreadful noise returned dulling his senses. However noises did not matter anymore, he was trapped and had to get free.

Having grasped the significance of the fact that he was under the upturned boat the situation rapidly became clear to him. His shoulders and arms were jammed under a thwart and his face was pressed against the loose bottom boards. He realised that the boat must have been blown over by the wind or by an explosion on the tanker and the fact that he had been trapped combined with the pocket of air below the boat had saved his life.

The immediate problem was to get clear. Now he appreciated the situation more fully it was a relatively simple operation to struggle free. His exertions made him aware of how bruised were his limbs although he decided that he was not seriously hurt, the thick padding of his life-jacket had prevented any injury to his torso.

The next move was to get from under the boat. Ben was contemplating this manoeuvre when the noise began to return. This time he realised what it was.

'A plane! Of course a plane searching!' This added impetus to his struggles but the life-jacket now became a hindrance, being too buoyant to allow him to duck under the gunwale of the boat. Half frozen fingers tore desperately at the bow fastening the tapes of the life-jacket but his clumsiness resulted only in pulling the loops into a hard knot.

Ben remembered the small pen-knife in his trouser pocket. He reached down and patted his thigh. Yes, it was still there! His numbed fingers searched for the opening of the pocket but could not at first distinguish it from the sodden folds of cloth. With every heave of the boat his aching head banged against the loose bottom boards and, floating nearly neck deep in very cold water, frequently his face received a dollop of it filling his mouth and stinging his eyes. He was weeping with rage and frustration when the plane passed over one more time. Thank God it was still there but how much longer would it stay? Ben almost panicked again.

After minutes which seemed an eternity Ben managed to get the knife from his pocket and a little later had struggled out of the life-jacket, the pen-knife already on its last journey to the bottom of the sea. Not a moment too soon. He heard the plane approaching once again.

Ben gripped the edge of the boat's gunwale under the water and, taking a deep breath, ducked below the surface. His arms and head were immediately enveloped in the folds of the anorak which, now released from the constriction of the life-jacket tapes, was quite loose. Completely disorientated Ben came up once again under the boat giving his sore head a further crack in the process. With his strength fast ebbing only blind fury kept him going. Holding the front of the anorak to his chest with his left hand and forearm he forced himself under water with his right.

Suddenly it was like being in a different world. From the almost complete darkness below the boat the transition to broad daylight momentarily blinded him and the noise was deafening.

'There it is!' The plane was almost alongside, its Maple Leaf insignia and numbers easily discernible as it screamed past but a hundred feet from the surface of the sea.

Ben shouted with joy. They must have seen him, or even if not they would on their next pass.

With what seemed his last reserve of strength Ben scrambled onto the bottom of the boat aided by the bucketed lifelines and the bilge grab rails. He slipped several times on a wide streak of half burned oil which crossed the bottom of the boat diagonally like a brush mark painted by a giant hand. The boat nearly righted itself during this process as Ben's weight combined with the weight of the engine attached to the bottom of it made it very unstable.

Ben spread-eagled to make himself as conspicuous as possible, his right hand gripping the keel and his right foot hooked over it, his left hand and knee on the grab rail.

'Thank God the nightmare was nearly over. How long would it be before he was picked up? Were there already ships in the vicinity heading his way? Where was his own ship come to that? Anyway it did not matter, relief would be on its way the moment the plane reported him if it was not on its way already. How long could he hold on? An hour? Even two if necessary and providing relief was in sight. If only his heart would stop beating like a trip-hammer so he could hear the plane as it returned.'

****

Three hundred feet above the sea the search plane slowly turned to port.

"One more sweep?" queried the co-pilot.

The pilot glanced at the clock and the fuel gauge before him. "No, I reckon it's time to head for the barn." He glanced over his shoulder as he spoke. The upturned boat was still visible floating forlornly in the oil-streaked sea. The black mark on it seemed more solid and distinct now for some reason.

Some trick of the light no doubt.

Chapter 4

It was some time before Ben realised that the plane was not coming back. When it did not turn and fly again over the boat he consoled himself with the thought that it had hurried off to inform the nearest surface vessel of his plight and position. He knew that the usual routine would be for the aircraft to return and circle his position to home other craft to him but this did not happen.

'Hope they hurry up,' he said to himself, 'it was well on in the afternoon when we reached the tanker so there can't be much daylight left.' It struck him that there was something wrong. Although the sun was hidden by low lying clouds it was still obviously high in the sky.

'Ye Gods!' He released his grip on the grab rail and brought his left wrist before his eyes. His watch was not there. At first he thought it had been torn off at some time during his struggles under the boat but then he remembered that he had dropped it onto his bunk when he went to wash his jersey that morning. But that must have been yesterday morning! The realisation struck him like a blow. He must have been unconscious all night under the boat, sixteen, eighteen hours possibly. It seemed impossible but true. That would account for the fact that there was no smoke from the burning tanker visible, though there was plenty of oil on the water. Ben decided that she must have foundered.

It must be well into the morning now. Which was strange because if that were so it was a long time since he had eaten therefore he should be hungry. By this roundabout route his throbbing brain relayed the signal and he realised he was hungry but more than that thirsty, desperately thirsty.

What could be done to relieve his terrible thirst? He forced his aching brain to concentrate on this problem. The rescue vessel could take an hour to reach him, maybe longer and he did not think he could last that length of time without a drink. There was plenty of rain about but….but… There was water within inches of him! Gallons of it in the plastic containers in the boat just below his aching body. He could duck back under the boat and fish around until he found one of the containers, however he could not raise much enthusiasm for this idea. Possibly he could turn the boat over? Goodness knows it had almost righted itself several times since he had climbed onto the bottom.

The three grab lines rigged under the keel from one gunwale to the other for just this situation had been removed when the boat had been prepared for launching as they would only increase the drag and endanger the propeller. But had they been removed completely? Ben seemed to remember their being coiled on the port side bench indicating that they had been released at one end only then hauled into the boat at the other. That being so they should still be there, or, more probably, trailing in the water. Port side, he was on the starboard side so it meant crawling over the keel to fish in the water over there.

It took a long time, every movement of his cold, wet, aching body was an agony but he eventually managed to hook one of the dangling lines with his foot and transfer it to his hand.

The next manoeuvre was to stand up holding the line taught and hope that by leaning back his weight would create enough leverage to roll the boat over. He appreciated that when, or if, the boat turned it would land on top of him with a great chance of being knocked unconscious and drowned – or killed outright – but that was a chance to be taken. He was desperate for water and any risk was worth hazarding.

It was a struggle to get to his feet on the slippery, lurching surface but eventually he made it. With his feet firmly wedged against the grab-rail he leaned back.

Nothing happened. Three times the boat passed over a swell but it was as if her gunwale was glued to the surface. The fourth swell was too much for the precariously balanced Ben. His feet went from under him and he landed with a crash on the bottom of the boat, fortunately managing to catch a handhold and avoiding being precipitated into the sea.

It was several minutes before he thought he had strength enough for a further attempt. On this second occasion Ben had hardly staggered to his feet and taken the weight on the line when, with the perversity of boats, it rolled over. He kicked with his legs as the boat turned and when it crashed down it only brushed his shoulder. Ben hauled himself back to the boat by the grab-line to which he retained his hold. Aided by this and the bucketed life-line along the gunwale, but mainly through sheer desperation, he managed to haul his heavy soaking body into the boat.

For twenty minutes he lay on a side bench gasping like a stranded whale before his raging thirst overcame his physical weakness and he began to fumble at the lanyard of one of the water-containers gleaming whitely below the surface of the water which filled the boat to the level of the thwarts. Eventually his clumsy fingers unfastened the lanyard enabling him to haul the container to the surface. He unscrewed the cap and drank.

The water revived him and to Ben things began to look a little more hopeful. Comfort being comparative sitting in cold salt water, battered, dispirited, exhausted and bitterly cold was infinitely better than being sprawled on the bottom of the boat – and thirsty.

Although all he wanted to do was to lie down and sleep Ben realised that there were a few things to attend to first. He struggled to get his priorities right.

The boat would be much more comfortable if it were not full of water. Ben contemplated the prospect of bailing it out with horror. It seemed to contain as much water as a Californian swimming pool. The sea was still slopping in at every other roll so it would be a waste of time anyway. But if the boat were more head to sea? Ben crawled to the bow of the boat and was relieved to see the sea anchor still under the thwart. After a struggle he managed to haul out the canvas cone and its tangled line and, after making the end of the line fast to the thwart, dump it overboard. He had not the strength to clear the line but fortunately most of became disentangled as the boat drifted away from the drogue.

What next? Ben slapped his hand to his head – and immediately regretted it. It felt like a hammer blow, sickening him. After a few minutes to recover he felt his cranium more gingerly. What a mess! His whole skull appeared to be a mass of cuts, lumps and bruises. Having found the first aid tin floating but anchored by its lanyard in the after part of the boat he padded his head with cotton wool and dressings then covered the lot with a large triangular bandage in the way of a gipsy's kerchief. He consoled himself with the thought that there was little chance of infection after all the salt-water soaking the wounds had received.

Next food, he was ravenous. The food tank, secured below a thwart, was mainly under water which meant it would flood the moment the cover was removed but although the cardboard cartons would be pulped Ben hoped the foil linings would protect the contents. Not that he expected to need much of it anyway.

Ben breakfasted, or lunched?..... or even dined? he wondered, on glucose, biscuit and condensed milk. The glucose looked and tasted like chalk and the biscuits scarcely more palatable but Ben consumed about a pound of the mixture before nature exerted itself and, leaning over the side of the boat, Ben vomited it all up. He took it more easily after that.

Having eaten a little more and kept it down Ben realised that his headache was much improved. Although his head still throbbed painfully it had lost some of the feeling that it would explode into fragments at any moment.

He started to take more notice of things after his meal. A search around the horizon when on the crests of swells revealed nothing in the way of ships. They could be another hour or two he decided.

The movement of the boat seemed a little easier and he realised that the sea-anchor had taken effect bringing the bow into the wind. Although water still lopped over the gunwale it did so much less frequently than before.

The bow was slightly higher than the stern of the boat so less water was slopping over the thwarts at that end. Ben therefore crawled there before deciding on his next move. His life-jacket had surprisingly stayed with the boat when it turned over so he used it to chock himself off in the bows. The boat cover had also survived, rolled up and stowed right in the bows. He used this to cover himself although it was sorry comfort soaked to the skin as he was.

He closed his eyes to ease his still throbbing head and the next moment was asleep.

****

He awoke in the same situation as on the previous morning, trapped under the boat and drowning. At least this was his first impression. He struggled to free himself and although his body rolled over his arms were still trapped. The shock of his lower legs suddenly becoming very cold and wet awoke him completely and he realised where he was and what was happening. He still in the boat but not under it, the constriction of his arms and shoulders was caused by the stiff folds of the canvas boat cover. The abrupt coldness of his legs was the result of their being immersed in the water in the boat. He quickly returned them to the side bench.

The blackness was that of the night. He must have been asleep for several hours. The drowning sensation was effected by heavy rain beating on his face.

Ben sat up on the bench, cowering under the boat cover in

absolute misery awaiting day light. His head was still painful and his hands and feet were numb with cold although the remainder of his body acknowledged a certain muggy warmth.

The heavy rain continued until daylight and then stopped quite suddenly. However the sky remained heavily overcast and rain was continuously in sight for the remainder of the day.

'They will have a job finding me in this weather', Ben thought, 'even with the best of Radar equipment'......Radar!, the low-lying boat would give a very poor echo, something would have to be done to improve it. The bulky radar reflector which was part of the boat's equipment had been removed before the launch as it took up a great deal of room and would only have been an encumbrance during the hour or so the boat was expected to be away from the ship. A galvanised bucket on the end of an oar? There were two buckets, he could see them under the water between the thwarts, and five oars. Being a motor life-boat it was not equipped with a mast and sail. A glance along the length of the boat told him that both boat hooks were missing, not surprising as they had been lying loose when they took the boat away.

An hour after daylight Ben had summoned up enough strength to move, but that was in order to obtain some nourishment before attempting to rig his radar reflector.

After a similar meal to that of the previous day Ben selected an oar, made a bucket fast to the loom of it and after a great struggle managed to jam the blade of the oar between the slats of the bottom boards and with a short piece of line, lashed it to the thwart.

The effort exhausted him and he was forced to rest for an hour afterwards. He wondered why he was so weak and decided that he must have lost a considerable amount of blood from his head wounds.

Lost in thought as he recuperated after his exertions he realised that the wind had died with the rain and the boat had now only the long swell with which to contend. Very little water was slopping over the gunwales. Ben appreciated that the weather could not last so if the boat was to be bailed out the sooner it was done the better.

At what he estimated to be about mid-day Ben commenced the monumental task. He started bailing with the remaining bucket alternately crouching and kneeling on the thwarts and side-benches. A more effective way would have been to stand in the bottom of the boat but he was reluctant to subject his cold legs and feet to this torture.

It was back-breaking labour and after about fifteen minutes of it he had to rest. When he had recuperated to a certain extent he crawled aft to the pump. Swinging on the pump handle was much easier labour but Ben thought the discharge was slower than by the bucket method. He kept up the pumping for nearly an hour trying to convince himself that the water level in the boat was getting lower.

During his second rest he wondered if the drain plug in the bottom of the boat had been dislodged and that the water was coming in as fast as he was pumping it out. To find out he had to reach down through more than two feet of water. Ben stripped off his anorak and shirt and, as quickly as he could, felt for the plug. It was still in position. Brief as the exposure was he was glad to re-don his shirt and the clammy but slightly warm coat.

With frequent rests and snacks he continued the work, alternating between bucket and pump until dark, by which time he estimated that the water level had been reduced by about nine inches. However he was convinced that he was doing better at the end of the day than when he first started.

'Getting into the swing of it,' he said to himself, 'A full day tomorrow should finish the job – if I am not picked up first'.

With this thought he curled his aching body in the boat cover with a packet of food and the water container handy. Within seconds he was fast asleep.

Wind and rain woke Ben several times during the night but he only snuggled more deeply under the canvas. There was nothing he could do to alleviate the situation anyway.

He was wide awake at daylight, cramped, cold and thirsty. A quick glance around the horizon and then a rough breakfast.

Ben searched the horizon at regular intervals throughout the day but slowly he began to admit to himself that the plane had not seen and reported him after all. The realisation did nothing to cheer him but it did have the effect of stiffening his resolve to save himself rather than just wait for someone to do it for him.

He toyed with the idea of checking the boat's equipment, particularly to find out if the distress rockets were still in the boat, but decided that this was only an excuse to postpone the back-breaking task of baling out the boat.

'Damn it, No, today is baling day, when that is done I'll see what I have in the way of gear, it will give me something to look forward to.'

He kept to his resolve and all day alternated between baling and pumping with only the shortest of breaks for rest and nourishment. His muscles screamed with agony but he kept at it. When the pump choked on one occasion it took about ten minutes to clear. Ben considered this a 'rest' period and carried on pumping the moment he had removed the obstruction. 'Rather heroic of me' he thought.

Only stubborn determination kept him going until the pump indicated that it was sucking air occasionally as the boat pitched in the swell. This was Ben's pre-determined signal for stopping for the day. It had already been dark for over an hour. He hardly had the strength to crawl to his canvas nest. As soon as he was curled up in it he fell into a sleep of utter exhaustion.

****

Ben awoke in broad daylight as cold, wet and cramped as on the previous morning but otherwise greatly refreshed.

The first thing he noticed was that there was about a foot of water in the boat. Then he realised that the wind and sea had increased considerably whilst he had been asleep and also that it was now raining hard.

Deciding that it was pointless getting soaked he waited until the downpour had eased to a cold light drizzle before partaking of his breakfast. That consumed he then pumped until the boat was almost dry, waiting this time until the water ran aft to the pump suction so that when he at last desisted there remained less than an inch of water in the hollow keel.

Around midday he set about checking the boat's equipment. His discoveries were met with mixed feelings. In the small gear locker below the after thwart he found, among other things, a clasp knife with blade and marline spike, slightly rusty but otherwise in good order. An electric torch, soaked in spite of its plastic wrapping and therefore useless. Spare batteries and bulb for the same. Fishing line and hooks. Ben did not think that raw fish would improve his menu to any great extent. A steel mirror heliograph securely wrapped in waterproof paper, he let it stay that way. Matches in a water-tight container and a few other odds and ends.

The things which were missing caused him some concern. There were no distress rockets or compass in the boat. They may have been lost but Ben thought they had more likely been removed for safety when the boat was prepared for sending away. The bulky canvas boat hood and its spreaders certainly had been taken out, how useful that would have been now!

Ben decided that something should be done about the flooded food tank before all the rations were ruined. The tank containing the cans of condensed milk could be dealt with later.

He opened the food tank and viewed with trepidation the prospect of hauling out the fifty odd soggy cardboard covered packets through the eight inch aperture. It would take ages and he had no way of drying them. Even when the tank was bailed out, and goodness knows how that was to be done, the packets would have to be restowed in it. There must be a better way. It suddenly occurred to him that there was. After several blows with an axe the tank was punctured at the bottom edge and the water poured out. Ben kept the holes clear with the spike of the knife, they could be plugged easily enough when the tank was fully drained.

By the time water stopped running from the tank it was nearly dark so, after eating again, Ben retired to the relative comfort of the boat cover. He did not fall asleep immediately but lay on his back thinking of the events which had led up to his present situation – about the first opportunity he had had for this since he left the ship. When was that? Two, three, even four days ago? Good grief! The chip could be in Seattle by now, she was only three days from the place when they diverted to the tanker. What happened to the two blokes with him in the boat? If the tanker had exploded, and he was not too sure on this point, did they and the earlier survivors escape? Hardly likely as their boat was not a great deal further from the tanker than himself. Even the ship was quite close. Good God! Could he be the sole survivor of the whole holocaust?

He thought of his parents. How would they take the news that he was dead? – 'Missing' anyway he corrected himself, or would it be 'missing presumed dead'? And Elizabeth, how would she feel? He tried to cheer himself up by imagining a phone call from the rescue ship, "Hello Elizabeth! Just checking to make sure you have not married someone else since I've been away......."

What rescue ship? He returned to reality. They would have found him by now if they were still searching. That plane was not heralding the beginning of the search but indicating the end of it! The only hope now was of a passing ship coming close enough to see him.

And what chance of that? They had not seen one ship since the day they left Nakhodka.

Not much point in hanging around here then, he decided, must make a move tomorrow to get under way. How? The engine? Both the starting handle and the tools had been lost so there was no hope there. Even if he did manage to get the engine running the amount of fuel on board would take the boat but a short distance and he was in the middle of the ocean.

No mast or sail either but surely something could be rigged from the oars and the boat cover? Thank goodness that had remained in the boat, if it had been in use actually covering the boat, as was usual in port, it would no doubt have been tossed aside when the boat was prepared for launching.

He was deciding how best to rig some kind of sail when he fell asleep.

****

Ben awoke just after daylight as cold, and wet and cramped as ever but with his headache greatly diminished. However the damp and cold were beginning to tell on him and he was most reluctant to drag himself out from the comparative comfort of the canvas.

After eating a little and drinking a can of milk, the refinement of puncturing the tin with the spike instead of gashing it with an axe was a slight improvement, he felt strong enough to start tackling the job of getting the boat under sail.

The first consideration was a mast. The forward thwarts each had large food tanks secured under them which would make the securing of the foot of the 'oar' mast something of a problem. Some kind of fairlead for the halyard at the masthead was another. For the latter he used one of the oar crutches, one jaw and the shank securely lashed to the loom of the oar the other jaw forming a hook over which

99

the halyard could be rove.

One of the belly grab lines was utilised as a halyard and another used to lash the foot of the 'mast' to the thwart and locker with its ends fast to the oar a couple of feet above the thwart and out to the gunwale stays on each side. Pretty low 'shrouds', Ben thought, but they should help to strengthen the arrangement.

The boat's painter, one end already spliced inside the bows, he led to the mast-head, hitched it there and led it to the after thwart where it was made fast. This he hoped would take most of the strain when the sail was set.

The next consideration was the sail itself. With the clasp knife he cut the boat cover roughly in half then cut off the pointed end. This left him with a piece of canvas approximately ten feet square. The machine sewn edges of the canvas he left as the leeches of the sail. Having no means of sewing he folded the narrowest cut edge twice to make a tabling of sorts, poked holed in it with the spike and bent it to an oar with lengths of lanyards which had previously secured various items of gear in the boat. Notches were cut in the blade of the oar in order to secure the sail at the end of the 'yard'.

The foot of the sail was a repeat of the tabling laced with pieces of small line and ropeyarn.

By the time all this had been accomplished the day was well spent so Ben decided that the actual setting of the sail could wait until the following day.

He spent what was left of the daylight pumping out as much water as he could from the bottom of the boat, rearranging his now reduced canvas 'nest', having a meal of sorts and then settling down for the night. Apart from a few light showers it had been mainly dry so Ben went to bed in relative comfort.

'Long may this weather last' was his final thought before he fell asleep.

Ben awoke much refreshed after an undisturbed night. He lay wrapped in his piece of boat cover and thought over his previous day's work. He was not satisfied with what he had done, the arrangement was far too weak. He had used the largest of the oars, the steering oar, as a mast but without much more robust rigging he could not see it lasting for long. The weakest point was at the top of the thwart. The blade reached well above this and here, where most of the bending of the oar would occur, the wood, although five inches wide, was only about one and half inches thick.

After considerable contemplation Ben decided on a tripod mast, as sometimes used on Polynesian craft he seemed to remember. Although short of line he still had three oars remaining, two of which could be utilised for this job. It meant dismantling most of his previous day's work but it would be worth the effort. It would be disastrous if the mast collapsed in the middle of the night.

After his usual rudimentary breakfast Ben set to to re-build his mast. First the original mast had to be taken down and the painter and crutch removed from the head of it.

The looms of three oars he lashed together then resecured the crutch 'fairlead' in a position to allow the halyard to run free.

After a great deal of labour the steering oar was once more in position with its blade jammed in the bottom boards and lashed to the thwart. Ben took the opportunity of replacing the original grab-line lashing with short lengths of lanyard in order to preserve the former for another job he had in mind. The blades of the other two oars, aided by notches hacked into them with the axe, were lashed to the nest thwart aft. The tripod gave a sturdy support for the yard and sail. Ben was well pleased with his efforts.

The morning's work was very tiring in his weakened state so a long lunch break was decided upon. At least it was intended to be long but, having just finished eating, Ben realised that the boat, which had been pitching with her head to the moderate breeze, suddenly began to roll and the apparent wind began to haul round onto the beam. For a moment he could not account for this, then with a cry, he quickly scrambled forward and found, as he suspected, only a handful of ropeyarn where the sea-anchor line had led over the gunwale. Ben cursed himself for not having checked it, he had not even given it a thought since he dumped it over the side days before. There was not the slightest hope of retrieving the sea-anchor so he decided to make a virtue of necessity and get the boat under way immediately.

There was still some work to be carried out on the sail. Tack and sheet lines to be attached to the lower corners and, to take some of the strain off the centre of the 'yard', a grab-line 'brace' led to each end of it. Four lines to handle instead of the single one of a lugsail would detract from manoeuvrability but Ben did not expect to do much in this line.

The quite violent movement of the boat added greatly to the labour but eventually the preparations were complete.

With the yard and sail across the boat forward of the mast and the four lines fast at what Ben estimated to be about their correct lengths the big moment arrived and he commenced to haul on the halyard. The yard lifted from the gunwales and, with the sail flapping furiously, slowly crawled towards the masthead. By the time it arrived there the boat was already swinging and within a few minutes was heading down-wind.

Ben adjusted the sheet and one of the braces then went aft to the tiller. The sail was merely a canvas bag so no niceties of sailing were expected but Ben was interested to see what the helm was capable of doing. After a few experiments he found that he could alter a course a point or two either way but that was all. The sail was too far forward to allow the boat to be sailed in any direction other than down wind.

'All to the good'. Thought Ben, 'I do not fancy having to sit here for any length of time.' A dollop of spray in the back of his neck quickly confirmed this resolution.

With all the sea room in the world Ben decided to leave all thought of navigation until the morrow and set about making himself comfortable for the rapidly approaching night.

Not relishing the possibility of the mast and sail descending upon him during the hours of darkness he was forced to relinquish his previous sleeping quarters between the two forward thwarts and establish a new position aft. By using some of the forward bottom boards he made a long enough platform alongside the engine to allow him to lie at full stretch if he felt so inclined.

After an evening meal he settled down for the night with what comfort his life-jacket and half boat cover afforded.

The wind increased during the hours of darkness and brought with it rain, frequent heavy, cold downpours.

After a fairly sleepless night Ben took stock of the situation as soon as it was light enough to see anything. As was becoming his practice he did this from the relative comfort of his canvas cocoon.

The sail had survived its first test he was pleased to observe. Water from both rain and spray had filled the boat to the level of the bottom board so pumping was going to be an early priority. The sky was completely overcast, the wind quite fresh and it was raining heavily. It was also very much colder.

On a more personal note Ben decided that he was cold, stiff with cramp, wet, hungry, lonely and very dispirited.

Considering the noticeable drop in temperature he decided, rightly, that the wind, after being basically from the south-west since he had been in the boat, had now veered to well north of west. He tried to cheer himself up with such thoughts as; 'At least we are now on our way' and 'California here I come' – which was a great improvement on Alaska – but he was not much impressed by the resultant effect on his morale.

However there was work to be done so reluctantly Ben hauled himself from the wet canvas and crawled forward to check the sail. He was pleased to see that it was still holding together so, with one slight adjustment to one of the braces he left it and moved aft to the pump. Then breakfast, such as it was.

Chapter 5

The weather changed but little over the next few days. Occasional squalls added to his labour, discomfort and anxiety but the odd dry spells allowed him to get some non-routine work done. This included constructing a second sail with the other half of the boat cover, which he continued to use as his bed, and fitting canvas and ropeyard chafing gear to the halyard where it was beginning to show signs of wear at the crutch lead. He also made himself a rough canvas jerkin from the very end of the boat cover. It covered his back and the holes for his arms he did not cut out completely but left as flaps to rest, rather than flutter in the wind, on his shoulders. The very end of the cover formed something of a hood when the 'shark's mouth' had been laced with ropeyarn. The front of the coat he secured in a similar manner. Not very elegant but it did give some slight protection from the elements. Ben often put his life-jacket on over everything else but it was too bulky to allow much activity so this was normally reserved for his 'off duty' moments.

The remaining oar he lashed to two thwarts and rigged his new sail over it in the form of a tent to shelter under during the worst of the rain. It was his intention to utilise one end of it in this manner and roll himself in the other at night but he found that the 'tent' deprived him of too much of his 'bedding' so after one night he reverted to his old system of rolling himself in the whole thing, sheltering his face from the rain by its folds.

Navigation as such was non-existent. Ben had no means of even roughly determining where he was. The position of the sun and the very occasional glimpse of a few known stars were his only indications of which way the boat was heading, and incidentally, the direction of the wind. Much more often than not the sun was obscured by the overcast and only a somewhat lighter part of the sky indicated its whereabouts.

Ben tried to estimate his progress. When he left the ship she was about three days from the Seattle pilots, say a thousand miles or so, he could not remember the 'distance to go' from the previous noon calculations. How long had he been in the boat? He could not rightly remember. Say five days before he commenced sailing. Drift down-wind with the sea anchor? Two knots? One? Say one and a half as a compromise, that would be thirty-six miles a day for five days, which would amount to... Ben wished he had something to write with – about one hundred and eighty miles in a north easterly direction, (little wonder it was so difficult to find anything as small as a boat when it was lost at sea). It did not knock much of a hole in a thousand miles but it was a start. What speed was he making now? That was difficult to guess. He thought of trying to rig some kind of Dutch Log with the fishing line but decided to do that later. What speed then? Ben decided on five knots. It was hardly likely to be more and anything less would be depressing.

Five knots was one hundred and twenty miles a day. One twenty into a thousand, allowing a little extra distance for hitting the coast further south than the Canadian/U.S.A. border, was, Ben scratched the calculation on a thwart with the spike of his knife – nearly eight and a half days. Not too bad, he should be able to hold out that long. But this was only if the sail held together, it seemed to be feeling the strain a bit even at this early stage.

To be on the safe side Ben repeated the calculation allowing an average speed of four knots. This gave him ten and a half days. He decided that if he allowed himself two weeks this would take care of any marked change in the wind or any breakdowns of gear. Two weeks seemed an awful long time but in a couple of days or so he would already have survived a week so double that length of time again seemed just possible.

If only it were not so bitterly cold and always so wet, he could not decide which was the worse. Even after all this time there had never been a dry enough spell to get the dampness out of his anorak. Probably the salt remaining in it after his initial soaking had a lot to do with it he thought. Maybe he would get a few warm dry days when he got further south and would be able to rinse it out in rainwater. The combined effect of the cold, wet and salt was causing painful raw patches on the skin of his hands and wrists but there was nothing he could do about this as he was using his hands constantly.

He tried to build a fire in one of the buckets using as fuel ropeyarn soaked in diesel oil from the tank. After the expenditure of half of his supply of matches he managed to achieve a very smoky blaze but any heat was immediately dissipated by the movement of air in the boat. He decided to keep the remainder of the matches for lighting a similar arrangement as a distress signal if a ship passed close enough to see it.

If only that oil lamp was still in the boat, that would have made an ideal little heater but it, like the compass, had either been lost or removed by the economy minded mate.

The cold, everything else was just bearable but the persistent, bone-chilling cold, that was the hardest thing of all to bear. If only he could dry his clothes out it would help but this proved impossible as the weather deteriorated steadily.

At first Ben thought that the increase in wind would last but a day or so but he was wrong, it persisted. If it eased at all it was only a temporary lull heralding the next of the depressions which followed one another with monotonous regularity across the North Pacific. The weather tried Ben as nothing had before. His earlier days in the boat took on the aspect of a pleasure cruise by comparison.

The howling, shrieking wind tore at the boat as if desirous of blowing it off the face of the sea. It was flung in all directions battering and bruising the exhausted Ben until he almost screamed in pain. Spray and rain kept him constantly soaked and the bitter cold almost drove him to distraction.

For the first two days of the first gale the sail held the boat's head down wind. In the trough of each sea it slatted and flapped and the boat yawed off course only to be wrenched back as it crested each sea and the sail filled with a crack like a gun-shot.

It was towards the end of the second day that the sail on filling with its usual loud report did not then become silent but made an ominous thrumming noise, just audible above the howling of the wind and the hissing spray.

Ben glanced up from the bottom of the boat where he sat wrapped in the spare sail. What he had dreaded had happened, the sail had split in two of three places and streamers of it were flapping in the wind.

Only sheer terror got him moving, he knew that once the boat got beam on to the wind it would be blown over. He automatically released the halyard and immediately wished he had not as the remnant of the sail might have held the boat's head down wind for a few more minutes. And then? It would only delay the end by so much longer. Was it worth while trying to do anything? If he did not die immediately it was only a matter of time – and little of that, a few minutes at the outside.

However Nature's instinct of self-preservation prevailed and Ben made one more effort to get his mind working. There was no hope of bending on the second sail in the present weather so the immediate call was for a sea-anchor. But what to make one with? The old sail and yard suggested itself but this would take too long to rig – and the need was urgent as was more than apparent when the boat crested a sea almost beam on to the wind.

It was nearly turned over, Ben flinging his puny weight to the weather side in a desperate effort to prevent it. Very urgent indeed. The new sail would not do, this left very little. The life-jacket was too light – but – Ben wrenched the two useless fire-extinguishers from their brackets, hurriedly lashed them to the life-jacket by its tapes and scrambled forward. The boat nearly went over again on the crest of the next sea but by the time the following one was reached Ben had the life-jacket and extinguishers fast to the end of the boat painter and had lowered the hurriedly assembled sea-anchor over the side.

The new anchor was not very effective by sufficiently so to prevent the boat broaching to. Ben sank into the bottom of the boat mentally and physically exhausted. If he dozed at all it was but fitfully, he seemed to be aware of every moment of the reeling, shuddering boat. It was the longest night he could ever remember.

Daylight revealed the extent of the damage to the sail although the morning was well advanced before Ben had summoned up enough strength to do anything about it. He was more reluctant than ever to leave the dubious comfort of his sail. In fact he may have stayed in its folds even longer if not for the fact that the water in the boat was already surging over the bottom boards.

After appeasing his hunger and thirst he pumped the boat reasonably dry, hauled the yard and tattered sail aft of the mast to where he could work on it and then, recalling an earlier disaster, frapped strips of the torn sail around the sea-anchor painter in way of the gunwale to prevent it chafing through. These activities were all he could manage that day.

For three days the boat lay at the sea-anchor. Time and again the wind shifted its direction, dropped to only a fresh breeze for an hour or two then increased to a gale with renewed vigour.

Ben lay in the bottom of the boat most of the time taking very little interest in what went on around him. Only occasionally did he manage to overcome his exhaustion and accomplish something practical. He vaguely realised that the wind was anything but steady in direction as was indicated by the feint glimmer of the sun through the overcast sky. Once or twice he attempted to work out the wind's direction but the mental effort was too much. He just hoped that the prevailing wind was taking him towards the coast.

It took him all of one day, in easy stages, to remove the old sail from the yard and bend on the new one. The following morning he prepared the yard for hoisting but decided to leave it lowered until the next day in the hope that the weather would improve. Apart from the actual sailing he wanted to retrieve the sea-anchor, a job he knew he had not the strength for unless there was very little wind.

But it was not to be. After several attempts during a relative lull the following morning Ben realised that he would not be able to haul in the sea-anchor even in a flat calm. His numbed hands could hardly grasp the line never mind haul on it. With the utmost reluctance he gripped an axe with both hands and brought it down on the painter where it led over the gunwale. Not only was he losing the anchor gear which might be urgently needed again but also the rough comfort of his life-jacket.

After a struggle Ben got the sail hoisted and once again the boat set off down wind. Whatever direction that was, he was beyond caring.

Well that is it, he decided. Even after an hour's rest he felt too weak to move. The old sail was beyond any repairing he could do to it so if the new one blew out that would be the end. If he was not picked up by a passing ship or failed to make the coast within the next day or two it would be the finish of everything anyway.

He should have sighted the coast by now he judged. How long

was it since he first got under sail? Ten, twelve days ago? Ben wished he had kept a proper tally of the days. With the knife he cut a small notch in the thwart for every day he could positively identify then added three more for days he had 'lost' one way or another. He totalled the notches. Seventeen! Seventeen days since he left the ship! It was incredible. He tried to cheer himself with the thought that he should, if his calculations were anything like correct, sight the land at any time now. Ben dragged his weary eyes to the horizon as it briefly came into view when the boat crested a sea. There was no sign of any land between the rain showers all around him.

For two more days Ben hardly moved from his cramped position in the bottom of the boat. Only making a supreme effort could he force his tired, aching body to crawl aft to the pump when the rain and spray had filled the boat to the level of the bottom boards. The pumping itself was an agonising nightmare. When he crawled back to his nest in the old sail he invariably slept for hours, undisturbed by the violent movement of the boat, the flapping and cracking of the sail or the rain and spray.

He forced himself to eat as much as he could but even that was an effort. Sometimes he struggled for several minutes just to open a packet of rations, his numbed hands and brain refusing to act in unison.

The boat, the sea and the sky were all that Ben had seen for weeks so when something different came into his line of vision he did not immediately realise its significance. Then his heart began thumping. A ship! Only a few miles away! His signal!, his smoke signal! Moving his cramped body from his position in the bottom of the boat felt like tearing his way through barbed wire entanglements or naked through dense brambles, his bruised, aching muscles seemed to scream in agony.

His fumbling fingers managed to open the food locker and withdraw the slightly damp ropeyarns he had stowed there. He dumped them in a bucket then scrambled to the fuel tank. He gripped the cap as best he could and twisted. No movement. Two hands, two hands and a scrap of canvas to prevent his numbed fingers slipping. Ben was frantic, almost weeping in frustration. He glanced over his shoulder, he had not much time. The ship was obscured by the boat's sail. The ten feet of canvas looked massive from but a few feet away, they must have seen it of course, that and the white boat itself must be very conspicuous on the empty sea. He was wasting his time trying to get his signal burning, when the ship came insight around the edge of the sail it would be right on top of him. She would be blowing her whistle at any moment heralding her approach, telling him that he was within a few minutes of succour and all that that implied. He glanced quickly around the boat, was there anything he wished to take with him – a souvenir of some kind? Nothing, he did not want to be reminded of his ordeal, all he longed for was warmth, security, food, the company of his fellow men and sleep, above all sleep.

Ben staggered to the side of the boat to look around the sail. What he saw caused his heart to sink. The ship was still on her original course but much closer. She should have altered course towards him by now, what was the matter with them? He tried to console himself with the thought that the vessel would have been on automatic steering so it would take a minute or two to get a man on the wheel. He could almost imagine the bustle on the ship now, the master called from his afternoon siesta, (he thought it was afternoon,) the engineers wondering why the telegraphs rang 'stand by engines' in the middle of the ocean, the deck crew dashing off for heaving lines and a jacob's ladder. And all for his benefit!

But nothing like that seemed to be happening. The ship retained her course relentlessly. Surely they had not failed to see him? Even an off duty steward leaning over the rail could not avoid seeing the boat. They must have seen him, they must! It would be far too cruel for the ship to have appeared just in time to save his life and then pass as if he did not exist and allow him to die!

The ship passed remorselessly a few miles away. Slowly the

realisation sank into Ben's weary brain that he had not been observed although the full horror did not register until the vessel was well past. He sank into the bottom of the boat and sobbed like a child.

What kind of a watch were they keeping? Were they all asleep or dead on the ship? It seemed so unfair that he would die just because some second mate had decided to correct charts rather than keep a proper lookout – the slight twinge of conscience at the thought that he had often done the same thing himself was immediately suppressed. And the man on watch with him, what was he doing? Sitting in a corner of the wheelhouse sewing canvas no doubt. The full magnitude of his hopeless situation almost unhinged him.

It was as if his tears had washed away the last atom of his physical and mental strength. He pulled the tattered canvas over his aching body and lay down to die. What was the point of struggling anymore?

In making himself as comfortable as possible on the bottom boards something hard dug into his thigh. Damn! What was he lying on? He shifted his position slightly but whatever was causing his discomfort was still there. 'Must be something in my pocket,' he thought. The knife? No that was secure on the side-bench, (blade open, his fingers had long been incapable of opening it should it ever be closed). What else was there? It felt like a coin but he carried no money in his pockets at sea. Keys? No keys either, they were only toted around in port when rooms were locked. Whatever it was it did not matter he decided irritably.

But it did. The mystery nagged his brain as the object jarred his flesh. Damnation! Was he not even to be allowed to die in peace? Ben struggled over onto his left side and investigated his right leg with numbed fingers. Yes, there was something in his trouser pocket. An odd shaped something. His fingers fumbled for the opening of his pocket. He vaguely remembered doing this before with the other pocket. Yes, it came back now, searching for his knife when under the boat. How long ago that seemed to be, a week, a month, a year? Ben gave it up and continued his struggle with the pocket. Eventually his fingers found their way into its depths and contacted something hard and cold. He withdrew it and held it before his blurred vision. The object slipped from his grasp as he brought it up but some small chain attached to it tangled with his fingers so it dangled before his eyes.

At first he was mystified as to what it was, then:

"Bring it back to me."

He did not remember the words, he heard them, and once again saw her tear-filled eyes as she spoke.

"Bring it back to me", "Bring it back to me", the words repeated themselves in his brain as he lapsed into unconsciousness.

* * * * * * * * * * * * * *

For two more days Ben Travis lay in the boat lingering between life and death. Occasionally he would nibble a piece of lifeboat ration or take a sip of water when he was awake but most of the tIme he slept, or at least drifted into a coma foretelling death.

His brain seemed to have lost all contact with his cold, soaked and exhausted body. Even when the accumulation of spray and rain water lapped above the bottom boards he did no more than to drag himself into a sitting position. A very small part of his brain appeared to survive with a viability of its own. It seemed to be about the size of a walnut, a small warm core entirely divorced from the remainder of his being. With it he thought of food, of home and of Elizabeth.

'Sorry I could not bring it back Elizabeth, God knows I tried.'

Maybe the pendant would be found on his body and somehow returned to her. The thought revolted him, as if she herself would discover it on his stinking, mouldering corpse. That would be too awful. He would have to attach it to the boat somehow, somewhere it could easily be seen when the boat was at last found. A leg of the mast seemed the best place. Yes, that was it. Ben struggled to retrieve the pendant from his pocket. With his right arm cramped against the engine he had to shift his position in order to withdraw his hand. He was therefore off balance when the boat gave a tremendous lurch which sent him crashing across the bottom boards. It was not far but it was a painful experience, Ben did not think he could feel any more pain in his numbed body but somehow further hurts to his shoulder and knee registered in his brain. A few seconds later a vicious lurch the other way threw his curled up body back to whence it came.

'Good God! The sail has gone again!' Ben looked towards it but the square of canvas was still there. Beyond it however, where the sky should have been, there was blackness. For a moment he could not make out the cause then realisation crashed upon his weary brain. It was a cliff, a great black heavily fissured cliff! And he was right on top of it! He was in the breakers at the foot of the tremendous wall of rock!

He stared at the cliff absolutely dumbfounded. How could it be? It could not just suddenly appear in his path, it must have been in sight all day, even allowing for the rain obscuring the visibility much of the time. When was it that he last checked ahead, a day. Two days? He could not remember.

He reached for the halyard to let the sail go. Then hesitated, what good would that do? Only delay the inevitable momentarily. If this was where he was meant to die he might as well get it over with as soon as possible. Instead of his body rotting in the boat it would be dashed fragments on the cliff. It did not matter much either way.

Elizabeth would never see her silver pendant again and that was the only thing that saddened him.

'I'm sorry Elizabeth, I did try to bring it back to you'. That seemed to be all that mattered.

Ben jammed himself as securely as he could in the bottom of

the boat as it was tossed violently in the surf. 'We may as well go together,' he thought. With only a few more minutes to live he retreated into the small, warm portion of his brain and concentrated his thoughts on Elizabeth. He wanted to be thinking of her when his life was eventually snuffed out. After all his travails he was quite reconciled to death, even welcoming it for the peace it would bring.

Chapter 6

Fate, however had one more trick to play on the tortured Ben.

Subconsciously he realised that it suddenly got dark, then a moment or two later, light again, then dark. He dragged open his heavy eyelids and saw what was happening. The boat was being driven by the wind and sea into a great cavern, a tremendous crack in the cliff face reaching up into the impenetrable darkness above him. Ben's only thought was that it was a pity that he was going to die in darkness, he would have preferred to have gone in the light outside.

The fissure sloped at about forty-five degrees and rapidly narrowed as it penetrated the cliff. Each face of it was serrated with jagged terraces of strata resembling the teeth of giant nut-crackers – with the boat and Ben the nut between its jaws. As the sea surged in and out of the cavern the surface rose and fell nearly thirty feet. At one moment ledges of rock were submerged, seconds later as each swell receded they took on the aspect of so many wild water-falls. Not that Ben appreciated much of this in the spume and spray filled darkness. He huddled as tightly as he could in the bottom of the tossing boat. Seeing very little and deafened by the thundering of the seas and rearing of the wind.

The boat was well into the cavern before it first struck. The mast was the first to go, crashing into the roof of the cavern, the whole structure of oars, rope and canvas was hammered instantly into a torn and splintered mass on the thwarts and over the side of the boat.

The next surge took the boat up the sloping floor of the cavern and in receding brought it crashing down onto the jagged rock. The bottom of the glass fibre boat was smashed like an eggshell. The rudder and propeller caught in a crack in the rock which served to slew the boat round before the stern was torn off and it tobogganed down the rock in the wake of the sea, catapulting Ben onto the top of the wreckage of the mast and sail. He frantically grabbed the top of the gunwale as the boat again surged up in the maelstrom of water.

Again the shattered boat crashed down on the rocks tearing the gunwale from Ben's numbed fingers. He grabbed frantically in the darkness and renewed his grip as once again the sea receded.

The boat again bounced down the steps of jagged rock, turning over and rapidly disintegrating.

To Ben's numbed brain came the realisation that he was not moving. The water was cascading past and over him accompanied by pieces of the boat which he could dimly see. He found that he was not holding on to the boat but to a thin ledge of rock! His knees were taking most of his weight on the ledge below. If only he could climb higher! But it was too late, already the rush of air heralding the next surge of water was roaring in his ears.

At the top of the next sea Ben's legs were torn from their resting place and floated with his body. Grimly he held on to the rock with his hands. Vaguely to his left he saw a mass of white objects rising with the sea, all that remained of the boat. He felt a twinge of pity to see the end of his faithful vessel before his knees came crashing down on the rocks and he lost all interest in boats.

'If only I could climb a little higher, six feet would do it'.

He had only seconds to work in but in that time Ben managed to haul himself up to the next ledge and get his knees onto his original handhold. This was mainly carried out by the strength of his arms, his legs, after their long lack of use in the boat and considerable injuries appeared to be almost useless.

The next surge came up to his waist but he managed to cling to his position. The process was repeated as the sea surged back. This step was higher and it exhausted most of his remaining strength. As his handhold was at the level of his eyes he could see that the surface of the ledge sloped back into the face of the cavern floor but in the dim light he could not see how far. It could mean sanctuary, with his last remaining strength Ben hauled himself over the edge of the shelf and rolled onto the ledge. Everything then went black.

****

Ben regained consciousness with the now familiar feeling that he was drowning. After a moment of panic he discovered that he was lying in a couple of inches of water. It took some time for him to remember where he was and the circumstances which had caused him to be there.

Nothing could be seen in the stygian darkness, not even a flash of phosphorescence in the surging water just below him. This decided him that it must be night. As there was nothing he could do until a little light arrived with the day he settled down to await it. Despite the constant showers of spray and the roaring of the sea and wind he once again passed into oblivion.

It was day when Ben awoke. There was a little light now at the entrance of the cavern. Not that this brought much comfort, he was trapped in the cave as surely as in his grave. He now became aware of his raging thirst and once this registered on his tired brain he could think of nothing else. He glanced hopefully into the depths of the cave to where the shattered remnants of the boat either surged up and down with the sea or lay jammed in the many crevices in the rock. No hope of water in that direction, if any of the full plastic containers had survived they would have sunk to the bottom.

But he must have water! Where could water be found in a cave? Perhaps further up, possibly rain could have trickled through and collected on a ledge above him away from the spray of the sea? He cast his gaze upwards but could see nothing but rock, damp from the spray for the next twenty or thirty feet and then it appeared quite dry.

Ben sat for some minutes with his head in his hands, puzzled. Something was odd but he could not drag his mind away from his maddening thirst to solve the problem at first. Then it came to him in a flash. He could see the rocks above him quite distinctly for some way but the white fragments of boat were only just visible in the end of the cave at half the distance. Of course! The cavern was really a long crevice in the cliff face and the light was coming from the upper part of it. If he could climb up there he might find water, it may even be raining, he could lick the water from the rocks if necessary – he must have something to quench his raging thirst.

It was the thirst that got him moving and the thirst that drove him on. His legs seemed to be no part of him, only so much more to drag with his aching arms. Every foot of his progress was agony and it took him three hours to reach the source of the light and to see the sky once again. A clear, blue, sunny sky with no trace of a rain cloud.

Ben collapsed on a flat expense of rock and, despite his thirst, once more lost consciousness.

An hour later when he regained his senses his thirst was agonising. 'Why was I not allowed to die in the boat? It was much more comfortable there.'

He looked out to sea but there was still no sign of rain although clouds were building up on the horizon. He turned his gaze upwards, nothing there but the overhanging rock. Perhaps there was a pool of rainwater behind him? Painfully he rolled over and instead of the blank wall of rock he expected he found that the fissure extended to the top of the cliff. He could just see a crack of sky there and – what was that? For a moment he thought it was someone waving to him but when he managed to get his eyes focused he realised that it was but the branch of a tree swaying in the wind. It cheered him slightly, even a tree was something after weeks of nothing but sea and sky – with latterly hostile rock.

The crevasse had, over eons of time, filled with boulders and scree making a very rocky path to the top.

'I might be able to manage it,' thought Ben, 'if only I can get my legs to work.' He dragged his weary gaze in their direction and gave a start. His trousers, torn and tattered revealed his knees to him for the first time since he had left the ship. In his thirsty, weak, light-headed state the shock almost robbed him of his reason.

"Good God! No wonder! They are not my legs! They are not anyone's legs!" he cried out loud – although nobody would have recognised either the words or his voice which, forced past his dried, swollen tongue, resulted in no more than a series of croaks. Ben gazed at them, bewildered. He knew he had seen something like it before. Yes, it came back to him now, the brown, yellow and purple marbling of the caves of Petra which he had once visited when his ship was at Aqaba. No wonder he could hardly move, towing stone legs around him. But when had it happened? He could remember no one removing his legs and replacing them with stone replicas. It must be a joke. Perhaps it was funny and he was supposed to laugh? He started to giggle then broke into laughter which even his painfully swollen mouth could not retard. Mad, hysterical laughter, shrieking and howling, the ghastly sound echoing from the cliff face.

The effort exhausted him and soon he collapsed gasping on the rock and passed out.

****

Again the raging thirst awakened him. He lay for some time before he gained the strength to move. He felt strangely light-headed. Although everything about him seemed perfectly clear, he realised where he was and what he had to do, the knowledge appeared to be a very fragile thing as if in the event of someone asking him a difficult question, such as his date of birth or the name of his last ship, the pressure would be too much and the whole of his present knowledge would burst into a thousand fragments.

Ben rolled over so he could look up the rock-filled gully.. His eyes refused to focus properly but he could see its uneven surface. Estimating its length was another matter. He could make out the blurred movement of the tree branch at the top but whether it was ten yards away or fifty he could not guess.

He looked down at his legs. They only had one more job to do then he was finished with them, they could drop off then.......Steady!

His black shoes were a silvery yellow from their constant soaking in salt water. Although relatively new they were rapidly disintegrating, the leather of the toes shredded by the recent rock climbing and the soles parting company with the uppers. He could not decide which were likely to survive the longest, his legs or his shoes. He checked the remainder of his apparel. His anorak was in not much better case than his tattered trousers, its white filling hanging out of rents in the nylon covering in numerous places looking like scraps of sheep's wool dangling from a barbed wire fence. The canvas jerkin was missing, he could vaguely remember becoming entangled in its folds at some stage and struggling out of it.

Ben glanced at the sun. Only a couple of hours of daylight left, he would have to get moving.

By holding on to the wall of rock beside him he tried to get to his feet but could not control them even to the extent of crouching. He managed to get one leg bent beneath him but his efforts to get the other to join it precipitated him onto his back.

Hands and knees it is then, decided Ben.

The climb up the gully took him until sunset. Every few minutes

120

he thought he could go no further but each time he managed to struggle on a few more feet, his lacerated hands and knees leaving a bloody trail on the sharp rocks. The maddening desire for water provided the driving force.

He lay at the top of the gully for several minutes, his breath rasping in his lungs, before he had the strength to raise his head and look about him.

The rocky edge of the cliff gave way to a few dozen yards of stunted trees as the land sloped downwards away from him. Beyond them were widely spaced pines of moderate dimensions then a forest of trees. They seemed to go on forever. So far as Ben could see they covered the ground right up to, and probably over, the high land beyond.

In the rapidly failing light Ben sat on the ground and gazed at the landscape. He had never seen so many trees at one time in his life before. Trees, trees, trees. No buildings, not even a trace of smoke or, when it became dark, even one twinkle of light to indicate that someone was alive in this wilderness of trees.

Above all there was no water. Not even any rain. After all he had endured in the way of cold, soaking rain during the last few weeks this struck Ben as the cruellest cut of all.

He sat with his torn and bloody hands between his lacerated knees and gazed at the trees until they merged with the darkness of the night. He watched the stars come out one by one. The wind had dropped almost completely and for the first time that Ben could remember his little world was at peace.

Ben could hear the swell beating at the foot of the cliff behind him and felt some slight satisfaction in having cheated it of its prey. It seemed almost a victory to die here, on dry land, after all the sea had done to kill him.

He was about to close his eyes for what he considered to be the last time when he saw a faint flicker of light in the trees. His heart began to thump. Moments later he realised that it was not a light at all, only the reflection of a star. His eyes closed and he rolled over on the rock.

Sleep did not come immediately. Something nagged his mind. Something he had heard? Something he had read?

Bayonets. Why bayonets? What made him think of them? Or was it rifle barrels? All very ridiculous anyway, he was not going to waste time on them, he was going to spend his last few minutes on earth thinking of Elizabeth. If he could for one moment stop thinking of his agonising thirst.

But rifle barrels? His mind gave him a picture of old fashioned troops in pith helmets in the heat of a desert their bayonets glinting in the sun. But something was wrong, there was something that should not be. Yes! The bayonets should not glint in the sun. The sergeant with his great moustache said to keep them covered or they would give the position away. Then what did he say? It seemed important. Ben racked his brain for the answer.

Yes, he had it now, the flashing of the bayonets would give away as the enemy knew that the only thing in nature that glints is water.

Water! That was it! The star must have reflected on water! And not far away. Where was it? Ben struggled back into a sitting position and moved his head about trying to recapture the reflection. He was not successful but the thought of water spurred his brain to further efforts. It was not far away, just through the widely spaced trees somewhere. Not further than that as he remembered that the land sloped up from there. Therefore the pool or stream must be just at the bottom of the slope.

The thought of water to quench his burning thirst once again set his tortured body moving. The way lit only by the stars the going was difficult although at least the ground was softer once he had crawled off the rock. He scrambled and slithered down the slope, occasionally encountering outcrops of rock and dead branches but eventually reaching the bank of the stream. The bed of it was wider than he expected, much wider. What was more a shock though was the fact that it was dry.

But it could not be! It could not dry up in the few minutes it had taken him to get there! Was that water there, towards the other side of the stream bed? There was something slightly different anyway, a long, narrow pool by the look of it.

Ben fell rather than crawled down the three foot bank and after recovering his breath, dragged himself over the bumpy surface to the pool. It seemed to Ben a strange bed for a stream. Instead of being flat or rocky it was furrowed, long furrows which seemed to stretch endlessly along it so far as he could make out. Some of the furrows had a strange herringbone kind of pattern in them, he seemed to remember seeing something like it before, a long time ago in some previous existence.

But all this did not matter, the important thing was that he was getting closer to the strange shaped pool.

At last he arrived. His left arm plunged into the water the other lay along the top of a ridge. He lowered his face into the water and drank deeply of the muddy liquid.

The refreshing drink revived him to the extent of clearing his brain for just a few moments. He struggled to take the pendant and chain from his pocket and looked around for somewhere to hang it where it could be seen. There! Just a few feet away feebly illuminated by the starlight, a tree stump, he would hang it there. His exhausted brain signalled his limbs to make one more effort. They did not respond. Ben groaned and his head fell back into the water which had so recently saved him.

His last thoughts were of Elizabeth.

Epilogue 1

Only the constant plop, plop, plop of the water dripping onto the roof above after the afternoon's rain disturbed the silence until the reporter's chair scraped the floor as he rose to leave.

Sergeant Joseph Brady, Royal Canadian Mounted Police, seated on the other side of the desk, stroked his black moustache once with the back of his forefinger. It was not a nervous gesture, he was just checking that there was not a hair out of place. He took pride in his appearance. He sat very upright in his chair with his hands and wrists resting on the desk before him. Not for the first time he wondered how old his visitor was. He always reminded Brady of a stork, or was it a pelican? Long beaky nose which seemed even longer and more beaklike when he looked up over his spectacles to ask a question. A few streamers of white hair dangling from either side of his almost bald head and his hunched shoulders completed the bird-like appearance. Nice enough though, as reporters go, at least he did not consider his mission in life was to deride the police at every possible opportunity as did some of the young fellows.

"What an awful waste," said Clinton Fuller as he closed the notebook, "Thirty years old and everything going for him, then this happens. It must be tough for his folks but at least they know now."

"And the identification for the second time," said Brady, "You can imagine what the body was like after a couple of weeks out there, plus the head injuries. Old Man MacLaren was in a hell of a state, Mrs. Mac couldn't even face it. Mind you it was a wonder he was found at all, those light planes don't do more than knock a few branches off when they come down in the timber, not like a 747. If those two Indians hadn't tripped over the wreckage on a fishing trip he might not have been found for years. And it should never have happened at all. Fancy taking off with only enough gas to get home when he knew there was so much rain about!"

"The other fella Joe, any more on him?"

Brady was expecting the question and with difficulty suppressed his irritation as he answered, "Nothing, we are right back where we started. Damn it Clint, anyone could have made the mistake, roughly the same age and build, head and other injuries and obviously been lost for weeks. It was a shock for all of us when the MacLarens told us it was not their son."

"You have no further news from the hospital then?"

"No, it is still very much touch and go. God! He is lucky to be alive at all, those loggers only happened to go up that track by sheer chance, had some drag chains or somesuch up at their old camp and decided that as things happened to be quiet they would collect them in their pickup. Found the fellow in the middle of the road with the back of his head in a puddle of water, if he had been face down he would have drowned in it."

"If only we had something to work on, he carried no identification, not even a tag on his clothes, apart from a Taiwan label on his jacket – and he is no Chinaman."

"What about the locket, Joe? Any hope in that direction?"

"We are working on it. It's a woman's pendant, roses engraved on it as you know. Made in England for both the domestic and export market – including Canada – 'initials engraved at no extra cost' no doubt. How many people do you know with the initials 'E.B.' Clint? There are two in this department alone. The date on it is not much help either, July 4th a couple of years ago. It suggests the States so we have had to start enquiries over the border. What I would like to know is how the hell he got there whoever he is. The state he is in proves he was in a crash a week or so back. Amnesia? The head injuries suggest it. We have tried endless theories, planes, campers, yachts, passing freighters with men overboard, all negative so far. My guess is that he has smashed up his car somewhere out of sight of the roads and just wandered north instead of south trying to get back to civilisation – and there are plenty of holes in that line of reasoning."

"Could be a story in it Joe."

"The medics give him another couple of days to pull out of the coma, if he does not I doubt we will ever know who he is, just another unknown in a known grave – then no story, period."

Fuller slipped his note-book into the pocket of his shabby tweed jacket and reached for his hat.

"Well thanks for your time Joe, and the coffee." The sergeant waved a depreciating hand.

At the door Fuller turned.

"You know I could swear there is a story there. After forty odd years in the business you sort of get a nose for it."

As the sound of the reporter's departing car died away the only sound in the office was the plop, plop, plop of droplets of water from the overhanging branch.

'Goddammit', said Brady to himself, 'Tomorrow I'll bring a saw and cut that damn thing off!'

****

Later they could never remember exactly when in the sequence of events Elizabeth dropped the book.

It was the evening of an otherwise very ordinary day. The room itself was as it had been ever since Elizabeth could remember, it had a lasting, solid cosiness about it, in striking contrast to the weather outside the window.

Already seated by the fire her mother dropped her knitting in her lap and reached for the 'Radio Times' to check on a programme she intended to watch later. Elizabeth herself picked up the book she had been reading before dinner and was deciding where to settle – she was still young enough to consider the hearth-rug as comfortable as an arm-chair.

Her father filled his post-prandial pipe and applied to it the flame of a match. He glanced at the clock on the mantle-piece through a cloud of smoke and said to no-one in particular, "Geof Waters said he would ring today about golf on Saturday, I hope he has not forgotten, it's gone seven o'clock."

'....a good ten seconds after by my trusty wrist-chronometer...', the words flashed through Elizabeth's mind. It seemed as if they triggered off the telephone in the hall which began to ring.

"That will be him," said her father as he moved towards the door.

****

Elizabeth's mother swore afterwards that it was whilst the telephone was still ringing that the book falling at her daughter's feet called her attention.

"What?.....Elizabeth! Whatever is the matter? You are as white as a sheet!"

Although it may have been when they heard scraps of one end of the telephone conversation. "Long distance?......Where?.....British Columbia?....." Words which in themselves told little.

Certainly it was before her father said, "Yes, she is here", as by then Elizabeth was rushing through the door to snatch the phone from his hand.

Wallaroo to Jeddah. Sept 21 to Oct 14 1982

Epilogue 2

Only the constant plop, plop, plop of water dripping onto the roof from an overhanging tree branch, a reminder of the afternoon's rain, disturbed the silence.

Sergeant Joseph Brady, Royal Canadian Mounted Police, touched his black moustache with the back of his forefinger. It was not a nervous gesture, he was just checking that there was not a hair out of place. Joe Brady took a pride in his appearance.

Sitting upright in his chair he looked at his visitor at the other side of his desk and wondered, not for the first time, how old he was. Ever since they had first met, many years before, he had reminded Brady of a stork, or a pelican, he was not quite sure which. Long beaky nose and a few streamers of white hair hanging down the sides of his almost bald head, the nose looking more beak-like than ever when he looked over his spectacles to ask a question. Nice enough though as reporters go, he did not consider it his mission in life to belittle the police as many of the young fellows were inclined to.

Clinton Fuller finished checking through his notes on the traffic accident he had just been discussing with the sergeant.

"Well I think I have got it all now thanks. Nasty business. One thing though, have you yet traced the owner of the car?"

Receiving a negative reply he continued, "Talking of identifications, is there anything further on that business up at the old logging camp?"

If it was not for his admirable self-control Brady would have raised his eyes to the ceiling. He never relished being 'police spokesman' for the press which in his opinion was only a shade better than being named, with all that implied, but he had hoped that the interview was over.

"Nothing, we are right where we were when the body was found. The track has not been used for over two years and the medics think it has been there almost that long. I wish those two Indians had never found it, why couldn't they have gone camping somewhere else? Now we have one set of human remains, male, Caucasian, within five years of thirty. No identification whatsoever except the zipper of his jacket which was made in Taiwan – and he was no Chinaman. Good set of teeth which is no help, no fillings or fancy bridgework to check up on. Nothing. But you know all this. So far as we can make out no one in the whole wide world has lost anybody like that in at least the last five years."

"The locket?" queried Fuller.

"No lead there. Made in England and exported all over. Engraved with the initials 'E.B.' – how many 'E.B.'s do you know for God's sake? We have two in this department alone. A woman's pendant at that, roses engraved on it – not that that means much in this day and age. The date on it, July 4th four years ago, just makes things worse. Suggests the States so we now spread our inquiries over the border instead of narrowing them down a bit. Anyway we are not at all sure it has any connection with the body, it was not around his neck so far as the forensic people can judge. It was only by sheer luck that it was found at all under the mud."

"Any new theories then Joe?"

"No. As you know we had two or three a week at first but they seem to have died down now. I'm still of the opinion, but don't quote me, that he was some hop-head who decided to crawl out into the wild to do a bit of dreaming and forgot to wake up. But how in hell's name did he get right out there? The track leads from nowhere to nowhere and he was right in the middle of it, with no sign of his having been living rough at the old logging camps at either end. Of course there could be something out there that we have missed, you know what that timber country is like, but we don't even know what we are looking for.

So, no identification and, after all this time, hardly likely ever to be."

"No story then Joe." It was not a question.

"No story, period."

Fuller slipped his note-book into the pocket of his shabby tweed jacket and reached for his hat.

"Well, thanks for your time Joe – and for the coffee." The sergeant waved a depreciating hand.

At the door Fuller turned.

"You know I could swear there is a story there. After forty odd years in the business you sort of get a nose for it."

As the sound of the reporter's departing car died away the only sound in the office was the plop, plop, plop of water from the overhanging branch.

'Goddammit', said Brady to himself, 'Tomorrow I'll bring a saw and cut that thing off."

Wallaroo to Jeddah. Sept.21/Oct.14. 1982

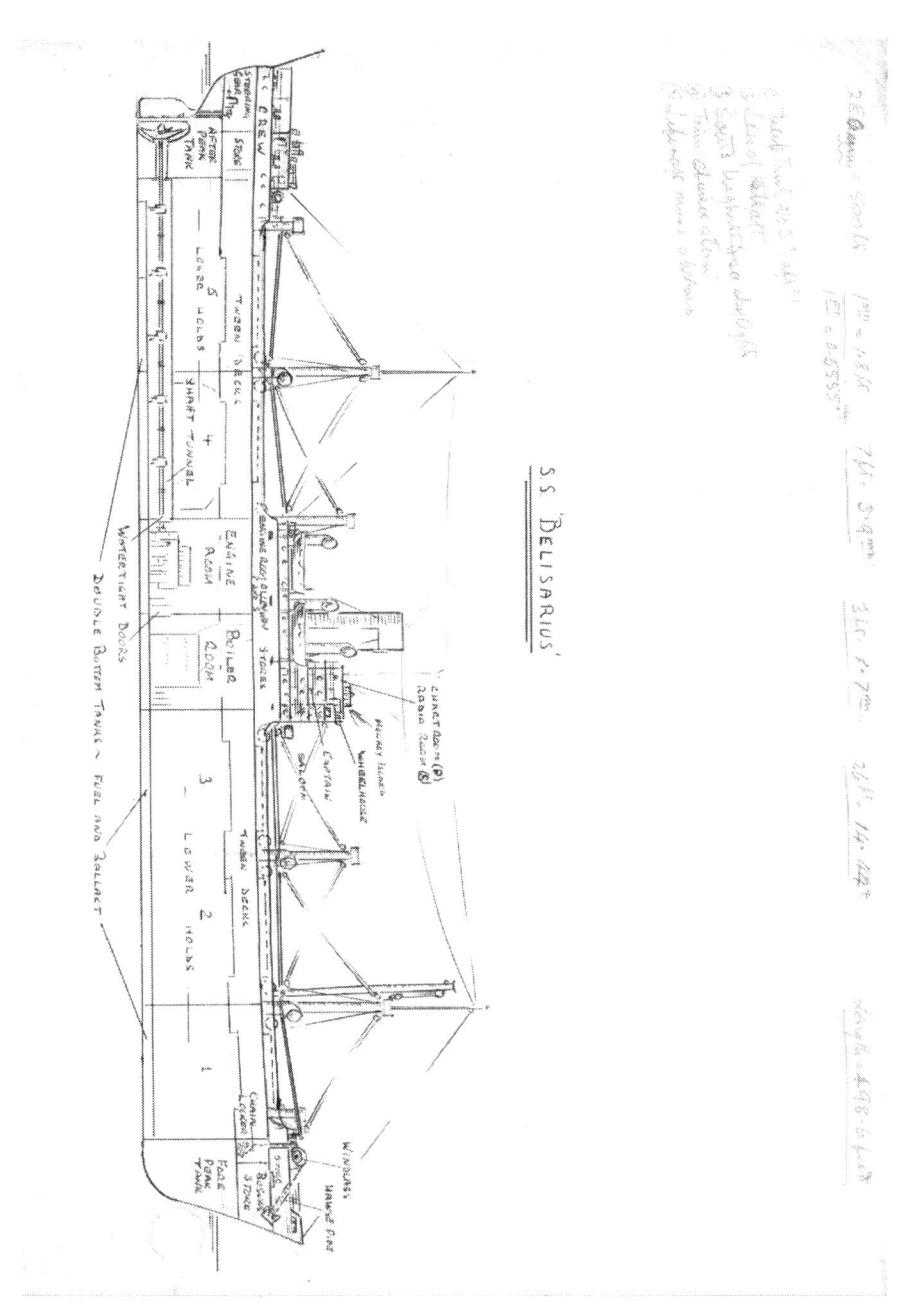

S.S. "BELISARIUS"

8 THE WOODEN MEN

'Wooden Ships and Iron Men'

Old 'Shellbacks' saying.

To: The Mate in his many trials

<u>Chapter 1</u>

The Nineteen Sixties marked a period of change in the shipping world. Changes in this and the following decade were as great as those covering the transition from sail to steam a century earlier.

Here follows a tale of one ship and the sea-change she and her people experienced at this time.

The voyage commenced in a routine manner and in fact progressed with no more upsets and frustrations than normally experienced on a journey half way round the world and back. The old 'Belisarius' had made more than three score similar voyages without serious incident and no one sailing on her had the slightest premonition that this would be any different.

*****

An observer would at first have seen nothing out of the ordinary in the man seated in the taxi rolling towards the Airport. Of average height, slim build and dressed in a suit which suggested Saville Row, a casual glance would have indicated a successful business man or eminent doctor. The iron grey hair merging to almost snow white at the temples might have given cause for second thoughts. It was the eyes which would have called for a complete reassessment. Although the man's lined features were composed the eyes were for ever on the alert. Noting every aspect of the landscape as it flashed past. Steel blue eyes which missed no detail, eyes obviously not easily given to smiling. Eyes of a man of strong will and considerable authority.

Captain Andrew Cowell Montague was in a mixed frame of mind as the taxi took him on the first stage of a very long journey. On the debit side the fact that he was to join a ship in the middle of what proved to have been a particularly pleasurable leave caused him considerable annoyance. Nor was he pleased to be appointed to the 'Belisarius', the oldest ship in the Company's fleet. Not that it was anyone's fault, his predecessor had to be relieved owing to the sudden illness of his wife and Montague was the only Master available to replace him at short notice.

However, he quickly reassured himself, these negative aspects were greatly outweighed by the credit side. He had left the Company's head office less than an hour before with the promise that this was to be his last voyage on the general traders. After this trip he was to take command of one of the Fairbell Line's cruise ships. Thus his life-long ambition was to be full-filled. To complete his happiness in this respect he was being appointed over the heads of several masters senior to him in length of service. This naturally greatly increased his satisfaction.

*****

James Carey Second Officer of the 'Belisarius', arrived at the airport in a red Aston Martin. A lingering embrace with the tawny-headed Leonora might have lasted a good deal longer but for the imprecations of other drivers wishing to park in order to discharge their passengers.

Carey eased his six feet two inches out of the car and relinquished the driver's seat to the very attractive girl. A few minutes and a long kiss later he stood with his matching luggage at his feet watching the sleek car weave its way skilfully through the afternoon traffic. When it was completely out of sight he picked up the two suitcases and carried them to the check-in desk designated by the Company's personnel department as the rendezvous for the various officers proceeding to the ship at Rotterdam. His thoughts were far from ships as he made his way through the multi-coloured throng of people.

Having obtained his ticket and deposited his baggage, apart from the small 'flight bag' slung over his shoulder, Carey headed for the bar. Having joined ships by air on several previous occasions he did not even bother to look for any ship's personnel at the appointed meeting place.

There were about forty people around the bar but Carey had no difficulty in identifying the seafarers. One or two of them appeared to have been there for some time as quite a noisy party was in progress. He stopped a few yards from the bar to look for familiar faces. Carey recognised Peter Gregson, Second Engineer, with whom he had made a voyage some years previously, Bill Parry, Chief Steward and Humphrey Smith, Third Officer, he had also sailed with at different times. The others were strangers to him.

"Is there another bar around here where a gentleman can have a drink in peace?" asked Carey with a grin as he joined them.

"Here he is!" yelled Smith, ('How many beers had he had?' wondered Carey), "God's gift to women. Come and join the party."

Carey greeted those he already knew and was introduced to the others, Ken Forbes, Radio Officer; Mike Crawford, Third Engineer; Charlie Ingram and Ted Lattimer, Fourth and Fifth Engineers.

"Congratulations on the new 'Ticket' James," said Parry.

"Yes, 'Master Mariner' now," laughed Smith, "Was it much of a struggle?"

"Months of clean living and constant self-denial," replied Carey, "As one who knows I can strongly advise you to get your nose into some improving books this voyage rather than pint pots young Hump, your day of reckoning will come."

He changed the subject.

"By the way, I have been rather out of contact lately. I have heard that Andy Montague is sailing as 'Old Man' but who is the Mate?"

"Jake Hatch is still carrying the white man's burden there," answered Gregson.

"Old Jake?" Carey was surprised, "I thought he had collected the 'brass hat' at last and gone to better things."

"You mean you haven't heard?" Smith's cherubic face glowed with pleasure in anticipation of being in a position to pass on a particularly juicy piece of scandal. "Actually," he continued in a more subdued voice, "We don't like to talk about it but, as you are the discreet type and won't let it go any further," the subject had been the main talking point in the Company for weeks, "The bold Jake hit a bit of a snag at the last minute which entailed a slight change of plan on the Company's part. A sudden dimming, as it were, of his promotion prospects......"

"For God's sake get on with it," urged Carey, "or we will be in Rotterdam before you get to the end of the story."

Gregson intervened. "As a matter of fact no-one seems to know the exact story. Rumour has it however that Jake lost his promotion owing to the fact that he was unable to resist a sudden impulse to throw beer cans at the chairman."

"I heard he tried to seduce the chairman's daughter," offered Lattimer.

"Could not imagine anyone allowing their daughter within a mile of Jake, anyway I don't think the boss has one," Gregson continued. "I have heard several versions of the yarn and they all agree that dear old Jake had gone on one of his magnificent benders at just the wrong time. It seems pretty certain too that the chairman was involved in some way."

"Poor old Jake," commented Carey, "His life seems to be a catalogue of disaster. I can't say I have much sympathy for him though, he certainly seems to ask for all the trouble he gets. I wonder what he will be like to sail with now? By all accounts he was bloody-minded enough before this happened."

This discourse was interrupted by the arrival of Captain Montague. Soon after the greetings and introductions Montague left the gathering with the excuse that he had 'things to attend to'. The Captain had in fact nothing of importance to attend to but had no intention of becoming involved with the others. He would see plenty of them later and at the present time would be happier with his own company.

Having purchased a copy of 'The Times' and a cup of coffee Captain Montague settled himself at a table out of sight of the bar. There, with the newspaper open but unread before him, he contemplated the officers appointed to the ship.

Of the men at the bar he was acquainted with Carey and Parry. The Second Mate was a first class officer, he mused, pity there are not more like him. Parry now? – the last time they had sailed together the Chief Steward had been pretty green but that was some years ago. He had shown promise then and had no doubt improved with experience. I remember his feeding was good so I don't expect to have any trouble with the crowd in that respect. The Second Engineer, Gregson was it not? – have not sailed with him before but seem to have heard he has a good reputation. The Third Mate, that must have been the stocky lad with red hair. Appeared to be half drunk – will have to have a quiet word with him before he is much older.

The others were but half registered in his mind. No doubt he would be able to connect the names with the faces when he had been on the ship for a few days.

Looking further afield Montague thought of the Chief Engineer whom he knew to be already on the ship. He had met Macquarie on several different occasions but never actually sailed with him. A first class man by all accounts – and goodness knows a ship the age of the 'Belisarius' needs a good 'Chief' he decided.

That left the Chief Officer, the 'Mate'. And there, mused Montague, we have our problem. He wished Hatch no harm but did, most sincerely, wish he had not been appointed to this ship. 'Correction! I am the one who is joining, Hatch has been there for some time. Which only proves what the Company think of him, their most senior chief officer on their oldest ship. There was only one way to deal with someone of Hatch's reputation, firmness! And to start right from the beginning in the way I intend to carry on. Although not much of a ship she will be _my_ ship, at least for this voyage and my reputation stands or falls with her. What is more not all the Hatches in creation are going to tarnish it, particularly at this stage of my career.'

Captain Montague's thoughts were interrupted by the calling of the Rotterdam flight.

*****

The agent's car deposited Captain Montague fifty yards from the 'Belisarius'' accommodation ladder, as close as the vehicle could safely approach with the quay-side a hive of activity as fork-lift trucks tore in and out of the cargo sheds with pallets and cases of cargo to feed the ever hungry hooks dangling from the ship's derricks waiting to snatch the packages from the quayside and swing them into the ship's holds.

The ship's agent, who had accompanied the captain from the airport, excused himself and departed to have a word with the stevedore. Left to himself Montague spent a few moments contemplating his new command.

Old fashioned now, she had been modern once. Montague remembered seeing her on her maiden voyage a decade after he first went to sea. She was of the 'three island type', her forecastle, midship structure and poop being a deck higher than the main deck with its three hatches forward and two aft of the engine and boiler rooms amidships.

Two buff-coloured masts forward and one aft with their similarly painted derricks served the hatches. The relatively high bridge structure contrasted with the single deck of accommodation immediately abaft it above the engine room. A pair of life-boats on each side of this accommodation took up much of the space there, the engine-room skylight and large cowl ventilators occupying most of the remainder.

Above all towered the large vertical funnel, its black paint relieved only by the Fairbell crest on either side.

'Not a curve or a rake in the whole set-up,' remarked Montague to himself, 'little resemblance to the stream-lining of our new motor ships.'

The black hull was a different matter entirely. The end product of centuries of ship-building experience even the battering the plates had received over the years could not hide the sweet run of her lines. In contrast to her top-hamper the hull seemed to contain no straight lines at all.

'Still a good sea-boat, probably a good deal more comfortable than my last ship in any kind of a sea,' mused the new captain – in an attempt to mollify the loss of creature comforts his appointment to this ancient ship would surely entail.

The 'Belisarius' was nearly a quarter of a century old and looked every minute of it. After more than a month of discharging and loading cargo in several British and Continental ports with the crew occupied in opening and closing hatches, cleaning holds, spending many hours 'on stations' entering and leaving ports, storing, bunkering and a thousand and one other activities entailed in 'turning the ship around' the vessel's appearance had been sadly neglected. Dirty white paintwork with numerous small streaks of new rust interspersed with orange coloured areas where repairs to various deck fittings had been hastily daubed with red-lead to preserve the metal from rust until time could be spared to attend to proper painting offended the eye. Empty bottles, discarded newspapers, piles of rubbish collected from the holds and loosely heaped planks of dunnage wood littered the decks.

The old ship had a two degrees list and leaned against the quay as if wearied with voyaging. She was looking her absolute worst as her new Master came on board.

Although, with the loading in full swing, there were men in plenty around the hatches, there was not a soul to greet the Captain as he stepped onto the deck. His experienced eye took in every aspect of the ship within his range of vision. What he saw did nothing to please him. With a frown which forebode trouble for someone in the very near future he made his way to the Chief Officer's office.

The room was similar to any other mate's office of the time. About ten feet square its main furnishing consisted of a large, glass-covered knee-hole desk fitted against the after bulkhead, a small padded bench under the port-hole of the outboard bulkhead with a battered steel filing cabinet at its end. Between the cabinet and a door leading into the chief officer's room was a small shelf supporting a typewriter of vintage aspect. A chair, a glass-fronted bookcase, a tall narrow locker and several large framed ship's plans screwed to the bulkheads completed the furnishings.

The furniture however was not immediately apparent. Nearly every square inch of the bulkheads was occupied by sheaves of boat-notes, stores lists, bills, invoices, mate's receipts, letters, forms, (completed and uncompleted), three calendars, (one left over from the previous year), advertising beer and ship's chandlers, each lavishly decorated with coloured pictures which could only be described as indecent and numerous other documents all secured with bull-dog paper grips hanging from cup-hooks. The 'settee' was covered by several ledgers, a broken life-boat compass, three cargo plans, an oilskin coat, the Deck Log Book, a hammer, several hanks of small line and an over-filled ash-tray. The filing cabinet was topped with an insecure heap of books and papers. The typewriter contained an unfinished letter whilst below it rested four small boxes marked 'Care of Chief Officer' – small items of cargo which were too valuable or hazardous to be stowed in the holds. Visible under the settee was a battered cardboard carton, two marline spikes, a large monkey-wrench some old rope and one sea-boot.

The desk was a veritable hay-stack of manifests, cargo plans, note-books, pens, pencils, ash-trays and sundry papers in current use. At one end of the desk stood two pint mugs and several empty beer cans bearing testimony to a discussion on stowage with the stevedore earlier in the day.

Sitting in the chair, elbows on the desk and head in his hands, sat the Mate.

Gilbert Henry Hatch was not a prepossessing figure of a man. Large and ungainly his uniform jacket and baggy trousers showed signs of long wear and remoteness from their last visit to the cleaners. What could be seen of his face gave the impression that at some time in its formative years someone wearing hob-nailed boots had walked on it. Shaggy black eyebrows and a furrowed brow were topped by rumpled black hair streaked with grey. Not, as some wit had it, the distinguished greying of the temples administered by the gentle hand of care but rather as if some passing seagull had decorated his head.

The Mate was a bastard.

To anyone familiar with ships this appellation will come as no surprise. However, in this case it was literally true, or, as Hatch himself occasionally announced when in his cups, "Anyone can claim to be a bastard but I am a bastard in my own right!"

To his credit let it be said that he always regretted these outbursts when he sobered up the following day.

"Mr. Hatch?"

The Mate awoke from his reverie and swinging his gaze to the doorway observed the trim figure in a dark suit whom he instinctively knew to be the captain.

Being in no doubt as to whom he was addressing the captain continued, "I am Captain Montague."

Hatch rose to his feet.

"Pleased to meet you sir. Yes, I am Hatch."

As they shook hands Montague said, "I know you are busy Mr. Hatch but I would appreciate it if you could spare me a few minutes. Have you got the keys to my room by the way?"

"Yes, they are here somewhere."

Hatch's hands plunged through the papers on his desk like a pair of snow-ploughs. After one or two other bunches of keys came to light he eventually held up a ring with three keys and a small brass tally inscribed 'Flag Locker' – an old dodge this, if the keys were ever mislaid, although easily identified by their owner they were of little value to any finder of evil intent.

The Captain accepted the keys, deciding not to comment at this time on the lack of security in leaving them lying about.

"Before you come up would you please send someone to fetch my gear? There are four pieces in the agent's car on the quay."

The interview in the Captain's room was short, in fact it terminated with the arrival of the agent after about ten minutes. However, the effectiveness of those few minutes could be deduced from the fact that the Mate arrived at the door with his uniform jacket unbuttoned and his tie askew and left the room with all buttons fastened and his neckwear amidships.

Hatch proceeded directly to the third mate's room from whence a considerable amount of noise was issuing.

The mini-bus bringing the relieving officers from the airport had arrived a few minutes earlier and the people leaving the ship were about to hand over their responsibilities to the new arrivals. In fact, the first few cans of beer were just being opened when the Mate burst in the room.

Hatch commenced issuing instructions the moment the brief introductions had been made.

"You can cut out this lot for a start," indicating the glasses of beer. "Before you hand over there is work to do. Bob," to the third mate about to leave the ship, "get a couple of men from the Serang and have them coil all the derrick guy-ropes tidily on the bulwarks," then, quoting the Captain, "'They are being used as door-mats at the moment'. And get a man to sweep the deck at the top of the gangway, 'it's ankle deep in rubbish'. You," he addressed Smith, having already forgotten his name, "get the life-boat and fire station muster lists in, Bob will show you where they are posted up, and get them up to date with the new arrivals entered on them. There will be a boat and fire drill before we sail tomorrow."

"The serang has all his men getting the derricks down at the number four hatch," protested Bob.

"I know that," snarled the Mate, "He can manage with a few less. And while you have the men get the rat-guards properly secured on the mooring lines."

"Why not let the poor little blighters escape?" suggested the second mate as he wiped beer froth from his lips with the back of his hand.

"You know I always thought the idea was to stop the rats getting on board," commented Carey with an innocent grin.

Hatch was in no mood for frivolity. He turned to Carey. "The Old Man wants all the distances to the discharging ports before we leave here and also, as soon as possible, the 'G.M.' for leaving here and for each arrival and departure at the discharge ports." He referred to the actual measurement of stability.

Carey ceased grinning.

"'G.M's? I thought this ship had stability and to spare? She is as 'stiff' as they come so I am told."

"All very true, the G.M. must be about six feet at the moment and I've never known it to get below three but that is the way he," nodding in the general direction of the captain's quarters, "wants it."

"Another thing," the Mate's change of expression indicated he was quoting the captain again, "if we are commiserating with the Dutch over the loss of their empire we are a bit late and also rather tactless."

The others gazed at Hatch uncomprehendingly.

The Mate continued, "So get the courtesy flag hoisted right up instead of a couple of feet below the yardarm – and see that all the flags come down at sunset and are hoisted at exactly eight o'clock in the morning. Not, repeat not, at any old time the gangway watchman happens to be passing by.

"Whilst on the subject of gangways the watchman is to be stationed there when not off on brief and very essential duties." With mock horror in his voice he continued, "The Master came on board this afternoon and no-one, absolutely no-one, was at the gangway to meet him!" A pause, then, "So get moving!"

"What is the Old Man like?" ventured Smith. Somewhat superfluously the others thought.

Hatch swung round at the doorway.

"He hasn't my sunny nature and easy-going temperament but we have discovered we have something in common – we hate each other's guts!"

*****

Having discussed with the captain various items of business the agent departed.

Captain Montague's predecessor had left the ship as soon as she had berthed at Rotterdam but had left a comprehensive sheaf of notes concerning bunkers, crew, cargo, outstanding repairs, the various idiosyncrasies of the bridge instruments and everything else he could think of which could be of assistance or interest to his relief.

Montague read the notes then glanced at his watch. Time enough for a quick look round before getting cleaned up for the evening meal he decided.

The Captain's gaze wandered around the day-room. Large enough and adequately furnished but he was going to miss the air-conditioned comfort of his previous ship. However, the two large electric fans fitted to the deckhand looked capable of moving the air fairly effectively once the vessel reached warmer climates. The pair of large arm chairs were well worn but were comfortable and the fitted settee seemed to invite afternoon naps once the ship got to sea. Old fashioned round brass-rimmed port-holes and the dark mahogany desk and other furniture gave the room an almost Victorian atmosphere but for all that a comforting sense of solidity. The framed prints on the bulkheads added a little colour to the room but Montague wished he had been able to bring his own favourite water-colours. However, this was impracticable when flying out to a ship meant bringing but the bare necessities for a voyage. He consoled himself with the thought that he would only be on the ship for one trip.

Montague climbed the inside stair between his accommodation and the deck above where, having selected the correct key from the bunch the chief officer had given him, he opened the door and entered the wheelhouse.

The wheelhouse was no modern, instrument packed ship's nerve centre stretching its armoured glass windowed front across two thirds of the ship's beam. Far from it, it had room enough only for the bare essentials and bare essentials was all it contained.

Although the five windows across the front of the wheel-house were close enough together their heavy teakwood frames reduced considerably the area available for glass. They were of the old-fashioned 'railway carriage' type. Designed to slide vertically in their frames and to be secured at the required height by leather straps to brass studs they invariably jammed at one stage or another. All the wedging in the world would not prevent them rattling or water gushing through in heavy weather.

A large sliding teak door led out to the bridge wing on either side. These doors had glass let in to the top panel and a further small window was fitted in the fore and aft bulkhead between each door and the bridge front.

Aft of the door on the starboard side was the flag locker. Montague noted with distaste the pieces of scrap paper, two dirty coffee mugs and a dangerously wired electric kettle decorating the top of it.

On the port side of the wheelhouse the position of the flag locker was occupied by an ancient radar console. A glance at it served to confirm the previous master's remarks on the instrument's unreliability.

The wheel, magnetic compass binnacle and gyro compass repeater took up most of the space in the after part of the wheelhouse. The console for the automatic steering gear, a very obvious recent addition, was situated under the windows towards the starboard side and a small table, hinged to the forward bulkhead, occupied a similar position to the port.

The engine room telegraphs were positioned on the bridge wings just outside the doors.

Three heavy telephone handsets, one each connecting to the engine room, foc'sle head and poop, ('I wonder if they work most of the time?' mused Montague), competed for space with several framed documents on the after bulkhead.

An Aldis signalling lamp, its battery, two battered megaphones and a large high bridge chair added to the congestion.

Two overflowing sandbox ashtrays screwed below the bridge front windows and a thin film of dust over everything completed the scene of desolation.

Captain Montague was not impressed.

The small chartroom aft of the wheelhouse and leading from it was somewhat cleaner but far from tidy.

'This mess will have to be cleaned up first thing in the morning,' said Montague to himself as he returned to his room for a shower and a change of clothes. At least this was his intention, in the event the shower refused to function and he was reduced to taking a tub bath in lukewarm rust coloured water.

Montague was not in a very happy state of mind as he made his way to the dining saloon for the evening meal. However, in uniform he felt more at home with his environment.

*****

The Captain dined in solitary estate.

Of the three officers normally seated at his table the Chief Engineer and Chief Officer had opted for sandwiches in their respective rooms and the Second Engineer was busy handing over to his relief. The few junior officers who had eaten in the saloon had left before Montague arrived.

On returning to his room after the meal Montague telephoned the Chief Engineer and arranged for that officer to visit him later in the evening when the Chief had completed the paperwork with which at the time he was engrossed.

Whilst awaiting his visitor the Captain read through the quite considerable pile of correspondence which required his attention. He also commenced writing, in his neat hand, the draught of a letter to the Chairman of the Company. The first of many adding meat to the bones of the various documents which gave details of the voyage as it progressed.

He had completed nearly a page of the letter when a tap on the door heralded the arrival of the Chief Engineer.

Alistair Macquarie was in his mid-thirties. Of average height his stocky figure gave evidence of considerable strength and endurance. His black hair was beginning to grey at the temples and his steady blue eyes indicated a man who did not suffer fools gladly. Strong hands from which no amount of scrubbing could entirely remove the dark stains from around the nails were demonstrative of the fact that the man was not afraid to use them.

The two men discussed the various aspects of the forthcoming voyage as it affected the engine room department and shortly before he left the Chief mentioned a problem which had been threatening for some time.

"If that strike comes off in London and we sail deep sea from here there will be quite a number of repairs outstanding but nothing we cannot handle ourselves or can't wait until we get back to the U.K."

'What a pleasant change from the last Chief I sailed with', thought Montague. That worthy had coped eventually with his problems but only after long discourses on their impossibility or the dire consequences if they were attempted. Montague warmed toward Macquarie, here was something like a Chief Engineer!

It was nearly eleven o'clock when the Chief got to his feet.

"Big day tomorrow, sailing day. Must get my beauty sleep."

"Yes, bed calls," replied Montague, "There won't be much rest for any of us tomorrow night."

Although the meeting had been both pleasant and constructive Montague was not sorry when the Chief departed. He was tired and the morrow would no doubt be a very busy day culminating in a night spent mainly on the bridge.

The morning's newspaper remained but part read on the settee. The world's troubles would have to await another day.

*****

The officers leaving the ship departed in the mini-bus fairly late in the evening. The scheduled time for departure from the ship, according to the letter thoughtfully supplied by the agents, was 2000hrs. but, what with one thing and another, it was but an hour or so before midnight by the time the patient driver had rounded up his passengers and started off for the hotel where they were to stay the night. At least he collected most of them, inevitably two of the junior officers had somewhat forgetfully drifted off towards the bright lights under their own steam.

When the old crowd had departed Carey, Gregson, Forbes and Smith settled down for a nightcap before turning in.

The conversation soon got around to the Mate.

None of those present had sailed with Hatch previously but Carey had met him briefly once or twice so was designated an authority.

"Is he always as bloody-minded as today?" queried Smith who had a vested interest in the subject.

"No," smiled Carey, "From what I know of his reputation we are lucky to find him in his present state of sweetness and light…. for him."

"Oh my God!" Hump Smith took a long swig of beer before his next question.

"How old is he?"

"I haven't a clue I'm afraid," replied Carey.

"About fifty, I would say," offered Forbes.

"Oh, have a heart!" from Gregson, "He can't be a day over forty-five, forty-six at the most."

"How did he get to be called 'Jake' anyway?" asked Forbes. "That's not his real name is it? Aren't his initials 'G.E.' or something?"

"'G.H.' actually," Carey answered, "Gilbert Henry, I do know that much. The 'Jake' apparently came during his early days at sea. The story goes that when he was a deck boy he had a mate nick-named 'Blondie' owing to his straw-coloured hair. The Master of the ship asked the Bosun this young fellow's name and the Bosun, who could not remember the newly-joined lad's surname, which was obviously required, blurted out 'Blondie'. The Old Man, presumably the sarcastic type, replied, 'And I suppose the dark-haired boy is 'Black Jake?' The 'Jake' part stuck from then on."

"Anything is better than 'Gilbert'," Smith said, "Whatever were his parents thinking of when they had him Christened?"

"I doubt if they really cared," muttered Forbes, little realising how close he was to the truth, "if the baby in any way resembled the end product."

This exhausted the subject of the Mate so Gregson turned to Carey. "What about the Old Man? You have sailed with him."

"Fine bloke, bit of a tartar at times, likes everything on the top line. If you do your job alright you will not have any trouble with him. A wonderful seaman too. I've seen him do some pretty fancy ship-handling at times. I remember once coming out of Charleston....."

The discussion continued until nearly midnight.

*****

The Captain came down to breakfast much refreshed after a goodnight's sleep. The temperamental shower had decided to co-operate which added to his feeling of well-being.

He looked in on the Mate on his way to the dining saloon.

"Good morning Mr. Hatch. All well I hope?"

"Good morning sir. Yes, as well as can be expected. They have sprung an extra fifty-odd tons of condensed milk on me but with all the space available it will be no problem to stow. The stevedore was in earlier, says he expects to finish at about ten o'clock tonight."

"I had hoped it would be earlier but never mind. Oh, by the way Mr. Hatch, the wheelhouse and chartroom......."

A few minutes later Captain Montague continued on his way to the saloon.

Hatch stuck his head into the pantry and ordered bacon and egg sandwiches.

Returning to his office the Mate reached across his desk and tore off the previous day's date from the calendar pad on the bulkhead. Automatically he read the motto printed below the new day's date, 'How do we know that this world is not some other world's Hell?'

"I know damn well it is.," muttered Hatch. Then, looking at the date again, he exclaimed loudly, "Good God! It's my birthday again." He made a quick calculation, 'Thirty-seven! I am getting old.'

*****

The day passed in the way of sailing days anywhere, the chaos mounting slowly to a crescendo during the last hour or so before the ship eventually left the berth.

The boat and fire drill was not an unqualified success. The Chief officer, nominally in charge of the exercises, arrived late, capless and with the tapes of his life-jacket fluttering in the breeze. None of the new engineers knew which life-boat they had been appointed to and the actual lowering of the two off-shore lifeboats left much to be desired. Captain Montague watched the performance with mounting irritation.

The fire drill was but little better. There was a few minutes delay awaiting pressure on the fire main and when the water did arrive it did so so suddenly a temporarily unmanned hose soaked the almost dry washing hanging on a barge alongside before it could be controlled. It was generally agreed that the invective this drew from the bargee's wife sounded just as fruity in Dutch as it would have done in English.

*****

Eventually the last sling of cargo was loaded and the last hatch covered, As the loading had taken a little longer than expected the tugs and pilot had been ordered for 2300 hours, even then they had arrived before the last few derricks had been lowered.

Pilot and Captain left the latter's room and climbed to the bridge. The third mate was in the chartroom entering the departure draft in the official log-book. The steering gear, whistle, navigation lights and engine-room telegraphs had been tested an hour before.

The Captain addressed the Third Officer.

"Mr.-er-Smith, nip down to the Chief Officer and tell him to make stations for departure right away. He can leave those derricks until the ship is in the river."

The Mate was completing some last minute calculations in his office when Smith arrived.

"Stations right away," Hump Smith was not quite certain how to address the Chief Officer. 'Sir' seemed too formal for someone like Hatch but he did not dare trying to use his nickname 'Jake'. He compromised by not calling him anything. "The Captain says to leave the derricks until we are in the river."

"Alright! I'll be along as soon as I can," replied Hatch in a very irritated tone of voice.

Smith had only been away a couple of minutes when he returned to the Mate's door.

The Captain says to hurry up. There is another ship moving down the dock and we will have to wait for him if we don't get away in the next few minutes."

"All right! All right!" replied Hatch testily as he got to his feet, "Let me get my coat on. Always a blind rush to get away, it's a wonder we don't have more accidents than we do now. Have you passed the word to the crew?"

"Yes, they are on their way for'd now and the Second Mate has started singling up aft."

On his way to the foc'sle head the Mate paused briefly to check that the two derricks previously plumbing the quay had been swung in and securely guyed to prevent them accidently swinging out again when the ship began to move.

"Hurry up Mr. Hatch!" shouted the Captain from the bridge, "We haven't got all night!"

Hatch muttered to himself as he continued his progress forward.

The first three forward mooring lines came in quickly enough but the fourth was securely jammed by the lines of the ship in the adjoining berth. This took several minutes to clear and by the time the forward end of the ship was 'singled up' to two lines which could be cast off the moment the order was given the vessel moving down the dock was judged to be too close for the 'Belisarius' to leave ahead of her in safety.

Captain Montague was fuming as the Swedish bulk-carrier moved slowly past. Someone should have ensured that the mooring lines were clear for leaving before the ship was due to sail. He decided to have some very strong words with the Chief Officer at the earliest opportunity.

The pilot sniffed the breeze and patted the dampness on the bridge rail.

"I don't like the way the breeze is dropping Captain," he said, "There could be fog outside the river."

"Let us hope not," replied Montague, suppressing a desire to say 'God, that's all I need!' Instead he continued, "there was no fog forecast on the weather report."

"Maybe just a patch or two."

'The man is almost wishing it on me.' Groaned the captain to himself. Aloud he said, without much conviction, "The breeze will no doubt return and clear it away before daylight."

The Swedish ship was eventually clear and shortly after midnight the 'Belisarius' drew away from her berth. The tugs let go when the ship was safely in the river and at last free from all ties she made her way towards the sea.

The pilot proved more accurate in his forecast that the radio bulletin. The first wisps of mist were encountered shortly before he left the ship off the Maas Buoy. Ten minutes later the 'Belisarius' ran into thick fog.

As every other shipmaster since men first went to sea Captain Montague hated fog with every fibre of his being. He had to decide quickly whether to anchor, with the possibility of having to stay for several hours, or to proceed hoping that the weather would clear, as he had prophesied, before dawn.

A slight thinning of the fog disclosed on the port bow the glow of the lights of a ship at anchor. A breath of a breeze felt on his cheek at the same time decided him.

Turning to his officer on watch he said, "I think we will carry on for a bit Mr. Carey. The radar appears to be behaving itself. Slow ahead and keep the whistle going. We can always haul out of the fairway and anchor if it does not clear. Tell the Chief Officer on the phone to keep a good lookout, he will have to stay for'd with the Carpenter until this muck makes its mind up one way or another."

The 'Belisarius' crept slowly past the anchorage, her steam whistle booming out at frequent regular intervals.

Between the Goeree and North Hinder lightships the visibility cleared with almost miraculous suddenness as an easterly breeze sprang up.

"Thank the Lord for that," said a very relieved Captain, "Right, ring 'Full Ahead' and tell the engine room we are now clear of the fog. We will make 'Full Away' in a few minutes. What time is it by the way?"

Carey flashed a torch on his watch.

"Three thirty-five sir."

"Tell the engine-room we will make 'Full Away' at three forty-eight then. Must start the sea passage on a decimal of an hour to make your arithmetic easier." Montague felt almost frivolous after the strain of the fog, brief though it had been.

"You can tell the Chief Officer to secure his anchors then that will do for'd. We only require one lookout on the bridge now, the other man can stream the log when he goes down."

The 'Belisarius' seemed to take on new life as her speed increased. Her bow wave became more apparent and for some minutes black, oily smoke belched from her tall funnel before the burners in her boiler furnaces were properly adjusted.

On his way along the foredeck after seeing the anchors securely lashed the Mate checked that there were a few wedges securing the tarpaulins of each hatch and that the derricks were properly housed in their crutches with a light lashing. As there was no immediate prospect of heavy weather the more permanent securing could wait until the carpenter and crew turned out later in the morning. This inspection he repeated on the after deck.

"All secure sir," he reported on reaching the bridge.

Montague looked up from the chart.

"Thank you Mr. Hatch. Sorry it has been such a long night for you."

"I suppose it is what I get my 'film star' wages for," replied Hatch without a trace of humour.

He glanced at the chartroom clock.

"Two minutes to four. I'll just nip down for a leak and be right back," he said to Carey.

The Mate's watch began at four o'clock.

*****

Chapter 2

There was nothing remarkable about the voyage. Rotterdam to the Suez Canal; the Red Sea; Aden for bunkers then the heavy weather of the South West Monsoon in the Arabian Sea. Singapore to commence discharge of the general cargo thence Bangkok and Djakarta, commencing loading in the latter port as the last of the outward cargo was discharged. The next ports of call were Padang and the Borneo port of Tanjong Mani for timber and finally Singapore again for general cargo. The most memorable feature of this part of the voyage was the heat, the tropical sun turning the steel ship into an oven by day, hardly relieved by the sweltering atmosphere at night when exhausted men slept fitfully in bedding stinking of sweat.

After Singapore came the long slog to the United States Gulf Ports. The mad rush there to get the cargo out, the holds cleaned and the full cargo of bulk soya bean meal loaded. Long hours and broken nights as the ship sailed as soon as the cargo programme for each port was completed, regardless of the hour.

However, the heat, toil and frustrations were forgotten as soon as each occasion passed. It was the good times ashore at such places as Savannah and New Orleans which remained fresh in the memory, to be relived many times in the future, no doubt with a certain amount of elaboration, when the participants again met. Even the shopping expeditions were fun as the visits to shops were intermingled with calls at bars. This often resulted in the happy shoppers returning to the ship in the early hours loaded with presents for friends and relations at home, which, although they seemed a good idea at the time, were viewed, as often as not, with some disapprobation in the cold light of the following day.

However, the last shore-side beer had been drunk and the last frivolous nightdress bought more than a week before as the deep-laden 'Belisarius' plodded her way north-easterly, away from the tropical weather and into the gales of the Western Ocean. Towards home. Towards her destiny.

*****

Captain Montague recalled some of the events of the voyage which was not drawing to a close. Nothing really noteworthy had occurred, no major calamities anyway, which was the main thing. The officers and Asian crew had proved more than satisfactory in spite of his earlier forebodings. In fact, he complimented himself on commanding a happy and efficient ship.

The main engines had suffered a few attacks of 'condenseritis' and other ailments which any ship the age of the 'Belisarius' was prone to but the Chief Engineer and his staff had worked hard and her performance this voyage had proved to be an improvement on her previous recent record. The electricity generators had been the main cause of anxiety throughout. At that very moment only two of the three on board were operational, the other being stripped down for overhaul. One generator was just sufficient to carry the present load but it was obviously best to have two running to share the burden. Montague smiled ruefully as he recalled the occasion earlier in the voyage when a fault had suddenly occurred on the generator then in operation. The ship 'blacked out' and slowed almost to a standstill before the reserve machine could be started up and 'got on board' to take the load. That was the only occasion he could remember of having to admonish the Chief Engineer. When all was well in the engine room after the breakdown the engineers immediately increased speed again to full without informing the bridge of their intentions. In fact, there had been no communication between the engine room and bridge during the entire period of the emergency. The bridge had been reluctant to telephone the engineers when they would obviously be busy rectifying the fault but thought they would at least have indicated their intentions on the engine room telegraph even if too pressed to use the phone. In the event there were no other vessels close by so no harm was done. However, the mild rebuke, administered over a drink after the incident, resulted in no ill-feeling.

The efforts of the deck department had exceeded Montague's expectations. There was no doubt in his mind that his original approach to the Chief Officer's attitude had been the correct one. After the first few days things had begun to run quite smoothly and at least the voyage had progressed without any major upheavals between them. In spite of this he could not help thinking that the Mate still looked on their relationship as a state of armed neutrality rather than one of close co-operation.

Judging by what he had previously heard of him Hatch had apparently been very subdued this voyage. However, Montague did not claim all the credit for this, the shock of his unfortunate meeting with the Chairman at the conclusion of his previous trip must have had a really telling effect.

For his own sake Montague wished the Chief Officer would try to be a little less abrasive and uncouth. Hatch's habit of ignoring the silver-plated butter-knife on the saloon table and taking cold steel to the butter like an engineer never ceased to irritate him and his tendency to refer to early morning as 'sparrow-fart' struck him as decidedly repugnant. Although very set in his ways the Mate was not so old that he could not improve his image with a little effort. He certainly had plenty of ability if only he would direct it in a more becoming manner.

In fact, Hatch had proved much more capable than Montague had originally contemplated. Although irked by the Mate's attitude and his general approach to things he had to admit that he did do his job, albeit in his own fashion. In his own opinion although the ship lacked the smart and neat appearance of which she was capable at least everything worked, which was the main thing. The Mate's habit of having any rust chipped off as soon as it appeared and the place touched up with red lead to preserve it until it could be properly painted at a convenient time later often left the ship giving the impression of suffering from a severe attack of measles. The Captain appreciated that with everything else to be done some details had to be postponed but this was one of several things that always irked him.

The second mate was all an officer should be. Always on top of the job and, although sociable enough, never the worse for drink. Which could not exactly be said for the third mate, mused Montague. A pleasant, friendly lad, did his job well enough but inclined to be rather harum-scarum at times. That business with the police earlier in the voyage for instance. Not that it was entirely Smith's fault, too easily led astray by the young engineers, that was his trouble.

All in all, it had been a reasonably trouble free voyage so far and, with but a few days to go, looked like concluding that way.

A bit of leave and then the challenge of his new ship. All the officers on her would be top-rate men, no doubt about that. Captain Montague looked forward to his next command with pleasurable anticipation.

The Captain was young enough to be able to adapt himself to the changes which were rapidly taking place in the shipping world. Although he often thought nostalgically of the comfortable 'family' atmosphere of the company as he first knew it he readily admitted that the new, more dynamic management was necessary in the fiercely competitive world of the day.

Of most of the modern innovations he heartily approved. Air-conditioned accommodation on the newer vessels meant that everyone could get a decent night's sleep no matter how hot the working conditions. The majority of deep-sea ships spent most of their working lives in hot climates. Comfortable living conditions increased efficiency and cut down on medical bills. As a side benefit the closed ports and windows shut out noise, flying insects and dust, also thieves.

Of all the electronic aids which had become available since the last war Radar was paramount. What a boon it was for coastal navigation and in traffic, and what a comfort in fog! As one wit put it, 'A great improvement on the old days when reliance had to be placed on a man in the bow with a long stick.'

However, the new aids had their drawbacks. They were inclined to be relied upon too much in Montague's opinion. Young officers nowadays were in the habit of doing most of their coastal navigation by radar instead of using it only as a check. It came as a very rude shock to most of them on the odd occasions the machine broke down and they had to revert to 'running fixes', 'four point bearings' and other traditional means of position finding. 'Old fashioned' methods the youngsters considered the Board of Trade included in the examinations solely to make them even more difficult.

Yes, meditated Montague, a lot of the old professionalism had gone out of with the advent of electronic aids. One man can obtain a fix as well as another with a Decca Navigator whereas previously an officer's navigation was his greatest pride. Sextants were still used of course away from the land but something was lost when many companies started providing sextants to their ships. Nowadays even personally owned sextants were lent and borrowed occasionally, a custom which filled the Captain with horror. When he first came to sea an officer's sextant was considered almost sacred. A man would no more dream of asking to borrow another's sextant than…. than to ask to borrow his wife.

The cruise liners would have nothing but the cream of the

Company's officers, that was a great satisfaction. Unlike a purely passenger ship company Fairbell's had room and to spare on its general cargo ships for any passenger ship officer who did not come right up to the very high standard expected. It was the standard Montague himself had achieved, but not without cost. He well knew he had made plenty of enemies on his way to the top, many among the ranks of his own colleagues. It was a case of the survival of the fittest and he had proved himself a worthy survivor. Not that he could claim all the credit himself, Beth had a lot to do with it, in fact he often wondered how far up the ladder he would have climbed without her. It was Beth who was the real driving force and had been from the beginning. He would no doubt have got on well enough without her constantly urging him on but not necessarily to the top, the very top almost certainly now provided he 'kept his nose clean' – and he had no doubt but that he would. Commodore Andrew Montague – and perhaps, was it too much to hope – Commodore Sir Andrew Montague?

Yes, the toastmaster announcing them at the Hunt Ball, "Commodore Sir Andrew and Lady Montague!" That would be the final accolade, the ultimate fulfilment of Beth's desires. How he wished he could complete the sentence...'for him.'

Yet he loved her. Or was it more true to say that he was proud of her? Montague could never really decide. Certainly pride held a considerable place in his feelings for Beth. Pride in her background and her beauty, a beauty undiminished in spite of her forty-six years. A lasting beauty which made many a woman ten years younger green with envy.

****

Montague thought back on how it had all begun.

Before the Second World War Fairbells ran a scheduled passenger service to the West Indies and South America from London and Montague, by reason of good reports from his superiors on cargo ships, was appointed to one of the liners. The young Montague took to his more sophisticated life like a duck to water. No more crawling around cargo hatches in baking heat, the nearest he got to that on the passenger ship was supervising the stowage and breaking out of the luggage – with plenty of men to do the donkey work, he was not expected to get his hands dirty.

Reminiscing in later years Captain Montague decided that these were his happiest days at sea. But they were not to last very long.

****

As the clouds of war were gathering Colonel Percival Hawthorne took a long leave of absence from his regiment and escorted his youngest daughter Elizabeth on a cruise to Latin America.

With two daughters satisfactorily married it is possible the Colonel had thoughts of getting the last off his hands, in spite of her youth, knowing with something skin to grim certainty that soon his movements, even his life, would be at the disposal of the Gods of War.

If it had been the Colonel's hope that his daughter would become emotionally involved with one of the rich young Americans who joined the ship at Bermuda on the vessel's way south – they would have to be rich in order to be there he conjectured – he was sadly disillusioned. With several of the desired category flinging themselves at her feet Elizabeth, with the perverseness of womankind, fell violently in love with a very junior ship's officer.

Nothing the Colonel said could make the girl see sense. He used the biggest guns in his armoury. The Family, (with a capital 'F'), there had never been a tradesman in it so far as he could recollect and there was no doubt that officers in the merchant service were definitely tradespeople. How did she know that the young fellow was not after her money? She did not actually have any but that was beside the point. The fact that even a Colonel's salary did not run to South American cruises and the present one was being paid for from his late wife's fortune was another point he avoided. He had married money but that was incidental, it had been a true love match and had resulted in a very happy, if all too brief, marriage.

He told his erring daughter she was too young to know her own mind, a theme he would have avoided like the plague had he known a little more about women, it did his case a good deal more harm than good.

And all the time he addressed his daughter as Elizabeth. The Colonel hated abbreviated names and throughout his life he never addressed his three girls other than by their full names of Adelaide, Florence and Elizabeth. Few things annoyed him more than having his honoured Christian name, long a family tradition for the eldest son, curtailed to 'Percy'. None of the girls liked their Christian names and Elizabeth was 'Beth' to everyone but her father.

Beth was adamant in her choice of husband and the Colonel, as many a better man before him, eventually was forced to give way.

The following summer Elizabeth, youngest daughter of Colonel Percival and the late Mrs. Alice Hawthorne, married her impecunious third officer.

The Colonel, in bowing to the inevitable, financed just as lavish a wedding for his third daughter as he had for the others but his heart was not really in it.

****

Within two months of the wedding the Colonel went to war. His regiment was one of the first to leave for France and one of the last to leave. What was left of it. It was those days of retreat culminating in standing waist, often chest, deep in the sea off Dunkirk which brought on the rheumatism that resulted in a Whitehall desk for the next two years.

Determined to return to active service Colonel Hawthorne plagued the powers who had charge of such things and brow-beat the various doctors to such an extent it was a relief to them all when he eventually had his way and was seconded to a regiment in North Africa.

The Colonel arrived in time for Rommel's last advance and was well behind the front line when his car, along with a considerable convoy of transport, was shot up by a pair of ME 109's. His driver was killed and he himself suffered a leg wound. It was not much of an injury but sufficient to get him sent, much to his chagrin, to a base hospital near Cairo. The army was heading in that direction in any case.

He was in hospital long enough to miss the battle at Alamein and to contract a mysterious disease which resulted in his repatriation to England and a return to the War Office for the remainder of the hostilities.

****

Andrew Montague did not go to war. The war came to him.

After a brief honeymoon in Scotland, the Continent where Beth's sisters had spent the first few weeks of their married lives being out of the question in the prevailing troubled times, Montague returned his bride to her family home and the following day joined his ship. This was a new vessel for him as his previous ship, the liner on which he had met his future wife, had with some degree of secrecy, been sent to the Clyde for conversion to an Armed Merchant Cruiser.

In early July tearful farewells were made on the station platform as Montague's trunk, two large sea-bags and a suitcase containing his sea-going gear were loaded into the luggage van of the train which was to take him away from his new bride. The polished mahogany box containing his sextant he carried in his hand. The last hopeful wish that the world would remain at peace and that he would be home for Christmas was almost drowned out by the hiss of steam as the train drew slowly out of the station.

Montague returned to his wife ten months later with the clothes he stood in, and those not his own.

＊＊＊＊＊＊＊＊＊＊＊＊＊＊＊＊

It was after the second torpedoing that Montague heard of his wife's efforts with her father trying to obtain an award of some sort for 'his bravery'. She would necessarily have been rather vague in her facts as, in common with most men at the time, he was loath to talk of the horrors he had faced. It was the cause of their first real quarrel and also, he was certain, the beginning of Beth's endeavours to push him ahead. However, it all came to nothing, such recommendations being outside the Colonel's sphere of influence, even had he been inclined to collaborate. And that was doubtful with the young husband of his daughter seeing more action in eighteen months of war than he had experienced in a lifetime in the Army, even including the long period in France during the First World War which was mainly spent behind the lines with the horses in the protracted, futile wait for the 'Big Breakthrough' when the Cavalry would come into its own.

Postponing a family until after the war, both Montague and Beth were young enough to have no doubts as to the eventual outcome, their one serious attempt resulted in a miscarriage. They were both naturally upset but Montague to a much greater extent than his wife. In fact, he strongly suspected that she used the misfortune to persuade him that any further pregnancies would be dangerous for her. There was therefore no further thought of having children.

Montague appreciated that Beth had few maternal instincts, she was nervous at the thought of even the best behaved children visiting the house, terrified that one of them would break a precious ornament or do some other damage. She seemed to be at a loss as to how to entertain or even communicate with young people. Almost inevitably after visitors which included children Beth would retire to bed with a headache the moment the front door had closed on the departing guests.

Children apart Beth loved company and to be asked to attend one of her numerous parties was considered both a pleasure and an honour to anyone fortunate to receive an invitation. She followed the tradition of her mother, one of the most famous hostesses in the county in her day, taking on the mantle at the tender age of seventeen at the death of her mother.

All this entertainment cost money. The fortune of the Colonel's lady was sufficient to keep the two of them in comparative luxury during their lifetimes but death duties took a great deal of what remained when the old Colonel, or Brigadier as he was then, died. This was shortly after Montague had first been appointed master of one of the Company's ships. The exchequer would have received considerably more from the estate if it had not been for Beth's stratagems. Often Montague arrived on leave to find a new bedroom suite or other expensive furniture installed in the house and, on one occasion, even a new car.

"A present from Daddy," Beth would explain as she fussed him, knowing how much he disapproved. "He knows he can't take it with him and when his time comes the government will grab most of the estate. What better than to make his little daughter and her wonderful husband happy whilst he can?"

"Then what of the others?" he once replied, "Surely he is just as fond of your sisters?"

"Oh, they don't need such things, they have pots of money," was the reply.

That hurt him. He considered his salary quite sufficient for their needs. If only she would cut down on her lavish spending they could live quite comfortably without being subsidised by her father. He did not begrudge Adelaide's Harley Street specialist or Florence's Q.C. a penny of their incomes and he was quite content with his own.

For all that he loved her and, he was quite certain, she loved him

– in spite of the economies he tried to impose on the household in an attempt to lessen the gap between income and expenditure. Beth never took them seriously, her attitude being that life was to be enjoyed and if money had to be begged, borrowed or stolen to achieve this end it was quite justified.

Beth used people unscrupulously, albeit always in the most charming way, to further her objectives and, as she saw it, her husbands' also. For instance, there was the case of the golf club selection committee. Both of them played golf, a game Montague enjoyed because of its challenge. He became quite good at it through sheer perseverance. Beth was good at it because she was good at anything she attempted. However, her interest did not end at the eighteenth green, she was deeply involved in the various ladies' committees and had for one year even been Lady Captain. That honour proved rather a tie as the duties involved interfered with her other numerous activities so was never repeated.

It was nearing the time of one of the club's twice yearly membership selection meetings when Beth, kissing Montague on the forehead as he read the morning newspaper, said, "Darling, will you please be a dear and propose Jonathan Woodward for membership at the club next week?"

"Who in Heaven's name is Jonathan Woodward?"

"Oh, you are becoming impossible, you know very well who he is, he was at the Barnley's dinner last Christmas."

"I remember now, round faced fellow, a 'something in the City' type. I've seen him a couple of times in the clubhouse, seemed to know me but I couldn't place him, wondered who he was."

"Good, that's settled then."

"It is not settled! I do not even know the man, how could I possibly propose him?"

"Well I know him, his wife anyway, and they are very, very respectable. They moved down here from Finchley when he became a director of his company." Which somehow proved it.

"That does not alter the fact that I do not...."

"Please Darling," Beth brushed aside the newspaper with her hips and sat on his knee. "Just to please me. I owe Julia Woodward a favour and promised you would only be too pleased to put Jonathan's name forward." She nuzzled him under one ear. He was weakening and well she knew it.

"Anyway, you know how much I hate those affairs."

"You have never been to one!"

"I know, that is because I don't like them. I would not know anyone there, except perhaps a few nodding acquaintances."

"Ben Caley is on the committee so he is sure to be there, you know how well you get on with him."

"If Ben is going to be there why does he not propose Woodward? He would carry a lot more weight than I."

"Because I promised Julia that you would propose him. Please Darling, just for me?" She had him licked.

****

As it so happened Montague met Woodward quite by accident a few days later. They chatted for a few minutes, Montague finding him very pleasant and friendly. It eased his conscience to a certain extent to think that he could honestly say that he now knew Woodward when the selection meeting took place.

Jonathan Woodward duly became a member of the club and so the matter rested so far as Montague was concerned.

For just over six months.

Montague had made a voyage after the golf club affair, had been on leave and was about to re-join his ship at Tilbury when he visited the head office for pre-sailing instructions and to discuss various topics with some of the department heads. As was often the case he also had a brief interview with the Chairman. He was taking his leave after their discussion when Charles Fairbell suddenly said, "I believe you play golf Captain Montague?"

Montague was somewhat surprised at the question as their previous conversation had been entirely of a business nature. Somewhat perplexed he replied in the affirmative.

"Good club too, difficult to get into I believe," Fairbell smiled.

This also was true, Montague himself knew he would have been considerably longer on the waiting list than had actually been the case had it not been for the late Colonel's influence. But what was all this about?

He was soon enlightened.

"Very good of you to get Woodward in. Cousin of my wife's you know."

Montague was speechless for a moment, then managed to stammer, "I…. I had no idea he was any relation of yours Sir!" His genuine reaction seemed to him an over-playing of a well-rehearsed part.

To say that he was furious would be to put it very mildly indeed. Sailing the following day Montague was not to see Beth for some months but he did speak to her on the telephone that evening. When he mentioned his embarrassment over the Woodward incident she took it all very lightly saying that the reason she had asked him to propose the man was as she had stated at the time, although she did admit that she thought she might have heard Julia mention some vague relationship with the Fairbells – now that he happened to mention the fact.

"Anyway dear, as it's turned out it must have done you some good so what are you so cross about?"

Being the last time he would speak to his wife for some considerable period Montague was reluctant to sour their farewells so let the matter drop, completing the phone call discussing more congenial topics.

Another occasion which rankled with him was the evening of the charity dinner in London. It was a maritime affair and the fact that the sufferings of destitute ex-seafarers were to be ameliorated by the proceeds of the grandiose meal prepared struck Montague as rather ironic. He hoped for their sake they received a fair cut from the obviously well-padded prices of the tickets.

The ship-owning fraternity was well represented among the guests and included several of the hierarchy of the Fairbell's Shipping Company. The Montagues spoke to various directors and their ladies and had a long chat with Marine Superintendent Dewar and his wife but it was the Fairbells themselves whom Beth set out to impress. There was nothing obvious about it, the whole thing was superbly carried out. The fact that both Samantha Fairbell and Beth were on committees of the charity, albeit of different local sections, was a talking point and Beth put it in to full use. If her efforts had not the slightest effect on the furtherance of her husband's career it probably did no harm and it helped to keep the name 'Montague' in the Fairbell's minds.

What it did do in the short term was to spoil Montague's evening, which he had not been enjoying much in the first place. He liked company when it was of his own choosing and often enough found pleasure in the functions he attended in his wife's wake, providing his fellow guests were not too overpowering – to him of course, not Beth, she could feel at ease with the highest in the land.

For all his qualms Montague could not but feel immensely proud of his wife. Her grace and charm coupled with her elegance and beauty made her stand out in any company. Even Samantha Fairbell's obviously expensive gown was outshone by Beth's which probably cost half as much. Somehow she seemed to radiate personality and always appeared, to him at least, the centre of any gathering she attended.

Montague was very proud indeed of his wife and this more than offset any doubts he might have had of her in some respects. It was not just Captain Montague who was heading for high places, it was very much Captain and Mrs. Montague.

And nothing was going to stand in their way.

Chapter 3

The 'Belisarius' shouldered her way through the heavy seas, pitching, rolling and occasionally shipping quite heavy water over the foredeck. The violent movement of the ship made any task on board more difficult and Carey often had to spread-eagle himself over the chart table to prevent the charts on which he was working from slithering onto the deck. He sighed with relief when he eventually completed erasing the pencilled courses and positions from the last of the charts used earlier in the passage. He removed the particles of rubber with a few sweeps of a four-inch paint brush kept expressly for that purpose, opened one of the wide, shallow drawers below the chart table and slipped the charts into their allotted places. Only the eight or ten charts required to get the ship to Rotterdam now remained in the left hand side of the top drawer. The remainder, cleaned and corrected, lay flat in their proper order in their respective canvas folders in the various drawers. Flat, Carey mused, folded once, or even occasionally twice if the particular chart was too large to go into its drawer otherwise. But definitely flat, not rolled up like a pirate's treasure map as Leonora had once intimated she thought they would be. What a nuisance they would be if they were rolled, one would have to iron them flat or pin them to the chart table before they could be used. And how much more space they would require that way. How many charts were there on board anyway? Must be well over a thousand and they only to cover the parts of the world the ship was likely to visit. What a panic there was when the ship was suddenly directed to proceed to a port not covered by her outfit of charts! No great problem when the charts could be flown out from home but often there was no time for this to be done. The local agents did their best on such occasions but often the charts they managed to acquire were so out of date that even the books of chart corrections retained on board for the previous two or three years failed to cover the period since the charts were last corrected. He remembered once having to tour the docks of Calcutta with his captain trying to borrow charts of an obscure port in Borneo from other ships.

Unless a message was received by radio indicating a new wreck or altered light there would be no more chart correcting this voyage. Any such corrections would be pencilled on the chart concerned to be inked in later when confirmed by 'Notices to Mariners'.

What a cumulative mass of information that little publication must have distributed in its time thought Carey. Every time a ship reported a shallow patch where deep water was indicated or a buoy was shifted to mark the end of an extending reef; each time a vessel sank in shallow water, the characteristics of a lighthouse were changed or anything else which could be a possible danger or of assistance to shipping was processed and published weekly in those small booklets. How many ships were there in the world? Twenty thousand? Thirty thousand? Carey tried to imagine thirty thousand second mates carefully noting thirty thousand identical corrections on thirty thousand similar charts. And this was just part of it. There were also lists of every navigational light in the world with its characteristics, pilot books for every port and coast and several other publications to correct and keep up to date.

Carey remembered explaining all this to Leonora. How bored she must have been but, being the girl she was, giving the impression of being really interested. He had described all the other things his job entailed. The four to eight watch at sea for instance. This had horrified her, never more than four hours sleep at a time for weeks on end! A healthy girl, she could dance until dawn with the best of them – providing she was not expected to be out of bed before lunchtime afterwards.

"Never mind," she had said, "You will soon be a chief officer and have a better watch so far as sleeping goes."

He meditated this theme as he went down to his room. The mate's job. It would only be a year or two before he was promoted to this position and all that it entailed.

The mate's responsibilities had not basically changed since the days of sail. Although the sails themselves had long since gone there remained plenty in the way of rope, both fibre and wire. Each mast and samson post was supported by several stays and shrouds of thick wire. Each derrick was rigged with a wire fall and topping lift. Two ordinary guys of wire with rope tackles to adjust them and a 'lazy' guy entirely of wire rope secured each derrick in its required position, plus the necessary blocks and shackles. What would that amount to? Four single or double blocks for the wires, four wooden blocks for the guys and a dozen or more shackles to hold the whole thing together Each block and shackle had its individual identification number stamped on it and, as with every wire on the ship, had its test certificate, all carefully listed and filed in the mate's office. There were sixteen derricks of ten tons safe working load on the ship plus one 'Jumbo' capable of handling weights of up to fifty tons. All this gear had to be stripped and lubricated at regular intervals by the crew and inspected by the chief officer. There were also numerous mooring ropes and wires, signal halyards, boat falls and a hundred and one other lines to be kept up to scratch. An old ship such as the 'Belisarius' also had a considerable number of canvas awnings, hatch tarpaulins and lifeboat covers.

Then there was the ship herself. Apart from the engine room and deck machinery such as cargo winches and the inside of the accommodation the remainder of the ship was nearly all the mate's territory. The hull and hatches, masts and bilges, decks and houses were all his to keep clean, scale and paint. The anchors and cables, the fresh water supplies and their tanks and plumbing, even the rudder itself was his.

The raison d'etre of the ship, the cargo, of whatever it consisted, was the mate's responsibility.

Leonora again, "But Darling, surely the cargo is not much of a problem? The stevedores put it in at one end and others discharge it when the ship reaches her destination. Surely it is all very simple?"

That remark really got Carey started. He explained to the attentive Leonora that there was more to loading a general cargo ship than just tossing the cargo in then hooking it out when she reached her discharging port. Ideally the cargo for each port should be evenly distributed between the hatches or the ship would be held up, at considerable expense, waiting for the 'long' hatch to complete discharging. Many commodities were incompatible, no shipper wanted his flour reeking of insecticide and nobody wanted a big hole where a mixed stow of acid jars and high explosives should have been. Rolls of newsprint could not be stowed on top of motor cars or cases of bank notes put where malicious hands could reach them.

Although cargo for several ports of discharge would generally be taken on board at each loading port it was imperative that it be stowed in such a way that the commodities for each discharge port in turn are readily accessible. This problem being aggravated by the fact that most heavy, bulky pieces have to be stowed in the lower holds and the lighter stuff in the tween decks above. No space is allowed to be wasted as a ship is normally full long before she reaches her maximum allowable draft. And freight is normally charged on the space the cargo utilises, not by its weight.

Stability was another important consideration. It was of little use having a ship nice and tight with a full cargo and the double bottom tanks pressed up with fuel at the commencement of a voyage if, towards the end of it, with fuel tanks almost empty, the ship was to become unstable. This had to be allowed for at the beginning of the programme.

Trim was yet another problem. This had to be kept in mind throughout the loading as it was pointless solving the main part of the jig-saw puzzle of stowage only to find that at one stage of the passage the propeller was going to be half out of the water or that the ship would be trimmed so far by her stern that her maximum draft would be too great to allow her to enter a restricted draft port on her itinerary. To a lesser extent the same applied in the athwartship plane as regards list.

A long discourse on stability had followed Leonora's question of how a ship stayed upright. She could not understand how a ship, with so little of her hull in the water when she was empty and so much above could possibly avoid rolling over. Carey explained as simply as he could the effects of centres of gravity and buoyancy, righting levers and metacentric heights, much of which went over the girl's head. However, she did appreciate the effect of loose liquids in tanks and the necessity of keeping then either tightly filled or completely empty. Slack tanks meant that the liquid in them was free to run to one side of the ship thus producing a list. The more slack tanks there were the greater the 'free surface' and thus more listing effect. This could create a dangerous chain reaction as liquid allowed to run to the low side of a listed ship would increase the list which in turn would cause more liquid to run down until, in extreme cases, the ship would roll right over. Carey demonstrated this with a plastic sandwich box in Leonora's bath.

He well remembered this little lecture and smiled as he recalled

Leonora's words at the end of it.

"And now James Carey, if you would kindly remove yourself to the other room I will be able to get out of this bath and get dressed."

The splashing and squeals of the following few minutes remained one of Carey's most treasured memories.

"Ah well," he said to himself, "Only a few more days and that lovely girl will be in my arms again."

It occurred to him that a girl's bathroom was a strange place to discuss the principles of stability. But how typical of their conversations. They would discuss politics and the population explosion on the tennis court or sex and the price of vegetables whilst waiting for a taxi in the early hours of the morning. The often ridiculous conversations were part of the magic of their relationship, a kind of warm secret they shared with no-one else. What a wonderful companion Leonora was and how dearly he loved her.

"Only a few more days!"

****

Carey's work in the chartroom had left him only time enough to get cleaned up before going to the saloon for the evening meal.

It was not easy to eat with the ship rolling more than thirty degrees either way. In spite of the 'fiddles', two inch high strips of wood fitted round the edges of the tables, ('Like eating over a fence' as one wit had it), and both the felt underlay and the table cloths themselves soaked with water, cutlery and plates slithered about with gay abandon and often disastrous results. Although each chair was secured to the deck with a short length of cord they still had sufficient scope to render sitting in them as tricky as riding a wild horse. Food was spilled and tempers frayed by the end of the meal but remarkably very little crockery was broken. Not that this was of any importance as most of it was never to be used again.

With no other diversion practicable after dinner Carey was soon in his bunk, thinking of Leonora as he awaited sleep.

Carey reminisced on the occasion of their first meeting, at a party in the flat of someone whose name he did not even remember. He had been reluctant to go in the first place but the blonde Dolly had insisted and how glad he was that he had allowed himself to be persuaded.

His first sight of Leonora as she arrived with the handsome Bill Some-thing-or-other and several others. The greetings and introductions. Of the various names he heard at that time only one registered in his mind, Leonora, a lovely name for a very lovely girl. Wonderful Leonora, far and away the most attractive woman of the twenty or so present. The problem of Bill, well aware of the fact, as attentive to her as any man could possibly be, never leaving her side, taking no chances.

On the one or two occasions he nearly managed to speak to the wonderful creature it so happened that Dolly attracted his attention elsewhere at the critical moment.

At the end of the party when Dolly and several of her acquaintances had passed out of the flat into the corridor he had hung back in the hope of either speaking to Leonora or asking someone, the host perhaps, who she was. Then the heaven-sent opportunity when Bill disappeared for a few minutes, a chance to be grabbed with both hands. He pushed through the crowd until he was right behind her, his heart pounding, trying desperately to appear cool and calm.

And all his fears of a rebuff unfounded, she was apparently as interested in him as he of her. Carey laughed as he recollected her telling him her version of that first encounter.

****

Leonora Graye listened with only half her attention to the story Bill Wright was narrating. It concerned a friend of his who was employed by a firm with Far Eastern interests. She liked Bill but that was as far as it went. He had brought her to the party and would no doubt take her home. So far as the door of her flat anyway which is as far as he got in that direction. The main attraction of Bill was that he had travelled. Some superior kind of salesman his job took him all over the Continent, France, Germany, Sweden, Switzerland, he could roll off stories of his experiences in any one of those countries. Leonora admired men who had travelled the world. She herself had holidayed several times on the Continent but that was not the same, to her it was obviously much more fascinating to have actually worked in foreign countries.

Tossing her long tawny hair Leonora glanced at the other party guests. There were two of three separate groups in corners of the large room laughing and conversing but at least half of those present were clustered around listening to Bill. He was an excellent raconteur. That was Bill's trouble she thought, he talked too much. Most of the people there she knew, or at least had seen before. One stranger however had caught her attention. A tall fair-haired man in a jacket and tie, unusual when most of the other men were more fashionably dressed in gaudy open-necked shirts or polo-necked sweaters with a fair sprinkling of pendants on chains. The slim stranger was suntanned, also unusual so early in the year.

'I wish I could remember his name,' thought Leonora, 'John? Jim?, everyone was talking at once as the brief introductions were made earlier and she had not since heard him addressed by name. He had arrived early with Dolly Meadowes, the fascinating blonde- who fascinated men at the rate of about one a week she thought cattily. Who was he? He said very little and then only the things people usually say at parties, nothing to give a clue as to where he came from or what he did.

Someone mentioned the fact that he had left his brief-case in a train a short time before which had occasioned considerable inconvenience. This had induced Bill to tell the story of his friend Davy who had once been given the task of taking some important documents from his office in Singapore to an obscure place in Borneo. After some days on his journey and when actually in sight of his destination the boat he was in struck a log and turned over. Davy and the crew were soon safe but the brief-case and its contents were lost.

"His company had sent Davy as they did not trust the post," Bill continued, "and anyway were in a desperate rush to get the documents to their potential customers at this place – I wish I could remember its name, it sounded like 'Two gins too many'."

"Tanjong Mani?" offered the fair-haired stranger.

"Tanjong Mani! That's it. However, did you hear of such an outlandish place?"

"Oh, I've been there."

Leonora was immediately alert. 'Oh, I've been there,' just like that. 'Oh, I've just been to Luton'….'Oh, I was at Brighton last weekend', as if it were the most commonplace thing in the world. She was about to ask him to enlarge on his remark when Bill, sensing competition, said to him, "You must tell us why you went there sometime." Then continued hurriedly with his story.

****

When the party started to break up some time later Leonora still had not managed to make contact with the slim man. Bill monopolised her which was one problem and a glance she caught from Dolly Meadowes as she towed her escort away to a far corner of the room indicated another. The fact that the stranger was apparently completely unaware of her existence constituted a third.

The departing guests were clustered in the hall of the flat making their farewells to the host when Leonora suddenly remembered she had left her handbag in the bedroom. Bill went off for it and Leonora took the opportunity to look for the fair-haired stranger among the people around her. Dolly was already outside the door, she could see her chatting to some friends so no doubt the man was out there too. Damn!

"Excuse me."

The voice behind her made her start. It was that of the man for whom she had been looking.

"Yes?" She hoped she had her voice perfectly under control.

"May I ask you for your telephone number?"

Before she could answer Bill's voice sounded from behind the crush of people, "I've found your bag Leonora!"

There was no time for playing the demure young maiden, she recited the number without preliminary.

"Thank you." He made no attempt to write it down.

"Do you think you will remember it?" she smiled.

"It is already engraved on my heart." Perfectly serious but she thought she detected a slight twinkle in his eyes.

Then Bill was with them and with scant apology took Leonora by the arm and hustled her towards the door. His departing remark to their host, "Must rush, I have an early flight to Stuttgart in the morning," might have been a reference to a visit to a maiden aunt in Kensington for all the effect it had on Leonora. So far as Bill was concerned his magic had gone.

Perhaps she would have been slightly disillusioned if she had seen, the moment she was out of his sight, the young man whip a ball-point pen out of his pocket and note the number on the palm of his hand before he forgot it.

As he did not know if the number Leonora had given him referred to a business or residence Carey made three calls at well-spaced intervals the following day. He reasoned that if it were a business number it would indicate a small business or she would have given an extension as well. If it were a home number and a matronly voice answered he would claim a wrong connection and ring again in the evening – as with most young men he had an aversion to girl's mothers. If, as he hoped, it was the telephone number of a flat there would probably be no answer it being a working day. This last alternative proved to be correct.

Carey rang again at six o'clock. After the third ring the phone was lifted and that lovely voice repeated the number.

"Leonora?" he asked.

"Yes," she replied, "Who is it?" She knew very well who it was but she still did not know his name and this was a quick way to find out.

"James Carey".

'Mrs Leonora Carey' she mused, 'Yes, I like it'.

"We met at the party last night," explained Carey hurriedly, wondering at the silence. "Sorry I did not have the opportunity of getting to know you."

"You completely ignored me!"

"A thousand apologies but what could I do with that hulking Bill fellow waiting to take a swing at me if I so much as looked at you?"

"Ah well, you are safe enough now. What was it you wished to speak to me about?"

"Have you eaten yet?"

"I was just about to," she lied glibly.

"Well please chuck it back into the fridge. I know a little Greek restaurant in Soho….. that is if you do not mind eating with an unimaginative, square oaf?"

"You are an unimaginative, square oaf?"

"I haven't exactly got it in writing but it comes from a very reliable source I assure you."

"I am intrigued, please tell me more."

"Well I was informed of this towards the end of the second party last night."

"By whom?"

"I cannot name names but take it from me it was very authoritative. The potted personality analysis was delivered shortly before my informant disappeared with some kind of guitarist who is reputed to be 'high on the charts'. I rather suspect on cannabis also."

Leonora laughed, "I would love to hear the rest of the story, do you know where I live?"

"You have but to tell me and my chariot with its team of snow-white horses will be at your door."

* * * * * * * * * * * *

Although the transport turned out to be a slightly more mundane elderly Aston Martin Leonora was quite satisfied.

On turning sharply into a Soho side street something rattled on the parcel shelf. Leonora reached out and picked up a lipstick. Holding it up she asked, "Yours? Or does it belong to your analyst?"

"Certainly not my shade," replied Carey.

With a flick of her fingers the lipstick and Dolly Meadowes disappeared from their lives.

****

During the course of their first evening together Carey found out a little about Leonora. She was four years younger than he and had a part interest in the small florists where she was employed. Although her parents had a house on London's outskirts she preferred to live in her small flat nearer the centre of things most of the time. He also learned that she owned a small car. It was not until some time later that he discovered she was a first class natural driver.

Leonora discovered most of what she wanted to know about Carey in the same amount of time. In her own charming way she literally pumped him dry. He also had a small London flat and had no desire to live anywhere else. He was second mate of a merchant ship, the middle one of the three normally carried on a deep sea vessel and he was at that time studying in Southampton for his Master's Certificate. This prompted her to ask if he would be a captain when he passed the examinations. To her disappointment she discovered that he would only be qualified as a shipmaster and would have to wait until a ship-owner decided to entrust him with a ship before he actually became a 'Captain', or more correctly 'Master' of a ship, the 'Captain' being merely a courtesy title. This would probably be in ten or fifteen years if he stayed with his present company.

They did not see a great deal of one another over the next few months. Although the weekends in London were frequent at first as time passed they became more rare until the last month before the examinations when Carey did not get to London at all.

On the last day of their third weekend together Carey got past Leonora's door, which was further than Bill Wright had managed – but only for a cup of coffee. On the fourth visit to London he managed to insinuate his hand into Leonora's blouse, but only very briefly. On the fifth and sixth occasion he got no further. After that there were no more weekends in London before the examinations.

Carey soon lost his sun-tan, suffered from eye-strain, lost weight and frequently his temper, drifted into brown studies and became inclined to talk to himself. In fact, he displayed all the normal symptoms of a man going up for his Master's 'ticket'. It put a considerable strain on his relationship with Leonora but she, with great understanding, suffered silently and did everything she could to encourage and cheer him.

They kept in contact by telephone. Carey rang two or three times a week in the evenings but his attempts at light-hearted conversation became progressively more dismal failures as the examinations approached at seemingly ever increasing speed.

The Saturday evening before the Monday morning start of the examinations Carey told Leonora on the phone that he intended to do no studying on Sunday in order to 'allow his brain to cool'. However, he would not come to London as that would constitute too violent and unsettling a change, instead he would go for a walk by the river, deciding at the time whether or not to throw himself in.

With considerable trepidation Leonora asked, "Would you like me to come and see you?"

A moment's silence, then, "Would you? That would be absolutely wonderful! It's an awfully long way to come just for a few hours though."

"It would be worth it even for just a couple of minutes," she replied. And meant it.

****

They walked by the river almost in silence. Carey obviously

preoccupied and Leonora trying to sympathise with his mood.

All too soon the visit was over and if Carey's hand did slip from Leonora's shoulder to somewhere slightly lower whilst they were kissing goodbye she raised no objection.

As Carey withdrew his head from the car window after the last lingering kiss Leonora started the engine, then motioned him back. Very pink of cheek she whispered in his ear, "I would not dream of going to bed with a man with no Master's ticket."

With that she let in the clutch leaving a stunned Carey staring after the retreating car.

Leonora drove back to London at high speed. Arriving at the lockup garage close to her flat she secured the car and walked rapidly home. She greeted a neighbour in her usual cheerful manner, smiled at some children playing hop-scotch on the pavement outside her building, tripped up the stairs, entered her flat and locked the door behind her. Dropping her handbag onto a chair she walked into the small bedroom, flung herself face down on the bed and burst into uncontrollable tears.

'Oh God!' What have I done? Of all the insane, idiotic, stupid things to do! Will I never learn? A woman's chastity was a thousand times more valuable to a man than any woman. I love him so much and now I have shattered all my hopes and dreams. What will he think of me now? A harlot! A common whore! Offering myself... my body, as a reward was just as bad as charging money for it in the normal manner. I wanted so much to prove my love for him and now, because of one mad, impetuous remark any love he may have had for me is destroyed. He must hate me now, no, not hate, despise, absolutely loathe me!'

Her body racked with sobs she lay on her bed for hours, her tears and makeup staining the frilly, flower-printed pillows.

****

The following week seemed to last for ever. How Leonora survived the endless days she could never afterwards remember. The lonely evenings were purgatory, listening for the sound of the telephone which never rang. James said earlier that to avoid losing his concentration he would not call her that week but circumstances had now dramatically changed. Surely he would ring if only to put her out of her misery one way or another? Often she thought of trying to phone James even though she knew it would be difficult but each time she decided to wait a little longer, another hour, until the next evening.

On the Wednesday Leonora made her decision. If he came back to her to claim his promised reward she would be ready to concede it. She owed him that much at least even if she never saw him again afterwards.

Taking time off from the shop she went to the West End and purchased a new dress, expensive lingerie and a nightdress which cost a week's salary. Leonora was not sure if courtesans wore nightdresses but bought it anyway.

She had booked an early appointment at her hairdressers on Saturday morning and dashed back to the flat the moment her hair was done. James had said he would ring round noon but of course he might make the call earlier. Or not at all.

Quickly dusting around the already immaculate flat she made the bed with freshly laundered linen and carried out final adjustments to the already perfectly arranged flowers in their large vase in the centre of the sitting room table. This was followed by a final general inspection of her apartment. Satisfied that nothing more could be done in the way of improvements to her home Leonora commenced her toilette.

She was in her bath when the telephone rang. Leaping from the water she rushed to the sitting room. The towel she grabbed on the way from the bathroom jammed on its rail and rather than waste time clearing it she raced to the phone dressed in nothing more than a shower cap.

Automatically she recited her number as she put the instrument to her ear then heard that well-loved voice say, "I will call on you at six o'clock". Nothing more. His voice was flat, expressionless. He sounded tired but that was all. No sign of elation or despondency. Had he passed? Had he failed? Above all did he hate her? Loathe her? Even, was it too much to hope, still love her a little?

The seconds ticked by in utter silence as Leonora waited for further information. Eventually she could stand the strain no longer, choked with emotion she managed to force out the one word 'Yes'. It was just a word, not an affirmative or a query, it could as well have been 'no' or 'abracadabra' for all the meaning it conveyed. However, it was apparently enough, there was a click as the receiver at the other end of the line was replaced.

For a full minute Leonora held the handset to her ear before she slowly returned it to its cradle.

What did it mean? She still had no means of knowing what his feelings were. Why had he not said something, anything, to let her know where she stood in his affections – if 'affections' could be considered the appropriate word?

Leonora returned to her bath, her mind in turmoil. The water was quite cool, had she been away from it so long?

No woman preparing for her lover could have been more meticulous in her grooming than Leonora that day. When finally she examined her reflection in the long wardrobe mirror even she was satisfied with the result.

'Leonora', she said to herself as she turned in front of the glass, 'you are quite beautiful', then ruefully, 'It is a pity you are such a disaster.' The only fault she could find were the feint shadows under her eyes which no makeup could hide, the result of a series of almost sleepless nights.

She glanced at the clock by the bed. 'Good Heavens! Gone five o'clock! He could be here within the hour.'

Leonora quickly tidied up the few things she had disturbed in the bedroom, the bathroom she had put in order before she dressed.

Attempting to soothe her jangled nerves she switched on her small television set – and immediately turned it off again in case the sound prevented her hearing the approach of his car. Picking up a magazine she glanced at its pages but it could have been a technical pamphlet in Chinese for all it conveyed to her. She stood up and sat down more times than she could remember, each time looking out of the window to see if the Aston Martin had arrived. Every time she stood up she fluffed up the cushions of the small settee – then disturbed them as she sat down again. She decided to discipline herself not to move again until James arrived so settled on the settee to wait with as much patience as she could muster. Her eyes, wandering around the room, noticed that the magazine she had looked at was not at quite the correct angle to the one below it. As it was just out of reach she had to stand up again to rectify the matter.

At ten minutes to six she suddenly realised that she was desperately hungry, which was not surprising as she had eaten nothing since a very light breakfast nearly ten hours earlier. Thinking there would be time for a quick sandwich she made for the tiny kitchenette but stopped half way and returned to the settee. Anything she ate now would be noticeable on her breath. Would he want to kiss her anyway?

Would he ever come?

The time dragged on with leaden tread. Five minutes to six o'clock. Four, three, two. One minute to go and still no sound of his car. Perhaps he had been held up by traffic? Or an accident? The tension was almost too much to bear. Perhaps he had changed his mind and was......

The triple tap on the door nearly startled her out of her wits. For nearly a minute she sat trying to control her trembling sufficiently to get to her feet and walk to the door. Opening it she stood back to allow him to enter.

He seemed even taller than she remembered him, paler and thinner too with dark shadows under his eyes which more than matched her own. She could make nothing of his expression, he was neither smiling or frowning. There was no sign of success or failure, loathing or love. That was all she could see before her eyes filled with tears, blinding her. Where did she stand in the life of this strange, silent man?

She felt her hands taken in both of his and lifted towards his face.

Then, only then, did he speak.

"Leonora, will you do me the honour of becoming my wife?"

Overcome with emotion, unable to believe that what was happening was not just a wild dream Leonora broke down completely. Wrenching her hands free she wrapped her arms around Carey's chest, pressed her face against his shoulder and broke into a fit of uncontrollable sobbing.

It would be putting it rather mildly to say that Carey was dumbfounded. One expected some sort of reaction from a girl who had just received a proposal of marriage but nothing like this. It was not what he had envisaged at all.

****

Elated at the success of obtaining his Master's Certificate on the first attempt he was so filled with confidence that he decided that very day to propose to the wonderful Leonora. Originally he had intended courting her properly as soon as he had got his 'Ticket', thinking of all manner of things to entertain and amuse her, presents to buy, (so long as his money held out), in an effort to persuade her that unworthy of her as he may be he was not really such a bad fellow. And to hope that slowly she would be brought round to loving him as much as he loved her. However, the news of his success that morning had radically changed his plans. He felt that he could conquer the world. If he could to that surely he could conquer Leonora's heart? On the face of it the latter appeared rather more difficult, she being so superior to him in every way. But what was there to lose? Adorable, kind-hearted Leonora would hardly laugh at him and surely nothing would be lost by proposing. If nothing else it would prove the sincerity of his love for her. She would certainly turn him down of course, the first time at least, but he would keep on trying.

Surely she felt some affection for him? The wonderful girl had been very kind and understanding throughout his recent ordeal, even to the extent of coming all the way to Southampton the day before the exams started in order to cheer him up and boost his confidence – he often wondered what she meant by that final remark of hers that day. She had always made herself available when he came up to London for those brief weekends earlier on, never once mentioning a previous engagement. What of the remainder of the time however? An attractive, popular girl such as Leonora could hardly be expected to spend her evenings alone in her flat watching television. She must have suitors galore ringing her up and taking her out, what happened to Bill Wright anyway? However not once did she mention her social activities knowing how jealous he would be.

Damn the whole bunch of them! He, James Carey, Master Mariner, was going to beat the lot and marry Leonora if it took the remainder of his life to achieve.

As he picked up the telephone to impart the good tidings to the girl of his dreams Carey changed his mind and decided instead not to say a word about his 'Ticket' – just that he would call on her that evening and tell her his news then.

Leonora's phone rang three times before she answered. Carey pictured her reclining on the small settee with her lovely legs curled under her. She would slowly put down the book she was reading and reach for the telephone with a graceful movement. Then that beautifully modulated voice would repeat her number and, when he had identified himself, ask, excitedly he hoped, if he had been successful. He would then answer, trying to keep the exhilaration out of his voice, 'I will call on you at six this evening and tell you the news.' Nothing more in case his voice gave him away. A flat statement to keep her curiosity aroused until he was actually with her and could observe her reactions and to bathe, he hoped, in her praise and congratulations. The fact that a second party could hardly be expected to be as excited as he himself at his achievement never occurred to him. Later, when the excitement of his news had died down a little he would propose to her. An excellent plan, he decided, absolutely faultless. Carey would have preferred not to have phoned at all but for one thing he had promised to do so and for another he would look a damn fool if he arrived at her flat unheralded and found her away.

Carey carried out his plan to the letter but the whole thing fell very flat. Leonora's reaction was not at all what he expected. In fact, there was hardly any reaction at all. Silence when he expected at least some interest in his affairs, then the single world 'Yes'. It meant absolutely nothing. She sounded somewhat breathless, distraught even. Was someone else with her preventing her speaking freely? The sooner he got to London the better.

His finger, poised at the cradle of the phone to cut the connection the moment he had passed his message and before Leonora could bombard him with questions, came down a few seconds after her mysterious 'Yes'. As soon as he had done so he regretted it and considered making a second call but decided that this would probably lead to his saying too much and thus ruining his original intention. Apart from this he was phoning from a call box and had no further suitable change.

Carey picked up the phone again and called the operator. Even as he waited for the telephone exchange to answer he toyed with the idea of reversing the charges and calling Leonora again but when the operator spoke he reverted to his original intention of calling his parents to tell them his good news. If he had the necessary coins he would have reversed the charges anyway as obviously all parents can well afford telephone bills otherwise they would not have telephones.

From then on it was a mad rush to get to London. His room quickly stripped of his personal belongings, bills paid, farewells made – avoiding like the plague the party at the local pub with other aspiring master mariners, to celebrate, or drown sorrows whichever was appropriate.

Soon he was in the car, his hastily stuffed suitcase, a carrier bag of shoes and laundry and a few bundles of books tied with string on the seat beside him, overflowing onto the floor below. Before starting the engine he took from his wallet the small, insignificant buff slip of paper which confirmed the fact that he had passed for master – the formal certificate itself would not be available for a week or two – gazed at it reverently for a moment, replaced it in his wallet, returned this to his coat pocket and set off on the road to London.

Carey stopped only once before reaching his flat, at an off-licence to purchase a couple of bottles of Leonora's favourite Riesling. Arriving at his flat he dumped his gear, stripped off, showered and shaved then dressed in fresh clothes. A glance at his watch informed him that it had just gone five-thirty, he could not have timed it better. He had said he would call on Leonora at six and he had time to make it comfortably. Regretfully there was not time to wash and polish his car, it had certainly been neglected over the last few months he mused ruefully.

Feeling elated, albeit somewhat nervous, at the prospect of the coming meeting he walked to the Aston Martin. Was there anything he should have remembered? He stowed the wine under the seat and patted his breast pocket to ensure his wallet was there. There was still a slight nagging at the back of his mind, something forgotten, what could it be?..... Damnation! Flowers of course! Women expected flowers on every possible occasion. The local florists would be closed by now. Damn! Damn! Damn! Short of going to the West End, and there was not time for that, there was nothing he could do about it. What a fine start to the evening he cursed to himself as he set off flowerless for Leonora's flat.

He arrived early. Having parked the car he sat in it for a few minutes then walked as slowly as he could to the flat, six o'clock he had said and six o'clock it would be. Silently he mounted the stairs and arrived at her door with half a minute in hand. He stood with his eyes riveted to the second hand of his watch until it reached the hour. His knuckle rapped on the wood and a minute later Leonora opened the door and stood back to allow him to enter. Leonora, looking more beautiful than he even remembered her, breathtakingly beautiful. His Leonora, his marvellous, wonderful, adorable Leonora. He looked into her eyes and saw in them not what he had expected. They looked troubled, fearful even. What had happened? Whatever had gone wrong? Even as he looked those eyes, those beautiful hazel eyes, seemed to moisten. Desperately worried by the turn of events Carey did not know what to say. Someone had to break the silence and Leonora appeared to have been struck dumb. He wanted to ask what was troubling her, what he could do to help but could not find words to express himself. Hammering in his brain was the sentence he had recited half seriously to himself all the way up from Southampton, old fashioned sentimental words but he found himself saying them.

"Leonora, will you do me the honour of becoming my wife?"

Carey's immediate regret at his clumsy utterance was accentuated by the fact that at his words Leonora flung herself into his arms and sobbed as if her very heart would break.

Whatever was it all about? For minutes on end Carey held the girl as she wept and trembled. Completely at a loss he muttered endearments in an effort to console her but to no avail. Suddenly Leonora's face seemed to slip on his chest. Fearing her legs were giving way he moved his right arm and lifting her carried her to the settee, the soft warmth of her thighs beneath the thin material of her dress did nothing to ease his confused mind.

Seated with Leonora still clinging to him it was several more minutes before he could get any sense out of the situation.

"I…. I thought you hated me, …..loathed me," Leonora sobbed.

"Good heavens! How could I possibly hate you? I love you more than anything else in the world."

"You…You did not phone!"

"But Leonora, we agreed that I would not call this week as you would be too much of a distraction," and in case this did not sound too good Carey hastily added, "If I heard your voice I would think of nothing but you for days and you know how much the 'ticket' meant to me."

"That was…. was before… Oh! I am so ashamed!"

Carey's heart sank to his boots. Whatever was she on about? What was it that he was supposed to know that he did not? Was Leonora already married? Had she a child hidden away in some orphanage? His soul was in torment.

"When things were different I thought you would have called me."

"Different? In what way?"

"After what I said as I drove away at Southampton …I… I felt like a ..a harlot!"

"What are you talking about? I don't understand a word you are saying. Please Leonora, explain what you mean, I can't stand much more of this."

"You must remember. I said…I said…" Carey could scarcely hear her as she pressed her face into his chest. "I said I would… would sleep with you if you passed your exams."

"You mean to say that is what is upsetting you? You pay me the greatest compliment a respectable woman can offer a man and you expect me to hate you for it? I know you said it on the spur of the moment to increase my incentive and I love you all the more for it if such a thing were possible." Firmly grasping the wrong end of the stick in true masculine fashion he continued, "If you think for one moment I would hold you to such a promise you may put your mind at rest right away. I would not dream of such a thing." Carey kissed the top of Leonora's head which was all he could get at at the time.

Leonora managed to gain some control over herself and began to realise that her traumas of the last week were quite unfounded. But how was she to know how James would react to her stupid remark? One never knew how men would interpret things. What extraordinary creatures they were.

"I thought you were not coming when I didn't hear your car at six o'clock. Where is it by the way?" Leonora was rapidly losing her tension but still kept her face against Carey's shirtfront.

"The ancient vehicle is parked two streets away, no doubt compromising some innocent maiden lady in the eyes of her neighbours – but I did not come here to talk of cars. What I want to know, Dearest Leonora, is whether.."

"Please James, please stop!" Leonora pleaded. With her face still buried in his chest she reached up a hand and, finding his face, pressed her fingers to his lips. She wriggled to escape from his knee. "Please let me go!"

Carey held the girl more tightly. What in heaven's name was

happening now?

Leonora continued to plead with him. "Please let me go! I don't want you to remember me like this. I must look an absolute fright!"

Understanding at last and greatly relieved Carey released his hold on the girl who immediately half rolled from the settee and, getting to her feet, fled to the bedroom and its adjoining bathroom with both hands spread over her face.

Carey sat for several minutes trying to fathom out the ways of women, gave up the impossible task and concentrated on the present situation. His eyes, wandering around the room, noticed the flowers on the table. Flowers! It was a pity he had not remembered flowers in time to bring some. It was just as well he had remembered the wine...the wine! He had left it in the car.

"I'm going down to the car....be back in a couple of minutes!" he called to the bedroom door but he doubted if Leonora would have heard him.

Leaving the flat Carey walked briskly to the car, retrieved the bottles from below the driver's seat and commenced his return journey. In his urgency to get back to Leonora he broke into a run, every moment spent away from his beloved was a moment wasted. Well not exactly his yet, in spite of his proposal he had not yet been accepted and therefore had no established claim. The sooner this situation was rectified the better. Carey increased his pace.

Carey rounded the last corner at speed. In two minutes he would be in Leonora's flat and within five could be engaged to that wonderful creature. With the home stretch before him he was about to put in a final spurt when he realised that the previously empty pavement was now obstructed by what appeared to be a posse of policemen. A second glance resolved the fact that there was actually only a single policeman but one of exceptional size. Although he appeared to materialise in the centre of the pavement Carey realised that in actual fact he must have moved out from the cover of a shadowy doorway.

Putting on his brakes Carey slowed to a dignified walk. Smiling sweetly he said, "Good evening Officer," and with a glance at the sky followed this with a chatty, "Lovely weather, should be a nice day tomorrow". In spite of the heavy overcast's imminent promise of rain. Carey knew his one-way conversation left much to be desired but his mind was on more important things. His attempt to side-step the minion of the law was thwarted by that worthy taking a sideways and once again positioning himself dead ahead. The law raised a large hand.

"Excuse me sir, would you mind explaining what all the rush is about?"

'Damn the officious blighter, what business is it of his?', thought Carey but decided that to put such sentiments into words would be far from diplomatic so settled for a more civil approach.

"Well I am at a sort of party and went out for some wine." It sounded reasonable enough to him but apparently it did not allay the suspicions of the policeman.

"May I inquire where you obtained wine at this time of night sir?"

'From the nearest pub of course!' seemed the obvious answer but Carey decided the truth to be more tactful.

"Oh, from my car. I brought it with me."

"You have a car sir? May I see your driving license?"

Carey failed to see how a driving license became involved when any speeding he may be accused of was purely pedestrian. However, in order to get the interview over as soon as possible he complied with the officer's request.

After examining the document the policeman handed it back.

"Would you tell me where your car is parked sir?"

"A couple of streets back there," Carey indicated the way from which he had come, "I'm afraid I don't know the name of it." This silly business had gone on long enough. "Do you mind if I go now, I'm in something of a hurry?"

The constable was obviously in no kind of hurry.

"If your party is along here," he jerked his thumb over his shoulder, "why didn't you park your car nearby? There are plenty of spaces."

Carey was about to say that there was no room when he arrived but decided that his inquisitor would either have been in the area for hours and know this to be untrue or would be so efficient as to have checked this point with his predecessor on the beat.

The truth was that Carey had parked the car well away from Leonora's flat to save her any embarrassment from the neighbours. Normally when he called for her of brought her home he naturally stopped as near as he could to her flat but on this particular occasion he intended staying as long as he was allowed. However, how does one explain that to a policeman?

The realisation that the officer of the law was gazing at his face intently did nothing to help Carey think up a plausible answer to the question. In fact, he could not think of one at all.

After what seemed an age the man in blue said, "I think we had better have a look at that car of yours sir."

"Good God Officer, it's miles away!"

"I thought you said it was only a couple of streets?"

"Well a couple of streets then, anyway far enough." Was this ridiculous interview going to go on all night? "As I said, I am in a hurry, a very important engagement." Carey's voice tripped on the last word.

"I thought you said you were at a party sir?"

It was going to take all night.

"A small party, in fact only a couple of people – and I am half of them." Flippant but true.

"May I ask where this small party is being held sir?"

The policeman had apparently temporarily shelved the subject of the car so to keep his mind off it Carey decided to oblige. The road fund license was only slightly out of date but the police could be rather sticky about such things.

"Yes, in that building," he indicated the large house converted to flats next to the one by which they were standing.

"I know most of the people there," said the policeman pleasantly, "Perhaps you would not mind telling me who is giving the party?"

Damn! He was hoping to keep Leonora's name out of it but now he could see no way of avoiding this.

"Miss Graye."

"Oh, Miss Graye. A very attractive young lady." The comment was obviously sincere enough but somehow Carey gained the impression the constable had managed to convey in his words the fact that he would have expected Miss Graye to have shown better taste.

"Well I don't think I need to delay you any longer sir."

Carey sighed with relief.

"So if we could just get Miss Graye to identify you," continued the officer, "I will get back to my beat."

Carey cancelled his sigh of relief.

"Is that really necessary?"

"It would save a lot of time sir."

It was the word 'time' that caused Carey to agree with the proposal. How long had he been away from the flat? It seemed to have been for hours.

****

Leonora spent a considerable amount of time repairing the ravages to her appearance. At first she intended just to wash her face and apply more makeup as quickly as possible but then reasoned that it being a very special occasion it would be as well to do the job properly.

Towel in hand she re-entered the bedroom and listened for the sound of the television in the sitting room but it was obviously not switched on. 'Poor James, he must be sitting there with nothing to read but women's magazines, what a bore for the man but it was all his own fault,' (womanlike she could see no reason to blame herself for the anguish of the last week if there was a man available to take the onus), 'so it would do him no harm to commiserate with his soul for a while.'

In the fullness of time Leonora decided that she was as attractive as she could get. She glanced at the bedside clock and received quite a shock to realise how long she had been at her dressing table. 'Poor James, he must be sick to death of waiting!'

Leonora opened the bedroom door and with her loveliest smile, which was very lovely indeed, entered the sitting room saying, "I am sorry to have kept you waiting for so......."

The sitting room was empty.

"James!" she cried. A couple of steps proved he was not in the kitchenette. The television set remained blind and silent, even the magazines on the coffee table were undisturbed. It was as if James had left the room at the same time as she herself.

"What now?" Leonora put her hands to her face and sat down on the settee with an inelegant thump. "Oh God! My nerves won't stand much more!"

She had no time for further thought before a triple tap on the door made her jump. This time she had it open in seconds.

A slightly dishevelled James stood in the doorway, the large, familiar form of Mr. Wilson, one of the local policeman, behind him.

"Wherever have you been?" exclaimed the startled Leonora.

"I went out to get the wine from the car," was the explanation.

"But that was nearly an hour ago, I heard you shout. Did you lock the door behind you? You should have knocked and I would have opened it."

"Actually I had a brush with the law," replied Carey, "and I can prove it." He glanced behind him but the large policeman had tactfully disappeared, just as silently and mysteriously as he had entered Carey's life. "No I can't."

"What are you talking about? But come in and close the door, we will have all the neighbours out on the landing any minute."

Carey followed the girl into the room and locked the door behind him.

"I will tell you the story of my adventures in crime later, at the present time I have far more important things to discuss. Firstly, I would like to state, with no possibility of contradiction, that you look absolutely ravishing. Always beautiful I have never seen you lovelier than you are at this moment.

"Secondly I have something to ask you and nervous breakdowns, arrests and restraints of princes, strikes and lockouts, riots and civil commotions, alarms and excursions generally excepted I hope to get an answer this time."

Leonora, despite the pains she had gone to as regards to her appearance, was more than ready to be taken into Carey's arms and become messed up again but the man had other ideas.

Carey took one of Leonora's hands in his and led her to the settee, saying, "Let us start again."

When she was seated Carey knelt on one knee, raised her hand to his lips, looked into her eyes and said, "Dearest Leonora, will you do me the honour of becoming my wife?"

Matching his mood Leonora solemnly replied, "Dearest James, I accept your proposal in all humility and with all my heart."

Which was pretty good for a pair of amateurs.

If the performance caused a fly on the wall to puke no-one noticed.

With those words spoken the dam of their emotions burst and clasping one another in their arms they kissed and hugged, laughed and prattled and swore undying love to one another.

****

If the local milkman had cause to wonder at the strange sports car parked with those of the residents a few streets away from the flat so far as is known, he did not remark on the fact.

Chapter 4

The usual crowd were in the officers' bar of the 'Belisarius' for the pre-luncheon session – if 'session' it could be termed as none of those present drank a great deal at sea. The word 'Bar' itself was rather an overstatement, it was a home-made affair and looked it. Constructed by the ship's people when the Company had decided that such an amenity could be allowed if it showed evidence of hard and constant use over the intervening years.

Due to the heavy rolling of the ship the sophistication of glasses had been dispensed with and the assembled company took their nourishment straight from the can. Spirits were available but the present assembly were all confirmed beer drinkers.

"Thank the Lord there is only a few more days of this to go," said Gregson, wiping from his chin the beer which had spilled by a particularly vicious roll of the ship.

"Roll on the day!", the Fiver turned to the third mate who had just entered the room, "Any word of our being relieved on arrival Hump?"

It was imagined that the third mate, being closer to the Master and the radio room in the course of his duties, would be in a position to pick up rumours more readily than the more isolated engineers.

"No good asking him," said Parry before Hump could answer, "He has been in his own little dream world since Bangkok."

Hearing the magic word the third mate started to take an interest in the conversation.

"What a place! What a place! I hope we do go there again next trip."

"It would be as well if you didn't," warned Hatch from the depths of an arm chair – literally the depths, the springs had gone years before, "Another week there and you would be just a smear of grease on the deck."

Hump took a swig from his newly opened can of beer and continued on his favourite subject.

"Has anyone seen anything like it? The alleyways and decks full of women before we even had the ship fast, absolutely screaming for it."

"And charging the earth," Gregson opened another can, "Just about broke you for a start Hump."

"Gone are the days when the third mates could get their rough for a bar of soap," contributed Hatch, "Even in my youth the going rate was about fifty cigarettes in most places."

"Absolutely unavoidable," Hump was stuck in his groove, "How could anyone deny those lovely girls what they wanted?"

"Some people managed to," the Fourth tossed his empty beer can into the plastic dustbin jammed behind the bar and reached for a full one. "The Chief for instance, I saw him ploughing through the whole lot of them like an ice-breaker, they did not even exist so far as he was concerned."

"Probably too old for it." said the Fiver.

"Trouble is he has a one track mind," joined in the Fourth, "Engines, engines, engines. I wonder if he ever thinks of anything else."

"I did ask him if he was thinking of indulging," said Parry, "But he just said something like, 'Once you have tasted champagne….' I can't remember the rest of it."

"'Beer's not the same'," Gregson completed the couplet for him. "Probably referring to some old flame of his youth."

"Do you think he was ever young?" the Fiver chipped in, "If he was it must have been long before women were invented."

"What kind of women do they have in the Outer Hebrides or

wherever his hermitage is?" inquired Parry, "I had always imagined they only had old widows in black shawls out there."

"Perhaps he is kinky on sheep?" suggested Hump.

"Maybe he is happy enough without women." Gregson took a long pull at his can of beer whilst the ship was momentarily upright at the top of her roll.

"I'd hate that to happen to me," answered the irrepressible Hump.

* * * * * * * * * * * * * * * * * * *

Captain Montague had intended that evening to inform both the Head Office in London and the Rotterdam agents of the ship's estimated time of arrival at the latter port but later decided to post-pone sending these radio messages until the following morning owing to the weather. The state of the sea to be encountered during the last part of the passage would greatly affect the speed of the vessel and Montague wished to obtain as good an estimate as possible before committing himself to radio messages. He took a great deal of pride in getting his ship to port as close as humanly possible to his 'E.T.A.'. Accuracy he considered one of the keynotes of his success.

Since leaving the Mississippi the weather encountered by the 'Belisarius' had been rather mixed but on the whole quite reasonable for the time of the year. However, over the previous few days Montague had been carefully tracking a depression as it was positioned by the various weather reports. By mid-day the centre of the low was calculated to be about three hundred miles astern of the ship and was expected to pass about seventy miles to the north in about eighteen hours.

Once the noon position was plotted on the chart the ship's course was altered to a more south-easterly direction in order to allow the depression to pass by a greater margin and thus relatively easier weather. The added distance to the passage would be more than compensated by the greater speed maintained.

The weather deteriorated during the course of the afternoon. The wind, strong from the south-west in the forenoon, veered due west and by the time the short hours of daylight had faded had increased to a full gale.

The Captain stood on the port wing of the bridge contemplating the situation. His 'heavy weather hat', an ex-Tank Corps beret, and his dark grey duffle coat were quite wet in spite of his ducking behind the teakwood dodger every time a sea exploded against the ship's side like a torpedo sending spray splashing and rattling over the bridge. Never one for 'wheelhouse watch-keeping' he required his officers to keep their watches on the wing of the bridge where a really sharp lookout could be maintained. Uncomfortable as he was he claimed no privileges in this respect for himself. In army parlance he 'led from the front'.

Sensing the chief officer behind him he turned.

"It will get worse before it gets any better Mr. Hatch," almost shouting in order to be heard above the shrieking of the wind, "Is everything secure?"

Ask a silly question, thought Hatch.

"Yes sir. In fact, I had the carpenter go round and harden up all the hatch wedges only this morning. The weather boards are secured in the port engine-room alleyway but it is no use fitting the starboard ones as the firemen just take them out again when they change watches."

"Should be alright, we will be well south of the worst of the weather although we are definitely due for a dusting. I wish she were not quite so stiff although the rolling is not quite so bad as it was this morning.

However, it will be worse tonight when the wind gets round onto the other quarter. She steers like a cow with the wind anywhere near astern. Talking of steering I think we will have a man on the wheel as from eight o'clock. I am always afraid that auto-steering gear will break down in this sort of weather, it is not all that reliable at the best of times."

'That will mean an extra man on each watch,' groaned Hatch to himself, 'The Old Man seems to think I have an endless supply of seamen.'

Hatch gave the necessary instructions regarding the calling of the extra man to the helmsman, who, with the helm on 'auto', was keeping a lookout on the starboard of the bridge. He used an odd mixture of pidgin English and Laskari, the lingua franca of the Indian Coast, mainly the former.

Montague, who had a flair for picking up a working knowledge of any language with which he came into contact, could not help thinking that the mate should be able to speak the 'bat' fluently after all his years with Asian crews. Hatch however was obviously of the school of thought which considered that 'it was a pretty dumb native who could not understand English provided it was shouted at him hard enough.'

By the time the third mate came on watch at 2000 the wind was howling over the hissing sea, screaming and moaning as it passed over the ship. The 'Belisarius' pitched and rolled, pounded and shuddered as she strove to master each successive sea. The spray by this time was almost continuous as the wind, now north-westerly and approaching storm force, sent the seas crashing against the port side of the ship. The port wheelhouse door was now closed against the weather and the watch was being kept on the starboard wing as Smith arrived to take over.

"When is he going down?" asked the third mate, indicating the Captain whose shadowy form was just visible standing by the man at the wheel. "I'll freeze to death if I have to spend the whole watch out here." Smith had no scruples about easing into the comparative comfort of the wheelhouse the moment the Captain went below.

"He looks like he's staying for a bit," answered Hatch. "You will enjoy your beer all the more when you go down at midnight after a breath of fresh air."

"Don't think I'll fancy one tonight, the fourth will have to drink on his own. All I want when I come off watch will be my bunk. I hardly slept a wink this afternoon with all the rolling."

"More likely a guilty conscience Hump. Are you going to make an honest woman of that girl of yours when you get home?"

"Which one?" queried Smith in all innocence.

"I am not going to get involved in a long discussion on your love-life, I'm for my bed. Have you 'got your eyes' yet?"

The mate's question regarding the other's night vision having been replied to in the affirmative Hatch completed handing over the watch, not forgetting to remind Smith that there would be a man on the wheel until the weather improved.

Having said goodnight Hatch took a last look at the sky and sea then made his way down to his room.

****

Chapter 5

Chief Engineer Alastair Macquarie slipped the various forms he had been completing in pencil into a drawer and sighed with relief. He was more or less up to date with his paper-work but the final typing would have to wait until the ship's rolling decreased considerably. The typewriter was screwed to the desk and although the keys could be manipulated the carriage was inclined to stay in one place when the ship was rolled over one way resulting in a large black dot instead of the intended row of letters or figures. When the ship rolled the other way the carriage shot across with a crash against its stop – problems unknown to typists ashore. With patience and a little dexterity short notes could be typed by timing the punching of the keys to the rolling of the ship but this was not practical with the masses of figures the 'Chief' had to deal with, a moment's inattention could result in a mistake causing considerable trouble to rectify.

Macquarie stood up and stretched his legs, cramped by their being tensed in the kneehole of his desk to prevent his being thrown over backwards by the violent rolling.

Five steps took him from his office desk to his domestic arm chair, another feature virtually unknown ashore. He withdrew the novel jammed between the cushions of the chair and sat down.

Finding his place in the book the Chief read a few lines then closed it. He had read everything on the ship which he considered readable during the course of the voyage and the present novel failed to hold his interest. Anyway, he would rather think of his bachelor cottage on the West coast of Scotland.

Well, he should soon be back there, within a week he should be in the cottage putting it back to rights after his five months' absence. Once the place was operational he would be able to get out his paints and settle down to putting onto canvas the scenes of clouds and sea that he loved so much. Macquarie smiled when he thought of this and wondered what the people on the ship would think if they discovered he was a sea-scape painter of no little merit. Not only were his pictures considered good but they sold well, at least in his native Scotland. Some had even been hung at exhibitions, twice at Edinburgh itself. And no-one on the ship knew a thing about it, it was a secret he hugged to himself, a small private world he found essential in the close confines of a ship.

The cottage would never seem the same though, not after last summer. What a week that was! More than a week in actual fact. Macquarie reminisced on that time as he had so often before. The occasion he at first thought he had been invaded by a troop of boy scouts.

****

It had been a hot, sultry day towards the end of summer. Macquarie had hurried through his various domestic chores in the morning in order to spend the afternoon painting as it was obvious to him that there would be quite a dramatic cloud effect later as even before noon the cumulus was building up over the sea to the west.

By the time he had set up his easel a hundred yards from the cottage the clouds were towering thousands of feet above the sea with lightening flashing in the slate grey of their base.

The painting was progressing quite well when the first few drops of rain caused Macquarie to beat a hasty retreat to shelter. After quickly stowing his painting equipment in the old outhouse a few yards from the cottage he dashed to the house, only just getting through the door before the rain came down in torrents.

'In for a really dirty night', he said to himself as he lit the fire in the living room. After the hot day the rain had already caused a considerable drop in temperature.

On the heels of the initial deluge the wind, veering to the north-west and increasing in ferocity by the minute, whipped the surface of the loch to a fury and caused the house to shudder on its foundations.

'Heaven help the sailors on a night like this,' he muttered, 'This is the place to be in this sort of weather.'

Macquarie made himself a supper of bacon, eggs and fried bread and, with the addition of a large mug of tea, sat by the fire to enjoy it. A very similar meal had constituted his breakfast, the reason for the duplication was that the bacon was beginning to go off and it was against his principles to waste anything. His catering arrangements were pretty rough and ready, meals consisted of generally a cooked dish at either end of the day, always something simple. Lunch he did not bother with as such, often just a mug of tea or coffee with very occasionally a slice of bread and a lump of cheese if he happened to be particularly peckish. Macquarie was no gourmet.

It was about ten o'clock, the fire getting low and Macquarie was contemplating his bed when he heard a sound above the howling of the wind. Or was it his imagination? No, there it was again, a thump followed immediately by another.

Damnation! Macquarie hauled himself from his chair. Something was adrift. It was the first real test his recently completed long front porch had had to endure and his immediate concern was that part of the roof had failed to stand the strain. He grabbed a small electric torch from the mantelpiece and strode off to investigate. A quick inspection of the underside of the roof indicated that all was in order in that direction and he was still wondering what had caused the sound when it occurred again, a thump followed by a faint rattling of the outside door handle. Macquarie wrenched open the door, it was unlocked but being new was inclined to stick in wet weather.

At first the beam of the torch encountered nothing but driving rain. He directed it towards the ground, something must have blown against the door to cause the thumping sound.

The light illuminated what at first appeared to be a heap of saturated clothing. Macquarie's surprise was increased when he saw on top of the pile a soaking red and white woollen hat under which could be discerned part of a small face.

Macquarie's startled "Good God! Who are you? What are you doing here?" elicited only a silent whimpering sound.

He was about to say, "Well come in," when he realised that the lad was probably incapable of any further movement at the present time. Placing the torch on the floor he reached down to lift his surprise visitor and immediately discovered a problem. There appeared to be an inordinate number of arms and legs for just one small boy. The implication was that there were at least two, if not more of them entangled in the cold, wet heap.

Macquarie eventually managed to get a grip on the one evidently uppermost and carried the helpless form to the living room. Dumping it on the hearthrug in front of the fire he returned to the porch for the second, there proved to be but two of them.

Only two? What were they, survivors from a wrecked yacht or lost boy scouts? Good grief! There could be more of them outside in the howling gale, maybe a whole troop of them. Macquarie hurried with the completely unconscious body to the living room and laid it with its companion.

He turned to the first, who at least showed some signs of life.

"Quickly, are there more of you outside?"

He had to repeat the question twice more before it seemed to register. A few whimpering sounds and gestures appeared to indicate that the pair of them constituted the whole party. At least that is what Macquarie hoped the answer conveyed.

A log dropped in the grate caused a bright yellow flame to complement the light from the lamp on the table. Another shock. Macquarie snatched the woollen hat from the small head. A mass of dark, wet hair fell over the dimly lit face. A girl! One of them was a girl! One of them? He directed his gaze to the other figure lying supine, face pinched, the mouth slightly open and a fan of wet blonde hair spread over the rug.

"What a turn up for the book," said Macquarie out loud, "Two soaked, frozen, helpless girls and not a woman for miles! What in hell's name do I do now?"

'Well it's not time for false modesty,' he decided, 'a little longer in this state and they will both have pneumonia.'

Macquarie dashed to the bedroom and hauled out his entire stock of towels. As he was leaving the room he thought of something else and added to his load his spare blanket and the one from the bed, he owned only two.

Both girls appeared to be unconscious when he returned but he gave priority to the blonde, the other had shown at least some sign of life earlier but the light-haired one could already be in a serious state. She was not wearing a great deal but what there was seemed to have shrunk onto her body like a second skin. Macquarie had quite a struggle with the sodden bootlaces and some of the fastenings of her clothes but eventually she was stripped. The girl had offered not the slightest resistance. 'Completely out', decided the man. There was nothing sensuous about the operation, 'just a job to be done, like skinning a rabbit,' he mused.

As he applied the towels with vigour he wondered what charges of rape and assault he was laying himself open to. 'Well I could not leave them as they were', he justified himself as he rubbed energetically. Front, back, arms, legs, hands and feet. He had to go easy on the feet noticing some blisters there. Finally head and hair. During the drying process the girl, or woman?, he could not attempt to guess her age, gave vent to a few groans which at least proved she was in the land of the living. Otherwise she showed as much animation as a rag doll.

Having thoroughly dried the girl and, he hoped, succeeded in getting at least some circulation moving, he wrapped her in a blanket and dumped the bundle in the depths of his arm chair. Her head was out of the top but he was not sure where her limbs were, she was so small the blanket obscured any indication in this direction.

Macquarie turned to the other girl who was gazing at him with large, frightened brown eyes as she scratched feebly at the front of her anorak with cold, wet fingers, trying to find the toggle of the zip fastener.

"I...I'll dry myself," she whispered in a tremulous voice. The first lucid words she had spoken so far.

"It would take you the rest of the night," said Macquarie in what he thought was a soothing tone but in retrospect decided it probably sounded to the frightened girl like a grizzly bear trying to be chummy, "I will give you a hand – just close your eyes if you are shy."

Trying desperately to convince himself that he was not warming to his work of succour Macquarie knelt down and commenced removing the dark haired girl's boots in spite of her timid protestations.

The removal of the remainder of the clothing was more difficult this second time owing to the girl's frantic, if feeble, efforts to protect her modesty. A picture flashed through Macquarie's mind of a sanguinary provost glowering at him beneath bushy eyebrows, then, after a final look of absolute loathing, turning to the two demure plaintiffs and saying, "Now please young ladies, try to tell me in your own words what the abominable wretch did then."

He did intend leaving at least one small item for the sake of decency – or subconsciously in the hope that it might contribute to the mitigation of his potential prison sentence – but everything was so saturated it was hard to differentiate between one article of clothing and another so the job was eventually accomplished leaving the girl as bare as the day she was born, curled up in as near as she could get to a ball in the centre of the hearth-rug.

Macquarie began the drying by vigorously rubbing the girl's back with a rough towel, this was thoroughly dampened by her thick hair which he dried next. Reaching for another towel he managed to extricate an arm and dry that. Rolling the girl over he found that the second arm offered less resistance than the first and the hisses and 'No! No!'s to which she at first gave utterance changed to little timorous squeals as she began to lose some of her fear. Expecting difficulty with her curled up legs he was agreeably surprised when the first straightened out when he pulled on the ankle and the second uncoiled almost as soon as he touched it. The girl rapidly relaxed under his ministrations and at the completion of the rough drying of the front of her body there passed from her lips a sound which could only be described as a sigh.

Quickly he wrapped her in the second blanket and laid her on the small sofa.

'Must get something hot into them,' he said to himself as he transferred the large black kettle from the hob to the fire.

Going into the porch, which was rapidly becoming his kitchen-cum-storeroom, Macquarie took down from a shelf some packets of dehydrated soup and three earthware mugs, (he had four in case of visitors), and returned to the fire and his unexpected guests.

The kettle was soon boiling so he poured the water onto the powder in each of the mugs. Then he turned to the girls, to find them both fast asleep.

In something of a quandary as to what to do next Macquarie filled in the time by scooping up the wet clothes and towels and dumping them in a corner of the porch.

'I can't leave them where they are,' he mused, 'they could get cramp or fall to the floor and hurt themselves.'

Deciding on the best course of action he one at a time carried the girls to his bed, tipped them out of their cocoons into the centre of the mattress then covered them with the blankets. The sight of their pink flesh in the light of the oil lamp through the doorway reminded him forcibly of a nest of field-mice he had come upon the previous Summer, soft, pink and helpless.

Macquarie added the worn green bed-cover to the blankets and then, for good measure the night having turned quite cold, his 'heavy weather' coat, tucking the sleeves under the mattress to ensure it did not slip off.

Having checked that his visitors were still fast asleep in spite of their disturbance he returned to the living room and made himself as comfortable as possible for the remainder of the night.

He sat in his big arm chair for some time collecting his thoughts. Reaching out he took one of the mugs of soup and sipped it as he pondered.

Damn! He should have asked the dark-haired girl some questions when she was still conscious. Who were they? Where were they going? Was anyone expecting them at their destination? Were people at this very moment trudging around in the wind and rain searching for them? Had the police been informed? Rescue services? Helicopters?

And were there really only two of them? Were there more of them even now within a short distance of his cottage in desperate need of assistance? The dark girl seemed to indicate that the two of them were alone but was 'seemed' enough? Macquarie half rose from his chair to awaken her. He sat down again trying to convince himself that there were only two. A minute later he got to his feet and took the lamp to the bedroom, he must make sure. Gently he lifted the edge of the blankets and looked down on the two damp heads of the girls, close together, absolutely dead to the world. Macquarie had not the heart to disturb them.

His line of reasoning then became that if there were others of the party somewhere out on the small peninsular on which his cottage was situated they would no doubt survive the night even if they were in a sorry plight by the morning. After all it was not as if it were mid-winter. He pushed from his mind the thought that the blonde girl at least could not have endured much more than she had without shelter.

Macquarie began to think of them as people. 'Girls' was the term he had mentally employed but were they? At first they had appeared very young, thirteen or so perhaps, but as he got to know them better – was that a tactful expression? – it gradually dawned on him that they were older, mid-twenties or even thirty. It was their diminutive size which had misled him. Yes, both fully formed women even if they were fashioned on the small side. At least that was what he thought now after some consideration, although it was difficult to judge their ages having seen them only in the shadowy light of the oil lamp and fire. The dark girl had a little more meat on her than the blonde but he doubted if either of them topped five feet in height.

Another question, how did they come to arrive at the cottage? It was far from any track and the nearest habitation was several miles away on the other side of the loch.

Well there was nothing more he could do.

Rising to his feet Macquarie collected the three empty cups, none of the soup had been wasted, and took them to the sink in his kitchen-porch to rinse.

Five minutes later he returned to the room, extinguished the lamp and by the light of the embers of the fire made himself as comfortable as he could on the far too small sofa.

Almost immediately he was fast asleep.

*****

Macquarie awoke cramped, sweaty and uncomfortable. He was not used to sleeping in his clothes. For a moment he did not know where he was but then recollections of the previous evening came flooding back.

Rolling from the sofa he crept across to the bedroom and peeped at the two tousled heads. The girls were still fast asleep, breathing evenly, in exactly the same position he had last seen them. Although the bedroom curtains were not exactly threadbare they were far from thick and the morning light was sufficient to prove to Macquarie that he had been right the second time, the faces were of mature women – and quite pretty ones at that. He left the room as silently as he had entered and closed the door.

Taking advantage of the fact that the women were not likely to awake in the immediate future Macquarie stripped off in the kitchen and sluiced down his sweaty body in what he termed a 'bath'. He found but one dry towel in the living room, this he folded and left by the sink for the girls, drying himself on the least damp of those on the porch floor. Using the lukewarm water from the kettle he shaved.

Wrapped in the ancient dressing gown which had served as his blanket during the night he crept back into the bedroom and silently removed a clean shirt from the chest of drawers. Back in the kitchen he washed his briefs and socks and exchanged these for their counterparts hanging on the string 'clothes line' stretched along the wall.

Dressed after his routine toilet he set about cleaning and rebuilding the living room fire, the only one in the house. It would no doubt be needed as the day had every appearance of being cold and wet even though the wind had dropped considerably. In any case it was his only means of cooking.

Feeling hungry he thought about breakfast and wondered what girls ate at that meal. He had porridge, a few eggs, bacon – but he had best reserve the latter for himself as it was definitely deteriorating rapidly – and of course bread. He could also muster butter and an almost full two pound jar of marmalade. Macquarie decided he had enough to tempt the most discriminating palate and no doubt the girls would be desperately hungry anyway. It was a pity he had none of the popular breakfast cereals but they were bulky to transport and impalatable without fresh milk. He was not at all that fond of them in any case.

Macquarie wished the young women would wake up so he could question them. It was already ten minutes to nine. He decided that if they were not moving by the time he had the fire lit he would awaken them then.

As it happened it was just as he put a match to the heap of old newspaper and sticks that he heard the faint click of the bedroom door latch. He turned in time to see the door close again and to hear the patter of footsteps behind it. One at least of the women was awake.

Macquarie crossed to the bedroom door and tapped quietly. Hearing a quiet "Come in", he entered the room.

The rather timorous face of the dark-haired girl was all that could be seen of either of his guests.

"Good morning. How do you feel after yesterday's adventures? Did you sleep well?" Rattled out Macquarie in what he hoped was a soothing tone.

"Wonderfully thanks," the reply seemed to cover both questions, the voice quiet but clear.

"And your friend?"

"She is still asleep."

"Look," said Macquarie, getting down to business now the polite preliminaries were over, "I'm sorry to bother you but I must know some answers to a few questions. Firstly, did you say there were only two of you, no more of your party outside?" he gestured vaguely towards the window.

"No, there are only the two of us."

"Is anyone expecting to meet you anywhere or do you think people are out looking for you?"

"No, no-one knows where we are, we are on a camping holiday."

The answer was spoken quickly as if in order to get the questioning over as soon as possible. Macquarie wanted to ask further questions but obviously they were upsetting the girl. Possibly they could be interpreted as checking that the authorities were not likely to descend before he murdered them in the bed or whatever she thought were his plans. He felt like a wicked baron in a fairy tale, so changed the subject in an effort to soothe her fears.

"Just stay in bed as long as you like." Instead of soothing the remark seemed to make the girl wince. "I'll bring you some tea right away." She bit her lip at this. Whatever was wrong? "And some breakfast if you would tell me what you would like." The young woman had gone quite white. Macquarie was at a complete loss. "Is something wrong?" he inquired in a concerned voice.

The girl's complexion made a rapid change from off-white to bright red as she whispered, "I want to go to the loo."

"Oh my God!" equally embarrassed Macquarie had failed to realise that women had plumbing the same as anyone else. He stepped back to allow her to pass.

"It's in the porch, at the opposite end to the front door."

No movement from the bed but a beseeching look from the girl.

Macquarie's brain became operational again and he realised the other part of the problem. He pulled open a drawer of the chest and hauled out a large black and grey jersey which he tossed onto the bed without daring to look at the woman. As an afterthought he took a pair of thick socks from a top drawer. "Tiled floor out there, cold on the feet," he offered in explanation as he added them to the jersey. With that he left the room to make an exacting examination of the fire. Seconds later he heard the soft patter of feet behind him. He glanced round and noted that the jersey enveloped the small figure like a woolly tent, the hem of the garment reaching well below her knees.

Giving the girl time to get back into bed Macquarie again tapped the door.

"The kettle will soon be boiling, would you like some tea?"

"Yes please, I would love some," the soft voice, seemingly relaxed now, replied, "But please come in."

Macquarie re-entered the bedroom.

"Any sign of life from your friend yet?" he asked.

"No, she is still dead to the world. She is a great sleeper at the best of times."

As if on cue there was a movement from the pile of bed-clothes and slowly the top of a tousled blonde head appeared in Macquarie's line of vision.

"Good morning Fiona," said the dark-haired girl to the emerging head, "How are you?"

Her question was answered with another.

"Where am I?"

"You are quite safe in this gentleman's cottage, he....."

Realising from this remark that they were a trio the girl apparently named Fiona brought her wide blue eyes above the level of the bed-clothes and saw Macquarie for the first time.

For the want of something better to say Macquarie said "Good morning," then, including them both in the same glance, "By the way my name is Macquarie, Alistair Macquarie."

"We have been rather remiss on introductions," replied the dark one, "My name is Morag and this is Fiona."

No surnames. For some indefinable reason Macquarie liked this touch.

"How do you do?" Fiona, still half asleep, reached out to shake his hand in an automatic gesture but noticing her bare arm quickly withdrew it. With a slight frown of puzzlement she lifted the edge of the bed covers, glanced down, uttered a shriek and disappeared like a startled rabbit.

After a moment or two's silence a hand appeared where the head had been which groped wildly until it found the neck of Morag's jersey by which that girl's head was hauled down to the slight gap between blanket and pillow. A rapid whispering ensued.

Macquarie, mistaking the reason for consultation, withdrew a second jersey, a dark blue one, from the drawer.

Only one of Morag's eyes was visible above the blankets and it smiled, if an eye can be said to smile.

"No, she just wants to know where your wife is," and, probably pondering the same question herself, "what shall I tell her?"

"I am afraid you will have to tell her," as if Fiona could not hear him anyway, "that you young ladies last night brought up at what is probably the only bachelor establishment for thirty miles."

This statement caused a muffled cry and more frantic whispering from under the blankets.

Considering himself temporarily surplus to requirements Macquarie started to withdraw. Reaching the door he said he would return with some tea in about ten minutes.

"Oh,...er...Alistair," how lovely the name sounded on her lips, "I think it would be as well if you left the other jersey," said Morag with a smile.

Macquarie glanced down at the garment, forgotten in his hands, and tossed it onto the bed. "Sorry. The socks are in the top drawer."

****

Having heard the various alternatives on Macquarie's breakfast menu both ladies selected toast and marmalade – two slices each as they were hungry. This did not seem much nourishment to the host but as most women appeared to be on some stupid diet or other for the major part of their lives he did not press them to have more.

Macquarie need not have been concerned about the women leaving the breakfast table hungry, their and his ideas of what constituted slices of toast varied to a degree. Fiona at least wondered if it would be considered facetious if she took a knife and fork to hers.

Over breakfast the young ladies related the story of their adventures leading to their arrival on Macquarie's doorstep.

Long time friends they had often gone on holiday together to various places on the Continent and in England but mainly, and particularly in recent years, to parts of their native Scotland.

The types of holiday had varied considerably and this year they had decided on a walking tour, carrying their camping gear and buying food as they went along.

Although in unfamiliar country they experienced no trouble for the first two days and nights finding that the localities visited agreed with their map so they had no difficulties in finding villages to purchase supplies or, for that matter, in obtaining permission from farmers to camp in their fields.

It was on the third day that they ran into trouble. They were walking from the north and making for the village across the loch from the cottage when they decided mid-afternoon to take a look at the sea, which, according to their map, was not far to the right of the track they were following. This they did but on arrival at the shore the sun disappeared behind clouds and they realised that the weather was beginning to look rather threatening.

The ominous clouds persuaded them to hurry to such an extent they neglected to check their position on the map, which had been stowed in one of the rucksacks at their previous stop. Their certainty that the village was on the coast, confirmed by a picture post-card seen only that morning depicting it with fishing boats drawn up on the beach, decided them to carry on down the sea shore rather than return to their original path. In theory this would save a little distance, thus lessening the chance of a drenching and they could not possibly walk past the cluster of buildings without seeing them.

This was their undoing. What the girls would have realised had they glanced at the map was that a sea loch extended northwards and the village was on its mainland shore. There was nothing on the peninsula but Macquarie's cottage and that was about half way up from the tip of the mull inside the loch.

The rain and wind commenced and the women were soon worried at not reaching the village at the expected time. They plodded on getting more wet and cold until they thought it best to pitch the tent and shelter under it until the worst of the rain had passed. This they had left too late. The tent was not even half erected before a fierce squall tore it from the girls' cold, wet hands and sent it whirling away into the rain and rapidly gathering darkness. With this disaster and the village their nearest known refuge they decided to make a dash for it, temporarily abandoning their packs.

The two women stumbled along, tripping and slipping on the rocks of the shore and becoming more wet, cold and frightened by the minute. Their soaked boots and socks rubbed on their feet and soon Fiona was complaining of painful blisters.

They attempted to cheer one another as they progressed, insisting that the village must be just over the skyline but each time they topped a rocky outcrop another ridge confronted them. Time and time again.

Struggling in the wind and rain, saturated and almost exhausted they eventually topped a rise and found no other rocks ahead of them. Only the angry sea! With sickening horror they realised the sea was also to the left of them. They had reached the very tip of the mull, although they did not appreciate this at the time.

Completely at a loss as to where they were and how the sea came to be almost surrounding them they were quite terrified. Feeling that if they sat down they would be unable to rise again they pressed on along the shore not realising that they had turned northward and were heading back almost the way they had come. Facing more into the wind and rain their progress was even more difficult and exhausting. In the darkness they could see but dimly the rocks close to them and the waves of the loch beating against the shore.

They staggered on in almost overwhelming fear and distress until they could go no further. The two young women sank to the ground, cold, soaking wet, and absolutely terrified.

A few minutes later the wind died down considerably and they thought the storm was over but their hopes were soon dashed in this respect. Within moments the wind resumed with increased fury. The brief lull however had allowed the women to look around them and both saw a small glimmer of light but a short distance away. It gave them the heart and only just the strength to stagger the last few score yards to sanctuary.

****

Whilst they breakfasted the rain stopped although the heavily overcast sky promised more to come.

The ladies, seemingly quite recovered from their ordeal, insisted on washing the dishes as their share of the breakfast chores. Macquarie did not take a great deal of persuasion to agree to this as washing up was not one of his favourite occupations.

"In that case I'll see if I can rescue your equipment if you can tell me where you left it," he said.

A five minute description of the place pinned down the site of the abandoned rucksacks, so far as Macquarie could ascertain, to somewhere on the coast between Cape Wrath and the Mull of Kintyre.

He decided that questioning them would be a more productive course to take, times and one or two identifiable points from which he could work.

Regarding times, the sum total of facts derived from his questioning was that the girls had left the previous village, which he knew to be nine miles north of his cottage, 'shortly after breakfast'.

If he could establish whether they had left their packs before or after passing Sbarbh Sbon, or Cormorant Point as he termed it, not having the Gaelic, it would cut down the search area considerably as this rocky headland was about half way down the coast of the peninsula.

His question, "Did you notice a mass of black rocks sticking out to sea for about half a mile on your way down the shore?" brought about the only definite answer on which the women could agree. They were positive and unanimous.

"No."

'Patience Macquarie', he said to himself.

"How far from the beach did you attempt to make your camp?"

Morag, "About thirty yards."

Fiona, "A quarter of a mile or so."

In unison.

"I am afraid we are not being very helpful," said Fiona with marked perspicacity as Macquarie released an unfortunately audible sigh.

He cheered himself with the thought that if he had to follow their entire route the brightly coloured rucksacks should be easy enough to find providing they were not in a depression in the ground. He should have asked this question earlier of course.

"What colour are your packs anyway?"

"Dark tan," replied Fiona.

"Olive drab," said Morag.

"I should have guessed that," said Macquarie evenly, "I suppose the tent was camouflaged?"

"Oh no," replied Morag, surprised at the question, "It was olive drab to match my rucksack."

"Well that should be enough to go on," said Macquarie aware that the sarcasm would be wasted on the women, "I'll get on my way."

"Would you like us to come with you to help carry them?" asked Morag, who must have known full well that he would have to refuse the offer for any of several reasons.

"No thanks, I should be able to manage." The girl's patently sincere belief that he would even find the rucksacks cheered him considerably.

"I hope it does not take you too long to find them," said Fiona. Then, as if in contradiction to this remark, "And thank you again for taking us in and looking after us." As if there existed a fair possibility of never seeing him again. 'Which is quite likely if I set my heart on not returning without the damned bags,' said Macquarie to himself.

"Cheerio then, help yourselves to anything you can find for lunch if I am not back in time. As a rule I do not eat at midday so do not wait for me."

Once clear of his guests Macquarie could think more clearly. The girls could not have been more than three or four miles from the village when they turned off the track as they said they expected to arrive there before six o-clock. Therefore they must have crossed to the coast just north of the loch. There were some small hillocks just above the loch head and these could have been sufficient to have hidden it from their view. He wondered how much one could see from a height of eye of about four and a half feet anyway. They were not doubt concentrating on the sea ahead of them in any case. Yes, they could have been very close to the top of the loch at that time so the beach opposite could be one fairly definite point of reference.

Next they carried their packs part of the way down the peninsula. How far? Hard to say. Call it half way, that would be close to Cormorant Point.

In from the shore? A quarter of a mile seemed unlikely, probably less than a hundred yards. Macquarie's legs were already carrying him rapidly across the mull in the direction of Cormorant Point.

On arrival at his search area he first looked along a sheep track just above the beach for a couple of miles or so to the south of the black rocks of the point.

Unrewarded by his search he returned to his starting point by a route approximately fifty yards inland from the sheep track. The land rose sharply upwards about twice this distance from the beach and as the girls had said nothing about climbing he made no further searches in this direction.

Macquarie continued his hunt to the north of the point. When he estimated he had completed about two miles he looked around for something to identify the spot so he would know how far he had progressed in his search when he returned with the girls the following day. Their clothes should be dry by then. He had already made up his mind that it was unlikely he would find the rucksacks unaided. The women may remember some landmark even if the weather and darkness at the time made this rather doubtful. By the time he had walked back to Cormorant Point fifty yards inside his northward track and then home he would have covered more than twelve miles – which was quite enough for one day.

He looked around for some kind of mark. The trouble was the terrain was all much the same. He could build a cairn of rocks but that would be too time consuming and anyway he did not feel like that much labour. Perhaps there was something inland? He looked in that direction. Nothing much, all very similar rocks, that is apart from that green one a quarter of a mile from the shore but that was really too far away to be of much use as a mark. A green rock? That was strange, all the others were uniform grey. It could not be, surely? Macquarie strode towards it and was soon relieved to find that he was right, it was the tent, wrapped around the boulder like a coat of paint.

Leaving the tent in position in case he needed it again as a leading mark and noting that it was, as he had expected, adhering to the north west face of the rock Macquarie set off in that direction for the shore.

On arriving at the beach he cast backwards and forwards towards the tent, his zig-zag course taking in every fold of the ground. After twenty minutes or so he found the first rucksack, the dark green one. It was sitting forlornly in a depression behind a large boulder, a few lengths of tent pole lay scattered nearby.

Approaching he noted that the rucksack had lived up to its manufacturer's guarantee of water-tightness as, owing to the flap having been left wide open, rain water had filled it to the brim. Anything which might originally have floated must have become water-logged and sunk.

'God!', he muttered to himself as he tipped the bag onto its side to run out the water, 'that is going to weigh a ton. I hope the other one is properly fastened.'

When he found the second rucksack, forty yards from the first, he discovered that the flap of it had been secured although this was not readily apparent as only a few inches of the bag could be seen above the surface of the small pool in which it had come to rest after its passage down a gully. Although only a trickle of water ran into the pool it had obviously been a raging torrent during the previous night's heavy rain.

Emptying the bags and wringing out their contents would considerably reduce the weight he intended to carry but Macquarie was reluctant to take such a liberty with the ladies' clothing, he therefore contented himself with tipping the rucksacks onto their side for a few minutes to allow much of the loose water to run out.

Adjusting the shoulder straps of one rucksack Macquarie secured this to his back and balanced the other on top of it, holding it in position with one hand. He collected the tent from its rock and this, added to the rucksacks and tent poles previously gathered, constituted a heavy and very cumbersome load.

Several times during the course of the journey home he thought of caching half of the equipment and collecting it later but in the event he struggled on with the whole load. Before he was even half way back to the cottage he decided that his first estimate of the weight of one bag could not have been far out.

The girls had been watching out and saw him as he topped a rise a hundred yards or so from the cottage. They met him just outside the front door, modesty concerning their attire preventing them from proceeding any further. The ecstatic welcome to him and their equipment and the numerous compliments heaped on his head caused Macquarie to consider his endeavour well worthwhile.

If our acquaintance had been just a little longer I am sure they would have kissed me, he decided.

Leaving the rucksacks and tent in the porch the two young women fussed over Macquarie like a couple of mother hens. At least it seemed so to him, unused as he was to such attention. They helped him off with his wet coat, it had rained for part of the journey back just to keep things interesting, and did not even look at their equipment until he was comfortably settled in his arm chair with a mug of hot tea and a plate of hot toast and cheese- the commissariat did not extend to jam and cake which the girls no doubt thought more appropriate to afternoon tea. Even then they showed signs of staying until he chased them off as they were obviously on tenterhooks to see what damage their property had sustained.

Although Macquarie could not see the women from his chair the subdued shrieks of anguish, the cries of, "Oh dear!" and the soggy thump of item after item as it was tossed onto the draining board or into the sink told their own story. He felt sorry for them so went out into the kitchen and told them so. Both girls were having trouble holding back their tears as they viewed the saturated mass of their belongings. Apart from identifiable items such as sleeping bags and sweaters there were many pink, white and pale blue articles which were apparently underclothes, a few soggy maps, wet shoes and, dripping from behind the tap, a camera.

Obviously the women had hoped that at least the contents of one bag would have remained dry so they could have shared the available clothing but everything was saturated.

Instinctively he put an arm around a shoulder of each and for a moment they allowed him to draw them to him. But only for an instant. They pushed away and, fighting back their tears, each put on as brave a face as she could.

"Never mind," said Fiona, "We are very fortunate to get the stuff back at all."

"Yes, I'm sure _we_ would never have been able to find the bags."

In their distress the women's compliments were anything but subtle but Macquarie appreciated them none the less for that.

There was something he had noticed when he first arrived home but had neglected to mention owing to all the activity since that time. It occurred to him that this was as good a time as any to rectify the omission.

As the girls' eyes returned to the scene of devastation Macquarie took each of them by the hand and with a quiet, "Come with me," led them back into the living room. Mystified they followed docilely.

Macquarie stopped beside the fire and with a gentle pressure on their hands, turned them until they stood side by side.

His gaze moved slowly from their eyes to the tops of their heads, his face taking on a somewhat overdone expression of wonderment.

At the same time both young ladies realised the significance of his actions and their expressions of puzzlement changed to embarrassed pleasure.

Macquarie made little noises of appreciation as he slowly circled the two women. They had obviously not been idle whilst he had been away hunting for the rucksacks, the most apparent result of their activities being the state of their hair. Instead of fuzzy dark brown and blonde mass each head was now very neatly groomed. Fiona's flaxen tresses fell sleekly to in-curling ends about her shoulders and Morag's dark, thick hair was brushed back and neatly plaited into a sort of long bun at the nape of her neck. The shining brown hair had taken on a coppery sheen that he had not noticed before.

"You are absolutely beautiful!" I thought I had a couple of pretty girls on my hands but this is absolutely breath-taking!"

"Oh, go on!" said Fiona, "You are just saying that to cheer us up."

Which of course was true to a certain extent.

Although both ladies were obviously pleased at the blandishments Morag could not prevent herself from saying, accusingly, "You have only just noticed!"

Macquarie of course denied this emphatically claiming that he had been unable to get a word in edgeways since he arrived home.

"You have tidied the place up as well," he added. This he really had noticed. The book he had been reading, (how long ago that seemed to be!), the broken door lock he had been in the process of repairing, the few tools he was constantly using and the other odds and ends he normally left ready to hand had either been neatly stowed or hidden away altogether. On sitting down earlier he had noted that the cushions of his chair no longer exactly fitted the contours of his body.

"A great improvement," Macquarie said admiringly. At least he hoped it sounded that way. "It was very kind of you indeed but really you should not have bothered, you both must still be very tired after yesterday."

The girls made depreciating remarks and insisted that the clearing up had only taken a few minutes.

Macquarie looked at his watch and remarked that it was time to start thinking about the evening meal. There was a clock on the mantelpiece but as this stopped regularly eight days after he wound it Macquarie decided it was more of a nuisance than an asset.

"We will look after that if you will tell us what you would like," Fiona's words caused Macquarie's chest to swell a little.

"We had a look through your stores," joined in Morag, "I hope you don't mind?" she added hurriedly. "There does not appear to be much selection, it must be near your next shopping day."

The statement surprised Macquarie as he thought he had food for a week or more having stocked up but a few days earlier. Fresh stuff was always a problem of course, even toasted bread tasted pretty awful after a week or ten days but the present loaves were recently purchased and there was nothing wrong with the cheese.

"Yes," he lied, "I intended going round to the village in the next day or two."

"How do you get there?" enquired Fiona.

"Walk, it is only a couple of hours or so around the head of the loch. When I have collected what I require I come back in MacNab's boat – he owns the local transport, such as it is."

"That cannot be very convenient," said Morag.

"Oh, it's handy enough although sometimes MacNab is busy so I have to wait until he can bring it across. That was a pest when I was building the porch and wanted something heavy which was holding up the job. Apart from everything else it meant either waiting until the boat was available or leaving the stuff for him to bring over when he had time and walking back – half a day gone."

"You built the porch yourself?" said Fiona in admiration, "But that is wonderful!"

Macquarie felt his head swelling. That young woman certainly knew how to boost a man's morale.

"Oh, it is of simple enough design, time consuming with all the fetching and carrying but easy enough to build. I intend buying my own boat sometime but so far when anything suitable comes on the market locally I have been too busy to go and look at it."

The conversation continued for another ten minutes or so before it was unanimously agreed that the evening meal would have to be prepared.

****

Macquarie was agreeably surprised at what could be achieved with his limited culinary resources. After the dinner, it could be termed no less, the ladies seemed to take it for granted that they would wash up so he went out to the old stone outbuilding he used as a store and workshop to collect a supply of logs for the fire. As the supply of sticks in his ready use bucket were getting rather low he decided to chop some more for fire-lighting over the next few days.

This done he carried the sticks and several logs back to the house. Usually he transported the logs in an old zinc bath he had inherited with the cottage but he noticed it was now, for the first time in years, bright and clean, apparently having been used for its original purpose whilst he had been away earlier in the day. Later he noticed that his hair brush and comb were also very clean and hoped the girls had washed them before they were utilised.

Macquarie automatically glanced out to sea before entering the house and noted blue patches between the clouds to the westward. It promised to be fine on the morrow after the grey skies, rain and drizzle of the day.

The girls' anoraks, jerseys and trousers, or whatever such garments were termed that year, still hung damply on the long clothes line between the store house and a corner of the cottage. It would do them no harm to stay out all night decided Macquarie as the wind had dropped away almost entirely and it had become quite mild. In fact, he was more than warm enough outside in his shirtsleeves.

Entering the living room with the ladies, who had just completed the washing up, he felt uncomfortably warm even in a shirt, the girls must be absolutely sweltering in their......

"Good God!" Macquarie dropped the logs onto the hearth with a crash. Swinging round to the startled girls he began to apologise profusely.

"Whatever can you think of me. You must be absolutely boiling in those jerseys. Please hunt around in the bedroom for something cooler – there are some shirts in the bottom drawer of the chest if nothing else."

"Thank you," said Morag, "We were thinking of asking you but did not want to make any more washing than we could help."

Macquarie waved away the thoughtful gesture, "If it piles up I will take it across to the village, one of the old ladies there would be only too glad to do it for me."

The women reached the bedroom door when, after a hurried whisper, Fiona dashed back to the kitchen and returned a moment later with two towels.

Ten minutes later the ladies returned to the living room already appearing considerably cooler. The reason for the towels was immediately apparent, each of them had one secured about their hips in lieu of a skirt.

"The shirts were rather short," explained Morag.

The towels interested Macquarie less than the shirts. Although those selected were obviously his thickest, and with pockets, even these were hardly of dreadnought canvas. The girls had, however, tried to arrange folds decorously in the fronts of the much too large shirts although, he was pleased to note, none too successfully.

The women, slightly pink of cheek, walked towards the sofa but before they sat down Macquarie cried, "Just a minute, those towels must be still quite wet. There must be something more suitable in the house. Let me think, yes, of course! The old curtains from this window," he indicated the glazed aperture in the wall separating the new porch from the living room, "I took them down to get a bit more light as they were not necessary after I bought new curtains for the porch."

Macquarie opened a cupboard under the bookshelves by the chimney breast and hauled out a large cardboard box. From it he removed a pair of old boots, a jar of rusty nails and a small hammer, "I wondered where that had got to," he muttered. Finally he brought out a pair of small, faded and well-worn curtains of indeterminate colour and design.

"They have been washed," he hastened to say in case the women had any doubts in that direction. Both girls' looks said, 'But not ironed.'

"I wonder if they are large enough?" continued Macquarie with a glance at the women's waists as he stretched the tape at the top of one curtain to its full extent. A few brass hooks fell to the floor in the process.

"They will do fine," said both girls in unison as they reached for them.

There comes the odd time in every man's life when one decision can alter the whole pattern of his existence.

Macquarie decided that this was one of them. To carry on as things were or to risk the whole potentially delightful friendship by one clumsy, stupid move? He pretended to take a great interest in the length of the tape as he pondered....for a good three seconds. With nerves on edge he decided on one clumsy, stupid move.

Morag was nearest.

Ignoring the outstretched hands he crouched and whipped the

top of the curtain around Morag's waist. It overlapped by a good three inches.

No violent reaction, just a surprised squeak. He was winning.

A few deft movements of his strong fingers pushed a couple of hooks through the material and the 'skirt' was secure, although bunched up owing to the towel under it.

"The towel will have to go." It was Fiona's voice behind him.

"Of course," Morag's fingers felt through the cretonne and after some fumbling the towel fell at her feet.

"Why that is excellent," she cried, stepping away from Macquarie and smoothing the material over her hips. "Just a moment though," she patted the front of her waist, "You have left a couple of hooks in the tape."

Then she stepped back to him!

It did not take Macquarie long to remove the maverick hooks, well no more than two or three times as long as the job should have taken. He then turned to Fiona.

As Macquarie passed the 'skirt' around her waist Fiona blushed slightly but made no comment. It was Morag who spoke first.

"Your towel looks even more secure than mine."

"Sorry," Fiona reached inside the loosely held curtain and untwisted the well tucked in edge of the towel but held it in place until the curtain was right round her before she allowed it to fall to the floor.

"Thank you," said Fiona when Macquarie had completed securing the curtain, "That is much better, those towels were a trifle damp."

The makeshift skirts reached to below the knees of the young women but they immediately had trouble controlling the potential gap where the two edges of the material were supposed to overlap. Macquarie thought of his half dozen blanket pins but could not remember where he had put them with other odds and ends in a cigar box under the sink. However, a natural feminine ability to adapt to such problems of dress came to the ladies' aid and within a few minutes they could move about without the slightest hesitation yet gracefully and effectively keeping their legs decorously covered. Macquarie's pulse throbbed like a pom-pom gun.

The remainder of the evening was spent around the crackling fire.

During a lull in in the conversation Macquarie suddenly remembered to inquire after Fiona's blisters. She could not think how he knew of them as they had not been mentioned in his hearing and her feet had been covered all day by the thick woollen socks. The look of surprise caused Macquarie to wish he had bitten off his tongue. Belatedly he tried to include Morag in the query by saying that he assumed they had blisters on their feet after the route march of the previous day but the damage was done. Fiona blushed crimson.

For nearly a minute there was a deathly silence before Morag came to the rescue with a tactful, "I do think you should get something on them Fiona," in the most matter of fact tone imaginable.

"I have some plasters in the outhouse," blurted Macquarie, as if this was the obvious place to keep first aid equipment. Not waiting for any comment he jumped to his feet and stumbled out through the porch into the darkness of the night.

A moment later he was back again, crossed the room wishing he were invisible, picked up the torch from the mantelpiece and, for the second time, set out on his errand of mercy. Morag supressed a giggle and even Fiona smiled faintly.

In a few minutes Macquarie returned with a rather dusty plastic sandwich box. "Remembered I left it there last Christmas, just as well you mentioned the subject or I might have lost it altogether." 'How?' he thought, 'Why don't you just shut up Macquarie? You are rambling.'

When he had pried off the lid the ladies were pleased to observe that the contents looked clean enough in spite of the box's grubby exterior.

"It is very kind of you to go to all this trouble," said Fiona quietly, "The blisters are nothing much really, hardly worth bothering about."

"Any blister is worth bothering about," replied Macquarie with the voice of experience, "If they get infected you could be in serious trouble. Let me have a look at them."

Fiona would obviously have preferred to attend to the blisters herself in the privacy of the bed room but she realised that this would mean taking the lamp with her or Alistair having to go to the trouble of lighting the small lamp by the bed.

Therefore, with some reluctance, she removed one sock and, holding the hem of her makeshift skirt as far over her knees as it would go, presented her foot to Macquarie. Morag tactfully refrained from offering her assistance.

After turning the tiny foot one way and then another – frantic adjustments of the skirt – Macquarie decided that although one small blister could be left alone the other two should have plasters so there he gently applied.

"That blister below your big toe must be painful to walk on, we should have attended to it much earlier. Right, let's have a look at the other foot."

"That one is quite alright," replied Fiona but noting the raised eyebrow and small gesture of the man's fingers she hastily removed the second sock.

A thorough examination of the dainty foot verified that Fiona had been correct. "Under that big blister you need more padding than just an old sock," said Macquarie. "I wonder how we could manage that?" He thought for a moment, then, "I know the very thing!"

He dived back into the cupboard by the fireplace and once again hauled out the cardboard box. After feeling around in it for a moment or two he drew out a piece of old sheepskin.

"It is part of a rug I inherited with the cottage," Macquarie explained, "It was pretty dirty so I washed it. It wasn't much good as a rug after that so I've been using pieces of it for odd jobs ever since."

Half kneeling on the hearthrug Macquarie placed Fiona's left foot on his knee – she was just quick enough to prevent the edge of her skirt sliding from her thigh – and placing the piece of sheepskin against the sole of it drew the outline of her foot onto the skin with a stub of pencil taken from his pocket. Folding the skin in various ways around the girl's foot and making pencil marks as he went along Macquarie soon had the pattern he required.

Contemplating the faint marks on the sheepskin Macquarie reached behind him and put his hand on the lower bookshelf. His fingers moved several inches along the plank without encountering that for which they were searching. He looked round, somewhat perplexed.

"Have either of you seen a handyman's knife anywhere?" he asked.

"What is that?" queried Morag in reply.

"Well, a sort of metal handle with a small blade in one end of it," was the best description he could think of at the spur of the moment.

"Oh that! I put it in the table drawer," Morag jumped to her feet and went to retrieve the knife.

"But why?" then Macquarie remembered the tidying up that morning.

"Sorry," apologised Morag, "We thought it looked rather dangerous lying there."

"Never mind," smiled Macquarie, "I'll no doubt find all my bits and pieces again in good time."

After a few deft stokes of the knife a very oddly shaped piece of sheepskin lay on the rug. Picking up Fiona's foot again he fitted the piece of skin around it flap by flap and on removing it trimmed off a couple of corners which did not meet with his approval. He then laid the shaped piece on the skin side of the largest remaining off-cut, which the ladies noticed was just large enough to accommodate it, and pencilled the outline of the first piece onto the second. This was then cut out. Next Macquarie went to the kitchen and returned with a ball of twine and a needle three inches long. Triangular in section near the point of the needle tapered towards the eye where it was round. He explained to the girls that this was a sail-maker's needle.

Expecting very woolly slippers to emerge from his efforts the ladies were surprised when Macquarie commenced sewing the seams with the wool inside.

The two women sat throughout the construction apparently entranced by Macquarie's skilful workmanship, hardly saying a word. Which rather surprised the man as he had almost arrived at the conclusion that they were physically incapable of not chattering.

"Try that for size," said Macquarie handing the completed slipper towards Fiona. "Second thoughts though, I had best fit it myself to make sure it is right."

This time Fiona was quick enough to grab the hem of her skirt before Macquarie took hold of her ankle.

"It fits perfectly," exclaimed Fiona a moment later, "Absolutely perfectly." Not that a handful of woolly sheepskin could do much else.

Soon the second slipper was complete and Fiona stood up to try them out.

"They are wonderful! They are the most comfortable things I have ever had on my feet – just like walking on clouds. How can I thank you enough?" then, wistfully, "May I keep them?"

"Of course," laughed Macquarie, "who else would they fit anyway? They are nothing to look at but at least they will be comfortable than shoes whilst you have that blister." 'What am I talking about?' he said to himself, 'they will be walking away from here in boots tomorrow.'

"I think they are lovely," said Morag, the faintest trace of envy in her voice.

"May I try them Fiona – when you have finished cavorting around the room?"

Fiona stopped sliding her feet along the floor as if walking on skis and replied, "Certainly but do you not think our hard-working cobbler deserves a cup of tea first? I will put the kettle on."

Macquarie, pretending to an aching back, sank into his arm chair.

As Fiona returned from the kitchen with the partly filled kettle, full to the brim she would hardly have been able to lift the heavy iron contraption, Macquarie smiled and said, "Morag."

"Yes?" replied that young lady looking up from her self-appointed task of picking up the tiny scraps of sheepskin and wool from the hearthrug.

"Nothing really," was the response, "I was just thinking that it is a pity you have no blisters."

Morag was obviously puzzled. "Why do you wish I had blisters?"

"Well you seem to like Fiona's surgical boots and I just thought….."

"What?" the girl asked eagerly as his words trailed off.

"There <u>may</u> be enough pieces of sheepskin in the bottom of the box."

"Would you?" she cried, "Would you, please?"

Who could have refused?

*****

It was whilst they were washing the cups after a pre-bed hot drink that Macquarie happened to notice that the girls' original underclothes were still hanging with his on the string clothes line. 'If they had draped them on a couple of chairs in front of the fire this morning as I often do they could have been wearing them by now,' he mused.

Noticing his glance Fiona said, "It is a handy wee clothes line you have there Alistair."

To which he coolly replied, "Yes it is a good drying spot when the sun is on the roof – and it keeps the place tidy, I hate clothes hanging around in the living room."

He had the grace to wince when his conscience whispered in his ear, 'You bloody liar Macquarie!'

Macquarie was pleased to note that the sleeping bags and clothing rescued that morning were still in a wet heap on the porch floor. Having as yet no cooking appliances he generally referred to the lean-to as the porch but since he had ordered a bottled-gas cooker, due for delivery in a week or so, he found himself referring to it more and more as the kitchen. So far the only fitting in the extension was the sink with its solitary cold water tap. That and the flush toilet he had installed with a good deal of labour and considerable ingenuity at the opposite end of the porch to the front door were items in which he took considerable pride. The fact that the toilet door opened directly into the intended kitchen worried him but little, he was a long way from the abodes of officialdom. Of course 'front door' was rather a misnomer as the cottage did not boast of any other door leading outside.

With a final glance at the heap of wet clothing and a hope for a nice rainy day on the morrow Macquarie left the kitchen. He was thoroughly enjoying the girls' company and would be sorry to see them go.

His two guests tried to persuade Macquarie to let them sleep in the living room and he return to his bed but he would not hear of it.

"Time enough for that when your sleeping bags are dry," As soon as he had spoken those words he felt a sadness come over him, for when that occurred the girls would leave him to continue their holiday.

It so happened that there was one final chore to attend to before they all actually retired.

A few minutes after they left the ladies returned to the living room and asked Macquarie if he had a pair of pliers or something similar, explaining shyly that they could not bend the curtain hooks to release their skirts. If he had such a tool handy he did not mention it, his fingers being more than sufficient for the job in hand.

Pink of cheek and with their hands holding their skirts tightly about them the two young women fled back to the bedroom.

Chapter 6

The following day broke clear and cloudless.

Macquarie woke at his usual hour and crept soundlessly into the kitchen to perform his ablutions. The two young ladies had asked to be called 'early' as they had a great deal to do if they were to get away at a reasonable hour that afternoon. However, Macquarie mentally translated the 'early' to as late as he could manage without being too discourteous, wanting to delay their departure for as long as possible. He could not remember ever being so happy in anyone's company.

Having indulged in his routine 'bath' he commenced shaving. The water from the kettle was colder than usual which was an irritation. Another was that owing to the recent rush on towels the only dryish one he could find, apart from the one the girls had shared, was so small it became sopping wet after his bath and when wrapped round him was hardly adequate to cover his hips. The sun insolently shining into the porch had already set him off in a foul mood.

Noting the time, he switched on the transistor radio at his elbow and with the volume turned right down listened to the local weather forecast. South-westerly breezes with sunshine and just the possibility of an occasional shower in the morning. The prospect for the afternoon was even worse, light southerly airs with no cloud at all. The announcer's cheery 'Hope you have a nice day,' at the end of the programme was answered by Macquarie's uncharitable snarl, "And I hope you choke on your breakfast kipper!"

A mouse-like squeak behind him greeted this remark. Macquarie whirled round and was in time to catch a glimpse of a blue-clad figure disappearing into the bedroom.

Damnation! The girls were awake already, at least one of them was so no doubt the other also.

Having dressed Macquarie laid and lit the fire. It would be required for cooking breakfast if not for heating the room. Having completed this with no further sign of the girls, who were no doubt waiting for him to get out of the way so they could use the washing facilities, he put a half-filled kettle on the fire for morning tea – or washing water for the women – then wondered what to do next. Getting out of the house for a while seemed the tactful thing to do. Glancing around his eyes fell on the girls' boots by the fireplace, where, stuffed with newspapers, they had spent the night drying along with two pairs of sand shoes.

Macquarie picked up the boots and shouted at the bedroom door, "I am going out for half an hour. The kettle is on the fire."

Hearing a response from one of the girls he proceeded out into the morning sunlight, collecting the polishing gear and his own boots from the porch in transit.

Examining the small boots as he dubbined them Macquarie decided they were of the finest quality, proving the women had shown plenty of sense in that particular direction.

When the boots and shoes were cleaned to his satisfaction he continued to sit at the top of the short flight of stone steps leading down to the beach. At their foot was the beginning of the rough path of flat stones he had almost completed laying to the point just below the high water mark. His 'causeway' as he termed it. Contemplating the path, he for the hundredth time came to the conclusion he had built it the wrong way round. Starting from the house he had naturally used all the best and most readily available flat stones first. Now it was nearing completion at the seaward end he had to go further and further afield for suitable flat rocks.

Macquarie was building the path in order to have a flat surface on which to trundle his wheelbarrow when heavy items of stores and building materials were landed on the beach. In theory he should have made the path before he commenced the porch but it was not until the construction was well in hand that the advantage of a properly constructed track became apparent. In the event the 'causeway' only progressed when the actual porch building was held up for one reason or another.

However, it would still come in useful, for instance when the heavy stove arrived by MacNab's boat. There being no road but only sheep tracks down the peninsula there was no other means of transporting to the cottage heavy or bulky items. Generally, the wheelbarrow was worse than useless on the coarse sand and scattered rocks of the beach itself so all the stones for the new path had to be carried to it by hand.

The seaward end of the causeway received most of the wear and tear from tide and weather so should have had the heaviest stones but now those suitably flat and weighty were becoming few and far between. There was still several feet of the path to complete and he was rapidly running out of time. Walking down to the water's edge he contemplated the work still to be done and decided he must get cracking on it the moment the women had departed.

A call from the house brought Macquarie back to the present. Both girls were standing outside the porch waving, the light breeze fluttering their makeshift clothing.

Greetings were shouted as he made his way towards his guests. God! How good they looked! He was so pleased to see them that his foul mood instantly evaporated. But only temporarily.

"Breakfast is nearly ready," called Fiona as he closed with the girls.

When Macquarie arrived at the foot of the steps the women thanked him for polishing their footwear which lay on a rock in a gleaming row.

"There is no bacon left so we have made you an omelette, I hope that is alright?" said Morag.

Macquarie made a polite rejoinder but rather absentmindedly as he was much more interested in the effect the wind was having on the women's clothing. With their hands busy controlling the curtain skirts the breeze was allowed free play to flatten the material of the shirts to the contours of their bodies. Well almost. On entering the porch Macquarie was able to confirm his surmise, only his own small clothes hung from the string washing line. They looked so lonely and forlorn he almost felt sorry for them.

Macquarie's spirits were soon revived by the large omelette and heap of pan-fried potatoes prepared for him. For once the toast was an even golden brown and but half an inch thick – in contrast to his smoky, piebald slabs.

In spite of his protests the ladies breakfasted on two small slices of toast and marmalade apiece claiming they could not possibly eat more at that time of day.

The breakfast things out of the way the women commenced what Macquarie considered a monumental laundry session. Brushing aside his objections they soon had the kettle, seconded by a galvanised bucket, providing hot water for washing sheets, pillow cases, towels and all of their clothes. Why the latter was thought necessary Macquarie could not imagine as it had only been soaked in rain water.

His offer to help was refused by a sharp "Certainly not!", sweetened by a smile, from Fiona. The implication received was that washing was not a man's work.

"Well in that case I may as well carry on with the causeway," he said.

If Macquarie had in fact been as tall as he felt at that moment the lintel of the doorway would have caught him smack on the bridge of his nose.

However, the mood of exuberance soon passed as the women's original clothing was replaced on the outside clothes-line by more and more as the washing progressed. In fact, some of the more flimsy items were already being retrieved and taken into the house as Macquarie noted at one stage when he was along the beach collecting flat rock. The clothes-line was obscured by the house when he was working on the causeway itself.

Macquarie lifted, shifted and carried rocks in the rapidly rising temperature, sweating and cursing, particularly when the length of iron he was using as a crow-bar slipped or his hammer knocked a corner from a rock as he was tapping it into place. The sun burnt his neck and the reflected glare from the water hurt his eyes. He could not remember ever having endured such awful weather.

Hearing his name called he turned to see Morag stepping gingerly down the flat stones of the path. Seeing she had attracted his attention she shouted, "Where is the flat-iron you spoke of Alistair?"

"In the tool-box under the sink," he yelled back automatically. Then realised that if he had the brains of a half-witted moron he would have tossed the thing into the sea earlier that morning when he had the chance. This did nothing to improve his temper.

Macquarie tried to think of anything that might delay the departure of his charming guests. Even the weather was against him.

Damn it all! Why did today have to be bright and sunny? Having rained every day since Hogmanay, (a slight exaggeration), why on the one day he wanted it to be wet and miserable the sun had to shine like mid-summer in the Persian Gulf? Why could it not have rained for a week or two longer, trapping the girls in the cottage?

The causeway building did not go too well. Every stone he fitted, wedged with slivers of rock and jammed as tightly as he could to its neighbours proved rickety when he stood on it to test its firmness. The stones were not big enough, that was the main problem. There was one just the right size to fit a space he had remaining but it was bordering on the maximum he could carry – and it was nearly a hundred yards along the beach. But he would have to use it, no nearer stone would do. After weeks of working at odd times on the causeway Macquarie felt he was personally acquainted with every rock on the beach.

Lifting the heavy stone he commenced to carry it back to his work site in easy stages, planning ahead each boulder on which he would rest it before starting out from the last. He found that stretches of about ten yards were about as far as he could manage without a rest.

Looking about him at his second stop he noticed clouds over the sea to the southwest. Not many of them as yet but inasmuch as there had been nothing but blue sky there earlier indicated that they must be forming. 'Could do with a shower,' he said to himself, brightening a little. The feeling was immediately erased when he saw Fiona, after touching them to her cheek, commence removing the sheets and pillow cases from the clothes line and take them into the house for ironing.

Damn! Damn! Damn! Damn! Damn!

Macquarie had staggered a few more stages when the sun disappeared attracting his attention to the fact that the clouds had developed rapidly and were now approaching. Grey, rain-bearing clouds. They were balm to his soul.

'It's going to pee down', he said to himself in a very vulgar manner, grinning from ear to ear. 'I hope the girls are too busy to notice the rain coming.'

The clouds loomed high and the rain imminent when Macquarie suddenly wondered if the women were aware of the situation and were already snatching in the remaining washing. After all he had not been watching the door closely, being far too occupied with the navigation of the rock. Perhaps the clothes were already in the house being ironed? They would certainly all be dry by now.

Plagued by uncertainty Macquarie balanced the rock on the nearest boulder and, hoping the girls would not see him, dashed towards the house. Reaching the cover of the bank in front of the building he ran along the beach with his head well down until he reached a position from which he would have an uninterrupted view of the clothes line.

Slowly lifting his head Macquarie observed with absolute delight that apart from a few gaps where items had been removed the line was full – and the heavy rain shower only a few hundred yards away! He could have shouted with joy. Almost their entire stock of clothes would be soaked once again in just a few minutes which would force his lovely guests to stay for at least another day.

A moment later his dreams were shattered by a cry from inside the cottage and Morag's voice shouting to Fiona, "Fiona! Look out here, it is going to pour any minute!" And Fiona's, "Great heavens! Quick, the washing!"

Macquarie could have wept. He stormed back to the end of the causeway cursing under, and when the distance from the cottage allowed, over his breath. He would be damned before he would go to help the women in their dire emergency.

Having reached the water's edge he remembered he was not working there but was in the throes of transporting the large stone so had to retrace most of his steps to where he had left it.

Having carried the stone another twenty or thirty feet he rested it on a boulder in order to catch his breath. The burden seemed heavier than ever and he was sorely tempted to leave it where it was and search for something lighter. The sweat poured from him. Why the hell did it not start raining and cool things off a bit? The grey clouds seemed to hover over the house but still the rain held off.

Macquarie shifted the stone another stage then contemplated the next and final one. With no convenient boulder on which to rest it between his present position and the end of the causeway this last stage was going to be the stiffest by far. It was twice the distance of any so far attempted and some of them had tested his strength to the utmost. He well knew that if he had to drop it on the sand it would be risking his back to try to lift it up again. Sucking in great draughts of the humid air he prepared himself for the final effort.

Whilst resting Macquarie tried to estimate how the ironing in the cottage was progressing. The women would have had the washing in ten, no fifteen minutes ago. Say half an hour for the actual ironing, allowing for the heating of the iron on the fire. Forty-five minutes at the outside so they would be finished in half an hour. He looked at his watch, just gone one o'clock, (whatever happened to the mid-day break?), they would complete the ironing by one-thirty at the latest. Half an hour to change and prepare for the road and they could be away by two o'clock. As they would not really need to leave the cottage until three at the earliest in order to catch the six o'clock bus from the village they had all the time in the world. At least they had asked him the times the bus ran so he assumed they would be using that mode of transport for the next stage of their holiday. He wondered if he should ask them about their future plans but, not for the first time, was undecided as to the dividing line between friendly interest and offensive curiosity. In any case he did not really care what their future plans were. He just wanted them to stay.

'Well I can't stay here brooding'. He looked over his shoulder. The clouds were blacker than ever and seemingly towering right above the house. Still it did not rain.

Heaving the heavy rock up to the level of his waist Macquarie staggered off on the last stage of his journey.

Then it rained.

It more than rained, it poured. A deluge that gave Macquarie the impression that the cloud was actually a huge canvas bucket upturned over his head. It would not have surprised him if the ground a hundred yards away was still quite dry. It seemed that the entire contents of the cloud were directed at him and at him alone. Within seconds he was soaked to the skin.

Macquarie's immediate reaction was to drop the rock and dash for cover but second thoughts decided him that this was pointless as he was already as wet as he could get and in any case he did not want to have to lift the rock from the sand later. No, he would take the damn thing to the end of the causeway if it killed him.

The sheer density of the downpour reduced the visibility to a few yards but Macquarie was unable to see even this far for with rivulets of rain running into his eyes he could look nowhere but just ahead of his stumbling, slithering feet.

Hoping he was heading in the right direction he staggered on, his breath rasping from his lungs.

It soon seemed that it was such a long time since he started on this leg that he must have missed the causeway and now struggling senselessly along the beach away from it. However, a moment's reflection convinced him that this was not possible as he would have to arrive at the distinctive stonework of the track or sea, just provided he could keep his feet moving.

When he thought he could not stagger another two steps he arrived at the causeway. Six feet from the end but definitely the causeway. This heartened him and gave him just enough strength to make the last few steps and hold the stone over the space reserved for it. Lowering the heavy rock to within nine inches of the ground he dropped it into place. The relief was enormous.

But only momentary.

On coming in contact with the sand the great stone split almost exactly down its centre.

So far as is known no-one from the village a mere two miles across the loch ever complained about Macquarie's language on that occasion. A worthy tribute to their forbearance.

For some time, he had no idea how long, Macquarie sat in the pouring rain on the causeway, his head in his hands. He could never have imagined so many things could go wrong in one day. The warm sun drying the clothes as if sent to order, the rain just when he least needed it and the broken rock, that fiendish joke at the end of all his efforts. But most of all the girls, his girls, leaving him. Yes, that was the hardest cut of all.

Perhaps he could persuade them to stay until tomorrow? Argue that it was too late in the day and that an early start in the morning would be a much more sensible idea. But would that be fair? They said they would be leaving that day and he had no claim on their time. If he did manage to get them to delay their departure it would only be to oblige him, a charitable act to mollify him. No! He could not endure that. The die was cast and he would have to put up with the situation.

Physically and emotionally drained Macquarie felt he could not face the women in his present condition. Climbing to his feet he set off up the beach in the rain. Although beginning to ease off a little the downpour was still sufficient to almost obscure the house.

He walked up the edge of the loch deep in thought. 'What a moody bastard you are! Getting all worked up just because a couple of attractive young women cross your path! You know damn well it's not the broken rock of the rain, it's those girls. You have had a couple of very happy days with them, why not let it go at that? Why spoil it for them? Even now they will be wondering what has happened to you – worrying even. Worrying about me? Good God, perhaps they were!'

Macquarie turned and began to retrace his steps and as he did so the rain ceased. Minutes later the sun came out and the rocks he passed were soon steaming as they dried rapidly. He felt the sun's warmth on his hands and face and only then realised how cold he had been. His wet clothes stuck to his body in increasing discomfort. Feeling a shiver down his back he said to himself, 'That is all I need, to catch a cold!'

Macquarie looked at his watch and was shocked to find that it was nearly two-thirty. The girls would no doubt be packed and dressed for the road by now and he, the host, was strolling along the beach like a half-wit. He increased his pace to a run.

On approaching the house Macquarie slowed to a more dignified walk, mainly in order to get back his breath.

The front door was open and Macquarie was in the porch before the women were aware of his return. There were shouts and both girls appeared from the living room.

"Alistair! Wherever have you been?" cried Morag.

"You are absolutely soaked!" added Fiona. Concern in the eyes and voices of each.

"Just went for a walk up the loch to…er….to let you get your packing done in peace." It sounded idiotic which was understandable as his mind was not on what he was saying. Immediately he had set eyes on the girls he realised that things were not as he had expected. Far from being ready for the road the young women were still dressed in his shirts and the curtain skirts.

'What the hell goes on now?' he thought, then, cleaning it up a little for general consumption, asked, "I thought you would be ready to leave. What has happened?"

"Never mind that for the present, you must get those wet clothes off immediately," said Fiona with considerable authority.

"And have a hot bath. The kettle is hot but I will get the bucket on the fire too, you will need lots of hot water," added Morag, equally adamant.

Pleasant as I was to be fussed by the girls, who were obviously sincere in their concern for him, Macquarie wanted to know why, after expecting them to be booted and spurred, they were not ready to move although time was passing. Was there some hope that a hitch had occurred and they would have to stay until tomorrow? In spite of the girls' protests he refused to do anything until they had explained.

Seeing that he was quite determined the girls said they had a little confession to make.

Standing side by side the two women resembled, in Macquarie's opinion at least, two naughty schoolgirls detected at some mischief. They were not exactly blushing and standing on their own toes but both had a look he had not seen before. Apprehension, was that the word he was looking for? Were they worried as to his reaction when they had told him what they had done? But what was it? There was nothing valuable in the house that they could damage and anyway that would not explain the curtain skirts.

It was Morag who spoke first, quietly, shyly even, "I'm afraid you will think we are awfully silly…."

"Absolutely stupid," added Fiona when Morag lapsed into silence.

"For goodness sake tell me what you have done, it probably does not matter anyway," Macquarie felt inclined to add that it was only an old one and he had intended to dump it in any case just to break the silence – but as yet he did not know the cause of the mystery.

"Oh, we haven't broken something or anything like that," said Morag quickly, "it is that we were so busy ironing and talking that…." she trailed off again into silence.

Fiona continued for her, "…we did not notice the rain coming until it was too late and everything on the line got soaked again."

Macquarie pushed past the women, swung through the old front doorway into the living room and through the back window saw, flapping damply in the light breeze, the clothes he had observed there earlier in the day. He was astounded.

Turning to face the two women who had followed him into the room he blurted, "But I......"

Suddenly realisation burst upon him like a thunder clap. Fortunately his heart, shooting up from his boots, missed its billet and very nearly choked him thus preventing his making any mention of the fact that he knew they had seen the approaching rain in sufficient time to have saved the washing.

They did not want to leave.

They did NOT want to leave!

THEY DID NOT WANT TO LEAVE!!

Macquarie felt as if he were shouting it from the roof-tops, from the peaks of mountains.

In actual fact he was merely flapping his arms and opening and shutting his mouth in a fair imitation of an expiring penguin, completely inarticulate in his relief and joy.

Macquarie could have hugged them. It was rather a pity he missed the opportunity as the two attractive, vital young women were ripe for hugging at that moment. However, he could hardly have been expected to have known this.

"But that is wonderful!" he eventually managed to say, making no attempt to mask his pleasure, "that means you cannot go today."

The ladies' expressions, bordering on alarm before he managed to speak, changed to smiles.

"Yes, I'm afraid you are lumbered with us until tomorrow," said Morag, "If we may stay of course?"

Macquarie's ecstatic reply left no room for doubt in that direction.

"Well now that is settled" said Fiona, "off with those wet clothes," she pointed to the bedroom door, "Morag and I will get the hot water."

Macquarie raised a delaying hand. "Just one more thing. Will you please take pity on me and stay, not just until tomorrow but for as long as you can?"

The ladies exchanged glances.

"I am afraid that would not be possible.", answered Fiona, her tone implying that such a thing would be very improper.

"Anyway there is not enough food for all of us, we are eating you out of house and home as it is," added Morag.

"And we both have to be back at work soon," continued Fiona. No mention of any specific date Macquarie noted so her first reaction was to keep the provisional date of their departure elastic, a very good sign. Nothing was said of any fixed plans for the remainder of their holiday either seemingly to indicate that they could stay as long as they so desired. It was therefore up to him to play the attentive host and delay their departure for as long as possible.

"Let us discuss this after you have had your bath," said Fiona, "If you leave those wet things on any longer you will catch pneumonia."

Macquarie could only agree. He did feel cold and shivery and in any case pressing his argument at this stage would probably do more harm than good. The time he took over his bath would no doubt be utilised by the girls in discussing the pros and cons of the situation and he could only hope that they would decide to stay at the cottage for a few more days.

Having the women organise his bath made Macquarie feel like an Eastern prince. He stripped off in the bedroom amongst various feminine fripperies and donned his old dressing gown. He would have felt more comfortable with a towel around his waist also but supplies of dry ones had not yet reached the bed-room.

Returning to the kitchen with his wet clothes he found the women had the bath-tub in the centre of the floor and soap and towel to hand. They were about to attempt to bring the kettle and bucket of hot water from the fire but fortunately Macquarie was in time to do this himself as both utensils were dangerously heavy for the limited strength of the girls.

With the ladies discreetly closeted in the bedroom Macquarie thoroughly enjoyed his hot bath. As the tub was far too small for him to sit in his ablutions were performed partly standing in and partly kneeling beside it.

Bathed and dried, Macquarie was pleased to observe that the towels were beginning to return into circulation, he emptied the tub down the toilet bowl and then realised he had neglected to bring any clean clothes with him. This meant turning the girls out of the bedroom and dressing there. Having done this, he returned to the living room to become immediately embarrassed by sounds from the kitchen. He dashed there to find Morag on her knees swabbing the floor with an old singlet he used as a floor-cloth, (the establishment did not extend to a mop), and Fiona just completing wiping out the tub.

"Hey! You should not be doing that! I was going to mop up after I'd dressed."

"Don't be silly, there were only a few splashes on the floor." The amount of water in the bucket into which Morag was wringing the floor cloth belied her statement.

"Anyway we need the floor dry in order to commence supper," said Fiona.

"What do you think we should have?" asked Morag as she wrung out the cloth for the last time and stood up.

Macquarie snatched the bucket from the floor, opened the toilet door and poured the contents down the bowl.

"Fish", he said as he reappeared.

The looks of puzzlement on the town-bred women's faces Macquarie assumed to indicate that they were wondering if there was a fish shop in the locality or if he had a deep-freeze hidden away somewhere.

Macquarie smiled, "Yes, come along, we are going fishing."

"What a wonderful idea," Morag clasped her hands together in front of her.

"Just a moment then whilst we get changed." Fiona turned towards the door of the bedroom.

"Why?" inquired Macquarie, "we will only be away half an hour or so." He had forgotten that the clothing the women had been wearing when they first arrived would be dry by now.

Two pairs of horrified eyes gazed at him.

"We can't possibly go out of the house like this," said Fiona glancing down at the shirt, draped in folds over her shoulders, and the curtain skirt. The latter he noticed for the first time was now smoothly ironed.

"Someone might see us." Morag was equally shocked.

"There is nobody likely to be on the shore, particularly after all that rain. I see only a dozen or so people here in the course of a year. Anyway you would be far too hot in trousers and jerseys."

Somewhat reluctantly the ladies agreed to go fishing dressed as they were but not without Morag saying for the two of them, "If anyone sees us we will never forgive you." She was not smiling.

"Don't worry," replied Macquarie, "If anyone does by chance happen to be there you can be back in the house in a few minutes," adding as an afterthought, "whilst I am poking their eyes out with my sea rod. I won't have other men ogling my women."

The ridiculous remark took the seriousness out of the air and soon the three of them were of their way to a shelf of rock running at an angle out to sea on the opposite side of the mull to the cottage.

Macquarie led the way by the shortest route, straight across the peninsula. It was an easy enough path, only at the seaward end was there a little scrambling to be done down to the shore.

An alternative route, round by the beach, was about half as long again and reasonably flat all the way. This was the route usually taken by Macquarie as it allowed him to check if any driftwood fuel had had been 'delivered' since he was last that way. It only took ten minutes or so longer then the direct path.

The only real disadvantage of the shore route was that it had no difficulties in the way of awkward rocks where the ladies would be certain to require his assistance. Macquarie knew what he was doing.

During the walk they discussed the possibilities of the ladies staying at the cottage a little longer. Both girls raised objections of various kinds which Macquarie demolished as best he could. Eventually it was decided that the guests would stay for another two, or at most three days and Macquarie had to be content with that.

One of the objections again raised was the question of the food supply which Macquarie had countered with the promise of going shopping the very next day if the women would make out a list of requirements.

The peninsula was a favourite haunt of numerous varieties of seabird, many of which Macquarie was able to identify to the two women. They showed considerable interest and were obviously thoroughly enjoying the outing, although continuing to keep a very sharp lookout for other people.

The clamber down the rocks to the beach was accomplished safely although causing considerable difficulties with skirts as one hand at least was usually required for balance. Macquarie was most attentive with his assistance however so when equilibrium was momentarily lost or sandshoe slipped he was always at hand to prevent a fall.

Twenty minutes fishing from the ledge resulted in a batch of three mackerel and a fair-sized Pollack.

"That's enough," said Macquarie as he unhooked the last fish, "they won't keep in this warm weather."

The women had been gazing apprehensively at the rocky cliff as Macquarie packed up his fishing gear. They obviously did not relish the ascent with him behind them. To spare their blushes he suggested that they returned to the cottage by way of the beach.

"It is considerably longer but will be easier with all this stuff to carry," indicating his rod, tackle box and bucket of fish.

The walk home was made in the highest of spirits. If it could be termed a walk. Macquarie proceeded at his normal pace but the women were forever on the move in one direction or another, frequently dashing off to examine some interesting looking object stranded on the beach or a small cave in the cliff, for all the world like a couple of schoolgirls on a day's outing at the seaside. At other times they would try to remember places associated with their original walk along the beach in very different circumstances. However, everything looked so different in the bright sunlight and they identified nothing.

Often they would return to Macquarie's side and bombard him with questions on tides and seabirds, fish and rocks as if he would know the answers to anything they cared to ask. Fortunately, he did know the answers to most of their queries which were generally fairly simple. In fact, so easy were some of them that at one time he formed a sneaking suspicion that the women were, to some extent at least, trying to boost his male ego. But why would they want to do that?

After a short questioning session something on the beach would attract the girls' attention and off they would go chattering and laughing. To Macquarie it was the sweetest sound in the world.

On returning to the cottage Macquarie deftly cleaned and filleted the fish whilst the women got in the now bone dry washing. He was pleased to note that on the sink draining board was a pan containing potatoes which had somehow got themselves peeled earlier in the day.

With dinner beginning to cook on the fire the ladies, having first obtained Macquarie's promise not to peep, got washed in the kitchen. To ensure some degree of privacy he hung an old, once wine-coloured table-cloth over the window between the living room and kitchen. The women suggested using the curtains themselves but he would not hear of it, they were currently serving a much more useful purpose.

The splashing of water and the girls passing through the living room in flapping shirts did nothing to help the concentration of the self-appointed cook.

Eventually the women settled in the bedroom. Morag's parting words of, "We will only be five minutes", brought the response from Macquarie, "If so it will be an all-time ladies record!"

In the event it was not more than twenty minutes before Macquarie heard the bedroom door open quietly behind him and felt rather than saw the women enter the living room as he was busy prodding potatoes at the time.

"Dinner is about ready although I am afraid the cooking is not up to the usual standard," he said as the potato he was poking with a fork crumbled in the boiling water.

His remark brought no response so thinking he had made a mistake in believing the girls to be in the room he replaced the lid of the pan and turned to check.

To say that Macquarie was surprised would be to put it very mildly indeed. Morag and Fiona not lonely had their hair groomed to perfection but were actually wearing dresses! Fiona's was a pale green affair and Morag's white with blue flowers.

The astonished man stood rooted to the sport at a complete loss for words. These girls would never cease to amaze him. How did dresses suddenly materialise? Some slight recollection of articles of similar colours on the clothes line earlier that day came to him vaguely.

Someone had to break the silence.

"I hope you like them," said Morag, "I am afraid they are the only dresses we have with us."

Macquarie's gaze of unstinted admiration gave her her answer. Still at a loss for words he pointed a finger at the floor and moved it in a circle. Obeying the signal, the ladies slowly pirouetted so they could be viewed from all angles. A perfectionist might have claimed that high-heeled shoes would have complimented the dressed but to Macquarie bare feet were fine.

Facing him again Morag queried, "Do we pass muster?"

"One hundred percent," replied Macquarie having found his tongue.

"Ninety-five percent," said Fiona.

Morag and Macquarie looked at her.

"Whatever do you mean?" asked the bewildered man.

"Ninety-five percent only," Fiona pointed to her chest, "You do not approve of the foundation garments." She could read him like a book.

The frankness of the remark took Macquarie's breath away. 'How in Hell's name did you answer a statement like that?' Completely flustered he said "Yes" and "No" with equal emphasis and then, more by accident that inspiration, "Well I suppose _some_ women need them."

At the implied compliment and smiling at his discomfiture the extraordinary woman further amazed Macquarie by dropping him a mock curtsey and saying, "Your wish is our command, Oh Master," then taking her astonished friend by the hand with a "Come Morag," retired to the bedroom.

They returned two minutes later. Macquarie stood exactly where the ladies had left him although by that time he had managed to get his mouth closed.

He got it right this time. Stepping forward with outstretched arms he clasped the two soft, unresisting bodies to him and showered kisses on the upturned, laughing faces.

So far as Macquarie at least was concerned this situation could have continued indefinitely but, after about a minute, it was interrupted by a pan starting to boil over.

The women broke away, each receiving a pat on the rump in the process, and dashed to the rescue of the potatoes. Reaching the fire place together they were both instantly drawn back by a large hand around either waist and Macquarie removed the pan from the flames. The ladies were obviously glad enough to be clear of the smoke, hot pan and spitting fire.

＊＊＊＊＊＊＊＊＊＊＊

The three of them spent the evening by the hearth talking of trivialities. Both women had seated themselves on the sofa at first but as time wore on transferred to the hearth-rug, or at least to the old dressing gown which Macquarie had insisted was used to cover the rug. "We can always wash it", one of them had said.

They seem to have a mania for washing things Macquarie decided.

There was a long discussion on sleeping arrangements. The ladies tried to persuade Macquarie that now their sleeping bags were dry they would sleep in the living room and he return to the comfort of his bed but the host would have none of it. Realising that argument was useless the women compromised by making the sofa considerably more comfortable by utilising the sleeping bags but, of course, could do nothing to remedy its shortness.

In spite of the earlier exuberance Macquarie did not touch the women, except occasionally to help make them more comfortable or to assist one or the other to their feet. With these small attentions his guests appeared to be quite content.

One subject discussed was the proposed shopping expedition the following day. Macquarie supplied a sheet of paper and a pencil and the two women composed a list, edited occasionally by the man when he thought the village shop did not stock one or two of the suggested items.

"Well," said Fiona as she checked through the list, "that seems to be all we can think of at the moment. If there is anything else we can add it in the morning."

"Do you think you can carry all that?" asked Morag, "There is rather a lot."

Macquarie had decided to walk both ways as he did not want MacNab and his boat anywhere near the cottage even if they were available. Looking through the list he decided that although the various tin-stuffs and jars would be heavy there was nothing too bulky to make up more than his ruck-sack could hold.

"No problem," was his verdict.

"Time for bed then," said Morag as she rose to her feet, (assisted by the attentive host), she picked up two empty coffee mugs by their handles, (they look like quart pots in her tiny hand thought Macquarie), and whilst waiting for Fiona to pass hers rested her free hand on one of the book shelves. Quickly removing it she studied her fingers by the light of the lamp. Her nose wrinkled slightly in disgust.

"Alistair, who do you get to clean this house?"

"Good grief, no one would come out here to clean a house," he replied. Then added modestly, "I do it myself."

"How often?" Fiona joined the conversation.

"Every week," replied Macquarie. Honesty caused him to add, "If I am not too busy."

"When was it last Spring-cleaned?" From Morag.

"Spring-cleaned?"

"Yes, Spring-cleaned, you know, everything out and scrubbed from top to bottom."

"Good heavens it doesn't need that, there is only me living here and then only for a few months in the year."

The two women exchanged glances.

"Tomorrow Alistair, whilst you are out shopping, this house is going to be cleaned." Morag's tone brooked no argument.

"So if you have any girl-friends' photographs or magazines you would not like us to see you had better hide them in the outhouse or somewhere," added Fiona with a smile.

In spite of Macquarie's protests the women were adamant and, as he would not be at the cottage to prevent them carrying out their plans he had to leave it at that.

Whilst the ladies were rinsing out the cups Macquarie, as he had previously mentioned to them, took the opportunity of retrieving the mirror from the bedroom. It was the only one he possessed and he would need it first thing in the morning.

On taking the mirror from the top of the chest of drawers he glanced around the room. Already it had taken on an aura of femininity. A pile of underwear on the bedside table, pretty flimsy stuff for hikers he thought, a regiment of small plastic bottles and jars of cosmetics on the chest of drawers and a neat heap of outer clothing on the floor beside the two rucksacks – he remembered the latter well!

Macquarie was amazed at the amount of stuff the women carried with them. That which had been evolved by experts over the years as essential equipment for hikers and campers apparently did not apply to the girls. Toilet articles, cosmetics and clothes seemed to constitute the main part of their gear although the sleeping bags, albeit of the smallest size, were one bulky and normal item. He smiled as he looked around. The room had certainly changed its character since he last saw it the morning after the girls' arrival.

But something jarred. At the foot of the bed were, neatly folded, two sets of what were obviously pyjamas. Frilly, feminine pyjamas but pyjamas for all that. Somehow they were in discord with his vivid picture of the two small pink bodies curled up in the middle of the bed as he covered them on the night they arrived at the cottage. Without really thinking he scooped up the offending garments and stuffed them into one of the rucksacks. With the mirror in his hand he left the room.

Macquarie never knew if either of the girls ever wore the pyjamas at all during the remainder of their stay but of one thing he was certain, he never saw them again.

Sleep came to him that night living again those first sweet goodnight kisses.

****

There was a change in the weather during the night and the following day dawned grey and breezy.

The weather report on the radio promised Macquarie a cool day with the chance of some showers. 'Always a chance of showers in this part of the world', he said to himself. However, a cool day was preferable to a hot one for the walk he had in mind. A hot, humid day carrying a heavy rucksack would be purgatory.

The fire lit for breakfast and a shout at the bedroom door to announce his going out for half an hour and Macquarie headed for the beach and his causeway. There he shifted a few stones around but did little to further the actual paving before he heard the girls calling him to breakfast from the kitchen window.

On reaching the house he found the girls neatly dressed in their own shirts, or whatever they were called, and tight fitting jeans. The hair of each of them was caught up in a tight bun at the back of the head.

"Our working gear," explained Morag as he kissed her, (she being nearest). Having kissed Fiona, who shyly muttered something about not having any skirts – to fill in the brief seconds between his reaching for her and the actual kiss – Macquarie said, "surely you are not going to work in those nice clean clothes? You have only just washed and ironed them. If you do insist on cleaning the place why not wear the 'house uniform', no one will come."

Morag looked at Fiona saying, "I don't think this man approves of ladies in trousers. However, I think it would be a good idea."

To Macquarie Fiona said, "Never mind Alistair, by the time you return we will be back in our dresses."

"How long do you expect to be away?" asked Morag.

"Oh it takes about five hours normally, often longer if I am delayed by anything. Generally, I leave here about ten and get back sometime after three o'clock in the afternoon."

"I doubt if we will get the whole place cleaned in that time," said Fiona, "we may have to carry on tomorrow."

"Not on your life!" cried Macquarie, "You are not going to spend your entire stay here cleaning the house. You are only doing so today because I am not going to be here to prevent you."

"Do not let us have an argument," joined in Morag, "we will see how we get on today. Come along or the breakfast will get cold."

The meal was eaten at the table. If Macquarie had any reservations about the women's leg-wear he could certainly find no reason for complaint from their waists up. The shirts were rather tight-fitting and apparently the criticism of which he had been accused the previous evening had been taken to heart. In fact, he saw nothing more of the unnecessarily misleading articles of underwear until the day the girls left.

It started to rain as they were eating but as Macquarie had all day for the shopping and there was no point in getting soaked the trip was postponed until the weather improved.

The rain continued unabated all the forenoon but shortly after mid-day it eased off and the sky began to brighten.

Denied the house by the women who entreated him not to come further than the porch Macquarie carried on with some oft postponed woodwork in the outhouse.

Shortly after noon he called out to the young women that he was about to set off on his tramp to the village. He had donned a light nylon jacket and shouldered his empty rucksack when the two somewhat dishevelled ladies appeared to bid him farewell. The kisses on parting had him walking on air.

Normally Macquarie walked to the village by what he termed the 'outside route' – across the peninsula to the ocean shore and up the coast to a point opposite to the head of the loch, around it and then down to the village. The reason for this was pure beachcomber instinct, he could check on the various pieces of timber washed ashore and it there was anything worth having, as was often the case, collect it later. This route increased the distance considerably but as he was then unladen this was no hardship. Returning burdened with shopping and possibly a little foot-sore was a different matter altogether, then he invariably took the shortest route around the shore of the loch.

Striding along thinking of the girls with both his feet and his head in the clouds he only vaguely realised that the rain had ceased completely and that the sun was beginning to indicate its presence through the remaining overcast.

He smiled in recollection of Morag's worried "Are you quite certain all that shopping will not be too heavy? Leave some of it if you think so." And Fiona's motherly "Are you sure you will be warm enough?" feeling only a shirt beneath the thin nylon of his jacket as they kissed goodbye.

'What wonderful young women they are,' he mused, 'so dainty, so feminine, so warm and cheerful, so.....'

Macquarie catalogued their virtues to such lengths that if the ladies concerned had heard half of them they would have blushed with embarrassment.

The happy man was well on his way before he realised his feet were taking him in the wrong direction. He was half way up the shore of the loch instead of on the beach at the other side of the mull. The discovery did nothing to dampen his spirits.

"Feet," he exclaimed looking down, "you are taking me the wrong way!"

Undismayed by the fact the offending feet continued in their chosen direction.

"Hey feet! We are supposed to be on the other side of the mull." Receiving no response Macquarie continued. "Your trouble is that you are so busy thinking of dainty little feminine feet you can't keep your minds on your job."

Deciding that argument was useless Macquarie continued to follow the direction his mutinous feet dictated. In any case he wanted to get back to his girls as soon as possible.

****

Arriving at the village shop-cum-post office Macquarie produced the list and soon a pile of groceries was accumulating on the counter.

The change from Macquarie's routine purchases of staples soon became apparent prompting the old widow who owned the shop to say, "You seem to be taking an awful lot of fancy things this time Mr. Macquarie."

Macquarie, prepared for such a question, replied, "Yes, I am thinking of improving my diet when the new cooker arrives."

The mention of the cooker apparently brought the subject of transport to the old lady's mind.

"I'm afraid you will have to leave your shopping here until tomorrow, MacNab is away in his boat today."

This news came to Macquarie as rather a shock. Not that he wanted to use the boat but for quite another reason.

"Where has he gone?" he asked quite sharply.

"That I don't know," was the reply, "He has taken a couple of English visitors fishing I believe."

Fishing! They could be anywhere. They could be out by the mull even now, they might decide to land there or even visit the house.

Observing the old lady's gaze he quickly collected his thoughts and said that it did not matter, he would carry the groceries back to the cottage.

"You will not be carrying all that weight right round the loch?" she exclaimed in surprise.

"Why not?" Macquarie tried to think of a good reason for not wanting to leave the provisions for MacNab to bring across the following day, he obviously did not intend devouring the lot that evening.

"The exercise will do me good, I have all the time in the world so will no doubt take a breather or two on the way back." It sounded pretty weak but it was the best he could think up on the spur of the moment. The main thing was it seemed to satisfy the widow.

The old lady was inclined to chat and Macquarie usually indulged her but on this occasion he could not pay his bill and stow the provisions in his rucksack quickly enough. Fortunately, another customer arrived to take the shop-keeper's attention so he was able to make a hurried goodbye and set off for home at a cracking pace.

Fear for the safety of Morag and Fiona lent wings to his heels as he strode along the shore of the loch.

Safety! What the hell was he thinking of? They were safe enough. Even if the worst happened and MacNab had taken the two Englishmen to the cottage the chances were that they were not homicidal maniacs or rapists. He tried to laugh at his fears but was not altogether successful. Anyway, he tried to console himself, there was not the slightest evidence to suggest that the boat had even headed that way.

Having eased his mind to a certain extent he found time to think of something else. The rucksack was very, very heavy. He slowed his ridiculous pace to a more comfortable walk.

Half way down the home stretch on the peninsula shore of the loch he was again assailed by fears. He should never have left them alone and unprotected, anything could happen, one reads of the most horrifying things in the newspapers every day. He worked himself into such a state that he almost dumped the rucksack on the sand in order to run the remainder of the way to the cottage. A few minutes later he was glad he had not done so as, to his great relief, the unmistakable patched sail of MacNab's boat appeared round a headland of the mainland shore.

Approaching the cottage, he found it ominously quiet.

'What the hell did you expect it to be you damn fool? It's a house not a dance hall!'

For all that he would certainly be relieved to arrive and confirm that all was well.

Coming to the door Macquarie was about to stride in and announce his arrival when he noticed just inside the door on the gleaming tiles of the floor his 'indoor' sandals. Grinning he took the hint.

With a sigh of relief he shrugged off the rucksack and dumped it on the ground. Divesting himself of jacket, boots and heavy socks he slid his feet into the welcoming cool leather of the sandals. Hearing sounds of movement in the living room Macquarie felt a surge of relief. All was well.

However, expecting a warm welcome he instead received a violent shock.

Macquarie's cheerful, "I'm home!" was greeted first with complete silence then, as he stepped towards the entrance to the living room, with the most ungodly screams and shrieks he had ever heard in his life. His heart pounding he leaped into the room, a primeval instinct preparing him to fight for his females – if necessary to kill!

He halted in the centre of the room utterly dumbfounded. The screams had died away to be replaced by deathly silence. The old zinc bath emitting a thin cloud of vapour in the middle of the hearthrug seemed to him a witches' cauldron – with all its black magic implications – accentuated by the fact that there was not a soul to be seen.

Macquarie's hair seemed to stand on end.

The sound of a slight movement behind the armchair attracted his attention. Knowing not what to expect he took a step forward to investigate and pulled the chair away from what appeared to be a bundle of dirty old clothes.

"Don't look at me!" shrieked the bundle of dirty old clothes.

Macquarie staggered back and in doing so felt rather than heard a movement behind him. He turned in time to see an almost identical bundle scuttling from behind the sofa towards the kitchen doorway.

Realisation dawning on him he quickly pulled himself together and headed the bundle off from the door causing it to go into rapid reverse back to cover behind the sofa.

"Go away!" shouted the second bundle as it rolled itself into a ball, "Don't look! Go away!" It could possibly be Morag's voice.

A glance over his shoulder and Macquarie observed bundle number one had achieved animation and was heading silently towards the bedroom. He fielded it neatly causing it to scuttle back behind the armchair.

Grabbing one of the wooden chairs from under the table he

swung it round and sat on it heavily, feeling his legs would sustain him no longer.

"You girls will be the death of me," gasped Macquarie to the chair and sofa.

"You said you would not be back for another hour at least!" Fiona's voice, accusingly and with a slight sob in it from behind the armchair.

"We were just about to get cleaned up," said the sofa, "you are not due back for ages yet. Go away."

"Yes, walk right out of here and don't come back for at least an hour," said the armchair, the voice steadier now.

Then in unison as Macquarie shifted his feet, a shrieked, "Don't look at me!"

Now any gentlemen worthy of the name would have conceded to the ladies' request and taken himself off for a long walk.

Macquarie considered himself a gentleman most of the time but there were limits and the primeval urges recently engendered in him had not yet subsided.

After a few moments planning he leapt to his feet, pushed the armchair out of his way and grabbed the bundle containing Fiona, as being the nearest to the sanctuary of the bedroom, before it could move. Swinging the girl through the air he deposited her in a sitting position on the sofa.

Bundle Morag made a dash for it but in two strides she was overtaken and despite kicks and squeals, in contrast to Fiona's silent capture, placed next to her friend.

The two young women sat in shocked silence, grubby knee to grubby knee above a line of dainty, dirty feet, each duster-covered head held in a pair of very grimy hands.

Before the surprised women could collect their senses Macquarie asked, "Right, who is to be first?"

Either completely bewildered or beginning to guess his wicked intentions Fiona said, "Morag..!"

"Morag first, fine," said Macquarie, cutting off whatever Fiona was going to say next.

Before the girl could give vent to more than frightened squeak he picked her up and, sitting back on the wooden chair, deposited her on his knee.

'So far so good,' thought Macquarie, wondering how far he would get before he would have to think up some way of explaining that it was all just a joke – which he wickedly hoped would not be necessary.

He whipped off the head-covering and, continuing his nefarious designs, reached under Morag's chin and deftly unfastened the top button of her shirt. On touching the second one he thought all hell had broken loose.

Morag suddenly came to life and snatched at his hands crying, "Stop it! No! No! Stop it!" and commenced thumping his arms with her puny fists. "No! You will not!"

Macquarie desisted and let his hands fall away from her.

He cursed himself. 'Of all the clumsy, mad, bestial things to try to do to one of these sweet, lovely, innocent, trusting young women! Are you completely crazy? You had a wonderful situation here and you spoil it all, absolutely and completely. They will march right out and it would not surprise me if they went straight to the police. Who do you think you are you useless, randy, bullying bastard, you........'

Macquarie would have continued his self-condemnation to even

278

greater lengths had not Morag, her face contorted with outrage and humiliation, hissed at him, "You will not bath me in front of Fiona!" Her eyes swung briefly to the sofa before continuing, as if her friend was not only out of earshot but also had no say in the matter whatsoever, "Send her into the bedroom!"

This sudden and surprising reversal of his fortunes nearly knocked Macquarie from his chair. For a moment or two he could only gasp for air, then, with his mental equilibrium almost regained, he realised that a Fiona under his eye was one thing, a Fiona in the bedroom was another kettle of fish altogether. There she could barricade herself in or escape from the window causing all sorts of complications. Even now he could see from the corner of his eye that she was beginning to rise from the sofa. What Morag was apparently willing to endure would not automatically extend to Fiona.

A compromise occurred to him to which Morag might agree. He swung his head.

"Fiona, turn my armchair around and sit in it quietly, facing the window."

To his surprise, as if anything more could surprise him, Fiona rose from the sofa and silently complied.

Macquarie had no need to worry that she might try to escape. To Fiona the fact that she was shortly to be bathed like a child by this husky, self-confident man whom she did not even know existed two days before was as inevitable as the coming day.

Apparently satisfied with the disposal of her friend Morag allowed Macquarie to continue to undress her, her tiny hands sometimes touching his, trembling slightly.

When the shirt had slipped from her shoulders Macquarie unhooked the skirt which dropped away. Then, taking her slight weight with his left arm he reached down and slipped off a tiny scrap of nylon to reveal Morag in all her natural loveliness and ready for the bath.

Standing up and stepping to the tub Macquarie gently lowered the girl into the water. With knees bent there was ample room for someone of Morag's diminutive size to sit in comfort.

With the girl safely in the bath Macquarie checked the equipment available. Scented soap, two face-cloths, one large sponge the women evidently shared, a plastic bottle labelled 'Bath Oil' and a bag of bath salts. He judged from the fragrance of the water that the condiments had already been added.

Picking up a dark green face-cloth, guessing it to be Morag's – to match her tent and rucksack – Macquarie commenced his ministrations. First he gently washed the grubby face, being careful to avoid getting soap in the tightly closed eyes, then the tiny pink ears and slim neck. Changing to the sponge he washed the back followed by one dainty hand and arm and then the other. Next it was the turn of the exquisite front with all its detail right down to the level of the bath water. The tiny right foot and its corresponding leg was carefully sponged followed by the left. Macquarie was surprised how easily the dirt floated from the delicate skin, when he was dirty it generally necessitated a scrubbing brush to remove the grime.

Throughout these stages of the bathing Morag was absolutely silent. It was not until Macquarie had put his hands under her arms and lifted her to her feet, dripping with soap-suds, and said, "Put your hands on your knees," that she, realising his intentions, rebelled.

"No!" she said, standing up very straight.

A moment later Morag's hands met her knees with a soft 'pat'. This followed a similar, if somewhat louder sound from a region about eighteen inches further north.

It was with three very pink cheeks that Morag submitted to the last details of her sponging.

The drying was very thorough, Macquarie lifted the young woman from the tub and standing her by the fire made a meticulous job of it. The subject of his attentions only spoke once, towards the end of the towelling, when she whispered, "It is a pity the talcum powder was ruined by the rain," but Macquarie could not decide by the tone of her voice if it was said in regret or apology.

When nearing the end of the drying Macquarie turned to the armchair and said to the top of Fiona's head, "Please get the two blankets from the bed Fiona." In actual fact the words were spoken to rather more than the top of that young lady's head as he observed beneath the duster covered crown two highly arched eyebrows and a pair of very wide sparkling blue eyes.

Fiona quietly left the room to return a minute later with the two blankets. One she placed on the back of the armchair and the other she handed to Macquarie who was decorously holding up a towel to shield from her eyes Morag's nudity.

Wrapping Morag in the blanket Macquarie picked her up and deposited her on the sofa. Turning her to face away from the tub he enjoined her not to peep.

Leisurely he dropped a handful of bath-salts into the water then added about an egg-cup full of 'bath-oil'. Hearing no protests he assumed this was about the correct dosage. He then poured the almost boiling contents of the kettle into the tub. Remembering at the last moment he discretely retained some of the hot water and added it to the lukewarm contents of the bucket on the hob. This he moved to a position close to the bath.

After checking that all the necessary appointments were to hand he looked up and said simply, "Fiona."

Since handing Macquarie the blanket Fiona had been standing by the armchair but at her quietly spoken name she stepped forward and stood before him, meekly waiting to be undressed.

Knowing how much women hated getting their hair wet, unless intentionally, Macquarie was relieved to observe when he removed its duster covering that Fiona's golden hair was still in a fairly neat bun at the back of her head – though he could have sworn that a few strands had been hanging below the cloth earlier.

As Fiona was standing Macquarie chose to remove her apparel in the reverse order to Morag's. First the curtain skirt followed by the wisp of nylon under it. Finally, the loose shirt which, when unbuttoned, fell away leaving the young woman in all her feminine, if rather grubby, beauty.

The bathing of Fiona was carried out as painstakingly as that of Morag, the only differences being that Macquarie used the water from the bucket to wash the lovely face, ears and neck with the pink face-cloth and that the final sponging was carried out in this instance with only two pink cheeks on the part of the recipient, Fiona having learned from Morag's experience.

The careful drying completed Macquarie gently enfolded Fiona in the second blanket then picked her up and carried her to the bedroom. Returning a moment later to the living room, to the apparent relief of the young woman on the sofa, he took her in his arms and a minute later placed her by her friend in the centre of the bed.

Stepping towards the door Macquarie turned and said, "I want you two ladies looking just as glamorous as you did last night," and, glancing at his watch, "I will give you half an hour."

With that he left the room.

****

Macquarie needed a full half hour to do all that he wanted. First the disposal of the bath water. As soon as he had poured it away he regretted not having kept a bottle of it as a memento. He then collected the wet towels and hung them out on the clothes line to dry as best they could.

The tray of soaps and lotions and the women's discarded clothing he left for them to pick up. Macquarie was no ladies' maid.

Naturally nothing had been prepared for dinner and the girls, unless they had escaped through the bedroom window and were even now fleeing towards the nearest police station, would be prettily dressed when they emerged. Macquarie therefore decided that the decent thing to do would be to peel a few potatoes. He had no idea what else was to be on the menu but considered potatoes almost certainly to be one item. In his enthusiasm, or perhaps because his mind was on other things, he peeled one or two too many so laid these beside the filled pan.

The final chore was to do something about cleaning up Macquarie. As the hot water supply was exhausted and there was no time to heat more he performed his ablutions in cold water. His original intention of stripping off completely to indulge in his normal standing up 'bath' had regrettably to be cancelled as there was not enough of the half hour left to risk such an operation.

Removing his shirt he washed hands, face and neck, then, after a sniff and a grimace, sloshed water into his armpits and thoroughly washed them. For good measure he added the scrubbing of his hairy chest to the agenda.

Quickly drying himself he combed his wet hair, he was a rather sloppy washer, and completed his toilet by poking a towel-covered finger into his navel to mop up a drop of water which had found its way there.

Macquarie reached for his shirt and cursed himself for not thinking of collecting a clean one from the bedroom before the girls took it over. The soiled one would have to do until the omission could be rectified, he could not go around the house shirtless with the ladies in residence. Remembering that the garment had served him during his route march to and from the village earlier in the day he lifted it to his nose and sniffed it which caused him to wrinkle his nose and give utterance to a disgusted "Yeuk!"

Thrusting his arm through one sleeve he turned to repeat the performance with the other and promptly received another shock to his fortunately robust nerves.

"Good God! How long have you two been here?"

Leaning gracefully in the entrance to the living room was an extremely attractive Fiona, her green dress seemingly moulded to her dainty figure. At her side, seated on the orange box in which Macquarie kept his shoe-polishing gear and old newspapers for the fire sat an equally breath-taking Morag, one slim ankle crossed over the other below the skirt of her blue and white dress. The young women had the appearance of two models posing for the cover picture of a fashion magazine – although again, a fastidious photographer might have commented on the home-made sheep-skin slippers which completed each ensemble.

After enjoying his discomfiture for several moments Fiona said, "Oh not long."

"Only ten or fifteen minutes," added Morag mischievously.

Macquarie had only been washing for five minutes or so at the outside but for all this he was embarrassed and nettled. How much had they seen? A man expected to be able to do some things without an audience.

"Is there no privacy in this house?" he demanded half seriously.

After what happened earlier the irony of his remark was not lost on the girls who promptly burst out laughing, which Macquarie immediately joined.

When the merriment had subsided a little Fiona said, "Actually we have come to start dinner."

"Dinner!" replied Macquarie in mock horror, "You exquisite, elegant, beautiful young ladies speak of such mundane things as making dinner?"

Gratified Fiona answered, "Have you any better ideas Alistair?"

The only possible alternative was for Macquarie himself to prepare the meal a prospect he did not relish. He blustered, "Well I was thinking of having barbequed walrus on the beach – or I could swim across the loch for a Chinese takeaway."

"Out of the kitchen!" ordered Morag, "It's formal tonight so please dump that shirt in the wash and put on a clean one."

Fiona, who had reached the sink, cried, "Oh lovely! The good man has peeled the potatoes. Enough for the rest of the week too," she added as she removed several from the pan and put them with the others on the draining board. "Very sweet of you Alistair, thank you."

As if he had done them a great favour. Macquarie realised he was being spoiled.

"My pleasure," he assured them in all honesty. "By the way, what are we having for dinner?"

"It depends on what you managed to buy," responded Morag as she locked around, "Where is the shopping anyway?"

Shopping? Was that today? For a moment Macquarie could not remember what he had done with it. Yes, of course, he had dumped it just before the girls started screaming.

"Just outside the front door," he replied, moving in that direction.

"It is lucky it did not rain. Why did you leave it out there?" queried Fiona.

"I did not expect to leave it quite so long," was the reply as he hauled the rucksack into the porch. Noticing his dusty walking boots he picked them up by the laces and swung them towards their usual berth under the small table. They were within an inch of touchdown on the clean tiles when a soft "Ahem" from Morag caused him to abort the landing. Taking a newspaper from the orange box he flipped it onto the floor below the table and gently lowered his boots onto it.

"Fiona!" cried Morag, "I think we are beginning to get the man house-trained at last!"

They opened the rucksack and spread the new purchases out on the table. If Macquarie had not got the shopping quite right the girls were very good about it.

Soon a delicious meal was being prepared.

****

Macquarie was lavish in his praise of the results of the women's labours that day.

"I did not know that wall was meant to be white!" – "It hardly seems to be the same house," (with the mental reservation that he hoped he would be able to find all his belongings again), - "What a tremendous difference you have made, I had no idea the old homestead had become so dirty."

"There is still a bit to do," said Fiona, "We only had time for the bedroom and most of the living room."

"And there is still this porch and kitchen," added Morag, "We only scrubbed the floor as it got so wet and dirty with all our to-ing and fro-ing."

"Well you have certainly done a tremendous job," said Macquarie with feeling, "but you must not think of doing any more, you are on holiday after all. I will finish it after you leave." He immediately regretted the last words, they reminded him that the present idyllic situation could not last indefinitely.

The women insisted on completing the cleaning of the cottage on the morrow, for their own satisfaction if for no other reason, and nothing Macquarie said could shake their resolve.

Much to his relief.

****

They spent a quiet evening chatting by the fire. All three of them were tired after the exertions of the day but Macquarie sensed a slight tenseness in the atmosphere which could not be entirely attributed to weariness. Perhaps his conduct with the bathing had really upset them after all? The subject was not even hinted at never mind mentioned but he had a feeling that it had made a subtle difference to their hitherto carefree relationship.

After the routine attempted insistence of the women that they sleep in the living room and Macquarie return to his own bed and his veto of the idea they made their goodnights and retired.

At least this applied to Fiona and Morag. Macquarie himself changed into his own suit of pyjamas, bought years before in case of hotel fires and suchlike emergencies – he generally slept in the raw, then donned his ancient dressing gown and sat by the dying fire to brood.

For the first time in his life Macquarie seriously thought of altering his Income Tax coding.

They were both wonderful young women, different from one another but both having in full measure the attributes he would require in a wife.

The question was which one to choose? He mentally set aside the fact that in all probability neither would have him, partly to satisfy his conscience but mainly to get it out of the way of his train of thought.

Damn it all! If there had only been one of them he would probably have proposed to her by now.

'Easy!' whispered the voice of his guardian angel, 'You are on a very dangerous ground.'

Macquarie was undeterred. A man should have sons to carry on his name – and anyway thirty-six was not really too young to start thinking of getting married.

'Steady on!' whispered the guardian angel. 'You have been quite content all these years, why change things now? These nymphs have you bewitched.'

If Macquarie steadied at all it was on the line of thought he had chosen.

Which one? That was the problem. Which one to assist in carrying on the noble Macquarie name? In spite of their diminutive size both had good hips.

For a moment he toyed with the possibility that, they being only half size, the law might stretch a good point and let him have both but had to concede that this was highly unlikely.

'For goodness sake watch it,' hissed the G.A., an afterlifelong bachelor himself, 'You are heading for the slippery slope.' He then added in a more reasonable tone of voice, 'Why not sleep on it? You will feel better in the light of the day after a good night's rest.'

'In a minute! First let me sort this thing out. Let me try the other way around, find some things I do not entirely like about them and discard the one with the most faults.'

After several minutes of concentrated endeavour he could not think of one tiny criticism to apply to either of the girls.

Had any man ever been faced with such a dilemma?

Why had neither of them ever married? He assumed they were not divorced on the strength of no evidence whatsoever.

It must be strange for a woman he thought, leaving school and wondering if in a few years she would become a drudge or a duchess. Probably a few wanted nothing but a career but most surely seemed to prefer getting married and having a family of their own. It must be so as the majority of them ended up that way.

For a man the pattern of life was entirely different, if he wanted to be an engine-driver or to dig holes in South America he just set about heading in that direction until he got what he wanted. In theory he could plan his life right from the outset. Decide say to be an eminent surgeon and retire to South Africa when he was fifty-five. He might achieve it, by hard work and a bit of luck but if not he could get somewhere near it, say a reasonably successful doctor with a holiday cottage in the Hebrides or the Cotswolds.

With women it was by no means the same. They could not decide when they started out in life that they would marry a surgeon who would eventually become eminent, (or whatever it was top surgeons became), and retire to South Africa when he was fifty-five, (she, of course being considerably younger). There could easily be a glut in the market for surgeon's wife material when her time was ripe. Therefore a woman's thought processes must be entirely different to a man's. Which no doubt accounted for the fact they were so difficult to understand. Fancy having to change one's surname, Macquarie side-tracked, after twenty-odd years of getting used to the original, the mind boggled.

Which brought him back to his girls. Why had they not married? He was gallant enough to assume that they must have proposals galore. Life was a gamble to anyone but for nubile girls more than most. To marry the first man to propose to her or to hang on in the hope of something better? How long to wait? In the first instance many a marriage had come a cropper he decided in his vast experience of the subject. The old story of the bride who thought that no matter what her man's faults when she married him she would be able to mould him to her requirements. The man just the opposite of course, firmly convinced in his temporarily unbalanced state that the girl would not change from the exotic creature who walked down the aisle at his side.

Had the fates decided that it was time he found his mate and sent the women to him under such extraordinary circumstances? If so why two of them? It seemed a lot of trouble for the fates to go to just to make things complicated.

If only he could decide.

****

Macquarie's train of thought was interrupted by the faint click of the door latch behind him.

Had one of the girls drunk too much bed-time coffee? He decided to remain very quiet and pretend he was asleep so whoever it was would not be embarrassed. The remains of the fire hardly gave enough light for anyone to see he was not on the sofa.

Soundlessly the visitor moved further into the room – but not towards the kitchen door. Macquarie felt rather than saw that she was approaching the fire.

The slight form of the jersey dressed girl was beside him before Macquarie recognised who it was. Although the face was turned away, the eyes no doubt looking for him on the sofa, he could just make out in the dim light of the dying embers that the hair was dark, not blonde.

"Morag," he whispered.

The girl gave a start and spun round.

"Oh, I'm sorry Alistair," she said quietly, "I thought you would be asleep. I could not sleep either and thought my tossing about would disturb Fiona so decided to sit by the fire for a while. I am sorry to have bothered you instead but I thought you would be dead to the world after your long walk yesterday."

Morag turned as if to return to the bedroom but stopped when Macquarie asked her to stay and keep him company for a while. She took a step towards the sofa before Macquarie took her hand and drew her down to the hearthrug at his feet.

They sat without speaking, Morag gazing into the fire lost in goodness knows what thoughts and Macquarie looking down on that lovely head and dreaming his dreams.

After a few minutes Morag allowed herself to be drawn against his knee by the gentle pressure of his hand on her shoulder. For a long time they sat thus in silence, the only movement being of Macquarie's free hand as he added more logs to the fire.

Some further time elapsed before Morag, with a slight wriggle, raised herself slightly and slipped the skirt of the jersey from beneath her hips. Not understanding her movement Macquarie asked if she were in a draught.

"On the contrary," she replied, "It is rather too warm." Her voice was but a whisper.

Ready to state instantly if necessary that he was only trying to make her more comfortable Macquarie reached down and gently drew the rough wool of the jersey away from the small of Morag's back. The almost imperceptible upward movement of her arms gave him his clue. Slowly he lifted the heavy material upwards. The girl's arms moved up, slightly leading the black and grey wool until the jersey was completely removed when her hands returned to her lap in exactly the same position they had occupied before. Morag's eyes never left the fire. It was if she did not realise that she was again completely revealed to the eyes of the man who had so recently bathed her.

With the firelight glowing pinkly on Morag's smooth contours Macquarie was in no doubt that he had never seen anything so exquisitely beautiful in his entire life.

What happened shortly afterwards was the most natural thing in the world.

******

Chapter 7

After the supreme happiness of the previous day the one following verged on the brink of disaster.

Macquarie arose at his usual time in order to avoid any questions which might compromise Morag in Fiona's eyes. He had had nothing like enough sleep, goodness knows what time the wonderful, lovely Morag had left him.

He cursed himself for every kind of swine he could think of. Seducing that sweet, adorable young woman and probably completely wrecking her long friendship with Fiona to boot. What right had he to take advantage of her affection in that way? The poor girl bewildered and in a strange house to be so treated! He deserved to be shot.

How could he dare face her when she got up? Or Fiona either come to that?

'Steady on! You are all of a twitch,' he said to himself.

'I am not all of a twitch,' he replied as he knicked himself with the razor.

His ablutions completed, not without cutting himself a second time, Macquarie dressed and commenced cleaning out the fire. As the fire had burned for hours longer than usual the grate was not as cool as normally, as he discovered by scorching his thumb.

On opening the outside door on his way to dump the ashes Macquarie was confronted by a large cardboard box. He immediately remembered Morag's words of the previous evening, "All the rubbish we have dumped outside in a cardboard box, you do not appear to have a dust-bin."

He had felt a twinge of apprehension at the time and meant to investigate as people's ideas of what constitutes rubbish vary considerably. However, he had immediately forgotten the remark so decided to rectify the slip then and there.

The first two items the box divulged, a hammer helve and a somewhat frayed but quite usable length of car tow-rope, confirmed his fears so he picked up the box to take it to the outhouse. Macquarie had no trouble lifting most of the bulky box, it was feather light as the rain during the night had ensured that its base and contents remained on the ground. This did nothing to improve his irritable state.

After last night the whole situation had taken on a different and somewhat frightening dimension Macquarie decided as he picked up pieces of wood, scraps of brass, padlocks which only needed keys and keys which only required locks in order to again become completely serviceable, plus a score of other useful items. These he transferred to the outhouse.

After laying and lighting the fire he placed a kettle of water on it and called out to the bedroom door that he was, as had become his habit, going out for half an hour.

He was answered by a cheery, "Thank you Alistair," in Morag's voice.

How the hell do they manage to do it? The man thought. Or did he perhaps detect that the words sounded just a little too cheery?

*****

Dressed in jeans and blouses, the curtain skirt outfits apparently being 'in the wash', the girls' good morning kisses were warm enough and breakfast passed as pleasantly as ever. Or almost so. Macquarie could detect a slight formality in the women's relations to one another even then.

The atmosphere became more strained as the morning's work progressed. Macquarie helped the women shortly after breakfast, shifting the heavy dresser away from the wall and taking the rugs outside for a thorough shaking but he was more than glad when his services were dispensed with and he could escape to the outhouse to continue the cabinet he was constructing for the kitchen.

Between the house and workshop Macquarie stopped to look at the sky. Sunny at the moment a great thunderhead of cloud was building up over the sea.

'Watch out for the squall,' he said to himself.

The cabinet did not progress satisfactorily. The still, hot, humid atmosphere seemed to dull chisels and set the grain of the wood at cross purpose with itself. Macquarie struggled on however, albeit rather half-heartedly.

He would have preferred to have continued the causeway but, having told the women he would remain handy in case there was any further heavy shifting to do he felt obliged to remain near the house.

Hot and thirsty he had his ears pricked when it neared noon listening for one of the girls to call him in for coffee.

Hearing a shout he downed tools thankfully and walked towards the house. Halfway there he heard another cry. Was something wrong? The girls had expected to complete the cleaning some time before, in fact they had said they would be out of their working gear and 'properly dressed' by midday. They must have run into a snag.

A loud shriek followed by both women shouting at once. Had there been an accident? Perhaps they had tried to shift the dresser back against the wall themselves and it had fallen on one of them? Macquarie broke into a run.

The women were not in the kitchen or the living room, he did not look behind the furniture this time as the shrieks and cries were obviously coming from the bedroom. Whatever was happening? It sounded like a cat-fight. Three strides and he burst through the door.

It was a cat-fight.

Fiona and Morag were at one another's throats in the centre of the bed, kicking and shrieking as they apparently endeavoured to claw out each other's eyes. Both of them were displaying far more of their legs than decorum dictated which in spite of his astonishment somehow shocked Macquarie.

With cats in mind the bewildered man's first reaction was to stop the fight with the time-honoured bucket of water but, apart from soaking the bed, there was obviously no time to carry out such an expedient. Macquarie therefore entered the fray by grabbing Fiona, who happened to be uppermost at the time, and hauling her off Morag, having to twist Morag's fingers out of her hair first in order to do so. He dumped the girl unceremoniously onto the floor. Morag tried to follow her, claw outstretched, but Macquarie grappled with her writhing, kicking form and deposited her on the floor at the opposite end of the room to Fiona. By this time Fiona was half way along the bed about to renew her attack. Macquarie grabbed one of her legs and jerked it causing the furious Fiona to flop onto her face. Hearing Morag behind him returning to the fray he quickly sat on the bed and swung his legs over the small of Fiona's back to trap her, meanwhile trying to fend off Morag's assault with his shoulders. In this he was only partially successful but with a few quick movements managed to smother

Morag's clawing hands and kicking legs – forgetting all he had been taught about avoiding the soft parts when manhandling a woman.

With both girls temporarily immobilised and unable to do further damage to one another Macquarie tried to reason with them. Not an unqualified success, for all the effect his words had he might as well have not been there. The women resembled a couple of opposing cavalry forces which in mid-charge had suddenly become bogged down in the slough of despond or something equally sticky when almost within slashing range of one another. The main difference being that the women were making a good deal more noise than a mere brace of cavalry regiments could ever achieve. And there was the rub. Although the women's flailing limbs had been subdued Macquarie could do nothing to quieten their tongues and the racket was making his head ring. His remonstrances were of no avail, the cold water treatment out of the question and at first Macquarie could see no end in sight. He had no idea that such small creatures could accommodate lungs of such power.

Something had to be done and the positions of the women themselves, Morag face down across his thighs and Fiona prone beneath his knees, suggested an alternative.

The room was suddenly and briefly lit by a tremendous flash of lightening followed almost immediately by a veritable cannonade of thunder. The storm was upon them.

*****

The storm was heavy but mercifully brief. Late that afternoon the sky was still mainly overcast but showing definite signs of brightening in the west. Macquarie, aided somewhat by a weather forecast on the radio, prophesised a fine, hot day for the morrow.

"How about going for a picnic now the spring cleaning is over?" he suggested.

"That would be wonderful!" smiled Fiona as she reached for the tea-pot from her kneeling position by the fire.

"A delightful idea," Morag handed her mug to Fiona across the back of the sofa on which she was leaning. "It's a pity we haven't our swim-suits though."

"The sea around here is always too cold for swimming," said Macquarie, "but we could go up the sea shore and have lunch by 'Cormorant Point' – as you say you have never seen it," he added with a smile.

The picnic was agreed upon with enthusiasm as all three found the house oppressive after the events of the day.

They made an early night of it. Each had been under a heavy strain all day, which the thundery weather had accentuated, and hoped a good sleep would effect a cure to their tenseness.

*****

Prepared for bed Macquarie again decided to have half an hour in his chair in order to compose his thoughts before putting his weary head to the pillow. If this was his intention it did not get very far.

He had just settled down when the click of the bedroom door latch caused him to turn his head. Morag again! No doubt at all who it was as she was silhouetted in the doorway by the light from the bedroom lamp. What now? He did not for one moment expect.....

"Fiona is crying," said Morag in a matter of fact tone.

"Why?" Macquarie stood up. Whatever was the trouble now? It seemed to be a day of tears.

"You had better ask her," was the reply in a quiet, flat voice.

"Surely you must have some idea?" said the worried Macquarie as he moved towards the door. Entering the bedroom he continued, "There must be some reason," only to find that he was talking to himself as the door had been closed quietly behind him. With Morag on the other side.

Mystified and more worried than ever Macquarie approached the bed. The sound of sobbing came from the blanketed hump in the middle of it.

"Whatever is the matter?" asked the very concerned man as gently as he could.

The reply was renewed weeping.

Completely at a loss Macquarie leaned over and slowly pulled the covers down to reveal the tear-stained face of Fiona.

"Please tell me what the trouble is." He reached out a large hairy hand to touch her brow but it was instantly seized by two tiny ones and wetted with tears as the young woman pressed her face against his fingers. It came as a relief to Macquarie to think that the gesture indicated that he apparently was not the cause of the distress. Fiona's movement caused the blankets to slip and disclose her neck and one smooth white shoulder.

"Tell me what the trouble is lovely Fiona," Macquarie attempted to stroke her head with his other hand but over-balanced, only preventing a collision by taking the weight on his elbow. Their heads were then but inches apart.

Releasing his hand Fiona suddenly wrapped both of her arms around Macquarie's neck and tried to pull his head down to her. Macquarie was so surprised he tensed and the girl's sudden movement had the effect of lifting her shoulders from the bed causing the blankets to slip down almost to her waist. In a split second Macquarie had relaxed enough to allow his head to be clasped to a soft white throat.

Although still bewildered Macquarie was rapidly finding things to think about other than mysteries.

Slowly between sobs Fiona spoke and her words made the situation slightly clearer. Her desire for him... "but I'm only a silly spinster.... I've never...I mean......but you must hate me...think I'm silly."

Macquarie soothed her as best he could and slowly the story unfolded.

Fiona could not get to sleep the previous night, animal desires burning within her which her inexperience did nothing to allay. Pretending to be asleep when Morag silently left the bed and went to the other room. Her listening at the door to the movements and quiet murmuring. Her heart on fire as she had never known it before.

"And when Morag.... squealed....at....at the end I nearly fainted. I was shaking and hot and cold and wanted to die. It was just that I could not stand Morag's......I wanted you then, I wanted you so...so desperately but I did not know what to do..... I still don't....don't know what to do. Oh, you must hate me....... loathe me......." Fiona's sobbing became uncontrollable and it took all Macquarie's wit and tenderness to soothe her.

It was another hour before Fiona was completely relaxed and a further one before.........

But such intimacies are no concern of ours.

*****

The picnic was a tremendous success.

The weather was perfect, hot sun with just the trace of a sea breeze to prevent it becoming absolutely sweltering. In fact, it proved to be the hottest day of the year.

Macquarie carried the rucksack containing the food the ladies had prepared and two large thermos flasks of hot water. Tea bags, powdered milk, a pair of large towels and a few other odds and ends completed the load.

The two young women wore the thinnest blouses and perforce their slacks as the curtain skirts were still in the wash. No doubt to the ladies' relief as they were almost certain to meet other people on such a fine day. Even Macquarie had to admit to the risk. Their only dresses were reserved to change into when they returned to the cottage.

Macquarie had never seen the girls so gay and carefree. 'Should I still think of them as 'girls'' he wondered wickedly, 'surely they can only be considered 'women' now?'

Fiona and Morag walked with him most of the time, their animated conversation keeping him highly amused. Every now and again they would dash off and examine some object washed up on the beach, rushing back after a few minutes to tell or question him of their discovery.

For devilment Macquarie led the young women off the beach occasionally to places of rocks and grass and ask if they could identify the spot. The first few times they said it was the place they had left their rucksacks on the night of their stormy journey, now seemingly so long ago. Each time they were laughingly told they were wrong.

On the way up the coast Macquarie pointed out the grim, ancient black rocks of Cormorant Point thrusting out to sea like a massive breakwater. He asked the girls how they could have been so blind as not to have seen it. Only 'his' girls could have given the answer Morag voiced for the two of them.

"It was certainly not there when we passed the last time."

Macquarie eventually led the way a short distance inland just north of the point and again asked them if they recognised the spot with its grass and massive boulders.

Caught too many times already both women gave an unhesitating negative.

"Well young ladies I am not surprised you manage to get lost so easily. This is the place you left your rucksacks – and a devil of a time I had finding them." Macquarie indicated a slight dip in the ground, "Morag, your rucksack was just there, sitting wide open to the rain. Yours was way down that gully Fiona, almost submerged in that little pool you can just see from here. Of course it was a fair sized pond after all the rain that night."

"It certainly looks much different now," said Fiona, "Quite a pretty spot in fact."

"Why don't we have our picnic here?" exclaimed Morag, "I think it is lovely."

This agreed they set out the lunch on a small chequered table cloth. Although Macquarie had no wine to bring this omission did nothing to dim the high spirits over the meal.

The al fresco luncheon over both girls lay back on the grass, their faces, arms and now bare feet soaking up the hot sunshine.

"It certainly is a pity we brought no swim-suits," said Fiona regretfully, "What a lovely day for sun-bathing."

"Don't let that stop you," commented Macquarie hopefully, "After all we hardly have any secrets between us."

"Whatever are you suggesting Alistair Macquarie?" Fiona lifted herself onto one elbow and continued in the same shocked tone, "Sunbathing in the altogether in public? You surprise me!"

"It is hardly very public," persisted Macquarie, "We have not seen anyone else all day. I could keep watch on that rock," he indicated a huge boulder some yards inland from where they were. "Not even a rabbit could get within a mile without my seeing it. What do you think

Morag?"

"It does seem an awful waste of this wonderful sunshine," was the reply. Turning to her friend she continued, "Perhaps if we kept on just our briefs and Alistair kept a <u>very</u> good lookout....." Then, with a sudden change of mind, "No, it would be too risky."

It took ten minutes of Macquarie's most ardent persuasion before both ladies agreed that to waste such a golden opportunity to sunbathe would be a sacrilege, so, having extracted his solemn promise to inform them immediately if anyone came within a mile of the picnic spot the girls assented to the proposal.

In spite of their remonstrances both Fiona and Morag were eager to commence their sun-tans. They waited impatiently for Macquarie to reach his lookout post on the rock and to give them an all-clear signal so they could commence removing most of their clothing.

Having mounted the boulder and looked carefully all round Macquarie gave no sign but climbed back down.

"Damn!" said Morag, but quietly as she did not want Macquarie to know she used such language, "I was really looking forward to sun-bathing."

"Be it ere so risky," Fiona continued for her, "But what a nuisance, particularly as we have not seen a soul all day." To Macquarie who was now close to them she asked, "Are people coming this way or stopped close by?"

"People?" replied Macquarie in a surprised voice, "There is not a living soul between here and America so far as I can see."

"Then why are you not keeping your lookout?" inquired Morag rather tersely, "You did promise."

"Going straight back there to keep my lonely vigil as soon as I have taken care of the comfort of my guests," he replied.

"There was no need to bother," said Fiona as Macquarie selected a flat stretch of turf and began laying the two towels side by side about two feet apart, "we could have done that."

Macquarie stopped at his self-appointed task and looked at Fiona silently for a moment before continuing to spread the towels.

"Oh!" said Fiona turning slightly pink.

Macquarie walked across to the rucksack and rummaged in it, his hand re-appearing holding a bottle of sun-tan lotion.

"Oh!" exclaimed Morag, turning even more pink than Fiona.

Taking each of the women by a hand he led them to the towels where he stood them side by side and uncovered the dainty forms to the extent that not even a small triangle of white skin would mar the intended complete sun-tan. Macquarie then arranged the young women in a prone position on the towels and gently applied the sun-cream.

The tanning preparations completed to his satisfaction Macquarie returned to his watch tower where he stayed until the ladies had finished their sun-bathing. Apart, of course, from the odd occasion when the thought the lotion required renewing or felt that the upper surfaces were becoming too hot when he would gently turn over the lovely, soft, smooth bodies.

Only once during his vigil did Macquarie see any other people, three men or youths walking down the beach from the north. They stopped when, he estimated, they were a little over a mile from him. After what appeared to be a consultation the three figures turned and retraced their steps. No danger to his females but Macquarie found himself as nervous as a wild stallion.

When the ladies decided they had had sufficient sun they tried to remove the surplus oil with the towels. Macquarie suggested assisting the process in 'Rucksack Pool' but the girls shivered at the very thought of the cold water. Both considered a hot bath would be necessary on returning to the cottage.

It made Macquarie's day.

****

On completing Fiona's bath Macquarie wrapped the warm, soft creature in a towel and carried her to the bedroom. Whilst helping her into her dress the girl wrinkled her pretty little nose and said, "Phew! This dress needs washing!"

At this Macquarie placed his hands beneath her ribs and lifting her up pressed his nose somewhere in the region of her navel.

"It smells lovely to me," he said.

"Put me down!" Fiona cried, and, looking towards the door, "And get back to your duties, the water will be getting cold."

In the fullness of time a glowing Morag was deposited in the bedroom where Macquarie slipped her dress over her head and checked that it was properly fitted. He then left the room to allow the women to attend to their hair. There were some things at least at which even he had to admit he was not expert.

****

Whilst the women were completing their toilette Macquarie emptied the bath and made himself presentable for dinner.

The evening was spent pleasantly but with a certain amount of nervousness as to how decorum was to be preserved. The arrangements were carried out with the smoothness of a well-rehearsed play.

Macquarie; (stretching himself), "Well, I think it is about time for bed."

Fiona; "But we must insist that you sleep in your own bed tonight. We have had it long enough and that sofa must be awfully uncomfortable for someone your size."

Morag; "Yes, we are adamant. One of us can sleep on the sofa and the other on the hearth-rug."

Macquarie; (evenly but still giving the impression of having his lines changed by the producer just before the curtain went up), "Well, if you absolutely insist."

Fiona; "Good, then that is settled at last," to Morag, "I bags the sofa tonight." (Which for a moment sounded rather selfish to Macquarie), "We will take alternate nights."

And thus it was arranged, with the slight addition of Macquarie insisting that the one on the sofa had a blanket as well as her sleeping bag as she would be furthest from the fire.

****

Eventually all was quiet and Macquarie, giving the girls ample time to fall asleep, (a good seven or eight minutes although it seemed longer), crept into the living room, half knelt on the hearth-rug and picked up the sleeping bag which lay by the fire. Ignoring the whispered protestations and the odd "Shush, you will wake Fiona" from its fold, (to Macquarie who was not making a sound!), he carried the bundle to the other room and tipped its warm, soft wriggling contents onto the bed.

****

The days were passed in extreme happiness. Picnics, fishing trips, washing, cooking and housework were indulged in with unbounded delight.

The nights followed a delicious routine, the only variation being in the whispered request not to awaken 'Morag' rather than 'Fiona' on alternate nights.

✳✳✳✳✳✳✳✳✳✳✳✳✳✳

It was shortly after the day of the first picnic that the two women started behaving slightly out of character. Until then they had been constantly together but from about that time they were often apart doing different things. Macquarie hoped he had not driven a wedge into their friendship.

He first noticed this one morning when seeing through the window Fiona making the bed by herself asked casually the whereabouts of Morag. He was told she had gone for a walk along the beach for an hour or so. Surprised, he asked if something had upset her.

"Of course not," Fiona laughed, "Everyone likes to get away alone sometime or other just to put her thoughts in order. You should know Alistair, you apparently spend months alone here."

"Oh, by the way," she continued, "as you are here would you mind shifting this chest of drawers away from the wall for me? I would like to dust behind it."

Such an operation seemed hardly necessary as the room had been thoroughly cleaned just a day or two earlier but Macquarie was getting used to the women's extreme views on cleanliness.

"Service is our watchword," he declared.

Macquarie kicked off his sandals and vaulted gracefully through the window. At least that was his intention but the window was rather on the small side for such acrobatics and he caught his foot on the window frame. Being put completely off balance he landed with a resounding crash on the floor.

Fiona was at his side in an instant – which was not really surprising as she was only inches away when he made his forced landing. No doubt she would have cleared the runway if she had expected him to enter the room other than by the door.

"Are you hurt?" she cried.

"Only a broken limb or two," replied the discomforted Macquarie, "Tell them in Athens... Or was it Sparta?"

"What?"

"I'm not quite sure, that is all I can remember of 'The Last Stand of Thermopylae'".

"You are talking nonsense, are you sure you did not hit your head?" Fiona was becoming alarmed.

"That is what I did land on fortunately, anywhere else and I might have broken some bones."

Macquarie rose to his feet.

"Now where do you want the wardrobe shifted to, or was it the bed?"

"Are you sure you did not hurt yourself? You landed very heavily – and you are holding your hand."

Macquarie promptly released his hand the thumb of which was giving him gyp as he had wrenched it on coming to earth. In fact, had he been by himself he would certainly have given utterance to one of those words which are never used in mixed company.

"Why so I am! I must be crazy holding my own hand when I could be holding yours." He gave the offending mitt a slap with the other and promptly rectified the matter. She was very close.

Anyway, what with one thing and another the chest of drawers did not get its behind dusted – or whatever had been Fiona's original intention. In fact, the housework developed a negative aspect as she was obliged to re-make the bed.

****

Another unusual thing happened that very afternoon. It had originally been planned that the three of them would go fishing to eke out the stores. At the last moment Fiona excused herself from the expedition as she said she thought she had the beginnings of a slight headache so perhaps a nap would do her more good. Macquarie was quite concerned but the women persuaded him that it would be better all-round if he carried on with his original intention and left Fiona to rest in peace. For the same reason Morag would still come with him, particularly as it was such a nice sunny day. Apparently she was developing into quite a fresh-air fiend. She brought with her a rolled up towel to sit on whilst Macquarie fished.

Macquarie was of course glad of her company and was also pleased that she was quite happy to be alone with him, proving that she had lost any fear of nervousness she might once have had in this respect.

On reaching the ledge of rock, his usual fishing place, Macquarie tackled up and soon had three fair sized Pollock in the bucket.

Morag, showing signs of boredom, picked up the towel and the bottle of sun-tan lotion she had wrapped in it and headed for some large rocks nearby.

From the corner of his eye Macquarie saw her move. He turned.

"Where are you off to, Morag?" he asked.

"Oh, the sun is so hot I thought I would sunbathe behind those rocks. Please give me a shout if you see anyone coming."

"I'm coming!" shouted Macquarie. Rather unnecessarily as Morag was only a few feet away.

Taking the smiling and unresisting Morag by the hand he led her to a sandy patch between large rocks which was perfectly sheltered from the wind but caught the full rays of the afternoon sun.

Morag stood silently and without movement until Macquarie assisted her to a prone position on the towel – unless the slight trembling as the gentle breeze first caressed her skin and at the initial application of the lotion could be considered movement.

****

Three Pollock were considered sufficient for the evening meal. Macquarie was quite willing to re-tackle, a fair sized codling or skate having apparently got bored with waiting and gone off with his original hooks and fair amount of line, but as it was getting rather late it was decided to head for home.

Fiona had the fire going well when they reached the cottage and was heating water, "in case Morag had been sun-bathing and wanted a bath". Rather shyly she admitted awakening after her nap "feeling rather sticky".

Macquarie beamed until his smile hurt.

****

At first the women did the laundry together but came the occasion, shortly after the washing had been taken into the cottage, Fiona happened to walk past the open door of the outhouse where Macquarie was working. Three or four weeks later he wondered where she had been going as the direction in which she was heading would have taken her across the mull and into the Atlantic Ocean.

"Hullo!" he called out, "I thought you two would be busy ironing."

Fiona looked particularly attractive to Macquarie that morning. She was wearing a very thin green shirt with the three top buttons unfastened – the fashion that year he assumed – and her curtain skirt.

The women often wore the skirts around the house in compliance with his desires, (if that is the appropriate word), but never again away from its vicinity after the first occasion.

"Morag is doing it all, there isn't much. Anyway I am not speaking to her." Fiona's smile removed any seriousness from this remark.

"Why, what is the matter?" Macquarie felt a moment of alarm but this was erased by Fiona's next remark.

"She said this shirt is indecent. Do you think it is Alistair?"

Now a profound question such as this cannot be answered arbitrarily. It took Macquarie a good twenty minutes to arrive at the conclusion that the shirt was eminently satisfactory.

Which did not really answer the question anyway.

****

One breezy morning Macquarie was chopping sticks in the lee of the gable end of the house when Morag passed carrying an overflowing bucket of washing to the clothes-line – the establishment did not extend to a laundry basket. He just had time to wonder how his supply of soap and detergent powder was holding out, the girls having got through more in the few days they had been there than he normally used in a month, ('no one could term it a dirty weekend' he mused), when Morag returned. She stopped beside him to ask a question about the type of wood he was cutting.

Using this as an excuse he said, "Sit down and I will tell you."

Other than the box he was using as a seat there was nothing but the ground to sit on so Macquarie very reasonably drew the girl onto his knee. Morag offered only a token resistance but in sliding onto his lap her curtain skirt was disarranged exposing her left thigh. Frantic efforts to rise and adjust the material were thwarted by Macquarie's hand on that very limb holding her down.

"Please!" she cried — but not too desperately, "Fiona might come out at any moment."

Ignoring her plea Macquarie held the girl gently but firmly until she desisted from her struggles.

They discussed different types of wood and their various uses and one or two other subjects for a good ten minutes. Although Macquarie was prepared to liberate Morag at the first sound of Fiona's footsteps, after the first minute or so the girl herself seemed to have forgotten her friend's existence. In fact, Fiona did not appear before Morag insisted that she must get back to assist with the housework, when Macquarie reluctantly released her.

The mere thought of their being discovered at their love-making by a third party added spice to its enjoyment.

It so happened that in spite of it all the chances taken during these little displays of affection with either of the young women not once did the other catch them and cause embarrassment. Macquarie thought this very fortunate indeed considering the times they tempted fate.

Seemingly there was no jealousy between the girls as regards himself. It was as if for all the world there existed an agreement that nothing was to interfere with the idyllic little life within a lifetime, a small cameo of pleasure entirely separated from the outside world. The happiness of the three of them seemed so sweet yet so very fragile that the slightest dissension seemed certain to cause the whole dream to disintegrate. The earlier one and only fight between the women was never mentioned. Like the summer thunderstorm with which the conflict coincided it built up, burst and was soon over leaving untroubled skies.

Macquarie often wondered what exactly caused the battle but had sense enough not to enquire.

The brief daytime occasions of caress and other displays of affection were never more than that in spite of, for instance, Macquarie's assiduous attention to his sun-bathing attendant's duties. Their actual mating was only consummated during the hours of darkness. Even then it never developed, or was intended to develop into a nightly routine. Macquarie was terrified of getting either of the girls pregnant and never knew whether or not they themselves were taking any precautions against such an eventuality. The women themselves were often so tired after a long day that they seemed quite content, after a little fondling, to cuddle their soft, smooth bodies against his muscular, hairy one and drop off to sleep with the innocence of children.

****

All this time neither Morag or Fiona suspected that, among other things, Macquarie was a landscape painter of some repute. With apparent mutual consent no questions were asked about the lives each led in the 'outside world'. Early in their relationship Macquarie had intimated that he was an engineer but he had not elaborated and the women had not pursued the subject. He had not the slightest idea of what the girl did for a living. Presumably the girls thought, almost correctly, that the cottage was his holiday home as obviously he did not ply his trade from it. It was as if each felt that to mention something outside their own small circle would somehow break the spell of their happiness. When they talked they spoke only of things which intimately concerned them, here in their own small, dreamlike world. There was never a suggestion that there might be a 'next time' as if they knew in their hearts that even if it was so ordained it could never be the same. Like a play, it had a very definite beginning and would have just as certain an end.

So they lived every minute of every day to the full, all three of them enjoying life as they never had before, knowing that as each day ended it was one less of the few remaining to them.

****

Regarding his hobby Macquarie did however receive on shock. He was on top of a step-ladder touching up a porch window frame with white gloss when suddenly Morag's voice from below him cried, "Macquarie the painter!"

The start he gave nearly tipped Macquarie from the ladder. For some reason he wanted to keep his painting a secret from the women, possibly because it constituted part, if somewhat vaguely, of the 'outside world'. All his painting equipment was kept in the outhouse as there was no room for it in the cottage. It was handier there in any case as often he sat just outside the storehouse door to paint the scene of sky and clouds as they appeared over the sea to the westward. The girls never entered the ancient, dirty building to his knowledge owing to 'mice and spiders'.

"What did you say?" Macquarie regained his balance on the ladder, his mouth agape.

"Macquarie the famous landscape painter, at least I suppose he is famous as I have seen pictures of his in one of the best art shops in Edinburgh," Mistaking his expression she continued, "Obviously no relation of yours or you would have heard of him. Do you know where Fiona is?"

Macquarie was relieved at this rapid change of subject.

"Yes, round the corner of the house ostensively peeling potatoes but more likely sunbathing."

****

Every day had its variations. The women washed their dresses one morning but owing to the showery weather they were still quite damp by the evening. Rather than dine in their curtain skirts, or, worse still, slacks, they pleasurably surprised Macquarie by making their appearances in thin blouses, artfully adapted by means of invisible stitching to achieve an 'off the shoulder' affect, combined with long skirts fashioned from a couple of chequered table cloths.

Macquarie was so impressed that he not only insisted in dishing up the dinner but also, for the first time since the women arrived, washing up after the meal. He claimed that it was utterly unthinkable that such elegant ladies could even consider such chores.

A pair of candles, unfortunately only of white wax, in a pair of mismatching bottles confirmed the formality of the occasion.

After dinner that evening the young women mentioned their intention of washing the two jerseys they were still using in lieu of dressing gowns before they left. Macquarie was horrified and immediately vetoed the suggestion.

"But they have been worn," said Morag as if this settled the matter.

"Even if I wear them they last all winter," Macquarie replied, "Your wearing them will only improve them. With luck they may retain your scent for ages."

"They will attract moths if they are not washed," contributed Fiona, then, "I know if our perfumes give you so much pleasure we could sprinkle on a few drops afterwards."

"It would not be the same. I just want to feel that you two were the last occupiers when I next wear them – with no washing in between. So that is final, no washing."

Realising that Macquarie was adamant the women desisted in their argument. They were probably much relieved to escape the labour for, as everyone knows, heavy woollen garments are the most diabolical things to launder, this being particularly so in the primitive conditions prevailing at the cottage.

Their insistence on cleanliness was just one of a hundred things Macquarie liked about the women, the cottage seemed to sparkle from their efforts. Every minute of Morag and Fiona's company was a pleasure to him. He even liked to see them at breakfast which demonstrated their charm, it being an established fact that normally no woman should be allowed loose on the public before midday.

Chapter 8

One of the many things Macquarie liked about the young women was their interest in everything he did. Having rarely had an audience, never mind an admiring one, it was all the more appreciated. His cabinet making, his causeway laying, even his sawing up of driftwood all met with their approval. Without actually saying so they always gave the impression that they had never seen such mundane tasks carried out so efficiently. Which was inclined to give the man a swollen head.

On one occasion his ingenuity brought him particularly lavish praise.

Whilst walking up the ocean shore one evening after dinner they came across a piece of timber which Macquarie was determined to bring back to the cottage. It was a deal, twenty or more feet long, twelve inches wide and three thick.

"Magnificent!" he cried when they sighted it stranded at the high water mark. "The things I could do with that back at the cottage! It is probably from the deck cargo of a timber ship, certainly it is too good to be a piece of dunnage wood dumped at sea, that is the usual stuff that drifts ashore here."

"It will be a big job sawing it up," said Fiona, looking at it from the practical angle.

"Oh, it would be useless sawn up, I want it all in one piece."

"It's a pity you can't then," said Morag, "obviously all three of us together could not carry it home."

Macquarie loved that 'home'.

"I quite agree," he replied, "we can't possibly carry it so we will have to persuade it to come with us."

"How?" chorused the girls.

"Ah, that we will have to work out." Macquarie seated himself on a rock. "Have either of you any ideas?"

"You could hire a tractor," suggested Fiona, "but that would be very expensive I think."

"I know!" cried Morag, "Push it into the sea – if we can get it that far," The thirty odd yards to the water's edge looked a long way to move such a heavy piece of timber, "and tow it round by boat."

"Nearly right," smiled Macquarie, "the only thing is I haven't a boat and don't want to hire one."

"Then it can't be done so far as I can see," said Fiona, "but obviously you are going to do it so please tell us how."

"Yes, please do." Contributed Morag.

The women's faith in him was appealing and Macquarie dearly hoped that the plan forming in his brain would be successful, to fail them did not bear contemplating. However, in case the plan he was mentally developing was not a success he decided to make a secret of it so it could be changed or modified at will if circumstances would not permit its accomplishment.

"I am afraid I can't tell you now, nor can we start the operation until the planets are in the right quarter and we have made sacrifices to the gods. By the way, what is the state of the moon?"

"What in heaven's name has the moon to do with it?" asked the surprised Morag.

"Quite a lot actually, in its own quiet way," replied Macquarie mysteriously.

Puzzled the girls tried to remember when they had last seen the moon. Even Macquarie could but vaguely remember observing it a week or so earlier. With light evenings and the hours of darkness spent in the cottage they none of them saw much of the night sky. However, between the three of them they estimated it was about half way to full.

"All to the good," said Macquarie as he studied the edge of the sea where it lapped some rocks below them.

"Can anyone remember some old green coloured rope half buried in the sand along here somewhere? I seem to recall it being back there," Macquarie indicated the way they had come, "but I did not see it this time."

"No, I think it was further on, just past that black rock," Morag turned to Fiona, "You remember it don't you? Alistair said it was part of a fishing net or something."

"Yes, of course," replied Fiona, "I think it is where you said, just the other side of that rock."

And so it was. The tangle of tattered rope was well buried in the sand but Macquarie was able to haul out and cut off a couple of lengths which, when knitted together, gave him a line of about twelve feet in length.

"Not very long but it should be enough to secure it," said Macquarie as they returned to the plank.

One end of the line was made fast to the plank and the other to a jagged rock protruding from the sand.

"Well that is all we can do for the time being, I hope it will hold," said Macquarie. It is getting late, let us head for home.

*****

The following morning the young women were surprised that Macquarie did not set off immediately for his piece of wood. Instead he just pottered about as if he had all the time in the world.

"I hope you haven't a big washing programme today," Macquarie said on one occasion as he passed through the kitchen, "I will need the clothes-line this afternoon."

"No, only these," Fiona indicated a few flimsy items on the now extended string clothes-line, "Anyway it is not a good day for drying."

It certainly was not, the morning had begun grey and cool with occasional patches of drizzle.

Macquarie spent some time examining his store of wood in the outhouse, eventually choosing two old pieces of three by three inch timber each about four feet in length. In these he drilled quarter inch holes about twelve inches apart. Taking a scrap of one inch wood about eight inches long he slashed a chip off each end and with his pocket knife then drilled two holes in it close to its centre. The three pieces of wood he placed on the porch table. When the mystified women asked what they were for they were told they were to propitiate the gods. They asked no further question.

By early afternoon Macquarie had added a handful of large nails, a claw hammer and the neatly coiled clothes-line to the wood collection on the table. Still he showed no sign of leaving the cottage. The pot of tea Fiona made was consumed in a leisurely fashion.

Just before two o'clock Macquarie rose from his chair and said he would get changed and be on his way.

"But the weather is even worse than it was this morning."

exclaimed Morag.

"Can't help that, time waits for no man," replied Macquarie mysteriously – considering his dilatory conduct earlier.

He reappeared from the bedroom a few minutes later in a very disreputable pair of jeans, an old sweater and a pair of dilapidated canvas shoes.

"I don't know how long I will be but if I can't make it in one go I will leave the plank and come home in time for dinner," said Macquarie as he headed for the porch and his waterproof jacket.

"But we are coming with you!" cried Fiona.

"Not in this weather surely?" Macquarie indicated the cold grey sky and threatening rain through the window. "It will be pretty boring anyway and there is no point in all of us getting wet."

"Oh please let us come," pleaded Morag, "We have been looking forward to seeing how you are going to get that great plank here."

"Well if it means that much to you please come but promise to return home if you get bored or cold."

The women immediately dashed off to don their 'heavy weather gear', which included the woollen hats Macquarie had not seen since the time of their dramatic arrival.

Attaching the hammer to his belt, stuffing into his pockets the nails and small piece of wood and slinging the clothes line and two four feet lengths of wood over his shoulder Macquarie started off with a girl on either side of him.

They walked across the mull and struck the ocean beach about a hundred yards south of where they had left the plank. The scarp above the shore was quite steep along this stretch of the coast but Macquarie led the way to one of its easier descents.

Throwing the wood, hammer and line onto the beach Macquarie assisted the women down the small cliff. The final obstacle was a ledge of rock about three to four feet above the sand. Macquarie jumped from the ledge then lifted down each girl with one arm around a slim waist and the other taking the main weight, little as it was. There was probably a more elegant way but he was quite content with this method.

Whilst Macquarie collected his scattered equipment the young women hurried ahead to see if the plank had remained where they had left it.

Morag crested an outcrop of rock first and immediately turned and shouted excitedly, "It's still there Alistair!"

Fiona added a moment later, "And the sea is right up to it!" as if Macquarie had personally arranged this convenience. Which in a way he had.

On sighting the plank himself Macquarie realised that he had left things rather late. The tide was right up to it, the wavelets actually wetting one end as they ran up the beach. It had been his intention to carry out the task he had in mind in his own good time but now. Owing to his misjudgement of the time of high water, it would be a race against time. The flood tide was nearly at its height and the sea would very soon be retreating down the beach. If he was not very quick with his pre-launching arrangements he would be faced with the prospect of either chasing the receding tide down the beach with the heavy plank trying to get it afloat or postponing the launching until the next high water in the early hours of the morning. Either prospect would be embarrassing with the two girls obviously waiting for him to work wonders before their eyes.

Macquarie hurried to the plank and quickly got to work. Taking one of the lengths of wood he had brought he placed It flat at roughly the centre of the deal. Pushing the points of four inch nails into the holes he had drilled he hammered them into the plank, adjusting the angle of the square wood until it ran diagonally to the centre line of the large deal. That is, if the plank had been lying in a north and south direction the piece of wood nailed to it would run about south-south-east and north-north-west.

Using the second piece of wood as a lever he managed, after quite a struggle, to turn the plank over. Flopping over it splashed water over his legs but Macquarie disregarded this as he expected to get a good deal wetter in the very near future.

Placing the second piece of wood on the now upper surface of the plank he nailed it in exactly the same way as the first. By this time one end of the timber was definitely afloat and an added task was to keep it that way and to avoid it becoming stranded again.

All this time the women had not said a word.

Taking the small piece of wood from his pocket Macquarie quickly nailed this to the upper surface of the plank, right at one end. The timber by this time was afloat completely and showing a distinct inclination to make it way out to sea.

Macquarie called to the women to throw him the clothes line, passing it was out of the question as there was now ten feet of water between the plank and the girls.

Struggling to control the plank with the cold sea well above his ankles Macquarie turned after a minute or so to see what was causing the delay. The ladies were trying to unfasten the clove-hitch with which he had secured the coils of the line.

"Don't bother with that," he called, "just throw me the whole thing as it is."

"But shouldn't we hold one end?" An obviously worried Morag was apparently of the opinion that he was going to swim round the mull with the plank in tow.

"No, as soon as I have it fast to this...." The large, heavy timber bobbed on a wavelet and caught Macquarie just below his right kneecap, "This... this plank I will be re-joining you."

Fiona threw the line to him. It fell only about four feet short and somewhat behind him so it only took a minute or so to release his hold on the plank, surge through the water, grab the coil of line and return to his labours before the timber got too far out to sea.

Macquarie took a turn of the line around one end of the plank and knotted it securely. A couple of turns around the cleat he had nailed there and the voyage was ready to commence. The original old mooring line had been released early in the proceedings.

Giving the great baulk of timber a shove out to sea a cold, wet Macquarie ploughed through the water back to dry land, paying out the line as he did so.

"You are absolutely soaked," said Fiona.

"You will catch your death of cold," added Morag.

Concern in both voices. Macquarie loved it.

"One can't catch cold from salt water, at least that is what the old sailing ship men claimed and they should know."

He returned to the work in hand. Walking down the beach at the water's edge to the full extent of the clothes line he turned to observe the plank. It was floating about fifteen feet from the shore and roughly parallel to it, apparently trying to make up its mind which way to drift. Macquarie was happy to help it in its decision. Giving the line a jerk to start the plank in motion he was pleased to see that it acted exactly as he expected. Instead of trying to follow the direction of the force applied to it it moved towards him but slightly away rather than towards the beach.

Macquarie resumed walking, slowly increasing his pace until he reached almost his normal walking speed, the plank at the end of the line docilely trailing him twenty odd feet from the shore.

"May we ask questions now?" queried Fiona as the girls fell in beside him.

"Of course," replied Macquarie trying not to sound too patronising. He thought they were never going to ask.

"Why did you nail those two pieces of wood to the plank?" The first question was from Morag.

"Well the idea is that the one underneath will act as a sort of out of line keel, a rudder almost, so that when the plank is pulled through the water instead of forever coming ashore and having to be pushed out to sea again it would try to steer itself away from the beach." Macquarie hoped his explanation was clear enough.

"How very ingenious," Fiona did not even try to keep the admiration from her voice. "But what does the piece of wood on top do?"

"That is in case the plank rolls over, it would be most inconvenient to have to pull the plank ashore to turn it back every time it did so and no doubt it will turn over a few times before we get it home unless we are very lucky."

"You should have thought of that yourself Fiona," said Morag who felt a little out of the conversation as Fiona had beaten her to the very question which had been mystifying her.

The first hundred yards was a simple walk along the beach. Then came a rocky outcrop which was actually an island at high tide. Macquarie had to tow his plank around the seaward end but suggested that the women go round the rocks inshore where it would be sand all the way. They demurred at this saying that they would get over the rocks without any trouble.

Fiona and Morag were quite capable of surmounting the obstacle before them or even a much more difficult scramble without much danger but if they got into the habit of doing so they might not require Macquarie's assistance so much in the future. Macquarie liked helping people. Particularly attractive young ladies over rocks.

Adjusting the tension on the line until the plank was moving beautifully through the water Macquarie said,

"Alright, but it is a pity just when the plank is moving along so smoothly."

"In what way is it a pity?" asked Morag.

"Having to tie the plank up at this stage whilst I help you over those algae-covered basalt rocks," Macquarie toyed with moray eels and crabs as big as frying pans but decided this might be overdoing it, "they are not dry land rocks you know."

"Oh, we will be very careful," insisted Fiona.

'Damn! It will have to be crabs and moray eels after all,' thought Macquarie but before he could give utterance he was saved from such extremes by a whispered conversation between the girls which resulted in a remark from Morag to the effect that they would not want to distract him when things were going so well. So, with an admonition that he himself be very careful, the ladies walked round by the sand.

Macquarie was glad the girls were out of sight as he rounded the rocks as the footing was very slippery and awkward and the plank decided that this was as good a time as any to commence a voyage to America. He lost his footing once, landing heavily on his left thigh and grazing his hand, which made him give vent to some comments which would no doubt have shocked the ladies had they been within hearing range and lowered him in their estimation. He held on to the line however and a few minutes later was reunited with Morag and Fiona.

It became a slow journey as they approached the tip of the mull. The plank sometimes behaved as an exemplary plank but most of the time it resembled a self-willed puppy straining at the leash, trying alternately to head out to sea and drive itself up on the beach.

The weather, not of the best to start with, became steadily worse. An intermittent drizzle set in and by the time they had reached a position roughly opposite the cottage the three of them were very wet and quite cold. Macquarie suggested that it was time the girls returned to the house to get the fire going and dinner prepared. The two women loyally gave all manner of reasons for staying with him to the end of the journey but eventually he managed to persuade them to head for home.

Macquarie missed the girls' cheerful company but he was glad he had insisted on their departure as they were obviously wet and cold in spite of their denials. He could picture them in the cottage with the fire crackling away, rapidly dispensing the chill damp of the day.

And it was a chill, damp day. Macquarie's legs were soaked and clammy and the worn sweater and nylon jacket were insufficient to keep him warm as he could not move fast enough to improve his circulation. His hands were cold and wet as were his feet in the scant protection of the tattering canvas shoes.

Macquarie experienced quite a struggle around the tip of the peninsula. Although there was no increase of wind during the afternoon, for which he was very thankful, the cross current off the end of the mull caused the plank to behave like a wild thing, sheering in every direction and constantly turning over.

Eventually he was round and cheering himself with the thought that within minutes he would be in sight of the cottage – if he could see it though the now continuous drizzle.

Then he saw them. Two small figures hurrying through the greyness towards him, both carrying bags of some sort.

The women saw him at the same time and shouted a greeting, increasing their pace as they did so. Macquarie noted that although they still wore their anoraks they had on trousers of a different colour to those worn earlier that afternoon.

"Here is the rescue party," panted Fiona as the girls reached him.

"We have brought you some hot coffee and another jersey," Morag added, "Sorry we have been so long, we hoped to get to you sooner."

"I really don't know what to say," said Macquarie with feeling, "except that you should not have gone to all this trouble and I think you are the most wonderful girls in the world!"

With Fiona towing the plank for a few minutes Macquarie quickly whipped off his jacket and donned the jersey, an old grey one, not one of those used by the girls he was glad to observe. It was dry and still warm. Replacing his jacket he retrieved the line from Fiona and with this in one hand and a constantly replenished coffee mug in the other continued his journey along the beach.

Nearing the cottage the ladies left him again to prepare the evening meal and Macquarie made the last couple of hundred yards alone.

In front of the cottage Macquarie hauled the deal as hard as he could onto the beach. It was then almost seven o'clock and he estimated that it would not be afloat again until around midnight.

Not trusting the thin clothes line as a mooring Macquarie rigged an additional one of a long length of rusty fencing wire.

By this time the wind had risen a little and it was raining hard. Macquarie was very cold and wet but far from miserable, in fact he was quite elated by the success of his labours. 'But what would I not give for a nice hot bath', he said to himself.

On reaching the cottage he removed his soaking, sandy shoes and leaving them out in the rain, entered the porch. The women heard the door open and came out to greet him.

"Here you are at last – and what a mess," cried Morag.

"We were just coming out to look for you," added Fiona as Macquarie removed his coat, "You must be chilled to the bone. Quick, come this way."

The ladies, still dressed in slacks and jumpers Macquarie noted, led the way into the living room.

Macquarie's earlier desire had been anticipated by the thoughtful women. In front of the crackling fire was the zinc bath half full of steaming water. Beside it was his carbolic soap on a tin try and a couple of towels. On the seat of his chair was a neat pile of clean clothes, corduroy trousers, thick checked shirt and woollen socks. He later found a pair of underpants shyly hidden between the shirt and trousers.

"Why this is wonderful!" Macquarie exclaimed, "It is just what I have been dreaming about for the last hour. How can I thank you enough? You two are far too kind to me."

"It is no more than you do for us," replied Fiona, then, realising the implication of the remark, blushed, as they used to say in Victorian novelettes, prettily.

"However you will have to manage by yourself as we have to change for dinner," laughed Morag and she moved towards the bedroom.

"Just give a shout when you are dressed," added Fiona, "and please do not be too long as dinner is nearly ready."

Macquarie revelled in his bath as much as the circumstances permitted. He would happily have spent more time enjoying the rare luxury but in deference to the ladies' wishes he was as quick as he could reasonably be. After thoroughly drying himself he emptied the tub in the usual manner. With so much water in it it was heavier and more awkward than usual but he managed the job without making too much mess. He then dressed quickly and gave the women the all clear to come out of the bedroom.

The ladies emerged immediately looking more glamorous than ever, a fact on which Macquarie was quick to comment. After quick kisses all-round the women commenced setting out the dinner.

For the want of something more sensible to say Macquarie commented, "Sorry I pinched all the bath water."

"Never mind," replied Morag, "there is plenty more where that came from."

"Yes," said Fiona, "Morag and I were thinking of having a bath just before going to bed."

Which he did.

****

Macquarie awoke as the first grey light heralded the dawn of a new day. With that instinct often well preserved in those who live alone he could wake himself up at any time he wished, a kind of natural alarm clock.

Gently sliding his shoulder from under Fiona's golden head and replacing it with a corner of his pillow he slipped from the bed.

Taking his clothes from the chair he crept silently from the bedroom, through the living room to the porch where he dressed.

Easing out of the door into the coolness of the early morning and feeling relieved that the weather was dry Macquarie pulled on his rubber boots and set out for the beach.

It was still quite dark but he could clearly see the wavelets at the edge of the loch twenty feet from the top of the steps where he was standing. Just after high water he decided so he would have to hurry.

Macquarie made his way to the water's edge and from there could just make out the plank floating about thirty feet away. Feeling along the ground with his fingers he found the clothes-line and gently pulled on it swinging the end of the timber towards him. As soon as it was lined up he pulled hard bringing the heavy deal surging to the beach, where, with a grating sound, it came to rest. As soon as the moorings were released he commenced the heavy part of the labour.

Heaving, lifting, pushing and pulling Macquarie eventually had one end of the heavy water-soaked deal on the bottom step of the five leading up from the beach.

With tremendous effort he repeated the operation four more times until he had the end of the plank on the top step.

Panting and sweating profusely in spite of the cool morning Macquarie then commenced sliding the timber over the top step. Gasping for air he eventually pushed the plank past its point of balance and one end flopped onto the grass at the top of the bank. The task would have been considerably easier if the pieces of wood nailed to it had been removed but to do this would have involved a considerable amount of noise hammering in wedges and withdrawing the nails which would probably have disturbed his guests.

The next part of the job was relatively easy, just a matter of slewing, heaving and sliding the plank until it lay, safe from the sea on the grass and stones at the top of the bank. It was quite light by this time and Macquarie, looking at the sky, decided that the day's weather was likely to be rather mixed.

As he sat on the ground recovering his breath a grin slowly spread over his face.

'Now where did I leave that piece of chalk I was using a couple of days ago?'

****

Macquarie carefully replaced his boots on the spot one of the women had put them, as distinct from the general area of under the porch table where they used to be tossed, then stripped off his clothes and rolled them together. He then stepped to the sink and washed off the sand and sweat as quietly as he could. Having dried himself and wrapped the towel round his loins he mopped the floor and crept back through the living room, his clothes in his hands.

If either of the women awoke and asked him where he had been he had his answer ready, 'Ladies do not ask that kind of question!'

His stealthy progress had taken him half way across the living room when he nearly jumped out of his skin, (he had little else out of which to jump). A voice behind him had whispered "Alistair".

It was Morag, her face just discernible in the early morning light.

Readjusting his skin Macquarie softly replied, "Yes?"

"Alistair, I'm cold." Nothing suggestive about it, just a plan statement of fact.

This put Macquarie in a quandary. The room was cold, he appreciated the fact. A damp towel might be acceptable at high noon in Bermuda but not at something like five o'clock in the morning of a cold grey day in Scotland. The rub was, as host should he attend to the comfort of the guest who was not only cold but awake or make some sympathetic remark and return to his legitimate bed and his hostess of the evening – who was asleep?

Lighting the fire would be one solution but this would be noisy, time-consuming and in any case would take too long before it had any effect.

A second alternative was unthinkable. To replace the doubled blanket which he noticed had slipped from the sleeping bag to the floor would be caddish if not downright insulting.

Macquarie stood undecided in the middle of the room growing colder by the second. How dearly he would like to climb back into the warmth of his bed.

Suddenly he thought of a third alternative.

Dropping his clothes to the floor Macquarie walked to the sofa and gently inserted his hand into the sleeping bag past Morag's face. As he expected she grabbed it with both of hers. Quickly moving his fingers, he trapped her hands then slowly drew them from the bag until her arms were stretched above her head. With a swift movement he released the girl's fingers and whipped a hand under each of her arm pits, high up to trap her arms and prevent her grasping the sleeping bag.

Morag did not say a word. She apparently could not decide whether or not the man's intentions were honourable. In fact, she was obviously not all that bothered either way.

Gently Macquarie drew the unresisting girl from the sofa, then, stepping back a pace, lifted her high in the air.

At this juncture two things became apparent to Macquarie at the same time. Firstly, that the laws of gravity operate just as effectively at that unearthly hour of the morning as at any other time of day and secondly that at least one of his girls did not wear pyjamas even when sleeping alone.

Lowering the gorgeous body to his chest Macquarie's right hand and forearm moved to a more comfortable position and his left encircled the smooth back. Morag's immediate reaction to the release of her arms was to wrap them tightly around Macquarie's neck, which action relieved his left hand to open the bedroom door.

Dropping the towel at the bedside Macquarie gently eased himself beneath the blankets. In doing so his right arm touched a soft warm back which immediately turned to present an even softer, warmer front. A gentle wriggling in the region of his left arm resulted in a similar situation on that side.

Could any man want for more?

****

Fiona was a trifle put out when she awoke at her usual time to find Morag sharing 'her' bed and was only partially pacified when the situation was explained. She relieved her ruffled feelings by saying, "Morag still has to make the tea this morning!" Then, remembering an omission of the previous evening, "Oh! She can't, we forgot to fill the thermos flask last night."

Macquarie had got into the highly recommendable habit of starting his day with a gentle fondling and caressing to take his mind off the current middle east crisis, income tax, the state the country was in and suchlike horrors but on this occasion, deciding that such a delightful awakening process might easily lead to complications, he said he would light the fire and make the morning tea. In spite of a few feeble protests he therefore rolled from the bed, transferred Morag to the part of it he had just vacated in the one movement.

Retrieving his towel from the floor he wrapped it around his hips before standing up – Macquarie was the shy type – and made his way towards the kitchen.

Noting that Fiona still looked rather upset he stopped at the bedroom door and warned the young women that there was to be no squabbling whilst he was away. His parting remark, "Don't forget you are both very vulnerable," caused both little bottoms to wriggle nervously.

After a quick wash Macquarie collected the clothes he had dropped in the living room earlier that morning and got dressed. He then made and lit the fire and put the kettle on for tea, making a considerable amount of noise in the process.

Singing rather flatly Macquarie clattered mugs and tea-pot onto the tray, made up some milk from powder – no milkman made a daily call – and added the jug to the collection. None of them took sugar.

As only enough water had been put in the kettle for a pot of tea this was soon boiled and the tea brewing. Refilling the kettle for washing water Macquarie returned it to the fire and then took the tea tray in to the ladies, tapping on the bedroom door before entering for some damn fool reason.

The women welcomed their tea in bed but, sitting up, had some trouble keeping themselves chastely covered as the slightest movement of one was inclined to dislodge the bunched up sheet protecting the modesty of the other.

Macquarie sat on the end of the bed making light conversation in an effort to justify his presence. He was there for two good reasons, the other being to impress on the girls' subconscious that he had never been out of their sight or hearing since he left the bed, certainly he had had no opportunity to go outside the house.

Macquarie busied himself with the fire and laid the table for breakfast as first Fiona and the Morag tripped through the room towards the kitchen, sponge-bags in hand. He followed Fiona saying that the weather looked as if it would be rather on the dull side that day. Draped on the doorway he started to enlarge on the subject but Fiona, guessing his shameful hopes, leaned a jersey-covered elbow on the draining board in a rather exaggerated way as if to indicate she was willing to listen to his weather forecast for the remainder of the morning.

Temporarily foiled in his evil lust Macquarie suddenly remembered he had not brought the hot water to the kitchen. This had become a routine chore for him as the iron kettle when full was rather heavy and dangerous for either girl to manage. He dashed to the fire, grabbed the steaming kettle and rushed back to the kitchen to find Fiona demurely clad in a towel. Macquarie's towels were none of them very big but the largest covered all the necessary territory of a woman Fiona's size.

"Thank you Alistair," she said sweetly as he poured half the kettle's contents into the washing up bowl in the sink, the nearest the Macquarie household had to a vanity unit.

Entering the kitchen later to collect more logs as Morag was lathing her face Macquarie heard her say, "Blast, I've lost the soap."

Immediately to the rescue Macquarie's first thought was that the soap might have slipped down the front of Morag's towel-sarong but he had only begun to explore this possibility when Morag found the errant tablet in the sink behind the bowl.

Breathing somewhat heavily Macquarie found it no wonder so many citizens of otherwise exemplary character discovered themselves in trouble in the courts.

It was not until Morag had dressed and joined the others in the kitchen that Fiona asked, "I hope your plank was not washed away in the night Alistair, is it alright?"

"To tell you the truth I have not had time to go out and look yet. I moored it well so it should be alright. Let us go and see whilst the breakfast is cooking."

Allowing the women to precede him Macquarie dawdled in the porch putting on his rubber boots. As he expected there was an excited shout.

"Alistair! Come quickly!" Fiona called.

"Yes! Something strange had happened, the plank is right on top of the bank," cried an excited Morag.

"On top of the bank! It can't be, however could it have got there?" Macquarie sounded astonished.

"Whatever are you doing Alistair?" cried Fiona, "Come and see, quickly!"

Macquarie with a mystified expression on his face was crouched down examining the door post. Looking up he said in absolute seriousness, "You may laugh but there is only one way the plank could have got there."

"How?" chorused the girls.

"Fairies," answered Macquarie solemnly.

"Fairies?" the women obviously thought Macquarie was joking.

"Yes, the 'Wee Folk'. I know you town people think it is ridiculous but out here we do sometimes see traces of them. I always leave some cake and a wee dram out for them on Hogmanay and this must be their way of saying 'Thank you'."

"Alistair, don't be absurd, what an extraordinary thing to say." In spite of her words Fiona did not sound too convinced. Something had deposited the heavy piece of timber on top of the bank during the night and it certainly could not have been a tidal wave.

"How else could it have got there then?" persisted Macquarie, "The only thing I don't understand is that they have not left any signs. You see when the 'Wee Folk' do a good deed they invariably scratch a message on a door-post or chalk it on a nearby rock. No one but fairies can read it of course as it is in their own lan....."

"Alistair!" Morag's shriek must have been audible in the village across the loch, "There is writing! Here on the plank! Look Fiona, that looks like an eye...."

"And a sort of flower and a triangle!" added Fiona in a voice as excited as that of Morag.

Macquarie could contain himself no longer. His knees buckling beneath him he sat heavily on the grass, threw back his head and howled with laughter.

No doubt with all the talk of fairies Morag and Fiona thought for a moment that Macquarie had been bewitched. But only for a moment. Realising they had been duped, albeit by some unknown means, they pounced on the man calling him every (lady like), epithet they could lay their tongues to and pummelled him with tiny fists.

"You brute! You cheat! You beast! You absolute horror, making fun of us like that!"

Words and fists bounced off Macquarie like hail as he lay back completely unable to defend himself being so convulsed with laughter.

Eventually he managed to gain an element of control of himself and wrap an arm around each furious female to prevent, to a great extent, their physical attacks, though he was unable to control their tongues.

After struggling for a while Morag suddenly stiffened, "The breakfast!" she cried, "it will be ruined."

"I had forgotten all about it, quick, let us go," joined in Fiona.

On being released the women scrambled to their feet and fled to the cottage leaving Macquarie lying on the ground still whooping with laughter.

At first the young women gave the impression of being extremely hurt by his teasing but soon Macquarie had them laughing with him.

The ladies breakfasted on their usual toast and Macquarie on the somewhat scorched porridge which he only just prevented being thrown away. He considered it his penance – and a cheap price to pay.

Over the meal Macquarie recounted his endeavours of the early morning ending with the fright he had received on hearing his name whispered as he crept through the living room.

Being brought right up to date the ladies made flattering remarks regarding his prowess with the plank which must have temporarily increased Macquarie's hat size by a good three inches.

Breakfast over the women decided a laundry session was indicated in spite of the indifferent drying weather. Macquarie was all for leaving it until a more sunny day but the ladies were adamant.

"There are all the clothes we wore yesterday," said Fiona, "and I must wash my dress, it is becoming quite unsociable."

"Mine too." Morag was as confirmed an addict as Fiona to this washing fetish, thought Macquarie.

As soon as the washing up was done, the bed made and various items of tidying up carried out to the ladies' satisfaction they commenced the laundry.

Having assisted with the hot water supply for the washing Macquarie returned to his plank. He removed to the battens with claw hammer and wedges, salvaged the nails and returned these items to the storehouse ready for their next assignment. This done he bethought himself of the women's imminent need of the clothes line so set off to find it. He had dropped it on a heap of tide-wrack at the top of the beach when he had started manhandling the plank early that morning but could not remember having seen it since. From the top of the steps he saw something white in the vicinity of where he had dropped the line but approaching closer it proved to be only the remains of a dead seagull. There was no sign of the clothes-line. Thinking that one of the girls must have recovered it he walked back to the door and asked Fiona, busy at the sink, if she or Morag had seen the clothes line.

"Yes, I have it here. Do you want it for something?"

Much to Macquarie's astonishment she lifted from the soap-suds in the bowl the coils of the clothes line. Apparently so desperate for something to wash Fiona was washing the line itself! Macquarie swore he would never understand women.

****

Later that morning as Macquarie was heaving, sliding, levering and generally persuading the plank to move from its previous resting place to the vicinity of the outhouse Morag asked him what he intended to do with it. To her surprise he said he did not really know.

"What! After all your efforts to get it here you have no use for the thing?"

"Oh, I did not say that," was the reply, "there are plenty of uses for it. At one end of the scale it could become the main roof beam of a new store house I mean to build and at the other it would be useful to run the wheelbarrow on over rough ground."

"Well after all the work I hope it finds a useful purpose," Morag said as she left him to return to the house.

"Oh, by the way," she turned and smiled sweetly, "Why don't you get the 'Wee Folk' to take it to the outhouse for you?" Then she ran.

****

The newly washed clothes hung damply on the line all day.

That night the ladies again dressed in their off the shoulder blouses and chequered skirts so obviously Macquarie was forgiven his escapade with the 'Wee Folk' that morning.

****

All good things come to an end and inevitably the sad day of their parting arrived. It was an often melancholy Macquarie who helped the young women prepare for the journey which would take them away from him.

After breakfast Macquarie shouldered the two packs and they set off, the girls' eyes moist as they glanced back at the cottage. Little was said as they walked side by side up the beach. By mutual consent to preserve appearances, ('for some silly reason' thought Macquarie), he would escort the ladies as far as the head of the loch from whence they would make their own way to the road and village and from there by public transport to their respective homes.

****

The surface of the tranquil loch glistened in the morning sun as they reached the place where their paths divided.

After brief, all too brief, hugs and kisses Fiona and Morag parted from Macquarie with mutual good wishes and thanks. It was a sad farewell but as the women had to make good time in order to catch the one daily bus from the village it could not be prolonged.

As soon as 'his' pack-laden girls disappeared over the brow of a low hill Macquarie retraced his steps to the now very lonely cottage. Having that morning checked the date for the first time in over a week he was shocked to realise that MacNab was due at any time with the new cooker. If the boat arrived within the next day or two he would have to manhandle the heavy stove the first few yards from the high water mark to his wheelbarrow at the end of the still incomplete causeway. The sooner he got to work on it the better.

****

Thus we reach the end of Macquarie's soliloquy but a brief record of Fiona and Morag's conversation as they tramped towards the village may be of some slight interest.

****

The two young women had walked nearly half a mile without speaking, which was a near record for them, before Morag broke the silence with a sigh followed in the sincerest possible tone of voice, "That really was a holiday to remember."

"I could not agree more," replied her companion, "I will never forget a minute of it as long as I live."

"And hardly a souvenir, apart from the sheepskin slippers – I will never part with them."

"Neither will I," Fiona then laughed, "It's a pity we haven't the curtain skirts too, what shocking memories they would bring back."

"They would certainly take a bit of explaining at home. I wonder what is in those packets Alistair gave us this morning? I am dying to open mine, what a pity there is not time to stop and open them now."

"Morag!" said Fiona in a shocked voice, "You solemnly promised not to open it until you got home."

"'Woman thy promises are traced in sand'", misquoted Morag in reply.

"We might be able to dig them out of our packs in the bus if it is not too crowded," Fiona had apparently appeased her conscience with her earlier remark.

"I hope they are photographs of him."

"Hardly likely," said Fiona, "he is not the type to pass out pictures of himself. Anyway I don't think he has a camera, the only photos we saw were those old family ones in that album…. which…which happened to fall open whilst we were spring cleaning."

"We will have to be careful opening them in case they are one of his jokes, a piece of curtain skirt stuck to a card or something like that," said Morag, hastily adding, "but I don't think he would do anything like that."

The women had no cause for concern. Each package contained a miniature painting of his cottage. They had been painted years earlier so did not include the new porch, however the omission was not apparent as one was of the north west aspect thus hiding the front of the house and the other a distant view, the rocks at the end of the peninsula providing the foreground. Each painting was neatly signed 'A. Macquarie' in the bottom right hand corner and both were accompanied by a card inscribed 'To Fiona (or Morag) In memory of a visit –Alistair'

The women walked silently for another hundred yards before Morag, thinking of her companion's earlier blisters, asked if her feet were troubling her. Fiona replied in the negative as regards her feet although she had to admit she would be glad to reach the bus and rid herself of the unaccustomed pack. In reciprocation she asked if Morag was quite comfortable. This brought the reply, "Yes thanks," then with a laugh Morag added rather coarsely, "For a man who has such a thing about bras he certainly knows how to fit them."

"I noticed he went to a great deal of trouble," giggled Fiona.

"No more than he did with yours."

Silence for several more yards, then, "How often should we write to him?"

"I really don't know. I suppose it would be best if we wrote combined letters," replied Morag doubtfully.

"I do not think much of that but let us agree that we will always let one another know when we each write to prevent it developing into some kind of race."

"We can sort that out later, let us not have an argument about it," then, turning to look over her shoulder in mock apprehension, Morag continued, "Not in this part of the country anyway, you remember what happened last time?"

"It is engraved on my heart," replied Fiona with feeling, "my bottom still tingles when I think of it."

"So does mine," Morag touched her rump, "Are you sure there were no blisters when you looked?"

"Quite sure," replied Morag with a laugh, "As red as a Hawaiian sunset but no blisters."

"Gosh, his hands can be awfully hard when he wants them to be."

"Yes, it is just as well we had changed into our dresses by then, it would have been torture trying to get back into jeans."

Morag laughed, "I wonder what our mothers' reactions would have been if they had seen us lying on the bed applying cold cream to one another's derrieres!"

"Mothers! Good grief Morag, Post-Cards! We haven't sent any for over a week."

"Wow! We are in trouble. I seem to have been on another planet for ages. What can we do, buy a stock at the first opportunity and write them on the bus?"

"Saying we could not find a post box?", suggested Fiona, "We will have to phone as soon as possible to let them know we are alright in any case."

Discussing their problem, the two young ladies tramped towards the village.

****

Chapter 9

Chief Engineer Macquarie sighed as he thought of those days, the happiest of his life. Did Morag and Fiona often think of him he wondered? Sometimes they did of course or he would not have received their occasional letters, sweet, friendly letters which told him little but indicated without actually mentioning the fact that both remembered him with great affection. These communications were few and his replies as rare.

Macquarie's letters told 'his girls' of the things he intended to do at the cottage, no dates specified. A small jetty of rocks and concrete and eventually a path of similar materials from it to the steps below the cottage. This would be built mainly over the rocks to the south of his original causeway and should be useable for at least half the tide. This done he might construct another outbuilding or possibly a lean-to on the south wall of the house, mentioning a large plank he had which might come in useful in this connection. He wrote of the fitting of his new cooker and his small culinary successes with it. He never mentioned the weather or daily happenings at the cottage as when he wrote the letters he had not seen his home for months.

To protect the intimacy of their friendship from the 'outside world' Macquarie never mentioned the ship at all. In fact, he often wondered if the young women even knew that he went to sea for a livelihood. The subject had never been brought up in conversation any more than what the women themselves did to earn their daily bread. As all his sea-going gear was left on the ship when he went on leave there was no evidence of his profession at the cottage so far as he could recall. As his letters normally went to the U.K. with the Master's official mail and were posted there, having been addressed and stamped before leaving the ship, they gave no indication of his whereabouts. If either of the girls wondered at the London postmarks or his habit of dating the letters only by the day of the week it extracted no comment.

'Never mind my landscape painting,' thought Macquarie with a grin, 'I wonder what the lads on board would think if they knew about my girls?'

He glanced at the clock on the bulkhead, 'Good God! Is that the time? I must get down below and have a word with the Second before he comes off watch.'

Waiting for the rolling of the ship to ease the process Macquarie rose from his chair and reached for the boiler suit hanging in his office, alternately slapping against the bulkhead then swinging slowly out from it, matching the movement of the ship.

The wind could not be heard in the engine room, the sound of it being completely overwhelmed by the noise of the machinery, however there was no doubt in the minds of the people there as to the state of the weather. The heavy rolling and pitching of the ship made the old saying 'one hand for the ship and one for yourself' as appropriate on the oily footplates as on deck.

All day number three generator had been neglected in its dismantled state, the two others producing the electricity required for running the ship. Although it had been hoped to have it reassembled by the evening and ready to take over from the straining number one no time had been found to even commence the job. The heavy rolling and straining of the ship had started a joint in a generator cooling line which, being in a very awkward position, caused a great deal of time and effort to be expended before it was tight. Hardly had this job been completed when one of the fuel oil pumps began to give trouble. It was late afternoon by the time the fault was rectified.

Chief Engineer Macquarie had spent most of the day with his staff on the various repairs and when he went up to his room shortly before the evening meal everything appeared to have been restored to good order. It had been decided at that time that the No.3 generator reassembly could probably wait until the following morning. However, on returning to the engine room an hour or so later a brief inspection of the generators gave the Chief cause for alarm. He turned to the second Engineer standing beside him.

"I don't like it Peter, I don't like it at all. That number one sounds worse than it did an hour ago, I doubt if it will hold out until the morning. We will have to box up number three right away after all."

"Gawd! What a prospect!" Peter Gregson had already had a very long day. "Surely number two could take the whole load, just for tonight anyway? It is going like a bomb."

"Too risky in this weather if that one packed up where would we be? No, we will have to get number three on the board as soon as we can. We will get the job started with the watch then call the Third out early so you can get your head down."

Work had not been long in process on the generator when, as if in confirmation of the Chief's fears, a loud banging suddenly drowned out all the other noises of the engine room.

The engineers lunged for the controls of the straining number one generator but with horror found they had been mistaken, the noise emanated from number two machine, the one 'good' generator.

Number two generator was quickly stopped but the additional load suddenly placed on the one remaining machine proved too much for it. It too 'came off the board' and thus stopped the fans, pumps and other auxiliaries. Also the main engine. The ship was at once dark and powerless in the wild sea.

It took several minutes to get number one generator restarted and even then it did not produce enough power for more than a few bare essentials. The lights came on again throughout the ship but little else resulted.

****

The Mate could not sleep. The violent motion of the ship was not keeping him awake, he had had plenty of practice sleeping in all kinds of weather over the years. No, something was wrong. He felt it rather than heard it, whatever 'it' might be. Somewhere in all the roaring of the gale, the crashing of the seas and the internal sounds of the ship was one small sound or vibration out of place, something that should not be. A very small 'something', something almost indiscernible. But definitely something.

Hatch concentrated, discarding one by one the sounds that did not matter, the books in the bookcase flopping from one side to the other, a marline spike rolling on his office desk, (anyone trying to sleep on the deck below the office is probably being driven mad by it, thought Hatch with some slight satisfaction), the creaks and groans of the wood panelling. No, it was something else. Once or twice he thought he had identified the sound then it was gone. Then, there! That was it a tiny sound repeated at intervals. Regular intervals, a faint 'clump' then a pause as the ship rolled, then again the sound. It was obviously some distance away, a door perhaps? No, a swinging door did not sound like that.

To the Mate it was the sound of something loose which should not be loose. Something that was slightly loose now could be very seriously adrift in a very short time in the prevailing weather. There again it could be something absolutely trivial what had nothing to do with him, a piece of equipment belonging to the catering department for instance, a tin of scouring powder rolling in a locker might make such a sound whilst doing no more harm than making an awful mess.

There were two alternative courses of action. The sensible one was to convince oneself it was nothing important and try to get to sleep.

346

The other was to get up, dress and clamber around the ship in an attempt to identify the noise in the almost impossible conditions prevailing in the screaming wind. The latter course would inevitably mean becoming soaked and frozen – and possibly hurt – quite probably to no useful purpose. The thought of leaving a warm, if not particularly comfortable, bunk to find that some damn fool had left a snatch block swinging from an awning spar or something equally stupid was vile in the extreme.

Hatch slowly eased himself from his bunk and started to get dressed.

'Might as well start from the top,' he thought, 'and let the bridge know that I am not wandering around with a torch having a midnight stroll or putting the cat out.'

Hatch stepped out onto the deck into the biting wind and made his way up to the bridge. The weather had worsened since he came off watch, the wind screamed maniacally through the rigging, the tone but not the volume of sound changing slightly with the violent rolling of the ship. Too violently, he thought, if she were not so stiff at least each roll would be longer and somewhat easier. However, nothing could be done about that.

"Touch of insomnia Mr. Hatch?" said the Captain drily as the Mate stumbled into the wheelhouse.

"Just taking a breath of fresh air," answered the Mate, then, more seriously, "There is knocking somewhere, thought I'd have a poke around to see if I can find it."

"Mind you don't break your neck. Let me know if you find anything, or even if you do not tell me when you have finished. Do not go near the main deck though as she is taking some big ones on board now and again. Anything adrift there will have to wait until daylight."

It took Hatch nearly half an hour to trace the source of the mysterious sound, it was the fore end of number two lifeboat. The motion of the ship had caused a bottle screw on the gripe wire to work loose, very slightly but enough to allow the boat to move about an inch away from the chock then back again with each roll of the ship. A small thing but it would have got worse during the night and might have meant a big job of securing by morning.

The Mate required but a few minutes to fetch a marline spike from his office, tighten the screw and secure it with a piece of seizing wire to prevent a repeat performance. By the time the job was finished he was very wet, particularly about the knees where neither his oilskin coat or seaboots gave any protection. He was also extremely cold and bad-tempered.

The Captain was still on the bridge when Hatch returned. He expected to be there all night unless the weather moderated considerably before morning, which appeared very unlikely.

Hatch reported the boat secured then turned to the Third Mate.

"Have you got a brew on?"

"Kettle's just boiled," replied Smith, "Tea or coffee?"

"Either so long as it's hot. The taste is the same the way you make it anyway."

With remarkable dexterity the Third Mate poured three cups of tea and added a dollop of condensed milk to each. A quick stir with a chart pencil, the spoon had been lost on the deck earlier in the evening, and each man picked up a cup from the sticky top of the flag locker.

"I hope this tastes as good as it smells," said the Captain as he put the cup to his lips.

It was at this moment the generators failed.

****

A brief conversation with the Chief Engineer over the battery operated engine room telephone confirmed to the Captain that the situation was bad, if not worse, than he had at first surmised when the power failed. Very little could be done in the way of repairs in the engine room unless the ship could be prevented from rolling so violently.

The many emergencies which could, and did, occur on a ship were never far from Captain Montague's mind. He had mentally worked out many times what his first, so often the most important actions, would be when confronted with a sudden emergency. 'Man overboard' for instance. The first thing was to throw the helm hard over towards that side which the man had fallen over to swing the ship's stern and propeller clear of him. If a life-buoy or any other marker could be dropped into the water at the same time so much the better. Stopping the engines for the same purpose was a mere pipe-dream, the ship would run a couple of miles before the propeller stopped turning. Fire in the engine room; one of the crew with a sudden heart attack; there were a hundred or more situations which would be encountered without warning.

One such emergency stared him in the face. Storm force winds, a raging sea and no power whatsoever. As things were the helpless ship would come round until beam on to the wind and sea. Then she would roll. Not the rolling of a ship under way which good steering or a slight adjustment of course could alleviate to a certain extent but the violent uncontrolled rolling of a dead ship. Rolling that was not only extremely uncomfortable but very dangerous, carrying away things which would normally be secure and making vitally necessary repairs in the engine room utterly impossible.

The way to avoid this was to bring the ship's head into the wind. The pitching in the longitudinal axis of the ship then encountered, although violent enough, would at least allow men to work and effect repairs. With no power available this could be achieved only by increasing the drag of the fore end of the ship or increasing her wind resistance aft. The latter method was used on sailing vessels by rigging a small sail on the after mast. Montague had often wondered if on Saint Paul's ship the 'throwing anchors over the stern' was some kind of misprint in the first place. The build of ships in those ancient days with their high poops and low bows would by their very design be inclined to bring the vessel's head into the wind. 'Several anchors' from the bow, (they were probably small enough to be 'cast' in those days), seemed to make more sense.

The problem of the 'Belisarius' was rather different. Her main wind resistance was amidships, her bridge, funnel and accommodation. Neutral from the point of heaving to.

Although sails had disappeared from steam ships half a century earlier the ship still carried canvas in the way of awnings and hatch tarpaulins. The awnings, of various shapes and sizes, were of such light canvas they had to be taken in in anything like a breeze in spite of their being fitted horizontally. Hatch tarpaulins were of sterner stuff. Of heavy waterproofed canvas the largest on the 'Belisarius', for number two hatch, measured thirty-eight feet by twenty-four. The new spare tarpaulin, neatly rolled and lashed, lay in the forepeak store. It could be raised from the store, carried aft, fitted with bolt-ropes and other re-enforcements and with a little ingenuity rigged aft as a sail. Given a few fine days to do the job! If rigged in the prevailing weather it might last two or three hours. Or five minutes.

And it would have no effect at all. A sheet of canvas weighing nearly a quarter of a ton seems a lot of material to anyone who has experienced the man-handling of it but to fifteen odd thousand tons of ship and cargo with a length of five hundred and a breadth of sixty-five feet it would resemble, in both appearance and effect, a pocket handkerchief.

This left achieving the desired effect by the reverse process, increasing the drag forward so that the stern would have relatively more wind resistance. One way of doing this would be by pumping fuel and water from the after tanks to the forward ones and thus increasing the forward draft and reducing that aft. But with no power the ship had no means of pumping anything anywhere.

The Captain recalled the 'good old Board of Trade' methods of rigging sea-anchors learned whilst sitting for his certificate. The practicability of rigging any kind of sea-anchor in the prevailing conditions was out of the question.

However, there was one piece of equipment on the ship which would help, if not actually succeed, in bringing the vessel's head close to the wind. An item which would, if all went well, be used without power.

The windlass on the foc'sle head was a powerful piece of machinery. The 'drum-ends' on either end of its main shaft were used for heaving on mooring ropes when berthing but its main function was to control the chain cable when dropping or weighing anchor. Power was required to heave in the heavy chain and anchors but dropping them was executed by releasing the brakes, one for each of the two cables. Each cable extended from the anchor, through the hawse-pipe, over the gypsies of the windlass, (large sprocket wheels with divisions each neatly encompassing one link of the cable as it passed over), down through the deck via the spurling pipes abaft the windlass and into the chain locker. There the 'bitter end' was firmly secured to a quick release attachment in case the anchor and cable should ever be required to be slipped.

Secured to each anchor was nine shackles of cable, each 'shackle' or length of chain being of fifteen fathoms. A total of two hundred and seventy fathoms or sixteen hundred and twenty feet of chain and two four and a half ton anchors. Hanging vertically from the ship's bow they would constitute a considerable drag in the water.

If it could be done.

Anchors by their very nature are meant to be dropped onto the sea bed. Four and a half tons of anchor backed by a considerable tonnage of chain cable dropping vertically through nothing more resistant than water takes a great deal of stopping. Massive and strong as they are no windlass is designed to take this kind of treatment.

However, it was a risk the Captain decided would have to be taken. It was the possibility of losing thousands of pounds' worth of anchoring gear, plus a fair chance of maiming the mate or carpenter, balanced against the safety of the ship and crew as a whole.

Captain Montague turned to Hatch. He had to shout to make himself heard above the shrieking wind.

"There is only one thing for it Mr. Hatch, we will have to lower the anchors to the full extent of their cables, that might bring her round. It will mean the chain locker will flood but that can't be helped. By the way, is the chain locker door secured? We don't want the whole forepeak store flooding."

The chain locker door, actually more of an inspection hatch in the fore side of the locker near the top, was securely closed but more by luck than design as normally it was hooked open and had only been secured by its dogs earlier in the passage when the hook had at last reached the end of its days.

"Yes sir, the door is closed but I am not too keen on letting go the anchors with nothing to stop them. As you know the brakes are not too good at the best of times, we could easily lose the lot."

"It's a chance we will have to take, the engineers can't work in this rolling so there is no alternative I can think of."

"O.K. sir," ('I wish he would not use those Americanisms,' thought the Captain), "I will collect 'Chips' and see what we can do."

Hatch was halfway down the bridge ladder when the Captain called out to him.

"If when you get for'd you think the job impracticable just leave it." (To himself, 'What I mean is for God's sake don't get yourself injured.') "Let me know as soon as you are off the fore deck, - And Jake, take care."

Only one of the last four words registered in Hatch's mind. 'That's the first time he has ever called me 'Jake'. The old bastard must be becoming human after all, he might even stand me a peg when I get back!'

* *

The ship's carpenter, Joseph MacMurdo was a Glaswegian in his mid-forties. The impression given by his permanently dirty boiler suit and rarely shaved jaw was belied by a pair of blue eyes which twinkled beneath bushy sand-coloured eyebrows. His stocky, muscular slow moving frame spoke of considerable physical strength but his large horny hands gave no indication of the delicacy of which they were capable when applied to a fine piece of woodwork. Although a confirmed bachelor there existed many a small niece of his who's pride and joy was a completely furnished doll's house and most of his numerous nephews spent much of their spare time sailing the model yachts he had made for them. At that very moment a carefully packed carton under the carpenter's bunk contained a beautiful Tudor style doll's house with all its fittings, destined for his latest niece. Carefully packed as that young lady would probably not play with it for a year or two as she had only entered the world a month previously.

Joe MacMurdo had spent most of his adult life at sea, several years of it on the 'Belisarius'. As the Chief Officer's right hand man he had always proved a pillar of strength, or, as someone once remarked, 'he was built like a brick shit-house and just as dependable'.

In emergencies the carpenter's place was with the Chief Officer. 'Chips' had been looking for the Mate since the engines stopped and his search was about to extend to the bridge when Hatch ran into him at the after end of the accommodation.

"We have a bit of a job on," shouted the Mate above the roaring of the wind, "Have you got your hammer?"

The carpenter was surprised he asked.

Chip's hammer was a byword on the Company's ships. Actually the tool in question was a topping maul, the head being flat at one end and tapering to a blunt point at the other. An ideal design for one of its many uses, hammering home hatch wedges and, when the hatch was to be opened, knocking them out again. MacMurdo would probably have been surprised to learn that identical mauls had been used at the Battle of Agincourt.

MacMurdo was very fond of his hammer and it would accompany him to any job where there was the remotest possibility of its being needed. He had carried it with him since he first came to sea and for years previously when he was serving his time in Clyde shipyard. It was brand new when he was handed it, as the yard's youngest apprentice, to knock away the last dog shore at the launching of a liner which in her day became well known on the North Atlantic. It had been with him throughout the recent war and he had never really lived down the story of how, when his ship was torpedoed in the middle of a tropical night, he dashed to his room from the deck on which he had been sleeping and moments later arrived at his lifeboat clad in nothing but a life-jacket but firmly gripping his beloved hammer. Of course the maul had been fitted with several new shafts over the years but MacMurdo vehemently denied that it had had a few new heads as well.

"Let's go then," said Hatch, "We are going to drop a brace of anchors, even though the water is three miles deep. The Old Man thinks they might not act as a sea-anchor, I only hope he is right or we will be right up a gum tree, the engineers can't do anything with the ship rolling like this."

A less garrulous man the carpenter's only comment was, "It's a rare night for it!" as the two men set off the foc'sle head.

Whilst still in the lee of the midship house Chips secured his hammer to the lashing around his waist and Hatch checked that the marline spike was still in the deep pocket of his oilskin coat and that his torch still worked.

Their progress along the foredeck was a nightmare. Hanging on grimly to the life-line stretched from the fore end of the accommodation to the foc'sle head ladder they liberally fought their way forward. As each succeeding sea thundered across the deck they were first submerged and then afloat as again and again their legs were swept from under them.

After what seemed an eternity to the two men they eventually arrived on the foc'sle head, battered, bruised and soaked to the skin. Eight feet higher than the fore deck the seas still crashed over them but at least it was not solid water.

After a brief 'breather' in what shelter the windlass offered they set about freeing the anchor lashings. First the 'claws', heavy double hooks of steel which hooked round a link of each chain just forward of the windlass. Each claw was secured to the deck by a bottle screw. With the aid of the marline spike releasing them did not take long although the job had its frightening moments as a particularly violent roll of the ship or a heavy sea caused them to hang on desperately.

The 'cross lashing' consisted of a heavy wire strop passed through the links of the two cables just above the hawse-pipes, the ends of the strop being secured together by another bottle screw. This was in an even more exposed position with nothing to hang on to except the cables themselves. The danger and discomfort was intensified by the solid water gushing up the hawse-pipes as the seas crashed into the bow.

It was when they had slacked off but half a turn of the screw they lost the marline spike.

Hatch's language would have wilted a cactus. He was about to start for the space under the foc'sle head where old wire rope, empty paint drums, broken pieces of winch and other junk accumulated in the hope of finding something to replace the spike when Chips called him back.

"One moment sir, if I can get my two hands on the screw I may be able to turn it."

It would mean 'two hands for the ship' and none for himself but it was worth a try. Anything to get the job over and done with so they could return to the relative comfort offered amidships.

The screw was released that way. It took all of the carpenter's quite considerable strength to turn the screw and Hatch's arms were nearly torn from their sockets time and again as he hung on grimly to both Chips and the cable in order to prevent both men being swept away. The job took several minutes of agonising labour.

The 'locking bars', two feet long and four by six inches in sections, each hinged at one end to their cast iron frames, rested between two links of cable abaft the hawse-pipes. These were soon swung clear although one required a tap from Chips' hammer to free it.

It was not intended that anchors would be dropped by accident at sea.

Normally the plugs in the tops of the spurling pipes would have been removed before dropping the anchors but this was not a normal occasion. Each of the two plugs were built up of a 'pudding', a cigar shaped bag of sacking stuffed with oakum which was supported by pieces of stick and stuffed around the cable in the mouth of the pipe. This was covered with a thick layer of cement and a tight fitting canvas cover laced over the whole thing. Being sheltered by the windlass this arrangement was sufficient to prevent the heaviest sea making its way below into the chain locker. It would not last a second however once the cable began to move.

All that now held the anchors in the hawse-pipes were the brakes of the windlass.

If the brakes were released and left open the anchors would plummet down increasing their momentum as more and more chain surged out after them. When the end of the chain was reached one of several things could happen depending on where exactly the cable parted. Wherever the break occurred a great deal of damage would be caused by the flying ends of the chain.

The task of Hatch and the carpenter was to try to control the speed of each anchor's descent by adjusting the friction of the brakes as the cable ran out. Difficult and dangerous enough in ideal weather conditions the prospect for the two weary, half frozen men in the present circumstances was appalling.

"Right!" bawled Hatch into the carpenter's ear, "The usual routine though as soon as you have tapped the brake handle free hand me the hammer. I'll hold on to it and give you a hand when things start moving. Stand as clear as you can manage and don't forget that the plug will be coming up in bits as soon as the cable starts to run. And Chips, when this job is over I'll give you the biggest peg of whiskey you have ever seen in your drunken life!"

Waiting for the ship to roll upright the carpenter gave the brake handle a couple of taps, passed the hammer to the Mate and grabbed each end of the steel bar handle. He quickly gave it half a turn to release the friction of the brake band and then, as the anchor left the hawse-pipe and the cable began to move, slammed the handle back to renew the grip of the brake. The cement and oakum plug was plucked out of the spurling pipe as the cable began to run out. Chips threw his whole weight onto the handle and although this did not stop the chain running it did at least slow its progress. The cable rattled and banged as if determined to shake the ship apart. Almost as soon as the cable started running the brake band heated by friction sufficiently to create steam from the salt water pouring over it. By the time half the chain was out the band would probably have glowed red hot but for its constant drenching.

The two men struggled to keep their feet on the rolling, bucking deck whilst keeping as much weight as they could on the brake. The Mate's right hand and arm backed the other's two whilst with his left he gripped as well as he could the frame of the windlass in order to prevent both of them being swept away by the pitiless sea.

With a sudden, final crash which threatened to drive the entire windlass through the deck the cable became silent. For a moment they thought the chain had parted. It was not until the mate had struggled to the ship's side and by the light of his torch caught a glimpse of the cable hanging vertically into the raging sea that he could persuade himself of their success. At least part of the cable was there and to the mate's experienced eye the way the chain appeared to cut through the waves rather than swing indicated that all the cable and the anchor also was still attached to the ship. He swung round to signal the good news to the carpenter and this was nearly his undoing. The moment's inattention resulted in a heavy sea tearing Hatch's grip from the guard rail and sending him crashing across the deck to bring up against the pipe casings abaft the windlass.

In spite of considerable bruising to both body and dignity the Mate's elation remained undiminished. Having climbed to his feet he decided that he might say a few words to honour the occasion. Spitting out a mouthful of salt water and a broken tooth he shouted into the carpenter's ear, "There you are Chips, nothing to it!"

The two battered, weary men hauled themselves over to the second windlass brake.

Apart from the fact that the operation had to be carried out in complete darkness owing to the loss of the torch during the Mate's tumble the second cable's release was a repeat of the first, at least until the final few fathoms of chain. As the last length of chain rattled over the windlass the over-hot, screaming brake hand could stand the strain no longer and parted. Fortunately, the ship was at her maximum roll at the time and the two men were flung clear of the flying piece of brake band. However, the tortured brake had done its job, the cable stopped running when brought up by the stenhouse slip attaching it to the bottom of the chain locker.

Stop it did but the effect of the suddenly checked forces resembled an earthquake. The noise was indescribable. The windlass was wrecked, the upper part of the hawse-pipe shattered, the spurling pipe smashed and the deck around it torn as if it had been of tin-foil.

However, below the bow were two anchors and two long lengths of chain cable the drag of which would slowly, very slowly, bring the ship's head close into the direction of the oncoming seas. The first of many things required to renew the life of the 'Belisarius'.

Chapter 10

Since the beginning of time the winter storms have howled their unchecked way across the Western Ocean.

Born of the whirling depression which follow one another from west to east the great grey seas pursue their relentless course until they batter themselves to pieces on the iron-bound coasts of Europe.

The wind, varying in direction according to the position of the centre of each depression, providing the energy to build up a sea which in a matter of hours can defy description. Running at right angles to the wind the waves form roughly parallel lines and are normally of a similar height.

Almost all of them. Occasionally, as a result of a combination of causes, a sea slightly different from the pattern occurs, a sea sometimes larger or steeper than its neighbours, sometimes coming from a slightly different direction. A sea which can catch a ship off balance when she is struggling in a storm. A sea which could have the same disastrous effect as a hurdle of a different height or at a different angle or distance from its fellows would have to a smoothly jumping athlete. A dangerous sea, a rogue sea.

Such a sea rolled in from the west shortly after the ship broke down. A rogue sea similar in every respect to the millions which had proceeded it since the oceans were formed. In every respect but one.

It had the 'Belisarius' name on it.

****

A change in the rhythm of the rolling caused the Captain to sense that something calamitous was about to happen. The ship continued further over to port when she should have started coming back. He flung open the weather wheelhouse door and lunged out onto the wing of the bridge.

What he saw riveted him to the spot. A great wall of water was poised above the port quarter of the ship, the grey foam at its crest faintly visible in the blackness of the night. Montague's hands gripped the teakwood rail and he leaned back as if his own puny strength would heave the ship over to starboard in order to take the sea on the ship's side instead of her vulnerable decks.

The huge sea caught the 'Belisarius' at the worst possible moment, just as she was at her maximum roll to port. Thousands of tons of water crashed onto the poop and then diagonally down the length of the ship smashing everything in its path. The permanent wooden awning of the poop flew to splinters, their two inch thick steel stantions bent like soft wire. Most of the hold ventilator cowls to port were washed clean over the side. Bulwarks were torn and buckled, unable to endure the forces against them. The noise was unbelievable as the sea sought to smash the ship beneath its weight. Everything moveable was thrown about as the ship writhed as if in agony. Thick glass ports were smashed and doors of two inch thick teak were shattered by the sea smashing into them or snatched from their frames as the water surged through the accommodation. The sea, tearing into the engine room alleyways on either side of the ship, virtually filled them before pouring through the doors into the engine room itself.

In the engine room it was Bedlam. It had been difficult enough to keep a footing in the violent rolling prior to the rogue sea. When it struck, men, engine parts and tools were flung from one side of the generator flat to the other. At the same time tons of water poured into the engine space through the doors above and the shattered skylight. It cascaded onto the turbine casings, the pumps and other auxiliaries. It poured onto the main switch-board causing the blue flashes to smoke.

Then all the remaining lights went out.

****

The worst structural damage was sustained amidships. The wall of water smashed into the superstructure, tore adrift the two port life-boats and sent them crashing into the funnel guys and the funnel itself. The funnel collapsed and the whole mass of wreckage went over the side taking the starboard boats with it. Part of the engine room skylight and the engine boiler room ventilators were torn off and the two inflatable life-rafts washed over the side at the same time.

The raging sea struck the bridge, surging into the open port door and through the wheelhouse carrying away everything in its path including the starboard door and most of the windows and their frames.

In the wake of the first great sea the scene in the wheelhouse was of utter chaos.

The third mate had been swept from one side of the wheelhouse to the other taking the helmsman with him for part of the way. They fetched up in the after starboard corner amidst the wreckage of the flag locker and bridge chair. Almost miraculously Smith escaped injury.

However, the helmsman had been underneath when they crashed into the locker and was soon whimpering with pain. The gyro compass repeater still stood unharmed but the magnetic compass binnacle rocked with every roll of the ship. Most of the bridge equipment had been swept out of the wheelhouse and over the side. This included the Aldis signalling lamp, one of the oil side-lights, both megaphones and, more seriously, the portable emergency radio.

The port window in the wheelhouse front had escaped injury as it had been somewhat protected by the bulkhead forward of the door. All that remained of the other four were a few pieces of splintered framework. The port door remained in its slides but only a few fragments of glass remained of its light. Of the starboard door there was no sign.

The main weight of water soon freed itself from the wheelhouse leaving only a few inches splashing furiously from side to side in the after end. Floating in it were various pieces of flotsam, a number of flags, both tightly rolled and in tangled bunches, the wheel grating and a very battered electric kettle. Not that any of this mess could be seen in the almost complete darkness.

The port wing of the bridge had taken the full force of the sea. When it had passed little more than the twisted steel framework and a few pieces of teak deck planking remained. Gone to oblivion were the scrubbed teak rails, the dodgers and the tongue and groove boarding below them.

Gone also was Captain Andrew Cowell Montague.

****

James Carey was fast asleep when the ship stopped. It had taken him some time to get to sleep when he first turned in owing to the movement of the ship, or possibly, he decided, an attack of 'The Channels', that syndrome symptomized by uncharacteristic behaviour of seafarers towards the end of a long voyage. However, when he did drop off he literally did. Although subconsciously aware that the rhythm of the ship had changed even the more violent rolling of the ship did not wake him. The first intimation he had that something was wrong was when he was flung from his bunk to the deck.

His first impression was that the deck was sinking beneath him like the floor of a lift. He had no time for a second impression before all Hell seemed to be let loose. The screaming of the wind, the roaring of the sea, the splintering of woodwork and the crash of loose and breaking objects combined in a tumult of sound. A wave of water poured into his room as the ship rolled.

Carey stared at it amazed. 'This is ridiculous, I am thirty feet above sea level!'

He was sent slithering and splashing into a corner of the room and had just managed, half dazed, to sit up waist deep in icy water when the lights in the alleyway outside his room failed and he was plunged into impenetrable darkness. After struggling to his feet he groped for the torch which hung from a hook by the bunk. He had just switched it on when a chair crashed into his legs throwing him off balance. By grabbing at his desk he remained on his feet but the torch was dropped and extinguished, once again plunging him into darkness. He tried to convince himself that it was all a horrible dream but was not successful.

It took all of his resolve to prevent himself from panicking. He tried to think of what should be done. It would be a waste of time looking for his flashlight, if it was not broken the salt water would have rendered it useless. The thing to be done was to get to the bridge and find out what was going on, someone there would know and tell him what to do. How long had it been since he was so rudely awakened? How long had he been messing around in his room when he was probably desperately needed on the bridge or elsewhere?

"Steady! Steady!" said Carey to himself, "You will soon be in a blue funk if you carry on like this. Think constructively. Are you ready to go on the bridge?"

Clothes! He soon found his wardrobe in the darkness and reaching in pulled out the first thing he came to, his old uniform. Getting into the jacket was simple enough in spite of the movement of the ship but the trousers proved difficult and by the time he had them on they were as cold and wet as the pyjamas beneath. Shoes? Carey fished around in the surging water and eventually found two, both left feet. It took a little time to find a third in the pitch darkness, fortunately a right. With his feet crammed into the cold, wet leather he snatched his duffle coat from the hook by the door and started for the bridge.

****

Radio Officer Kenneth Forbes was looking forward to the end of his watch. He was cold, cramped and lonely. He had not spoken to anyone since the third mate had stuck his head through the communicating hatch to the wheelhouse to collect the latest weather report. A very garbled weather report it was too, the radio interference had been terrible all evening. He had not touched the key all watch, there were no messages to send and not even a 'Sparks' on another ship he could 'chat' to in the prevailing atmospherics. All he wanted to do was to go to sleep. He only hoped it would be possible when he did get to his bunk, the rolling was even greater than anything he had experienced before.

Forbes had hardly moved since he came on watch hours earlier. He found that the only way he could stay in one place was to wedge his chair against the inboard lockers with his feet against the work bench on the outboard side of his 'shack', as he invariably termed the radio room. He was in this position when the power failed on the first occasion. It occurred to him to switch on the battery operated emergency light but the switch for this was out of reach by the door. Anyway, he decided, the main generator would be back on the board in a few minutes. The indicator bulb in the main receiver gave all the light he required once he had switched that instrument onto battery power.

It was a little later, after the mains lighting had temporarily returned, that he realised that the bulkhead fastenings of the mains transmitter were even more loose than they had been earlier in the watch.

"How the Hell am I going to get a lashing around that?" he said to himself as he started to disentangle his legs from their cramped position.

It was then that the rogue sea struck. Everything seemed to happen at once. The violent roll to port pinned him to his chair for a few moments, all the books and papers which seemed perfectly secure a minute before flew across the room. A couple of drawers slid out from under the bench and he caught his foot in one of them.

The starboard roll caught him completely off balance and he fell, slamming his head against the main receiver with stunning force. He lay with head and shoulders sprawled over the bench when the heavy transmitter tore itself from the bulkhead.

The lights then went out for the last time.

* *

For several minutes the mate and the carpenter lay in a battered heap, hanging on desperately to the guard rails at the after end of the foc'sle head. It was some time before the shock of their sudden departure from the windlass wore off sufficiently for them to realise that the lowering of both anchors had been successfully accomplished.

"We've done it!" shouted Hatch, "We've done it you old bastard!" and would have thumped MacMurdo on the back if he had not needed both hands to hang onto the rails.

"Aye!" howled Chips, "An' I hope yon bottle of whiskey has no taken a tumble with all this rolling." And, as an afterthought as a deluge of spray cascaded over them, "An' I'll no be wanting any water wi' ma dram!"

Elated by their success almost to the extent of being light-headed it struck the exhausted Hatch that under the circumstances the carpenter's remark was funny. He commenced to laugh and, although uncertain of the joke, Chips joined in with loud guffaws.

They were still laughing when the great sea engulfed them.

****

Chapter 11

The darkness was so intense and the movement so violent that it took Carey some time to fight his way to the bridge. The door at the top of the inside staircase was jammed shut but he put his shoulder to it and, assisted by the ship's roll, burst into the chartroom. A foot of water surged from side to side. Floating in it were charts, pencils, books and papers but he saw nothing of this in the impenetrable darkness as he groped for the door to the wheelhouse.

Compared with the blackness inside the accommodation it was almost light in the wheelhouse. Carey's first impression was that the windows were larger than they should be, it was not until later that he realised that what he saw were the holes in the steel bulkhead where the windows and their frames once were.

Slowly his brain took in the scene of desolation. The first shock was to see no man at the wheel, he knew that there had been one there earlier in the evening. In fact, he could see no-one at all at first. Then a slight movement in the fore end of the wheelhouse caught his eye.

"Who is that?" he shouted as he stumbled towards the dim figure. It was not until his hands touched the man's back and the head turned that he realised it was the Third Mate. Smith's "Thank God, there is someone else left alive!" was a cry from the heart.

"What the Hell has happened?" screamed Carey in the Third Mate's ear, "What is going on?"

Hump Smith had been severely shocked by the catastrophe and, when no-one came to him in the first few minutes had convinced himself that he was the only soul on board left alive. The whole calamity was too much for him and it was taking him all his time to bring his senses together. However, the sudden appearance of the Second Mate came as such a relief he was almost his old self in a few moments. Carey's questions however soon reminded him of the seriousness of the situation. It seemed at first that everything was going to be alright now the Second Mate was with him. James would have everything taped, he would know exactly what to do to control the nightmare. It came as a shock to him that Carey did not know that the Captain was dead, even greater was the effect on him of James' reaction to the news. Although he could not hear the words above the shrieking of the wind he could almost feel the other repeating over and over again, "My God! My God!..."

"Where is the Mate then?" yelled Carey.

"He went for'd with Chips," was the shouted reply.

"What in Heaven's name for? He should be up here now the Old Man is..is gone."

"The Mate doesn't know, he went for'd before.... before...." Smith suddenly realised what his words implied.

"He is dead too!" Then, after a slight pause, he almost shrieked, "He's dead too! He is dead I tell you! Everyone is dead!" Smith was almost hysterical.

Carey gripped his shoulders, "Steady Hump! Take things easy, take it easy! Everything will be alright."

To himself, 'Ye Gods! I wish I thought so.'

"Sorry," said Smith, "Must not get excited." Carey could not hear him but knew he was going to be alright. He felt almost paternal in spite of the but few years' disparity in their ages.

Desperately he tried to clear his mind in order to think constructively. He remembered doing the same thing in his room only minutes, or was it hours? ago.

The full realisation of his position hit him like a punch in the guts.

He, James Carey, as senior deck officer and regardless of whoever else might be alive, was in command of the ship! For minutes on end he did not speak as the full weight of the situation slowly filled his mind. This was not how he had dreamed it would be, this was not the gallant young Second Mate bringing the ship into port after all the more senior officers had died of plague, (Plymouth preferably on a bright sunny day, the escort of scores of yachts crewed almost exclusively by bikini clad girls, cheering and waving). No, this was the reality. This was what separated the men from the boys. This was actually happening – and to him, James Carey.

'Oh God!' he thought, 'I don't want it. I want to resign. I should never have come to sea. This is too much! Why did the Old Man have to die? Why? Why? Just when he was most needed. Even Jake, if the Captain had to die Jake should have lived. It was the Mate's job to take over if the master died, not his. Jake, drunken, bad-tempered, uncouth, bloody-minded Jake. Why did you have to die?'

Carey tried desperately to control himself. This would not do. What has happened has happened. The first thing was to decide what should be done to alleviate the situation. If anything could be done!

First the ship. To Carey, even after less than ten years at sea, the ship always came first. When her wants had been attended to thought could be spared for the people.

What of the ship? Was she even at this moment sinking beneath their feet? The tremendous sea must have smashed its way below somewhere. If so where? And to what extent? Were the hatches intact? It seemed impossible to believe that any of the wooden hatch covers had survived being stove in. But if this were so why had the ship not sunk already? She still seemed lively enough, far too lively in fact. However, there was nothing that could be done about inspecting hatches whilst the seas were thundering unchecked across the decks.

Carey realised that the Third Mate was looking into his face waiting for him to say something, some instructions, anything to lead them out of their terrible plight.

"Why did I not think of it before!" yelled Carey, "The radio, we will get off a distress message – if Sparks hasn't already sent one off his own bat."

They found a torch hanging by the chartroom door and with its aid the log book, a coverless, soggy wad of paper. It took some minutes of careful opening of the saturated pages before they arrived at the entries for that day. Although very smeared they could just make out the figures of the ship's position at noon. With so much else filling his mind Carey found it impossible to mentally calculate the ship's present position.

"To Hell with it. We will just send the noon position, course and speed before we broke down. Let someone else work out where we are. Anyway Sparks can transmit a signal for other ships to home on. Come on Hump, let's get the message off. I only hope there is at least one aerial left standing."

The radio room door was wide open, hooked back when Forbes came on watch. It seemed strange to see the room in darkness, it had always been so brilliantly lit when Ken Forbes was there, and full of his idea of good music competing with the Morse and atmospherics.

The powerful beam of the bridge torch found Forbes almost

immediately. He was on the deck by this time with the two hundred pound weight of the transmitter still on top of him. Everything on the radio room deck, books, drawers, tools and coils of wire accompanied the transmitter and the crushed form beneath it as they slid the short distance from one side of the room to the other.

Momentarily sheer horror froze Carey to the spot before he rushed forward to try to lift the heavy apparatus, knowing full well that it was far too late to do Forbes any good.

Smith clung to the door frame retching.

The two men felt very much alone in the terrifying world.

It was then they heard voices. A few moments later Second Engineer Peter Gregson arrived at the top of the stairs followed by the Fourth and Fifth Engineers and a handful of Asian firemen. Even before identities had been established Gregson shouted, "How are things up here?"

"Pretty bloody," answered Carey, "We did not even know there was anyone else alive. What are things like down below?"

"The Third is hurt and a couple of the crew, the Chief and the Steward are doing what they can for them in the saloon."

'At least more and more people appear to be alive' thought a somewhat relived Carey. 'I wonder how many?'

"What are the chances of getting some power, or at least some lights?"

"Not a chance in Hell, ever." replied Gregson, "There must be six feet of water over the plates now and it is coming in fast."

Cold fear again gripped Carey's vitals. "You mean she is making water, more than is coming in from the top?"

After seeing to the closing of the water-tight doors leading to the boiler room and shaft tunnel Gregson had joined the Chief in trying to locate the source of the inrush of water to the lower part of the engine room. They continued by flashlight until the amount of water surging across the foot-plates forced them to abandon the search. This leak was, to Gregson's mind at least, the ship's most urgent problem and his major preoccupation so he was surprised the bridge knew nothing of it.

"Something has carried away at the ship's side, a discharge or intake I should imagine. Nothing we can do about it. Anyway, what are you lot doing up here? When do we expect to be rescued?"

Slowly, often having to repeat himself owing to the roaring of the storm, Carey told Gregson and the others of the catalogue of disaster. The engineers listened with mounting concern. In the engine room conditions had been terrifying but, each to himself at least, had buoyed his hopes with the thought that a distress message had been sent and even at that moment ships were hurrying to their succour. Now, it would appear, things were worse than they had anticipated and, with the engine room flooding rapidly, deteriorating all the time.

As the full realisation of the position was absorbed Gregson, in his soaked boiler suit, had cause to appreciate that he was cold, very, very cold.

"Ye Gods! It's freezing," he turned to his two juniors, "Hey, Charlie, you and Ted go down to the cabins and grab all the warm clothing you can find, anybody's, and bring it up here – No," glancing at the shambles around him, "Take it to the Old Man's room." He almost said, 'He won't mind.' "- and life-jackets too. I'll go and tell the Chief."

'Why did I not think of that?' thought Carey as the engineers stumbled off down the staircase.

What was next? People.

"God knows how the crew are faring down aft," he shouted to

Smith, "Nothing we can do about them until the weather eases up a bit, the main deck is awash. I only hope they have got themselves battened down for the time being."

The mention of the crew reminded Smith of something which had been in the back of his mind for some time.

"The secunny! I'd forgotten about him. He was in the wheelhouse earlier on. I don't know how badly he was hurt."

They scrambled back into the wheelhouse and soon found the man, still wedged in the corner. He was soaked to the skin and half frozen but, as it transpired, not seriously hurt. He sat with his head in his hands waiting for the nightmare to end – of his life to end, he was not particular which.

Carey and Smith stayed on the bridge. They had half carried and half dragged the groaning helmsman to a safer place on the chartroom settee then searched around for anything useful they could salvage. The distress rockets they removed from a chart room locker and secured on the table. At least they appeared to be alright, their plastic container having kept the rockets themselves dry. A couple of the emergency oil navigation lights were added to their find and a dry box of matches sighted in the chronometer box. A second torch was found as they continued their search.

The engineers left the Asian crew members in the saloon and climbed to the captain's accommodation below the bridge. They included Mike Crawford the Third who was in great pain from a broken wrist and a dislocated shoulder as well as numerous bruises and abrasions. The others had been fortunate in suffering only minor injuries. Bill Parry the Chief Steward, who was with them, soon discovered a couple of dry blankets in the top of a wardrobe and Crawford was made as comfortable as possible across the bed.

Alistair Macquarie the Chief Engineer left the crowd in the Captain's accommodation and climbed to the chart room. In his twenty-five years at sea he had experienced his share of calamities but nothing to compare with the present situation. So far as the ship was concerned he was a marine engineer pure and simple. He lived for his engines and would defend them against all criticism although, of course, he did not love them. Now that they were of no more value than scrap metal he felt rather lost. He was also very weary and considerably frightened. This latter he tried desperately to hide as, being by far the oldest officer on the ship, he felt a need to set an example to his 'lads', which term now, he could see, would include the deck officers as well.

The Chief was rarely on deck in bad weather as nothing called him there apart from the odd exceptional occasion. Although he always had his problems when the ship was rolling and pitching in a heavy sea it was on these occasions he would say he was glad he was an engineer. Those who were paid to stand on the bridge staring into a wet and stormy night were welcome to do so so far as he was concerned. He was less voluble on the subject on calm tropical nights when moon and stars were reflecting on the water – and the temperature in the engine room was over one hundred degrees Fahrenheit.

The sound of the storm was bad enough below but when the Chief entered the chart room the noise had twice the volume. The wind screamed unchecked through the wrecked wheelhouse with the sound of a thousand banshees. Even with the door closed speech in the chart room had to be carried out by shouting.

Carey and Smith tried desperately to light the oil masthead lamp rescued from the wheelhouse. Cold wet fingers resulted in a damp box of matches and this, combined with the draught, made what should have been a simple job extremely difficult. With the newly arrived Chief's help it was eventually accomplished and the lamp cast a yellowish glow over the scene in the disordered chartroom.

Concentrated as they had been on the lamp the Chief's first words brought the other two men's minds back to their main predicament.

"What is all this the Second tell me, that we can't send an S.O.S? Surely there is emergency gear of some sort?" In trying to keep his voice calm he only succeeded in giving the impression that there would have been such equipment if <u>his</u> department had been in charge of such things.

"We might be able to rig up something but I doubt it," replied Carey, "The life-boat transmitter is lost and the radio room is a shambles. Sparks might have been able to rig something but......" his voice trailed off to silence.

The Second Engineer and Chief Steward joined them and the five men tried to devise some plan, make some suggestion to alleviate their plight. They mentioned the distress rockets, they discussed the fact that they would soon be missed when radio messages were not received or expected ones sent by the ship, the fact that the last known weather report had indicated improving weather. Nothing constructive.

They got progressively colder and more depressed as they sat in a row on the chartroom settee. No one had even noticed that the helmsman had slipped off to join his countrymen below.

"Nothing can be done until daylight anyway," said Carey.

"We may as well be a bit more comfortable then," commented the Chief as the cold sea water surged over his lightly clad feet, "Let's join the others, at least it is a bit drier down there."

"Good idea," replied Carey, "Careful with that lamp Hump", as Smith commenced to unleash the large oil lantern, "Let's all get below until morning."

Before any of them could reach the straining chartroom door it suddenly burst open. In a night of fear, the crash of the door and the sudden inrush of wind and noise startled them. But to nothing like the extent of the shock they experienced a moment later.

The glow of the oil lamp faintly illuminated the figure of a man leaning on the door frame. He was clad in torn and soaking rags through which exposed white flesh gleamed in several places. The apparition's downcast head presented only a view of wet, black hair. No clue to the man's identity.

The man coughed once, twice. Deep rattling coughs. Then he slowly raised his head.

Even in the full light of the lamp it was some moments before the shocked men recognised the torn, battered, bloody face.

Chapter 12

"Jake!" Their voices sounded as one.

They leaped to their feet but Hatch waved them aside before he half stepped, half swung to the chartroom settee where he sat down with a crash.

The relief to Carey was as of a tremendous physical burden being lifted from his shoulders. It was if his prayers had been answered. Someone had arrived to take over the responsibility of the ship, someone to give orders, someone who would know what should be done.

"Jake! Is it really you?" ..... "Where have you been?"....."What happened to you?"......."Are you badly hurt?".... they all shouted at once.

Hatch silenced their questions with a harsh, "Never mind all that. What is the score up here?"

By the light of the lamp the men could see that Hatch was hurt, badly hurt. His face was so battered and cut it was devoid of any expression but his eyes, when the light caught them, showed intense pain. His breath came in gasps as if his first few words had exhausted him, as if even to breathe was agony. Occasionally he gave a gasping cough but none of them could establish if the blood on his chin was from his mouth or the lacerations of his face. They all wanted to comfort him in one way or another but Hatch would have none of it. The ship first, then the people.

Hatch listened as the others told him of the various aspects of the disaster, interposing questions. "Was a radio message sent?" – No. "Are the water-tight doors closed?" – Yes. "How many of the crew are known to be alive?" – Only the half dozen or so in the saloon. "Where was the lookout man?" – Not known although Smith thought he had gone aft to call his relief a few minutes before the disaster. And a dozen more queries.

Hatch then started issuing orders and instructions, interrupted with bouts of coughing.

"It's your watch Jim, get one of the crew to help you keep a lookout, a damn sharp lookout! There should be a heavy coat for the man somewhere, see he gets well wrapped up anyway.

"Chief, will you get a couple of your lads to go round all the accommodation they can get at and see if there is anyone else around? There may have been some men in the galley. Don't let anyone try to get aft though until I say so. Any men there will be better off where they are for the time being.

"Hump, if there are any more oil lamps in the wheelhouse get them down below and lit, we will need all the light we can get.

"If you could get a few men together and secure as many doors and ports as you can it would help Chief. Chips has had it I'm afraid." This only confirmed what had been guessed of the carpenter's fate.

"And Jim, I see the rockets are alright but they are not to be set off until I give the word O.K.?" Hatch did not want them wasted at the first sighting of a glimmer of light on the horizon, there were only a dozen of them.

"Right, let's get cracking. Let me know how you get on and report back here every fifteen minutes or so, I don't want anyone getting adrift and have to send out search parties."

The effort of talking had brought on another long spasm of coughing and it was some minutes before Hatch spoke again. All but the Chief Steward had by then left the chartroom.

"Bill, have you got your first aid gear with you?"

"It's down below, I was fixing up the Third earlier on."

"Bring it up here then will you? I think I am leaking a bit in places."

"You seem pretty knocked about," replied Parry, "Better if you come down below where there is more room and I can get some help."

"No, I'm staying here, I won't be going far until we reach port."

'The bastard doesn't realise the ship is sinking under our feet in spite of what the Chief has told him,' thought Parry, 'Ah well, I won't remind him.'

"Anyway," continued Hatch in a most matter of fact tone, "I wouldn't be able to make it, I think my leg is broken."

Parry's "Oh my God!" was quickly followed by Hatch's "And before you ask, it does bloody well hurt so the sooner you get the damn thing fixed the better."

It required more than the first-aid bag to fix up the Mate. Parry, aided by Carey, who had handed over the watch to Smith, and by various other willing helpers as they came up at different times to report progress, struggled for an hour tending to Hatch's injuries.

Trying to do anything other than hang on in the heaving room was bad enough. Attempting to work without adding to the patient's agony was impossible. With the room battened down to the greatest extent possible it was still freezing cold. The available light, from the oil lamp and two electric torches, was inadequate to say the least. The injuries were enough to keep a hospital operating theatre ashore busy for some time. Hatch's face was horribly bruised and cut, blood dribbled from his mouth where a couple of teeth had been knocked out and there were several deep gashes in his legs and body. These really required stitches but as that was impossible sticking plaster and wound dressings took their place.

The left knee horrified the first aid team when they saw it uncovered. The joint was twice its normal size and terribly discoloured. The lower leg stuck out at a slight angle demonstrating that the knee was not just badly bruised. Hatch almost passed out when Parry first touched the limb. Nothing much could be done except to pad it with cotton wool and roughly splint it with a couple of bookcase rails and other pieces of wood.

The Mate's left hand was badly lacerated but apparently none of the bones were broken. The whole arm was badly bruised from wrist to shoulder.

The main injury was however to his side. The whole area of his body from left armpit to waist was one large contusion. The unevenness of the surface and the discolouration indicated fractured ribs but how many and how severely could not be determined. As there was no cotton wool remaining kapok filling from a life-jacket was used in lieu to pad the area. A shortage of sticking plaster resulted in the padding being secured with strips of a sheet from the Captain's bed and chart repairing tape.

It was hard work for Parry and his assistant and it was agony for Hatch. With the ship's dispensary under water the only anaesthetic was half a bottle of whisky, most of which was consumed by the patient.

Hatch was nearly unconscious by the time the dressings were completed

"There, you should be reasonably comfortable now," said Parry in his best bed-side manner, "Particularly now the ship is riding a little easier."

The words were out of his mouth before either he or the others realised their import. Hatch returned to full consciousness with a start. The ship had lost much of her violent, uncontrolled rolling. Although the wind still screamed through the shattered wheelhouse and the ship continued to shudder as the great seas struck her she was definitely moving more easily. The wind, which had previously been on the port beam, was now decidedly on the port bow. Although still helpless the ship had taken the first step in her struggle to survive. The drag of the anchors and cables hanging from the bow was at last beginning to take effect.

There was no time for congratulations.

"What time is it?" asked Hatch.

Smith flashed a torch on the chartroom clock, they had all lost track of time.

"Nearly half-past six."

"It should be getting light in an hour or so," the Mate continued, "As soon as it is light enough a few of you try to get aft and see what the score is with the crew." His mind was already racing. "Where is the Chief?"

"He should be back shortly," replied Carey from the doorway, "He's been up a couple of times, says most of the doors and ports are secured but there are quite a few he can do nothing with at the moment."

"Fresh water will be a problem, see if you can close the valve to the bridge tank Jim, the line may be carried away somewhere and water escaping."

Carey had just got back from closing the valve when the Chief and his repair party returned to the bridge.

The Chief Engineer's news was mixed. He and the others had managed to secure many of the ports and some of the doors, not without a good deal of danger, hard work and ingenuity. Most of the ports now had their steel deadlights screwed down over them so were almost as strong as the bulkheads themselves. The engine room was still flooding but there was little water in the boiler room, what there was had apparently come from the engine room before the watertight door had been closed.

The weary men were discussing their grim situation when daylight began to filter into the chartroom.

Smith's frightened face appeared at the door.

"Number two hatch is stove in!"

"God! That's all we need," growled Hatch, "Is it very bad?"

"So far as I can see about half a dozen hatch covers gone and the tarpaulins ripped right away to the second locking bar."

The Mate contemplated this latest catastrophe. Each portable cover consisted of two nine inch deals secured edge to edge and was about ten feet long. This means a hole about ten feet square for the sea to pour down, apart from the water making its way between the other covers now the tarpaulins had been torn from them.

"Is there much water going down the hatch now?"

"There is plenty of water on the deck but only the odd bucketful getting over the coaming and down the hatch when she rolls," replied Smith.

"That will have to be fixed as soon as possible." Hatch followed this observation with further questions then instructions which resulted in Carey, Gregson and Parry making their perilous way aft, Parry with a newly replenished haversack containing what he could scrape together in the way of first-aid equipment.

The steel storm doors at the fore end of the poop were still closed and appeared undisturbed since they had been first secured at the onset of the bad weather. The three men climbed to the poop, passing the crew galley where the two sections of the steel doors on either side swung back and forth with the rolling of the ship disclosing the shambles within.

The after end of the poop house enclosed the crew's showers and toilets. Only a few pieces of splintered door frame remained as evidence of the two teakwood doors which had once given access to the deck.

Carey led the way to the ladder leading to the crew accommodation below. He switched on his torch, dreading what they might find when they descended.

Two or three feet of water sloshed about at the foot of the ladder with shoes, shirts and other clothing floating about in it. There was no sign of life and the only sounds were those caused by the storm.

The three men made their way below. After the slowly growing daylight on deck the accommodation seemed to be in complete darkness.

The first room they came to was devoid of human life. The sodden bedding on even the top bunks gave evidence of the height the water had been thrown at one time by the rolling.

The second room was the same, they began to despair of finding any of the crew.

The third room therefore came as rather a shock. It seemed at first to Carey that half the crew were there, stuck to the deckhead in some magical manner. A closer examination disclosed that actually there were eleven men hanging on grimly to the top bunks, one another and anything else handy.

When the initial shouting had died down the three officers established that none of the men were badly hurt so, after reassuring them as best they could they continued their inspection.

A fourth man joined them, the old Deck Serang, the bosun. Not until later was it appreciated how much was owed to old Ali. Although as terrified as anyone after the great sea had struck it was he who had calmed the men and persuaded them not to try to leave the poop. It was he who had managed to get them to stick it out on the top bunks in the belief that they would soon be rescued. He tried to get them to believe that the officers would soon sort things out even though he had grave doubts of this himself. Now if they had been officers of the calibre he had sailed with when he first came to sea! Then there would have been no question. They had been real Sahibs, they did not just think they were superior beings, they were. So called officers nowadays were, when all said and done, only so many white men. Ah, well! best not to tell these young seamen of his thoughts. However, one officer was remote enough from the Serang, a man on whom he could concentrate his thoughts, the Captain. The Captain Sahib was a good seaman, he would soon have things back to normal and bring this nightmare to an end.

Little did Ali know that the Captain had been dead for several hours.

****

The pattern of the search continued, some rooms empty others crowded. The spirits of the officers rose as the tally of men mounted. It was with heart-felt relief that they found that no-one was missing. Nearly all the men had bruises and cuts from their earlier buffeting but none was seriously injured. Only one or two had suspected fractures.

Having enjoined the men to put on their thickest clothes, even if they were wet, and to wait until told to come amidships Carey and Gregson went about the second part of their mission. Parry stayed with the crew to minister to their hurts, arranging to re-join the others before they returned to the bridge.

The two men climbed onto the top of the poop house. There on the open deck empty oil drums, old coils of wire ropes, spare hatch covers and other timber was normally stowed.

The big sea had just about swept the top of the house clean. The brass emergency steering wheel and its mounting were still there but of the compass binnacle the only sign was the base of it still bolted to the deck. The oil drums and most of the timber had disappeared and only one length of rusty wire remained, festooned over the starboard rail. All the spare hatch covers had gone but, against the rail was found what would serve almost as well. They counted seventeen hatch deals and five lengths of spar ceiling, the latter used as permanent dunnage in the ship's holds. This precious bundle of timber had been saved owing to the fact that it had been very securely lashed to the rail stantions with wire and bulldog grips earlier in the voyage, more to avoid its being stolen in eastern ports than in the expectation of the sea trying to tear it away.

"There is more than enough there for number two hatch," said Carey, "Let's get back and tell Jake."

After picking up Parry they returned to the bridge via the starboard side of the afterdeck, visually inspecting the hatch covers on the way. All seemed well so far as the security of the after hatches were concerned.

The news of the finding of the deals which they brought to Hatch and the others did little to alleviate the gloom caused by the latest development. The ship, now with the wind and sea about four points on the port bow, was pitching quite considerably but the rolling was much less. However, now the ship was more steady, what they had all dreaded, although they knew inevitable, was now very apparent. The vessel now had a very decided port list.

"Well it is no good sitting and brooding about it," Hatch was still worrying about the broached number two hatch, "Jim (Carey winced, 'I wish he would call me James, he knows how I hate 'Jim'.'), the sooner we get that hatch tight the better. Nip along aft again with a couple of the others and get some of those deals along. Get the Serang and all the men he can muster on the job too. The sick, the lame and the halt can come along at the same time, doss them down in the saloon or somewhere. Then at least we will know where everyone is."

Turning to the engineers Hatch continued, "Chief, can you spare a couple of your blokes to go with Hump and raid the carpenter's shop? We will need his bow saw, a bag of wedges and a hammer or two. In fact, it might be as well if they brought along any other tools they might think will be handy now or later, as many as they can safely carry. Have you a crow-bar or something to open the shop? Lord knows where the keys are."

It took over two hours of soul-destroying labour to secure the damaged hatch. There were many more cuts and bruises before the job was completed, apart from two men nearly swept over the side as a dozen of them struggled to bring a new tarpaulin along the deck from the forepeak store to the hatch.

When the utterly exhausted men returned to the bridge and saloon they were met with a marvellous surprise. Parry and some of the others had not been idle whilst work had been going on at the hatch. On various containers, designed for more mundane purposes, was food! It was not very elegantly exhibited on the chartroom table but was not the less welcome for that. There were several large loaves of bread, some already sliced, butter, cheese, a tin of marmalade, a pan of cold meats, a saucepan of extremely mixed salad and several jars of pickles.

In fact, the entire contents of the ready use refrigerators in the pantry had been shared between the officers on the bridge and the crew in the saloon.

"Don't make pigs of yourselves," said Parry, "It may have to last."

They all knew that the main storerooms were awash.

"Might as well tuck in then," someone said, "Is everybody here? Where is the Chief and Second?"

As if on cue the two missing men arrived at the door carrying a bucket, literally a bucket, of hot tea.

"How in Heaven's name did you manage to make that?" shouted Carey.

"Never you mind," answered the Chief, "We engineers are bloody clever." He was grinning now but had not smiled much during the previous half an hour as he and Gregson had been battered about struggling to boil a bucket of water collected from the pantry and galley. The assembly of the oxy-acetylene burner had been difficulty enough. However, the result was a great success. The brew was thick and contained far too much sugar and condensed milk for the discriminating palate, it soon grew cold and tasted strongly of diesel oil. It was voted the most wonderful tea any of them could remember drinking.

The meal had only just started when Hatch chased the Third Mate out into the wheelhouse to keep a lookout.

"God! Does he never let up?" grumbled Smith to himself, "As if things aren't bad enough without freezing out here."

As soon as the al fresco meal was over it was back to work for all hands. Some went to sound around to check the amount of water that had entered the ship, others set off in an attempt to obtain more food from the flooded storerooms. Macquarie the Chief Engineer and one of his juniors proceeded to the steering flat to explore the possibility of obtaining fresh water from the afterpeak tank. Parry descended to the saloon to see to the welfare of the crew. It had been arranged that the crew took over the saloon and its environs and the officers the decks above.

Hatch was not content to remain on the chartroom settee, he felt frustrated there unable to see what was going on around the decks. The wheelhouse was where he wanted to be and that was where he was going. No one else thought the idea was a good one, the Mate was obviously a very injured man. He was also a very obstinate one.

After considerable argument several officers, egged on by Hatch, rigged up a fairly comfortable seat in the port, forward corner of the wheelhouse. The main structure consisted of one of the Captain's arm chairs on top of a strong coffee table from the same source, the whole affair being very securely lashed.

When the seat was completed it at first appeared to be a wasted effort. Hatch's iron resolution was hardly matched by his shattered frame. Although his injured leg and side had 'stiffened up' as he put it they were still extremely painful even at rest. However, eventually his strong resolve won. Even though assisted by many willing hands it was undiluted agony making the short distance from the chartroom to the seat in the wheelhouse. By the time he sat down his face was grey and creased with pain. His breath came in short, bubbling gasps and it was some time before he could speak.

There was still much remaining to be done before dark. Many of the hatch ventilator coamings had to be plugged one way or another as their cowls had been smashed or entirely removed by the great sea. The shattered glass in the now closed port wheelhouse door was replaced with a sheet of plywood. Blankets and bedding was accumulated so that at least most of the people could have a chance of some rest during the coming night. These and many other pressing details received attention.

Towards the end of daylight nearly all that could be done had been done. The ship was as water-tight as the weary men could get her. Additional lamps and kerosene had been brought from the stores under the foc'sle head. Several sacks of very mixed canned provisions had been obtained from the 'Dry' store – which was nearly half full of water. A few buckets of fresh water had been obtained from the afterpeak tank by the efforts of the engineers who persuaded the hand-pump to work after years of disuse. Clothes had been secured from the officers' quarters and crew's accommodation.

A second scratch meal was prepared and consumed whilst there was still daylight enough to see.

After eating most of those not on watch made themselves as comfortable as the circumstances permitted. Some fell asleep immediately through sheer exhaustion, others lay awake for hours. Most however obtained some measure of rest.

Around Hatch's chair the more senior officers gathered and discussed the situation as it now stood.

On the credit side could be said the ship was still afloat. There was enough food and water for at least a few days. No one was so seriously injured that he required immediate expert medical attention. Hatch's contribution this last. None of the others commented on the remark.

On the debit side the ship was definitely still making water and also increasing her list. As Macquarie said with wry humour, it was a toss-up which happened first, her going under or going over. Apart from their life-jackets, now constantly worn or kept close at hand if this was impracticable, there were no life-saving appliances remaining.

Hatch explained that owing to the alteration of course to the south a day or two earlier to avoid the worst of the depression the ship was now at least fifty miles south of the main steamer lanes. However, as he was quick to point out, in the prevailing weather every shipmaster had his own ideas as to the best course to take so they were almost as likely to be found where they were as they would have been further to the north.

The excellent American Amver system which would have been following the ship's proposed progress would have been misled by the alteration to the south, which, so far as he and Carey knew, had not been reported.

Their main hope was that the Head Office in London would appreciate that something was seriously wrong when they failed to receive radio messages from the ship heralding her arrival.

"But," cautioned Hatch, "I doubt if they would put the wheels in motion for a full scale search right away. So far as I know the first step is to ask ships in the vicinity to keep a lookout and report if they sight us. For all the office knows our trouble may only be a radio failure. It will probably be a few days before a serious search is put in hand. We will just have to hold….."

"A ship! A ship!" screamed Smith from the starboard wing of the bridge.

Instantly there was a scramble to see the dim glow of lights on the starboard beam. Hatch, forgetting his injuries in the excitement was instantly reminded of them when he tried to twist round and burst into a paroxysm of agonised coughing. No one had time to comfort him as the men made for the rockets in the chartroom.

"Easy…Don't…" Hatch could not complete the sentence as he gasped in pain.

Eager hands tried to help Smith open the rocket container, eager, impatient, cold, wet, clumsy…. fatal hands.

Where all had been pleasurable excitement a moment before there was shocked horror as the men dimly saw the rockets, their main hope of salvation, bounce on the deck below before disappearing into the maelstrom of the sea.

Some of the officers below dashed up onto the bridge to discover the cause of the commotion which they had heard rather by vibration than by sound.

The disastrous news was soon known to all on board and bitter were the recriminations. Hatch and the Chief tried to mollify their emotions by saying that the ship was probably too far off to see the rockets. This did nothing to alleviate the fact that if and when another ship was sighted they would be unable to signal their distress.

"Can't we set fire to something?" suggested the Fourth Engineer.

"Too late Charlie," replied the Chief, "the ship has gone now." It was only too true, where the lights had been there was only a blank grey horizon.

****

The 'Belisarius' settled down for the night once again. This time everyone was more dispirited than ever. Everything appeared to be against them.

The gale, which had decreased during the day, dropped to only a strong breeze in the course of the night, less water was coming on board and the ship rode easier although more sluggishly. She was deeper in the water and the list increased as the night wore on.

****

And so daylight found them, at least what passed for daylight, the rain and drizzle following the depression made a grey mockery of the day.

"A ship would have to hit us in order to find us in this," observed Parry when he came onto the bridge in the morning.

Hatch knew that this was no less than the truth. A ship finding a stopped vessel on her radar screen would in the prevailing visibility assume her to be without radar and moving cautiously for reasons of safety. The drizzle still further lessened their hopes of succour.

It was Hatch who suggested a design for home-made flares and the Chief and Second, aided by many willing hands, who constructed them. Two forty gallon oil drums were found in the engine room top store and man-handled to the wheelhouse where the heads were cut out with hammer and chisel and numerous holes pierced in their sides. They were then hauled up to the monkey island, the deck covering the wheelhouse, and lashed to the rails with lengths of radio aerial. The drums were then filled with anything dry and combustible that could be found, many charts, (at a couple of quid apiece passed through Carey's mind), crushed into balls, a few curtains, broken furniture, torn up books, all were grist to the mill. When filled the contents of the drums were soaked in kerosene and each then covered in pieces of canvas and some scraps of plastic sheeting discovered somewhere. A two gallon can of kerosene was kept handy in the wheelhouse and one of the few dry boxes of matches wedged behind some wiring just inside the chartroom.

It was on the second day that they buried the remains of Radio Officer Forbes. His body had not been forgotten but everyone had been so busy looking after the living they could spare no time for the dead. In fact, it was not until that day that anyone really began to hope that the ship would, after all, survive and not become the tomb of Ken Forbes and, for that matter, themselves.

The disposal of the body was both a difficult and unpleasant task. His former colleagues did their best but the operation turned out far from the usual dignity of an interment at sea.

To start with the corpse had stiffened in its grotesque attitude of death so the sickening job of straightening the limbs to a certain extent had to be performed before the body could be wrapped and lashed in a canvas awning. The pitiful bundle was then man-handled through the wheelhouse and down to the deck below. To sink it several pieces of machinery and old tools were lashed together.

There was no hope of sliding the body in a dignified manner over the side, it took several men to even lift it to the top of the rail as the average list was then about twenty-five degrees and the ship still rolling considerably. The low port side would have been easier but there would have been too great a chance of the corpse being washed back on board if this side had been used, apart from the likelihood of some of the living going with it. The weights had been lifted over the rail and when the body had been manoeuvred to the top of it the weights were secured to the canvas.

No one had been deputed to read the burial service, had even a copy been found. The Chief's "goodbye Sparks" and the others' muttered words had to suffice as the grisly bundle dropped from the rail and, after brushing the ship's side, hit the surface of the sea and quickly sank.

Hatch had seen nothing of all this from his position in the wheelhouse. He had not left his chair since he first reached it the day before.

When the others returned from the travesty of a funeral he asked if any of them knew anything about radio, the subject being just so much black magic to him. "Surely there is something in that shack which could send some kind of signal?" Hatch concluded.

Carey and a couple of the engineers spent part of the afternoon trying to get some of the equipment operational but then found they had been frustrated from the start, the battery room had been flooded and the batteries ruined.

During the day the height of the water in the engine room levelled with the surface of the sea, at least so far as could be judged. The tunnel well had remained relatively dry, only two and a half feet of water had leaked into it from the engine room and stern gland. Number two hatch sounding was about eight feet but the sea entered the hold from the deck and thus had to percolate through the cargo, make its way to the bilges and then up the sounding pipe so this could not be considered anything but a rough estimation of the depth of water in the hold.

The only other sea water in the hull was in the boiler room and that which filled the chain locker. Fortunately, the starboard hawse-pipe was shattered only above the main deck level so the fore peak store below remained dry.

The list had increased but slightly to about thirty degrees.

****

The third night enclosed the ship and her people in its mantle of darkness. Everyone on board had got into the habit of timing his life from the moment when the great sea struck. All happenings before that time seemed a dim and distant memory. A feeling of hopelessness pervaded the slowly sinking ship as the weary men made themselves as comfortable as possible for the night. The still considerable movement of the ship kept muscles constantly active even though there had not been a great deal of manual activity that day, but, weary as they were, no one slept well.

The main worry of everyone on board was the boiler room bulkhead. The two thousand odd tons of water surging back and forth in the engine room was causing the bulkhead to bulge ominously. Jets of water shot into the boiler room through strained seams and leaking rivets.

The possibility of shoring up the bulkhead had been mooted but instantly dismissed. Even if the great balks of timber required for such a purpose had been available the men would not have had the strength to fit them. Apart from this the danger of the bulkhead bursting at any moment made any such attempt unjustifiable. It if collapsed it would almost certainly have meant the death of everyone working there. In the event of the bulkhead carrying away the water from the engine room would pour into the boiler room thus doubling the free surface effect and rendering negative what little stability remained to the ship. With her already considerable list it would be but a matter of moments before she rolled over and sank. On deck the men at least had a chance of jumping clear and living a few more desperate hours in the sea.

Chapter 13

In London the November night had closed in early.

Only a few lights glowed in the offices of the Fairbell Shipping Company as the Chairman, Charles Fairbell, pulled on his coat. Although often one of the last to leave he was not surprised to see Soames of the Operations Department still at his desk as he passed through the main office. Mr. Fairbell often wondered what kind of a home Soames had to go to after his day's work.

"Any word of the 'Belisarlus' yet?"

"Nothing so far sir," replied Soames, "I thought we would have received her 'E.T.A.' today."

"So did I. No doubt the weather is holding up the old ship again. Who is on duty this weekend?"

"Mr. Williams sir, and er...," glancing as a sheet of paper in front of him, "yes, young Thomson."

"Tell them to let me know as soon as the message arrives then, I'll be home all weekend. It really is too bad of Montague, he well knows he should inform us on a Friday if his three day estimate of his time of arrival is otherwise likely to arrive over the weekend. These Masters just don't seem to realise how much has to be organised before a ship arrives."

As he turned towards the main door he said, "Well goodbye Soames, have a nice quiet weekend."

However, it was not destined to be a quiet weekend for either of them.

*****

It was during the morning of the third day that the fast container ship 'Contania' found them.

For half an hour the third officer of the ship had been mystified by an echo on the radar screen. After plotting it for several minutes he called the captain on the telephone.

"Rather a strange echo on the radar sir, seems to be stopped."

"Probably one of those Russian fishermen, they seem to be all over the ocean these days. How far should we pass from it?"

"About three miles sir but I don't think it is a trawler, seems too big although it is difficult to tell at this range."

"Not likely to be a ship to hove to, the weather is not bad enough for that. Bring her up a few degrees and we will have a look at her. Put her on a course to pass a mile off. I will come up to the bridge."

At this stage it was merely idle curiosity on the Captain's part, another ship stopped and minding her own business in the middle of the ocean was no concern of his. Little did he visualise the scene which was about to be disclosed.

When three miles off the vague grey shadow of the derelict could be discerned through binoculars by the two officers. They could make nothing of her at first. A few minutes later details became clearer and then, as a thick patch of drizzle moved away like a veil, the full drama of the scene was displayed before their shocked eyes.

394

"Stand by engines," snapped the Captain, "and ring 'Emergency Stations', that will get everyone moving."

It was at this moment that Carey, on watch and scanning wearily and hopelessly the grey drizzle surrounding the ship, saw the approaching vessel.

"A ship!" he yelled, "There, on the starboard bow and close!"

Several officers had drifted onto the bridge at the coming of daylight and there was instantly a mad scramble for the monkey island and the flares. Carey had rushed to the chartroom for the matches so the Chief and Fifth Engineers were the first to arrive at the drums of combustibles. The excitement was intense but the memory of the loss of the rockets was in everyone's mind. There was to be no mistakes this time.

The first-comers tore the covers from the drums.

"Quick, the matches!" shouted the Chief, "Let me have them."

"She must see us!" prayed Carey as he handed the Chief the box of matches.

"Careful with that kerosene Fiver," said someone as Lattimer slopped the stuff from the can onto one of the drums and its contents. However, no one was in the mood to do anything but as quickly as possible.

The first two matches the Chief struck were blown out by the wind. He grabbed a bunch of four or five and as they flared up dropped them into the oil saturated drum and stepped back.

****

As the 'Contania' tore past at twenty-one knots her powerful whistle commenced booming. She had seen them!

However, the vengeful sea had not yet claimed its full reckoning. As the oil drum flared up the 'Belisarius' gave a particularly heavy roll. Carey and the others, there were several people on the monkey island by then, grabbed hold of whatever was handiest or slithered across the deck until brought up by the rail.

The Chief was not so lucky, with nothing to hold on to he skidded straight towards the blasting drum. He automatically put out his hands to save himself and a moment later was curled up on the deck trying not to scream out in the agony of his burns.

Everything else was forgotten as the others rushed to his aid. Parry was with them in a matter of moments and soon burn dressings and bandages embalmed the Chief's blistering hands. Hands which had unscrewed nuts most men would have required a wrench to turn, hands which had created exquisitely beautiful cloud scenes on canvas. Hands who's nearest touch could send at least two women into the realms of ecstasy.

Chief Engineer Alistair Macquarie, so long a pillar of strength, so long the man the others looked up to, not only to know what to do but be capable of doing it, was now, just when everything was about to come right, greatly through his efforts, no more than a liability.

****

At twenty-one knots an eighteen thousand ton ship takes some time to stop if she is not going to put an undue strain on her machinery. It was therefore nearly fifteen minutes before the 'Contania' returned to a position to leeward of the 'Belisarius'.

The prospect of imminent rescue, of comfort, warmth and safety affected the men of the 'Belisarius' in several different ways. To most of them, after the terror and discomfort of the last few days it meant a dream coming true. To the Chief Engineer it would mean release to some extent from the excruciating pain of his burnt hands, only later would he be able to concentrate his thoughts in other directions.

To Carey, Gregson, Smith and one or two others their relief was somewhat intermingled with a certain reluctance to leave the old 'Belisarius' even though she was so obviously near her end. However, she could not last much longer to their way of thinking so it would certainly be pressing their luck to stay with her a moment longer than was absolutely necessary. It would be sad to turn their backs on the old ship as she had done so well in holding them all above water for as long as she had.

Hatch was not affected by the prospect of abandoning the ship. The thought had never occurred to him.

Admittedly most of the crew would have to leave as soon as a vessel arrived to take them off. Under tow there was nothing to do that a handful of men could not manage. Hatch had been working on the theory that when a ship did eventually find them that vessel would take them in tow. He was cold blooded enough to admit to himself that should no one find in the very near future the problem would solve itself. The 'Belisarius' had stayed afloat now for nearly three days since the disaster, if she could hold out for another three or four she could make port. He had to admit however that now the boiler room bulkhead was about to collapse at any moment it would be criminal to risk other men's lives in the hope of getting the ship home.

Close alongside the 'Contania' looked huge from Hatch's viewpoint twenty odd feet from the sea's surface. Big, safe and surging with power. But she was someone else's ship, the 'Belisarius' was his. The old rusting, soul-destroying and now sinking 'Belisarius'. But his! She had done a lot for them all and if there was anything more he could do for her he was willing to do it. But nobody else, no one else was to stay.

Old Ali the Serang came to ask how many men would be required to help the Mate down to the boat which had been lowered from the 'Contania' and was on its way to them. Hatch told him he was going to stay on board.

Ali, knowing that all the crew were only too eager to leave the vessel, thought he was going to have some difficulty in persuading a few of them men to remain on board to assist in the expected towing operation.

"How many men you want to stay then Sah'b?"

"No men Serang, all men go other ship."

"Achah Sah'b," said the such relieved Serang, "I tell men then come back."

"No! You don't come back, you go too Serang."

Ali was horrified.

"Nay Sah'b! Chief Officer Sah'b stay, Serang stay!"

Hatch would brook no argument. "No Serang, you go too, that is an order!" He then added rather lamely, "You needed on other ship to look after men. That ship all white crew, no savvy Lascar sailor. Serang's job look after crew now."

There was more argument before a very reluctant Serang departed after giving the Chief Officer a very big 'Salaam'.

The effort of talking started Hatch coughing again. Tears streamed down his battered face. Coughing often has this effect.

Carey and Gregson had listened to the conversation with growing concern and when the Mate's coughing had somewhat subsided they questioned him eagerly.

"What is all this about staying? The bulkhead could go at any moment and the ship sink like a stone!"

Hatch was adamant in his decision.

The argument was still continuing when the 'Contania's boat

arrived alongside.

The life-boat came as close as it dared in the heaving swell. Occasionally it was enveloped in a cloud of spray but under the lee of the 'Belisarius' conditions were good enough to attempt to take off her crew.

A heaving line was passed to the boat and a minute later Smith scrambled onto the bridge with a canvas bag containing a small 'walkie-talkie' radio transceiver. Hatch was immediately in contact not only with the officer in charge of the boat but with the 'Contania' herself.

Arrangements were soon made for the transfer and the first batch of men, mainly Asian seaman but including the Third Mate, were quickly on their way to the rescue ship. Smith was reluctant to leave in the first boat but Hatch insisted as he wanted him to put the master of the 'Contania' more clearly in the picture as regards the situation on the 'Belisarius'.

It was soon established that the 'Contania' would not be attempting to tow the derelict. She had a very tight schedule to keep in addition to the fact that, with forty foot containers three or four high from one end of her deck to the other, her crew would have great difficulty in even trying to connect a tow. When Hatch intimated that he would wait for another vessel the 'Contania's master said he would send off a radio message informing ships in the vicinity of the situation. He had already sent a general message to the effect that he had found the damaged 'Belisarius'.

The first boat-load of men transferred to the container ship without undue incident, a feat of seamanship which reflected no little credit on all concerned.

In the second boat went the injured men, including the Chief and Third Engineers. The operation proved much more difficult this time as some of the injured had to be lowered into the water then hauled into the boat, at considerable further suffering to them.

Whilst this boat was on its way back to the 'Contania' further information was received by the wreck. A Dutch tug, homeward bound after towing a dredger to South Africa, was only a few score miles to the westward and expected to be on the scene before dark.

Hatch smiled for the first time in days.

"A tug in the offing and a good solid Dutchman at that! At last things are falling our way!"

Hatch's 'our' included only the 'Belisarius' and himself.

Seamen are not good at saying goodbye even at the best of time so as the boat arrived alongside for the third and last time the farewells and unfunny jokes were clumsily made. All of the officers asked Hatch if there was anything more they could do for him and all asked to stay but the Mate would not even consider such requests. They had stowed all the food and water they could find close to his chair in order that he could reach it easily and every packet of cigarettes they could muster was crammed beside him. The two junior engineers hooked a couple of life-jackets to the bulkhead behind the chair with the words,

"Found these spare ones, they might come in handy if you have to jump in a hurry."

By an odd coincidence the two young engineers were not wearing life-jackets when they left the ship.

"Could you just put a match to the other oil drum before you go?" said Hatch to no one in particular, "Just in case it is dark by the time the tug gets here."

All too soon for the many details the last of the men were fussing with, the boat returned for the third and final time.

"Away you go the lot of you," said Hatch with forced cheerfulness, "Don't keep the big ship waiting, it is probably costing him a fiver a minute hanging around here."

The last farewells, a few distant shouts and then all was silent except for the groaning of the ship's fabric, the thudding of the sea against her side and the sighing of the wind.

It was not until the boat came into his line of vision, rising and falling in the heavy swell between the two ships, that Hatch felt really alone.

'I should have said something to them, told them that they had done a good job, told them that they were a good crowd.....Damn it!....Told them that they were the best bunch of bastards I'd ever sailed with! Ah well, it is too late now.'

The sudden squawking of the 'walkie-talkie' on his lap startled him. It was the master of the container ship calling to inform him that all of the 'Belisarius'' people were now on board his ship. He would wait until the tug arrived if.......No, Hatch would not hear of any further delay to the 'Contania', it was his decision to stay on board and he would not have anyone inconvenienced solely on his account.

Hatch thanked the master of the 'Contania' for all his assistance and the latter responded by offering to send the boat over again if the Mate wanted to change his mind. The offer again refused the large ship quickly gathered speed and, with the last good wishes over the hand radio and a prolonged blast on her powerful whistle, she soon disappeared into the mist.

Noticing he was still holding the small radio Hatch consoled himself with the thought that the container ship would probably have sets and to spare. It would no doubt come in handy in communicating with the tug.

Thinking of the tug reminded Hatch that he had not heard anyone go on to the monkey island before they left the ship.

"The bastards have forgotten to light the other flare!" he said out loud.

"We will light it before dark," said a voice behind him.

Hatch half turned, startled. Coming through the door leading to the chartroom were Carey and Gregson.

"Compliments of the 'Contania'," said Gregson holding out a small plastic bag, "Spare batteries for the 'walkie-talkie'."

Hatch ignored the proffered package.

"You bastards. You damn fool useless bastards! Why didn't you go with the others?"

Carey and Gregson were taken aback by their reception. The Mate's 'yard-arm was clear', he had ordered them to leave and they had 'officially' left the ship so no one could accuse him of risking their lives unnecessarily. They were not all that fond of Hatch as a man but felt obliged to help him now that he had elected to stay on the ship.

Hatch however was quite sincere. The last thing he wanted was people trying to help him personally and that was why they had remained, not, as they assured him, to help get the towline on board when the tug arrived. They all of them knew that the tug's people would be quite capable of making their own arrangements in this respect.

Hatch wanted to be alone for reasons the others could never have guessed.

It was mainly the perverseness of his character which had caused him to stay when he could quite honourably have left for the safety and comfort of the 'Contania' but to his own way of thinking he had reason enough to stay alone with his old ship. In his terrible physical pain his almost delirious mind convinced him that he was soon to die and he wanted, for the last time, to dream his dream in solitude.

The tug came out of the mist at full speed whilst it was still daylight. Clouds of spray were flung high over her superstructure as she crashed into the seas. She carried her aura of strength, efficiency and complete reliability with an accustomed air. Water streamed from her decks as she pitched and rolled. The red paint of her bottom showed below the black of her sides as she climbed and dipped in the heavy swell. In large white letters on her bow and stern, repeated in black on her white accommodation, was the name 'Opus'.

Appropriate enough though Carey.

The tug slowed as she approached and then completely encircled the 'Belisarius'. On the bridge of the 'Opus' could be discerned several figures inspecting the derelict through binoculars.

The circuit complete the tug came close under the lee of the old ship and lowered a boat. A few minutes later one of the largest men Hatch had ever seen appeared at the wheelhouse doorway. He seemed to more than half fill it. Clad in a suit of glistening yellow oilskins with an inflatable 'Mae-West' life-jacket lashed to his massive chest he was a picture of solidity. Bare headed, his short, straw-coloured hair was plastered to his scalp by the spray. A confident grin completed the picture.

"I am the Mate of the 'Opus'," he introduced himself, "O.K. I start the job while it is still light?" His very good English contained a trace of American accent, "Must hurry up, more bad weather coming."

Agreeing to this Hatch suddenly remembered that he had switched off his 'walkie-talkie' earlier to conserve batteries and had forgotten to switch it on again in the excitement of the tug's arrival. Having rectified this lapse the two ships were soon in communication with one another. Various details were discussed between Hatch and the tug's skipper and mate, Hatch not forgetting to insist that the tow be attempted under the terms of Lloyds Salvage Agreement. This was answered by a confident, "Ja, Ja, Lloyds Agreement, 'no cure no pay'", from the master of the tug, "Don't worry Captain, we will get you to Falmouth O.K."

Hatch was human enough to like the 'Captain' touch and said

nothing to dispel the illusion.

One question of the tug's mate was the position of the slipping gear at the locker ends of the 'Belisarius'' anchor cables. Hatch told him they were secured at the bottom of the locker and under sixteen feet of water and not, as in the more modern practice, handily at the top of it.

Obviously the ship could not be towed with two anchors hanging eight hundred feet below her, they would have to be removed. The tug's mate had allowed for the fact that the cables probably could not be slipped.

"That's O.K., I have burning gear in the boat."

After a few brief words in Dutch with the tug over the hand radio her Mate said to Hatch, "I get started now," and strode from the wheelhouse.

'Get started' was to signal the beginning of efficient team work which was a pleasure for the three men in the wheelhouse to watch. Carey and Gregson had offered to help but their assistance was declined. The Dutch mate was obviously capable of doing the job with the men he had. Two of them were soon on board from the boat with oxy-acetylene burning gear, a compact, portable outfit. The remaining man took the boat away from the ship's side and, by adjustments to the engine throttle and helm, kept the small boat in position a few yards off with the nonchalance of a riverside ferryman awaiting a fare. No small feat in the heavy ocean swell.

The three Dutchmen made their way to the Foc'sle head whilst the tug manoeuvred her stern close below them. A heaving line snaked up from the tug and was quickly grasped, passed through a fairlead and hauled on by the men. The light line brought up the bight, not the end, of a line of three inches in circumference, the 'messenger' for heavier stuff to follow. The bight of this line was dropped over the after post of the heavy mooring bitts a few feet abaft the starboard side of the windlass.

A curt hand signal from the Dutch Mate and the messenger began to move. The slack of the line was quickly taken in by the capstan on the tug's afterdeck and then more slowly as it felt the weight of the tug's towing wire. The heavy wire rope, fast to the other end of the messenger, slowly slid like a black serpent into the water and across to the bow of the 'Belisarius'. There was a slight hitch as the eye of the wire caught at the roller fairleads but the mate and one of his men leaned over the bulwark and, grasping the heavy wire, 'jumped' it over the edge of the fairlead from whence it continued unhindered its progress to the bitts.

When the eye was slightly round the after side of the bitts the mate signalled the tug to stop heaving and then, by planting both his feet and all of his twenty-odd stone on the wire just inboard of the rollers, trapped it for the brief moment necessary to allow the other two to pull the eye of the wire over the after post of the pair of bitts. Although the bitts were no doubt strong enough to take the weight of the tow by themselves the men made sure that this would not be the weakest point of the tow by unreeling one of the 'Belisarius'' mooring wires and passing this two or three times through the eye of the wire and around the foremast.

The next task was to cut the chain anchor cables. Although theoretically safer to burn through them forward of the windlass this was not practicable owing to the frequent bursts of spray, it was therefore decided to cut them in the slightly more sheltered position abaft this machine.

Some line was found under the foc'sle head and this was used to lash the cables to the eyebolts of the claws just forward of the windlass. These lashings would by no means prevent the cables from running but it was hoped would to a certain extent at least, stop the suddenly released cut end of chain whip-lashing across the foc'sle head creating more damage and even possibly cutting the towing wire.

Sheltering the flame of the oxy-acetylene burner with their bodies as best they could the three men set about burning through the more than two inch thick metal of a chain link. They had cut through one side of the link and had just commenced burning the other when the link opened up as if made of lead, demonstrating the tremendous weight on it. The men flung themselves clear as the chain parted with a tremendous bang and accompanied its anchor towards the bottom of the sea.

Hatch watched the operation forward with mixed feelings. He thought of all the effort and danger involved in getting the anchors and cables to their position as a sea anchor. The fact that they had apparently made that slight difference between the life and death of the ship hardly compensated for the loss of his old friend the Carpenter. Chips! he had hardly time to think of him since they were washed off the foc'sle head together. MacMurdo had been on the ship for years even before Hatch joined her and together they had dropped and weighed those anchors countless times in the bone-chilling wet of a North Sea winter and the grilling heat of the tropics. He remembered their idiosyncrasies, the way the starboard anchor was inclined to stick in the pipe when the ship was trimmed well by the stern and the habit of the port one of coming up with the flukes inboard and its reluctance to swing, with all the time and effort that caused before it was properly housed. Well, never again, the whole shebang was on its way to the bottom of the ocean and out of his life forever.

After the second anchor and cable had followed the first the tug slowly took up the slack of the wire and stood by to pick up her boat.

The three Dutchmen reported briefly to the bridge and again Hatch tried to get Carey and Gregson to leave whilst the opportunity offered but they were now as adamant as the Mate himself on staying with the ship. The tug men listened to the argument with growing impatience. The Dutch mate tried unsuccessfully to persuade all three of them to leave, insisting that there was nothing any of them could do on the ship. He might just as well have talked to the wind.

In the gathering darkness the boat made its way back to the tug and, once it was on board, the 'Opus' took the strain on the wire and the long tow commenced.

* * * * * * * * * * * * * * * * *

Chapter 14

All the prospects of a quiet Saturday prevailed at the home of Mr. Charles Fairbell when the telephone rang. Mrs. Fairbell answered it.

"Charles!" she called, "It's for you. Mr. Williams from his home."

"Right ho, I'll be there in a moment. It will be the 'Belisarius'' E.T.A. no doubt, we were expecting it yesterday."

Samantha Fairbell cupped the mouthpiece of the phone in her hand,

"Please hurry dear, Mr. Williams is most upset."

"All right, I'm on my way," Mr. Fairbell came down stairs with his half combed hair in sharp contrast to its usual neat perfection. "No doubt interrupting his T.V. programme."

He took the receiver from his wife's hand.

"Hello Williams, what is the problem?"

A moment or two later he knew.

Samantha, who had started to walk away, stopped and turned as she heard the serious tones of her husband's voice. She did not learn much from his "Yes.....Yes....Good God! No!" but obviously something awful had happened. This was soon confirmed by the instructions given to Williams.

"Can't run it from here....Get the office opened up....I'll be there as soon as I can.....Yes, get someone on the switchboard....Get Soames to open up, he lives nearest.......You stay by your phone until we have the switchboard operational.......The marine and engineer superintendents....No, you phone them....Yes....No....I'm leaving now then." He replaced the receiver in its cradle.

"Charles! What is it? Whatever had happened?"

"The old 'Belisarius' darling, she's been found all smashed up. I don't know any details but there should be a message soon so I'm going to make a dash for the office. If anyone calls that is where I will be."

"Is anyone hurt?" Ships were mainly just names to Samantha but people were a different matter altogether.

"They don't know yet." Ships were Fairbell's whole life. He felt a twinge of conscience over the fact that he had not even asked about the crew. There was nothing in the message from the ship which had found the 'Belisarius' anyway, it was only a brief signal from her master on first sighting the derelict and before communications had been established between the two ships.

Fairbell's mind was racing as he shrugged on a jacket and his sheep-skin motoring coat before dashing to the garage. His blue jaguar was half way down the drive before he suddenly braked and shouted through the car window to his wife standing by the front door.

"Tell Dad will you darling? He will probably be interested."

A moment later the car continued on its way.

'He is in a flap,' thought Samantha, 'That is the first time he has gone to the office without kissing me goodbye – and he has left the garage doors open!'

****

408

Apart from in the vicinity of the telephone switchboard the main office was as silent and deserted as on any normal Saturday afternoon.

The Chairman's room was in complete contrast. Seven men were there when the second message from the 'Contania' arrived. Mr. Fairbell, directors Aldred and Cuthbertson, (who had been contacted and insisted on coming to the office), Soames and Williams of the office staff, Captain Dewar the Marine Superintendent and Robson the Engineer Superintendent.

The message contained more detail of the state of the 'Belisarius' including the fact that she was in a sinking condition. It also gave a slightly inaccurate casualty list and implied that all the crew were being taken off as this was thought to be the case when the message was sent.

The men in the room were deeply shocked by the message, particularly the news of the three deaths.

"Poor Andy Montague," said Dewar, "What a thing to happen, just when he was to get the cruise ship he wanted so much. We will have to let his wife know."

"I will tell her," Fairbell did not relish the prospect but was not one to shun responsibility. "You know her well, perhaps you would have a word with her afterwards?" After a pause, "The trouble is it sounds so very definite, it would be cruel to offer any hope at all?"

"Aye, it is too long ago for there to be any kind of chance, particularly in the kind of weather they must have experienced at the time." Dewar thought of Beth Montague. Extremely pleasant but rather ambitious on her husband's behalf. She too had been looking forward to the prestige that went with the command of a liner.

"The other young chap too, the Radio Officer, does anyone know anything about him? Married? Family? And the Carpenter?" Fairbell continued.

The carpenter was known to Captain Dewar but no one present acquainted with Forbes. Soames went off to look up some files.

It was then that 'Old' Mr. Fairbell arrived.

Henry Bartram Fairbell had followed his father, the founder of the originally styled 'Fairbell Steam Ship Company' as Chairman and Managing Director. Although retired for some years he still dropped into the office occasionally to see how things were progressing under the chairmanship of his only son. Although proud of the way the company was contending with the rapidly changing shipping world he could not help 'straightening out these young fellows now and again' as he put it.

"A serious business, a serious business," he said as he came into the room. Then, suddenly remembering his manners, "Good afternoon Gentlemen."

"You should not be out in the cold weather Father," said his son with some concern.

"Why not indeed? Why not?" Mr. Fairbell senior had in recent years got into the habit of repeating himself when upset. "The 'Belisarius' was one of my ships. Of course she was brand new then, a lovely ship. What exactly had happened anyway? Sama...., hem! your lady wife couldn't tell me much and I did not want everything second hand so I came to find out for myself."

Old Mr. Fairbell was soon as much informed of the situation as the others.

"I see the 'Contania' will radio when all the men are off so there is no point in your sending a message asking silly questions. They say the 'Belisarius' is sinking, how do they know? What is her cargo anyway?"

"Bulk soyabean meal," replied his son.

"Huh!" This response could have implied anything from the fact that Old Mr. Fairbell did not know what this commodity was to 'Fancy having to fill our ships with that low-freight rubbish, in my time they came home from the States with cotton and tobacco.'

The third radio message arrived later in the afternoon. The 'Contania' was proceeding on her voyage having taken off most of the crew of the 'Belisarius' whom she would land at Le Havre the following day. However, three men had remained on board awaiting a tug which was due to arrive before dark.

"The tug should be arriving about now then," said Dewar after a glance at the window.

"She can't really be sinking if the men have stayed on board and they think she can be towed in. I wonder why the others were in such a hurry to leave? It just doesn't seem to add up," remarked Mr. Aldred.

"Just a minute!" Mr. Cuthbertson had detected something odd. "Didn't the earlier message mention that the chief officer had been injured? Yet this one indicates that he is one of the three people who have stayed on board. There must be some mix up here."

"Probably only slightly hurt," said the Chairman. "If she is in any danger of sinking the three men probably intend moving over to the tug when the tow-line is fast. After all someone will have to get the line on board. I assume if the three men think they could do that any others would be superfluous. In any case the tug would not be able to accommodate the whole crew. By the way Captain Dewar, something I meant to ask earlier, who is the Chief Officer, anyone I know?"

Dewar had been rather dreading this inevitable question for some time.

"Hatch, sir,"

"Hatch? Hatch? Oh my God, not Hatch."

The Marine Superintendent was not all that fond of Hatch, in fact even that would have been understating their relationship. However, as an ex-seafarer he felt an automatic reaction to protect 'his' men.

"He is a good seaman sir, even though he has his faults."

"Faults!" almost shouted Mr. Fairbell, "Faults! The man is a dipsomaniac." He felt like saying that if it had not been for Dewar the man would have been dismissed long ago but decided this would be unfair.

"I wouldn't go as far as that sir. He is inclined to drink a bit too much in port I understand but he doesn't let it affect his job. The affair you recall was most unfortunate."

"Very unfortunate for him. I know your main argument was that it was a Saturday afternoon and who would expect an unheralded visit from the Head Office at that time? As I explained to you at the time it was a most extraordinary series of circumstances which led me to be passing the ship in the first place and deciding to drop on board but that does not alter the fact that the man was in a disgusting state for a senior officer of one of our ships."

Charles Fairbell cooled a little, "Well that is all over and done with now but it would have to be Hatch."

"I think he will do a good job sir, he is not one of our best by any means but he has a great deal of experience. Many of the younger Chief Officers would not do so well under the present circumstances I'm certain."

"I would be much happier if Montague was still there," re-joined the Chairman, "There was a man I had confidence in but I suppose we will just have to hope for the best."

Soames and Williams brought into the Chairman's room various files from the personnel section and soon telegrams were being sent and phone calls made informing the next of kin of survivors of their safety. An overseas telex message performed the same service for the Asian crew.

Mr. Aldred, who held the brief for personnel, got the switchboard operator to book him a flight to Le Havre and to obtain a connection to the company's agents there in order to inform them of the situation and to have repatriation and any necessary medical arrangements organised for the 'Belisarius" crew.

It occurred to Aldred that Miss Bates had been keeping a lonely vigil at the switchboard for some considerable time now.

"Sorry to drag you to the office on a Saturday afternoon and keep you so long. We will try to get someone to relieve you shortly."

"Not at all Mr. Aldred, and please don't dream of getting anyone else, I am only too glad to be of assistance and am willing to stay as long as the switchboard is required."

Miss Bates had been anticipating a long, dull afternoon with her cat watching an ancient film on her small television set. With all the excitement in the office wild horses would not have dragged her from her post.

****

The afternoon soon turned into evening. As the central heating was turned off for the weekend it was cold at first so the men retained their overcoats. One after another they removed them as the Chairman's electric fire, the only one in the whole office, began to take effect. Williams relieved Miss Bates who soon had a kettle boiling and minutes later they were drinking tea around the fire in its ornate marble surround, a reminder of earlier days.

"I suppose the tug will let us know when they have the 'Belisarius' in tow?" remarked Cuthbertson.

"I was wondering that myself," answered Charles Fairbell, "We will give them another hour and if we don't hear by then we will send them a message."

"I'll feel happier when all the men are off," said Cuthbertson, "I assume they do intend going over to the tug when they are connected up? If things are as bad as they appear it would be risky staying."

"What kind of radio do tugs have anyway Captain Dewar?" Fairbell asked, "I should imagine those deep sea chaps have......"

He was answered sooner than anyone expected. The telephone on the Chairman's desk shrilled and everyone leaped to their feet. Fairbell reached the phone in one stride and Miss Bates' cup and saucer nearly came to grief as she tore from the room to take over the switchboard from Williams' amateur hands.

Williams' voice came on the phone.

"A call from the tug 'opus' sir, I'll put him through."

Fairbell glanced up from the telephone receiver.

"One of you listen on the extension," he indicated the set on a side table, "and take notes."

The telephone call lasted for more than twenty minutes. Fairbell spoke to both the Master and Mate of the tug and soon the whole situation became clear. Mr. Robson was first to reach the extension phone and recorded the facts in an abbreviated form in his precise hand. The others leaned over him to read his notes as they emerged beneath his pen.

"Yes, I've got all that thank you Captain but please, if the ship is in such a sorry state get those men off. Tell them that is an order from me personally. Tell them that they have done a magnificent job but there is nothing more they can do so they must leave." Fairbell listened for a few more minutes and then continued, "Yes I appreciate you are busy and am sorry to have taken up so much of your time. What you have done is much appreciated. Right ho, I'll close now but please let us know the moment those men are on your ship. Goodbye then and thank you."

Fairbell put down the phone.

"Well there you are gentlemen. She is under tow but that bulkhead, boiler room bulkhead was it?, could burst at any moment and the ship go down like a stone. Why? Why in heaven's name did those men not get off when they had the opportunity?"

The question remained unanswered. Captain Dewar had been in command at sea for some years and might have had some inkling of the reason but if so he kept it to himself.

****

It was well after midnight when a brief message from the 'Opus' confirmed that the three men on the towed ship refused to leave her. Fairbell replied with renewed insistence that they did so immediately or at the latest at daylight in the morning.

"Well there seems little point in all of us staying here," said the Chairman, "there is little chance of any further messages or developments tonight. I suggest we take turns, 'watches' Captain Dewar? here at the office, a couple at a time. I'll take my father home now," he glanced at Old Mr. Fairbell who was half asleep in the most comfortable chair in the room, "catch a few hours' sleep and return first thing in the morning. Oh, I think we can chase Miss Bates off now too, she can leave the switchboard open. I will have a word with her before she goes."

****

As the jaguar sped through the night the two Fairbells, father and son, were each engrossed in his own thoughts. Old Mr. Fairbell did at one stage break the silence with the words, "Poor old 'Belisarius', I remember her well. Old Carmichael was master on her maiden voyage, just before he retired."

The observation, receiving no response, allowed the old man to return to his reverie.

As the car pulled up at his home Henry Fairbell invited his son in for a nightcap.

"It will have to be a very quick one then," said Charles Fairbell, "It has every prospect of being a long day tomorrow and I must get a little sleep."

With his study door closed and two large whiskies poured Henry Fairbell opened the conversation.

"This Hatch fellow, I didn't like to bring the subject up with the others present but isn't he the young man who celebrated his promotion a little prematurely? I seem to remember you mentioning the incident some months ago."

"Yes, the same. He was lucky to have kept his job, he would have got the push if Dewar had not talked me out of it."

"Very wise of Dewar if you don't mind me saying so Charles. The shock of finding you on his doorstep on such an occasion could go a long way in straightening the young chap out."

Charles Fairbell was incensed at this remark.

"I do not agree Dad, there is no room for drunks in the business in this day and age."

"For all that he seems a solid enough man, look at what he is doing now for instance."

"Is he doing more or less what anyone else would have done? Anyway, we don't know the whole story yet, and besides, it is hardly the point. If the company is to be run on efficient lines, there is no room for people who can't stick to the rules."

"It takes all kinds," re-joined Henry Fairbell, "'And there are....'"

"Please do not quote to me," interrupted his son, "'If I am paying the drummer I am calling the tune,' to misquote one for you. We are recruiting some very efficient men into all levels of the company at the moment and I have no regrets at seeing some of the old die-hards go."

"All very well Charles but don't forget that those die-hards as you term them are the people who kept the company going during the lean times. You won't remember much of the slump before the last war.....but that was long ago now." he paused, "The other side of the coin, your 'efficiency experts', how long do they stay with you? Just a few years most of them then they are off to pastures new. How many of them get involved in the company as a company and not just as a means to exercise their theories? That 'brilliant' young man you brought into accounts a few years ago at a phenomenal salary, what was his name? Broke eggs with a big stick for eighteen months, upset everyone in the department and then emigrated to Canada." He continued with a malicious grin, "Have you got that mess sorted out yet?"

"He did not leave a 'mess'," replied Charles Fairbell defensively, "Of course it took a little time to reorganise things in accounts but we are still using some of his ideas."

"And most of the old ones no doubt. But to get back to ships, you recall that Captain Bretherton you used to rave about?" Henry Fairbell was quite enjoying himself, "Couldn't go wrong in your eyes, 'He is going right to the top' you used to say. And what happened? The first voyage he makes in a liner he gets an American heiress with child, ruins his career and damn nigh wrecks the company's cruise business."

"Oh Dad! You are exaggerating! Bretherton might have got the high jump but as you well know cruise ships are like film stars, any publicity is better than no publicity. The Press had a ball at the time I will admit but the passenger booking did not fall off. The ships were almost full every voyage, with more American heiresses than ever." This last was just a guess but Charles Fairbell thought it likely to have a good deal of truth in it.

He glanced at his watch and rose to his feet.

"Thanks for the drink Dad. I'll get off home now for a few hours' sleep. I will keep you informed regarding the 'Belisarius'. You go off to bed now and give the office a ring sometime in the morning."

Goodnights were said and the Jaguar purred off down the dark empty road.

★★★★★★★★★★★★★★★★

Further brief messages were received in the office from the 'Opus' at intervals the following day. They contained information regarding the weather experienced and expected, the fact that the boiler room bulkhead still held and that the three men still refused to leave the derelict.

"Well it looks a little more cheerful," said Cuthbertson when the latest messaged had been read, "The weather seems to be holding out and the ship appears to be in much the same condition as last night. They have not mentioned an E.T.A. for Falmouth though, when do you think she will get there Hamish?" The variation of Dewar's first name was often used by his colleagues, particularly if they had any reason to want to remind him of his Scottish origins.

Captain James Dewar, sharing the vigil with his associate, thought for a moment before replying.

"It will take some time before they settle down to a steady speed on a job like that. No doubt they could tow at six or seven knots in good weather but the swell out there will make it considerably less. If they try to tow her too fast it would increase the strain on her in the swell – like attempting to rush an old lady up a flight of stairs, more haste, less

418

speed. Any deterioration in the weather will, of course, set them back too so I'm not surprised they are reluctant to give an estimated time of arrival."

"So are you obviously," smiled the Chairman as he entered the room, "Say I gave you, well let's say five knots average speed to Falmouth, what time would she arrive then?"

Captain Dewar examined the chart, brought earlier from the Marine Department. He took some rough measurements with the aid of the edge of a piece of paper, scribbled a few figures and then answered.

"At five knots, about ten o'clock on Tuesday morning."

"Tuesday, and now it is Sunday afternoon. Let us hope the weather gets no worse and the ship holds together," remarked Cuthbertson.

"I do wish those men would get off the ship. There is absolutely no reason why they should risk their lives any longer," Charles Fairbell was patently worried, "The ship herself really doesn't matter anymore, she will be finished after this. She was to go of course anyway before her next quadrennial survey, neither we nor anyone else can afford to run a steam ship which burns twice the fuel a motor ship does, not at today's oil prices.

"It's a hard thing to say but that ship is now just so much scrap iron, just so many tons of scrap."

Chapter 15

Like a great wounded animal dragging its tormented body towards the sanctuary of its lair the 'Belisarius' shouldered her groaning frame into each succeeding sea. Her bow, cascading water, slowly rose and then, as the crest of the swell passed amidships, fell slowly again into the trough. One sea after another, slowly, painfully up and then down again. Four times every three minutes, eighty times an hour. Every sea a torture to her strained hull.

****

All through the first night of the tow the three men on board the 'Belisarius' attempted to convince themselves that their troubles and privations would soon be over. They tried to cheer one another up with the optimism none of them really felt. At least Carey and Gregson discussed the ship's chances, Hatch said very little. In fact, the other two were never quite sure when the mate was awake or asleep. He seemed to exist in a state of limbo somewhere between the two. Occasionally he gave utterance to a half supressed groan as a slightly different motion of the ship caused movement to his pain seared body but otherwise he remained silent most of the time.

When the long awaited daylight at last arrived an analysis was taken of the situation.

The ship was riding rather more deeply in the water so far as could be judged but the port list had increased but slightly. The hatches were still secure and everything else around the decks appeared to be much the same as on the previous evening.

Carey and Gregson set off for an inspection below and on their return were able to inform Hatch that although the bulkhead between the engine and boiler rooms was still holding it was, so far as they could ascertain by flashlight, bulging and leaking more than it was the previous day.

"I've been talking to the tug whilst you two were below," said Hatch, "They suggested putting on board a portable salvage pump to try to get the level of the water in the engine room down a bit. However, this would mean discontinuing the tow for some time as they would have to make a lee for their boat in this weather so we have decided against it. It probably would not do much good anyway as there must be a fair sized hole in the ship's side and she appears to be floating on the buoyancy of the remainder of the ship mow so the idea is cancelled. We will just have to press on and hope for the best."

'He might have discussed it with Peter and I', thought Carey.

Hatch did not divulge the fact that the main reason for declining the offer of the pump was that it would mean one the tug's men being on board to run it and he had no intention of risking further lives. He was still irritated by the presence of Carey and Gregson.

Food of a sort was doled out but none of them felt much like eating. All they wanted was sleep, hours and hours and hours of completely undisturbed, luxurious, dreamless sleep. And if the Gods decreed that the most beautiful woman in the world was to share the bed with any one of them she would have been lucky to receive as much as a civil 'goodnight'.

Carey and Gregson decided to keep watch and watch on the bridge. Hatch was not even considered as they did not know when he was awake and when asleep. The arrangement was not very satisfactory. Although it was to be a system of four hour watches whoever's turn it was to lie on the chartroom settee dozed only fitfully. Nerves and strain prevented deep sleep and after an hour or so the 'watch below' man would return to the wheelhouse and insist that the other tried to get some rest.

Carey clung to a window frame in the fore side of the wheelhouse. He could have arranged something to sit on but preferred to stand, it seemed the correct thing to do whilst on watch. His thoughts were far from pleasant.

'On watch for what? Why on watch anyway? Why here at all? Why not miles away indulging in the comfort of the 'Contania' with the rest of the crowd? Why? Why? Why?' Carey's weary brain fired the questions at him.

He tried to answer them. He was not here for the sake of the job.

He was not here for the good of the ship. He was here to look after that bastard Jake! Carey almost snarled the name out loud. Jake! He was the cause of it all. He could have gone when the others did, then he and Peter Gregson would not have been here enduring all this horror and discomfort. Carey really hated Hatch at that moment.

Why had Jake chosen to stay? – another question. Why indeed? Jake was certainly not the type to court glory, just the reverse in fact. Being injured he had every excuse to leave even if one were needed. Above all he had no reason to be interested in protecting the company's property to this extent, not after they had dangled his 'brass hat' before his eyes and then snatched it away, wherever the fault might lie. An explanation had not emerged from Hatch and one did not seem likely now. What was he thinking of when he decided to stay? Come to that what was he thinking of at the present moment? Just sitting there hour after hour, day after day, gazing forward through half closed eyes. Asleep? Awake? If awake what was he thinking of?

****

Hatch's eyes gazed for hours on end at the rising and dipping foc'sle head but most of the time he did not see it. The bow of the ship could have been a barn, the tug a distant tree. Seas cascading over the bitts and windlass but clear, fresh water trickling over stones in a Lakeland stream.

His mind returned to that period of time between his last voyage and the present one. Over and over and over again.

He generally flitted quickly over the first few painful days. The elation at hearing, albeit unofficially, that after several people junior to him had been promoted to master, he was at last to receive his long awaited 'brass hat'. The celebration that afternoon which had started out mildly enough. The relieving chief engineer's whisky and the chief steward's gin which, combined with his tiredness after only a couple of hours sleep after docking the night before and a substantial amount of his more customary beer had provided the fuel for the disaster.

His cheerful, drunken, "Come in you old bastard!" in answer to the knock on his door. The ghastly horror of seeing, instead of the relieving chief officer he was expecting, the Chairman of the Company standing there when the door opened. The grande finale on coming to his feet completely off balance, tripping over a chair and crashing headlong into a pile of empty beer cans. It still seemed a bad dream. A horrible nightmare start to his leave.

He well remembered his visit to the Head Office the following Monday. Although spared an interview with Chairman or any of the directors a very long hour with the Marine Superintendent had left him even more white and shaken than he had been on entering that gentleman's sanctum.

Hatch's first reaction on escaping to the street after the interview was to head for the nearest bar. However, it was mid-afternoon and the pubs were shut. This gave him time to reflect that the nearest bar to the head office would hardly be the most tactful hostelry to visit. He therefore started walking and having no particular destination in mind let his feet guide him.

As Hatch walked he brooded. He thought of his life so far. Nothing at all to be proud of he decided. He recalled much of his childhood, the orphanage, his first going to sea as a deck boy. He reminisced on the various ships on which he had sailed, the adventures he had had and, above all, the fun. It was always much easier to remember the good times rather than the bad. He recalled 'parties' which in retrospect must have caused considerable anxiety to various authorities of one kind or another, if not actual damage. The most glorious booze-ups were remembered with relish, but rarely their subsequent hangovers.

Hatch had led quite a hectic life.

'Jake,' he said to himself, 'you are nothing but a disgusting animal. You will definitely have to slow down a bit, things are getting dangerous. Apart from everything else your liver is not going to stand much more of the treatment you have been doling out to it.'

So engrossed in his thoughts was Hatch that he failed to notice that a hostelry he had just passed was opening its doors for the evening custom.

He did not notice the next half-dozen either, so deep was he in thought. Hatch, as so many a better man before him, had decided to turn over a new leaf.

He was not exactly going to completely reform he hastened to assure his prematurely rejoicing liver but he was going to use a bit of sense from now on. His first intention in this direction was to avoid his old haunts and cronies. London was out for a start. Hatch did not like cities generally and London in particular now he came to think of it. The life and excitement were there but it was all so artificial – and Hatch was about as artificial as a log of wood. As he was known in about half the pubs on the south coast and west country they were out too.

Somewhere entirely different was required, somewhere he could book into a small hotel, licensed of course, talk to people other than bar-maids and lushes, walk up and down a hill or two and throw stones into ponds if he felt so inclined. Part of the world where he could pat passing cows and generally give the impression that he had never been a bit of a drunk, never mind a reformed one, which to Hatch was considerably worse.

North seemed to be the only direction left to go but what was up there? A place with hills, cows, lakes.....lakes! that was it, the Lake District!

Suiting action to his thoughts Hatch went down to the nearest Underground Railway Station and proceeded to his hotel. After making inquiries he decided to go north on the first available train in the morning. What was left of the evening was utilised in packing and making plans.

****

Hatch arrived at Windermere station in the late afternoon. There he bought a map of the Lake District and on consulting it decided he was not deep enough into the country so caught a bus heading north-west. After obtaining local advice and taking another two bus rides he eventually discovered a hostelry which suited him admirably. Being a Tuesday business was slack so he had no difficulty in obtaining a room.

Using the small hotel as a base Hatch spent the first few days exploring the country around it and the local points of interest. Later he would take a bus ride in whatever direction took his fancy and, on alighting, walk off on what appeared to be the most attractive route. He became acquainted with several of his fellow guests and occasionally walked with them or shared a meal but avoided becoming more involved preferring his own company.

The weather was rather mixed and Hatch soon joined the tourists in adding to his wardrobe a nylon anorak, a pair of boots and thick woollen socks. He toyed with the idea of a walking stick but decided that this would be rather overdoing it.

Hatch threw stones into Windermere, Ullswater, Grasmere, Derwentwater and sundry pools of less renown. He patted three cows, (actually one was a bullock), walked over numerous hills – and became somewhat bored. For all that he had no intention of leaving the area until his leave was up. He had given the London office the telephone number of his hotel on arrival there and after two weeks began to wonder when the call would come. A fortnight was more than enough of virtually his own company. The office generally gave at least a week's warning of the date of returning to a ship so he thought he had at least a week or ten days more of lakes and trees.

It was at this stage that it happened.

Hatch had taken a long bus ride that morning to what was, for him, a new area. He climbed the nearest mountain, admired the view from the top and then, by various footpaths and sheep tracks, wended his way slowly down towards the village he had seen in the distance from the top of the mountain. Or was it a hill? Hatch did not know how high a hill had to be before it qualified for the title of 'mountain'.

He was strolling by a tree bordered stream when the silence previously only broken by the sound of running water, was suddenly shattered by the barking of a dog, apparently almost under his feet. Being unable to see the source of the commotion Hatch crossed to the other side of the stream to obtain a better view. From this new position he saw under the bank and ensnared in the tangle of a blackberry thicket a small, very muddy Jack Russell Terrier. The dog was alternately barking at him and down a rabbit burrow. Hatch did not know a lot about dogs but decided that the animal, though lively enough, had probably been entangled for some time. There was no one in sight so it seemed obvious that it had escaped from its owner and its being so thin indicated it may have been trapped for days.

Hatch based his knowledge of Jack Russells on the only other specimen of the breed to which he had had close contact. This was the pet of an old lady who had asked him if he were feeling unwell when he was nursing a monumental hangover sitting on a bench on Brighton Promenade. The old lady insisted on chatting to him for a considerable length of time. Hatch, who's head was splitting to the extent that he wondered how the crevasse was not clearly visible, could not remember much of the lady's long life history but he did recall her insisting that her dog was a very fine, pedigree Jack Russell. He also retained the impression that this particular breed existed on a fairly heavy diet of sweet biscuits and chocolates.

Rescuing the dog posed rather a problem. It was under a fairly dense layer of prickly brambles about four feet above the stream. Hatch balanced precariously on two boulders in the stream bed and, at the expense of several scratches on his hands, managed to get hold of the dog which was now barking hysterically. To avoid being bitten he tucked the terrier under his left arm and grasped its collar with his right hand.

Carefully turning on the two stones Hatch was put off balance by the sudden violent struggling of the animal. He tried to step onto another stone, performed a pirouette which would have done credit to a professional ballet dancer and, with a loud oath, sat down with considerable force on the very edge of the bank.

About to extricate himself from his undignified position Hatch was startled to find that after all he and the dog were not alone.

A voice emanating from the top of the high bank on the other side of the stream said, "Hey!"

Hatch looked up and saw, standing but a few yards away, a girl. Not just a girl but the most beautiful girl Hatch had ever seen in his life.

She was wearing brown brogues, a tweed skirt, some kind of anorak and carried in her right hand a dog leash. All this Hatch took in at a glance. His eyes had stopped when they got to her face. It was more radiantly beautiful than any face he could ever have imagined. The indescribably lovely smile on it slowly dissolved.

"Are you hurt?"

This magnificent apparition was actually speaking to _him_, Jake Hatch! He managed to prevent himself looking over his shoulder to see if she were not, after all, talking to someone behind him.

"Are you alright?" A trace of concern now in her voice – if one could term such dulcet tones in so mundane a word. She was actually concerned about him! She actually cared whether he, Jake Hatch, had or had not broken his back! Those large, wonderful green eyes were beginning to look slightly worried – worried about him!

"You _are_ hurt!" A catch in her voice now.

427

How wonderfully those green eyes complimented her hair. And such hair, never had a woman's crowning glory reached such perfection. The dense copper-coloured tresses fell in waves about her shoulders, shining in the sun. For all the world like the bunches of fine copper winding from a broken electric motor...No!...Hatch frantically searched his bewildered mind for a more suitable simile.

The silent soliloquy might have gone on for some time longer if the dog had not decided to alter her tactics. Apart from the fact that she was not used to being handled by strangers she had marked objection to being clamped like a rugby football beneath the arm of a rather rough Cardiff quarterback. Having tried vocally for some time to get her message across she suddenly whipped her head free and buried her teeth in Hatch's wrist.

This brought the day-dreaming Hatch back to earth with a jolt. Figuratively of course, in the actual physical sense he could not have been closer to it.

The suddenly released dog sprang into the stream, splashed across, scrambled up the opposite bank through the blackberry bushes and stopped at her mistress' feet.

Hatch clambered up from his damp, undignified seat, unfortunately slapping his hand in a cow-pat in the process, and stepped slowly from the stream. He had landed dry-shod initially but the appearance of the girl had caused him to neglect the precarious position of his feet on a flat rock and they had slipped into the water where his boots had slowly filled.

Hatch stood on the bank considerably bewildered, extremely embarrassed, wet of foot.......and in love.

****

To Hatch the remainder of the afternoon passed in a golden dream. His memories of it, and how hard he tried to recall every detail, were blurred and in no particular order. He remembered her concern at the few drops of blood oozing from the marks of the little dog's sharp teeth. Her offer of a ridiculously small lace-edged handkerchief in lieu of a bandage – how he wished he had accepted it to hold as a keepsake! His insistence on using his own, luckily fresh that morning. Not that the tiny punctures required attention, he really wrapped his wrist to shield the sight of blood from her gentle eyes. His scarred hands gave ample evidence of far more serious injuries.

He remembered how she gaily chatted but little of what she said apart from the fact that her name was Marion, his favourite name as he told her in all sincerity – and without a twinge of conscience over the fact that until that moment he had always insisted that this was 'Penelope'. He also recalled that the dog's name was Cleopatra which was hardly relevant. He would never forget her expressive eyes, the way they wrinkled at the corners when she laughed. He often wondered why she laughed that afternoon, he could not remember saying anything funny, in fact he could not recall saying much at all.

Above all he remembered that magnificent hair as, with a graceful toss of her head, she shook it from her face when she looked up to say something.

Marion….he only knew her as Marion although he felt that he should have addressed her as miss Something or other although she had not offered her other name when they had introduced themselves……Marion had said that she often walked her dog by the beck in the late afternoon. This remark had led Hatch to immediately commence planning ambushes, 'accidental' meetings of course, it would not do to frighten the girl off, she came from another world and was far, far too good to become involved with the likes of him. However, it would be marvellous to see her again, even if only to say 'Hello' as they passed.

Hatch squelched along at her side as she prattled on, loving every minute of her company. He hoped they would never reach their destination.

Their parting was rather sudden. At some time, Hatch must have given Marion a general idea of where he was staying as when they arrived at a bus stop he was told by the girl that the bus just arriving was the last to head in that direction that evening. Hatch was sorely tempted to say he would catch the first bus in the morning, take a taxi, walk back or sleep under her window, anything to delay the parting but decided he had tried the lovely girl's patience long enough. She no doubt had other things to do that evening and had been very kind to have already given him so much of her time. Anyway, reasoned Hatch, being apparently so close to her home she would not want any of her acquaintances to see her talking to a man nearly old enough to her father. How old would she be? Nineteen? Twenty? Twenty-one at the most.

"I hope I'll see you by the stream in the next day or two," said Hatch as he boarded the bus, then for some involuntary reason, knowing his leave was nearing its end, "If I don't get suddenly recalled."

From his seat he watched Marion waiting for the bus to pull out. She was smiling but what did he detect in her eyes? They did not give the impression that she was glad he had left her at last. It was almost as if they held a look of slight disappointment.

Hatch was very confused.

****

Jake Hatch had sadly underestimated his effect on Marion. Her mind was in a whirl as the bus turned a corner of the lane and passed from her sight. Living in the quietness of the country virtually all of her life she had not experienced a great deal of excitement. The young men of her acquaintance, although of different temperaments, were, she decided, all of a pattern. She knew all about them, their families, their ambitions, their sports and foibles. Jake had crashed into her life like a marauding elephant. He was strange, entirely different to anyone she knew and so appealed strongly to her feminine instinct for mystery. Although she had elicited a fair amount of information from Hatch, almost completely without his knowing it, he was still mainly an enigma to her. She felt an urgent desire to talk to someone about her mysterious stranger. And who better than her sister Charlotte?

After brief apologies to her parents for being late home, very vague explanations and a hurried meal Marion made her way to her sister's house on the other side of the village. Charlotte was nearly nine years older than Marion, a long enough period of time to have created no childhood jealousies between them. They shared all of their secrets....within reason.

Charlotte opened the door to her sister.

"Well this is a surprise. I didn't think you were coming until Friday."

"I've come to talk to you about something – uh – is Harry in?"

"He left only five minutes ago, club meeting or something. Why, did you want to see him?"

"No, just you."

"This sounds very interesting," said Charlotte, "You haven't won the pools or something, your eyes are absolutely sparkling?"

They reached the pleasant little lounge and Marion burst forth with her story. It took long enough to tell. Marion's version of the afternoon was very detailed, slightly embellished and not entirely accurate. In fact, her description of Jake would have made him writhe with embarrassment had he heard it. Charlotte made suitable comments and asked a few questions when the occasions arose.

The two ladies made a pot of tea, consumed it, put Charlotte's two young children to bed, washed the cups and saucers, ironed quite a pile of clothes and then settled down to a second pot of tea without a break in their conversation.

At the conclusion of the narrative Charlotte exclaimed, "Wow!" and then after a moment's pause, "Wow!" again.

"It seems to me that my kid sister has fallen very violently in love!"

"Of course not!" Marion blushed furiously, "I hardly know him."

"For someone you have only just met you seem to know quite a lot about him, from the fact that he goes to sea for a living to his size in socks. And quite frankly I do not like this going to sea bit at all, 'you know what sailors are'."

Marion defended her Jake as best she could but even she had to admit that there was a great deal more she would have liked to know about him.

Charlotte continued her interrogation.

"You say you found this sailor in a ditch....."

"It was not a ditch, it was the beck by the big ash tree, you know, where the bank is quite high on one side. Anyway he was only there because he was rescuing Cleo. I think it was very sweet of him, he got awfully wet and muddy doing it."

"Did Cleo need rescuing?"

"Of course not, she always chases rabbits down those particular burrows. Anyway that is beside the point, he thought he was doing Cleo a good turn."

"Obviously she did not think so or she would not have bitten him."

"Charlotte, you are being impossible!" Marion stood up as if to leave.

"Sit down, sit down. I'm sorry if I've upset you, I didn't mean to. It's just that I feel a bit responsible for my little sister."

"Little sister indeed! I am a fully grown, responsible woman. May I remind you that I am twenty-five years old, twenty-six in just a few months," she trailed off rather ruefully. (In common with the majority of men Hatch could not have guessed a woman's age within ten years for a large bet but, as with most, he was inclined to err on the gallant side).

Charlotte allowed Marion's outburst to pass without comment. Although she had married at twenty-three she could well remember at the time of her twenty-first birthday deciding that she was destined to become an old maid.

"He doesn't seem to be a very ardent suitor. Do you mean to tell me that he did not even ask for your telephone number or address or anything?"

"He was far too shy, I had to do all the work," said Marion with a slight pout, "I think I overawed him a little." The thought of herself overawing anyone made her giggle.

"Didn't he even ask to take you out that evening? He might at least have given you tea."

Marion had all the necessary excuses ready.

"How could he? He was covered in mud," which was an exaggeration if not a downright fib, "and he must have been terribly uncomfortable with his boots full of water."

"Sounds quite a Romeo, after rescuing a damsel in distress he walks with her for hours on end without saying a word with river water and tadpoles oozing out of his boots and doesn't even ask the girl for a date. Are you sure he didn't bang his head when he fell in the ditch...sorry, beck?"

Seeing the expression on Marion's face Charlotte was

immediately contrite.

Sorry, darling," she gave her sister a hug, "That was horrid of me. I am sure he will be clean and dry when you meet him tomorrow or whenever. I'm dying to meet him, he sounds terribly interesting."

Marion was only slightly mollified.

"I don't really know when that will be, I remembered after he left that I won't be walking Cleo tomorrow afternoon as I've promised to take Mum shopping and to her dentist. In fact, I may not even see him before he goes away as when he was getting on the bus he said something about being recalled at any moment. Anyway he said he would certainly be back for a holiday in November so I will definitely see him then."

Although Hatch had every intention of returning, even if it meant spending the whole of his next leave searching for the girl of his dreams, he would have been extremely surprised to know that he had actually mentioned the fact to Marion. However, he hoped to have at least discovered her address before the end of his present visit.

November seemed a strange time to take a holiday in the Lake District but Charlotte did not comment on the point. Her mental picture of this strange young man of Marion's was slowly acquiring some substance. She desperately wanted her sister to become happily married, Marion was definitely not the 'career girl' type, but she retained her reservations about seafaring men. She decided to withhold her judgement until she had actually met the mysterious 'Jake'. Unusual name 'Jake'....Jacob? it sounded rather west country.

The two of them were still discussing Jake when Charlotte's husband Harry returned from his meeting.

****

434

Chapter 16

Sunday night passed into Monday morning. The 'Belisarius' was deeper in the water now and her list was more pronounced. She had come 'into soundings', less than one hundred fathoms beneath her keel, but this first indication of the nearing of land made no difference to the situation of the men on the ship even if they had known of it. Daylight brought scant relief although they were thankful enough to have survived another night.

As soon as there was light enough for them to find their way around the slanting decks Carey and Gregson made a cursory inspection. So far as they could see most of the doors and ports were still tight. The straining boiler room bulkhead had increased its bulge and water was squirting through it in an increasing number of jets. However, it was still holding and that was the main thing. If only it could last two more days, less than two days, the old 'Belisarius' could survive.

Carey and Gregson discussed the prospects of the ship staying afloat. The 'Opus' was keeping them informed over the hand radio of the expected weather. A depression was approaching from the west but this was expected to pass well to the north of them so an increase of sea and swell was not anticipated. Provided the weather got no worse than it was at present they stood a fair chance.

Everything depended on the bulkhead. The ship's now slow rate of sinking was such that she should still be afloat on Tuesday evening but not much longer than that. If the bulkhead went she would not last five minutes.

When the two men returned to the bridge they scrambled down the slope of the wheelhouse deck to report to Hatch.

With the cold light of day shining in his face Hatch's appearance horrified them. The black stubble of his beard combined with the frequent soaking of salt water had removed much of the sticking plaster which earlier had covered most of the wounds on his face. His skin had a deathly pallor, the cuts glaring black and red as if some savage beast had slashed him with poisoned claws.

It was however his eyes that really shocked them. Sunk deep in their sockets they were screwed up in an infinity of pain. His chin, the front of his coat and the sodden rag clutched in his hand were stained with blood.

"Good God Jake! You've had enough! I'll get that tug which arrived last night to take you off, you should be in hospital!" Carey reached for the 'walkie-talkie'.

"No! No, Damn you No!" Hatch croaked as he snatched the radio from Carey's hand. "You two can go any time you like. No one asked you to stay. I am staying here until she gets in!"

With all his previous dashed hopes and disappointments even this was to be denied him.

****

It was late on Sunday afternoon that a more complete picture of the state of affairs on the 'Belisarius' became available at the London office. After meeting the survivors at Le Havre Mr. Aldred made a long telephone call to the Head Office before taking the first available flight back to London.

"There is no question about it, those men must be taken off, in particular the Chief Officer if he is anything like as badly injured as reported. He should be in hospital." Charles Fairbell was obdurate.

"The damn fool," said Dewar with some heat, "What is he trying to prove?"

"How can we get them off now? The tug can't do much whilst she is towing apparently, are there any other vessels there?" Fairbell continued.

Dewar glanced at some rough notes by the telephone.

"There is a tug from Falmouth, she should arrive tonight and the press boys are chartering everything from trawlers to canoes to get to the scene so there will be plenty of craft there shortly."

"What about a helicopter? Surely one could reach the ship and get that man to hospital in a few hours? And get the others off too whether they like it or not."

"I'm afraid it's not flying weather down there by all accounts," said Cuthbertson, "I did hear on the radio that there is a Coastal Command plane 'in attendance' as it were but it is only more or less in radar contact. The cloud is just about down to sea level apparently."

"There is sure to be a break sometime," insisted Fairbell, "and those helicopter fellows pull off some pretty tricky jobs at times."

"It would be a pity to abandon the ship completely now she is so near home."

The assembled gathering swung as one to gaze at the instigator of this remark.

"What?" Fairbell was clearly horrified, "You mean you suggest those men should be left on board Captain Stone?"

Assistant Marine Superintendent Ralf Stone eased his athletic six foot three frame in the chair which was patently too small for him.

"No sir, what I suggest is that I go out on one of the helicopters and take over from them," and before the Chairman could protest, "I know the ship well, she was my last command before I came ashore you will remember. And I am big enough and ugly enough to make a jump for it if the worst happens."

"It is good of you Stone but the idea is not to be considered."

"It might be a good idea from the point of view of insurance," offered the canny Cuthbertson.

"Not really, even if there is no one on board we are not abandoning the ship, she would still be our property in the eye of the law," said Fairbell.

Captain Stone pressed his point. "I could borrow any necessary gear from the flying people."

Cuthbertson came to his aid.

"Although the agents know to have riggers ready it would be as well to have someone from the company on board when she berths."

"Possibly it might be worth considering," Fairbell conceded reluctantly.

****

With the ship steadily under tow there appeared little to be done on board. To Hatch this was wrong, there was always something requiring attention on a ship. If only the pain of his cold, battered body would ease up for a while, just time enough to allow him to think constructively. Eventually when the agony did subside for a few minutes his thought immediately returned to Marion and it was an effort to tear them away. After considerable concentration his numbed brain could think of nothing requiring immediate attention. What then of later on when the ship arrived at Falmouth? Of course, papers! Cargo plans, manifests, custom declarations, stores indents and a score of other documents to satisfy the various officials, stevedores, office staff and others who would descend upon the ship the moment she berthed.

To Hell with them! Let them come and help themselves – if they would find anything of interest in the mess below. It was a waste of effort even thinking of trying to salvage any of the numerous forms so painstakingly completed in the latter stages of the voyage. The damn ship would quite probably sink before she reached port anyway so there was no point in trying to collect anything in this line. Hatch's imagination pictured a pompous pin-striped individual reeking of after-shave lotion and tut-tutting over the loss of the log books.......Log books! Yes, they would certainly be required at any official inquiry later on. The ship's register too, it would be as well to have that and the log books on the bridge in case the worst happened.

The Mate swung his weary gaze to Carey who clung to a window frame in the fore end of the wheelhouse watching the tug wallowing in the seas ahead of the ship.

"Jim," he croaked, "I think we should have the ship's register and other papers handy in case we have to leave in a hurry. Do you think you could nip down and get them? If they are anywhere they will be in the top, right hand drawer of the Old Man's desk. The drawer will probably be locked so take something with you to force it with. If they are not in his desk they must be in his safe in which case, they will have to stay there along with anything else in it as no doubt the Old Man took the keys with him."

It occurred to Hatch that also in the safe was money belonging to the ship, kept in hand for any purchases of stores, to pay off a member of the crew or other small disbursements during the course of the voyage. Possibly hundreds of pounds and dollars but a worthless commodity at sea, it could buy them no comfort or sanctuary. More ironic was the fact that the 'dangerous drugs' were also safely locked away there. Drugs which would be used only in dire emergency and on the Master's authority alone. Morphine! he squeezed the thought out of his mind. He was past that now, pain, which had become a way of life for him was now being overcome by a numbness, as if he were dying by degrees.

Hatch dragged his mind back from his reverie when he realised Carey was speaking to him.

"Anything you want from your place whilst I'm down there?"

"Yes, now you mention it, that log book we completed a couple of weeks ago should some with us if you can find it, providing it is not just a soggy mess. It was in one of the top drawers of my office desk."

He remembered something else also.

"If you get as far as my room, in the top drawer of the chest is my wallet, discharge book and so forth. There is a big brown envelope there too, personal papers." Were they worth rescuing he wondered?

"Be as quick as you can if you do go and don't take any chances." At least that was Carey's interpretation of the Mate's words, his voice being but a hoarse croak.

The second mate did not relish clambering around inside the accommodation just to rescue some documents however important they appeared to be to Hatch. To relieve his feelings to some degree he took with him a fire axe in lieu of something smaller with which to force open the drawers.

As he passed the chart-room door Carey muttered "All right for some people," to the exhausted figure of the second engineer snoring on the settee.

Several minutes later he returned to the wheelhouse with everything the mate had asked for, plus a bundle of thin clear plastic.

"Courtesy of the local friendly dry-cleaners," said Carey as he displayed the large plastic bags he had taken from a couple of his suits which were miraculously still hanging in his wardrobe.

"Thought they would be just the job to wrap this library of yours in, it should keep the stuff reasonably dry if we have to toss it over the side in a hurry."

"Good idea," approved Hatch, "In fact it might be a good thing if we lash the package to one of the spare life-jackets then it might even float off if she does goo. We could easily have better things to do than collect souvenirs."

'He's a great one for the understatement,' thought Carey.

The contents of the envelope Carey had retrieved from his room with his other papers gave Hatch cause for considerable thought. His tired mind struggled with the problem. What if they fell into the wrong hands? There was no address on the envelope to indicate for whom the package was intended. Really there was only one sensible solution, dump them, that was the only safe way. This decided he turned his head.

"Jim…." He said, then realised that the second mate was no longer in the wheelhouse. His attempt to shout brought on another prolonged spasm of coughing.

It was some minutes later that Carey returned bearing in his hands the plastic covered bundle.

"There, that should hold it together even if it spends a week in the sea and gets washed up on the beach," he said as he admired his own handiwork. "I've sealed your envelope and written your name on it so it won't get mixed up with the ship's papers."

By the time he had finished speaking Carey had reached the fore end of the wheelhouse and could see Hatch's face.

"Good God! Are you alright Jake?"

The Mate waved him away. The pain was almost unbearable. What the second mate said hardly registered in his tortured brain but he did observe the efficiently wrapped package and realise that it would have to be opened and re-wrapped if the envelope was to be destroyed.

God! Was everything he tried to do, every move he tried to make, every decision he arrived at to be frustrated in one manner or another?

What did it matter anyway? What did anything matter anymore?

Later, when the coughing and pain had subsided a little Hatch decided he would have to give some sort of instruction regarding the envelope. Perhaps it would be best left in the second mate's care for a while, at least until he was out of hospital. Jim was not the type to pry into its contents.

"Jim," he gasped, "Look after the envelope for me."

****

Chapter 17

Hatch retained no recollection of the bus ride after leaving Marion. In fact, he was to all intents and purposes in another world until he realised he was back in his hotel walking towards the staircase.

Someone appeared to be trying to attract his attention.

"Mr. Hatch! Mr. Hatch!"

Suddenly becoming aware of the fact that the rotund manager of the hotel was attempting to impede his progress Hatch stopped.

"Mr. Hatch, I'm so glad you are back. There have been three phone calls from London since you went out, urgent phone calls!" The manager stressed the 'urgent', such calls were a rarity in this quiet hotel. "They want you to call them back the moment you get in. The number is....."

"I know the number all too well," interrupted Hatch, "No, just a minute, it is late evening, it will be someone's home number."

The manager handed Hatch a piece of paper on which was scribbled a telephone number.

"My office, please use my office phone," he fussed, "it's more private." The manager was making the most of the 'urgent call from London'.

"Thanks, that is very kind of you. I'll reverse the charges of course."

"Oh that does not matter," smiled the manager although secretly pleased as calls to London could prove expensive.

He had no need to worry, Hatch would not have dreamed of not transferring the charges when phoning anyone connected to the Head Office.

Only a few days more leave thought Hatch as he waited for his connection, although the 'urgent' gave cause for some foreboding. A week at the outside. How many hours in the course of only a week could he manage to spend with Marion?

"Mr. Hatch? Stone here."

The voice on the telephone brought Hatch back to the present with a jerk.

The conversation with Captain Stone was brief, the Assistant Marine Superintendent's message consisted of even worse news than Hatch had anticipated. As it progressed his bowels seemed to turn to water, horrible cold water with an abundance of ice-cubes in it.

Hatch replaced the receiver as a man in a daze. He was full of a seething mixture of hate, frustration and sheer fury.

He hated ships, ship-owners and the day he first decided to go to sea. Above all he hated George Reid. George who had accompanied Hatch on many a wild escapade. George whom he had known for years. George, who with thirty odd years to choose from, had chosen this day, this particular day, this day of all days to fall off a hatch ladder and break a leg!

Reid had relieved Hatch at London when the ship first arrived from her deep sea voyage and in the normal course of events would have stayed with the ship whilst she was discharging and loading on the coast and until Hatch returned for the next foreign voyage. Now at Hull, with Rotterdam and London to go, Reid was a casualty. As Hatch's leave had all but expired he was the obvious man to take his place.

Hatch's main concern of course was Marion. How was he to see her now? He could not even contact her. The only solution he could see was to dash up from London when the ship returned there and try to locate the girl. It would take a couple of days but to Hell with what the office had to say about it! Hatch was sorely tempted to ring London and tell them what they could do with the job but cold reason prevailed. Such an action could solve nothing at all. It was not as if he meant anything to the girl but what would she think if he did not appear by the stream in the next day or two? Would she already have forgotten their vague arrangement? Come to that had she already forgotten him? Hatch was completely out of his depth.

How long he sat by the telephone in the office Hatch did not know. It was not until the fact registered in his mind that the manager's face appeared at more and more frequent intervals at the glass panel in the door that he emerged from his thoughts.

With apologies Hatch opened the door.

"I'm afraid I will have to leave for Hull on the first train...."

"Er, yes," the manager looked slightly abashed. "They did mention it, asked me to look up the trains for you in fact to save time. Your account is ready. There is a train at......."

'How bloody efficient people get when they are doing someone dirt?' thought Hatch uncharitably.

****

A long taxi ride got Hatch to the station with only a few minutes to spare. After a long night of travelling he arrived on board the 'Belisarius' just in time to go 'on stations' for leaving the dock. The ship proceeded to Rotterdam in due order and commenced loading there.

Shortly before the ship was due to leave the long threatened Tilbury dock strike occurred. This resulted in the London call being cancelled so it was therefore from Rotterdam that the 'Belisarius' proceeded on her deep sea voyage.

She was loaded with only five thousand and thirty-eight tons of general cargo. Nearly two hundred thousand cubic feet of unused cargo space remained which nearly reduced the freight department to tears.

What Hatch had to say about the matter will remain unrecorded.

****

Marion was disappointed at the non-appearance of Hatch but, being a sensible girl, took it philosophically. If nothing else, it was good training for any young lady interested in becoming involved with followers of the sea. In spite of her sister's occasional raised eyebrow she refused to accept any other reason than that Hatch had been recalled earlier than expected even if she was surprised by the remarkable suddenness of it. She felt in her heart he would return and for the first time in her life began looking forward to the month of November.

The life style of Marion continued much as it had before the meeting. She still went to parties and other occasions with her friends. Her mind still occupied itself with such maidenly thoughts as to what she should wear for the forthcoming tennis club dance, whether she would look younger with her hair fashioned in a different way or wonder what it would be like to be raped by a barbarian horde. However, her musings always returned to Jake and their next meeting, whenever that would be.

****

To Hatch it remained just a dream. She was too young, too sweet, too good in every respect for the likes of him. However, where there was life there was hope. Seventeen years between them was not too great a gap really, he tried to convince himself. He knew of one or two married couples with an even greater disparity of ages getting along together in perfect accord. The thought of spending the rest of his life without Marion was too dreadful to contemplate.

Although their acquaintanceship had been brief Marion loomed large in Hatch's tortured mind, taking on an importance which, had his brain been lucid, would have struck him as being utterly ridiculous. With great effort he could stretch his mind to the affairs of the ship when required but immediately his concentration lapsed his thoughts sprang back like a piece of elastic to memories of the girl of his dreams.

It was never Hatch's intention to abandon the ship until she was about to take her final plunge, which, during the brief periods he was not in actual agony, he hoped would not happen. However, as the long, painful hours dragged into days his weary mind started making plans to salvage something more than just the ship.

Although convinced of his unworthiness so far as Marion was concerned he thought that perhaps something could be done to redeem his past, squandered life and this could be the opportunity. Any kudos resulting in the saving of the old 'Belisarius' he would willingly lay at Marion's feet. Promises and good intentions were no good, no good at all.

Hatch's weary, tortured brain drifted off into fantasy.

A fairy-tale princess did not want her gallant knight returning with exciting stories of how he frightened the living daylights out of the local dragon with his trusty sword or had given the animal a nasty buffet in the short ribs with his lance. She wanted the dragon's head on a platter or she did not want to hear about the creature at all. In fact, in the event of an unsuccessful encounter she might prefer the knight's head in lieu of the dragon's as something to weep over.

The 'Belisarius' was Hatch's dragon. Or, he thought, would the sea itself be more appropriate?

In any case what reward would there be? There could be no monetary recompense for helping to save one's own ship, that is what I am paid for, Hatch soliloquised. He could not imagine the Chairman delivering a pretty little speech before presenting him with a suitably inscribed silver salver – not after their last encounter! His hazy mind tarried briefly on something he had read in a novel of the Napoleonic era. The brave young Captain, after a particularly dashing piece of enemy frigate sinking, being presented by an appreciative Admiralty with a 'sword to the value of fifty guineas'.....

A wave of intense pain struck Hatch and the scene of the presentation of the sword and of the dragon dissolved. The water tinkling over the stones of a Lakeland brook became once more the cold sea cascading off the foc'sle head.

****

Marion was rather breathless when she arrived at her sister's house early one evening. Greetings over she immediately got down to the reason for her visit.

"It is still there! The green dress is still there!"

"So?" said Charlotte slowly, "What of it? I thought you had decided that it was trifle too decollate for you?"

"I've changed my mind," replied Marion.

"Bit dicey with the possibility of sailors around at any moment though," smiled her sister.

"Oh Charlotte! I wasn't even thinking of him." Of course she was.

"Anyway," getting back to the main point, "Greenbows say they will hold it for me until tomorrow." After a slight pause, "I wondered if…."

"How much?" interrupted Charlotte with a mock frown.

"Only five pounds, seven if you could manage it, I have the rest. It's awfully good of you."

"I haven't said I would lend you any money yet, you know what an old skin-flint that husband of mine is." A slur on the honest man.

"Shall I ask him?"

"No you won't, you get a man of your own to cadge money from. Anyway I'm just about skint myself with Christmas getting near and everything."

"That is what Mum and Dad said. I didn't like to ask old Lomax for an advance, you know what an old misery he is, and I can't wait until I'm paid on Friday as the dress will have gone by then. It's only Tuesday now."

"Alright, but only five mind," Charlotte laughed, "Anyone would think the man was on the doorstep you are so excited. I hope he is on a more reliable ship than that old wreck being towed up the Channel."

"How is the poor old thing doing? I saw a bit about it on television last night. Isn't it due in port today?"

"Yes, this evening sometime. But don't worry dear, they mentioned the names of the three men on her on the radio again this morning, I can't remember what they were but there was certainly no 'Jake' among them." Looking over her shoulder Charlotte continued, "The morning paper is over there, why don't you look at your horoscope and see if a tall, dark man is about to re-enter your life?"

In spite of herself Marion picked up the paper and glanced at it briefly.

"I wonder if there is anything in this sort of thing – or dreams come to that? I've been dreaming a lot just lately, all sorts of rubbish. Last night for instance, it seemed as if someone was trying to give me something. I don't know what it was, so far as I can remember it was a battered iron thing on a kind of tray – it could have been a rusty old knight's helmet or something like that. I wonder if it means anything?"

"Too much supper by the sound of it," grinned her sister.

An hour or so later Marion left for home, a crisp five pound note in her handbag and the green dress as good as hers.

Her happiness would have been complete if only her Jake would appear.

"If only he could have written," she said to herself.

* * * * * * * * * * * * * * * * * * *

Hatch <u>had</u> written. The first letter, a clumsy, school-boyish affair, was completed after several false starts whilst the ship was at Rotterdam. The idea behind it was that when he got back to the Lake District from London, as he was determined to do, he might find someone to pass it on to Marion if he was unfortunate enough not to find her. He destroyed this letter when his hopes were dashed owing to the ship sailing direct from Rotterdam.

Later in the voyage he wrote three more letters with much the same end in view although the possibility of not meeting Marion later in the year was too awful to contemplate.

The three letters were not much of an improvement on the original. He had just finished re-reading that which he had written in the third letter when he said out loud, "To Hell with it!"

Hatch tore the offending letter to fragments then took the previous two letters from a locked drawer and treated them in the same way.

Taking a fresh sheet of typing paper, he wrote in his very best handwriting, 'My Dearest Marion,'

'That is decidedly better,' he mused.

As a love letter it left much to be desired but it was a start.

The letter was followed by others which improved considerably as the voyage progressed until Hatch was pouring out his heart with an aptitude and fervour he had no idea he possessed and which no-one who knew him would have dreamed possible. All the love of which the frustrated soul of Hatch was capable was recorded in his rapidly deteriorating handwriting. Often for hours at night on coming off watch he would sit writing, engrossed in his dream. Amateurish at first the later instalments improved out of all recognition, almost equalling those of Napoleon to Josephine.

Hatch appreciated that even if by some miracle he was given Marion's address he could not have posted such letters to her considering the brevity of their acquaintanceship but the urge to pour out his love was irrepressible.

Perhaps he would give them to her sometime in the future? He allowed himself to be carried away by his fantasies. On her birthday maybe? Or possibly a wedding anniversary? Hatch had decided that by some quirk of fate he would at this stage be some kind of gentlemen farmer.

If one is going to dream one might as well make a job of it.

Yes, an anniversary. Hatch formed the picture of the occasion in his mind. The children safely asleep upstairs, the panelled dining room glowing in the soft light of the log fire and the candles in their silver candelabra on the long polished oak table. Marion looking ravishing in a bright red gown. This colour could have clashed with her shining copper tresses but this did not occur to him. The first present, a mink coat? No, too bulky, something small was required. A diamond necklace? Yes, that would do fine. The look in her eyes as she opened the velvet-lined box.

"Darling! Just what I've always wanted!...." Oh Gawd, thought Hatch, do they really say things like that? He floundered for a few moments then decided to leave that part of his dream and proceed with the next act.

A few minutes later.

"And this big envelope, is this for me too Darling?"

(Awful lot of 'Darlings' in this monologue mused Hatch, however, I like it, I can't remember anyone calling me 'Darling' before.)

"Yes, it is for you. It always has been."

"Always has been? How mysterious, whatever do you mean Darling?"

"Why not open it and see?"

Towards the end of the voyage the letters amounted to over two hundred closely written pages. They were kept in a large manila envelope carefully locked away in a drawer in Hatch's room.

****

Chapter 18

Few as the hours of winter daylight were they passed with agonising slowness before darkness enveloped the 'Belisarius' once again in seemingly endless night.

During the day another tug and several assorted craft arrived but were kept at a distance by signals and, in the case of one intrepid trawler crowded with newspaper reporters, by an excellent demonstration of what an irate Dutch tug skipper could achieve in the

451

way of colourful language through a bull-horn. Before dark most of these vessels had disappeared from the vision of those on the 'Belisarius' as the rain increased from occasional showers to a thick steady drizzle.

Bishops Rock Light was passed unseen in the grey blanket of rain during the early hours of Tuesday morning. It was late in the forenoon when the tug attracted the attention of the weary men on the derelict to something on the port bow. Carey and Gregson gazed for some minutes in that direction before the former suddenly shouted,

"There! There it is! Land! England at last!"

Faintly through the patches of drizzle the vague form of the Lizard could be discerned.

"We've made it then!" Gregson did not try to keep the excitement out of his voice. "Tonight proper beds. I'll sleep for a week at least."

Even Hatch tried to say something but the whispered croak which issued from his lips started him coughing again. He did not attempt to repeat his observation.

****

The people assembled on the cliffs of the Lizard saw nothing of the ship and her by then appreciable escort as they passed. However, the weather had cleared to a certain extent by the time the convoy had reached the vicinity of Black Head and the considerable crowd there had a panoramic view of the shattered 'Belisarius' faithfully following her tug and the score or more vessels accompanying them.

It was in the sheltered waters off Black Head that the master of the 'Opus' commenced to shorten the two-line in preparation for the more precise manoeuvring that would be required in Falmouth Roads.

Between bouts of body racking coughing Hatch managed to

convey to the others that it might be a good idea for them to check the towing wire where it passed through the fairlead on the foc'sle head. The continuously breaking seas over the decks had previously made any attempt at such an inspection too dangerous to justify.

Although aching in every muscle and weary beyond belief the two men were almost light-hearted as they slipped and stumbled along the foredeck, supporting themselves as best they could on the sloping deck.

They eventually reached the very eyes of the ship, panting from their exertions. The heavy wire showed no sign of wear in spite of its punishment over the previous few days.

"Well that should last us," said Carey.

His words were almost drowned by the sudden clattering of a helicopter which appeared from the murk almost overhead. Momentarily startled both of the men were soon grinning and waving although unable to see any of the helicopter's crew.

"Just as well we did not have to rely on those things to lift us off," observed Gregson. "It's a wonder it found us anyway, this seems to be the only patch of reasonable visibility for miles. Look! The land is disappearing again in the rain."

"Heavy stuff too by the look of it, the sooner we get back to the wheelhouse the better," replied Carey.

After two circuits of the ship the helicopter, as if disappointed its assistance was not required, headed back from whence it came. Within seconds it had disappeared from view and a minute later could no longer be heard.

Having watched the helicopter out of sight Gregson slowly turned to look down the length of the ship.

"Good God!" The words caused Carey to swing his head sharply. He immediately saw the cause of the exclamation.

From their viewpoint on the foc'sle head, so far removed from the one which had impressed itself on their minds during the recent long days, the ship appeared completely strange to them. Previously during their inspections they had concentrated on details, the hatches, plugged ventilators and doors. In the danger and discomfort of the then prevailing weather it was never possible to view any considerable part of the ship in its entirety. Prepared as they were for extensive changes in her appearance the sight which they beheld shocked them. A wreck of a ship completely foreign to their eyes. Carey at least was conversant with the 'Belisarius' from this angle but this was not her at all. Lying in a drunken fashion to port with her bulwarks at the after end of the foredeck alternately emerging and dipping in the swell, the fore side of the bridge structure streaked with rust in contrast to the fresh white paint applied to it but ten days earlier and looking strangely lop-sided with the port wing of the bridge missing and its fellow pointing to the sky. The missing hold ventilator cowls changed the whole vista of the foredeck but, more than anything else, there was just open sky, grey with an approaching rain squall, where the top of the funnel should have been. It seemed hardly possible that she was the same old 'Belisarius'.

"You poor old cow," Gregson spoke for both of them, "Never mind, we will soon have you home."

It was at this moment that the fatal bulkhead, having survived the earlier heavy weather, proved unable to stand the strain any longer in spite of the ship's more gentle rolling in the lee of the land. It burst like a dam and a thousand tons of water thundered into the boiler room.

A few seconds passed before the enormity of the disaster translated itself to the horrified minds of Carey and Gregson.

"Jake!" shrieked Carey as he lurched towards the ladder at the break of the foc'sle head. Gregson tried to follow but missed his footing and slid across the deck until brought up with a crash by the port rail.

The journey back down the foredeck, which had taken five minutes of struggle in the reverse direction, Carey covered in seconds. With his heart pounding his straining body drew on every last remaining atom of strength as he leaped, tripped and stumbled towards the midship structure. His flying feet hardly touched the hatch coamings, winch beds and other fittings as he gained fleeting foothold before his next leap on the rapidly tilting deck. His whole being resembled a machine racing unlubricated and out of control, which, if not stopped, would ensure its own destruction. By the time he reached the ladder at the end of the foredeck he felt his heart was about to burst but he managed to scramble to the deck above and to the ladder leading to the bridge.

The 'Belisarius' had commenced her upward roll when the death blow in her vitals occurred. She stopped and for long moments the world seemed to stop with her. She appeared to be taking a last agonised look at the sea she served so well before she commenced her last roll to port.

At first slowly then with ever increasing speed as the loose water in her completely destroyed what little stability she had, the old ship rolled further and further over. Her port bulwarks disappeared below the surface for the last time and the hungry sea surged triumphantly towards the hatches. The midship structure crashed onto the surface of the water and soon the cold grey sea was pouring into the great holes where the funnel and engine room sky-light had been. As the relentless sea smashed in doors others burst open from the air compressed by the incoming water. Loose gear crashed across the ship adding volume to the roaring of the escaping air and the thunder of the devouring sea.

As if directed by some omnipotent hand the heavy rain squall moved across the scene, mercifully hiding from the eyes of men the 'Belisarius' in her final agony.

****

The foundering of the 'Belisarius' was but one small brush mark on the larger canvas of the passing of an era. Within a decade all but a few of her ilk had disappeared from the seas. With the rapidly escalating price of oil the steam ships, no matter how efficient in other respects, gave way at last to the diesel powered vessels with their greatly reduced consumption. The graceful sheer and sea-kindly lines of the old ships were replaced by severely functional horizontal decks with massive hatchways required for the carrying of ubiquitous containers, which also necessitated large, unobstructed square holds.

The general cargo vessels, now Americanised to 'break bulk carriers', lost their mixed cargoes to the containers and their grain and ore cargoes to specialised bulk ships with their hopper shaped holds which did not require the fitting of time-wasting and expensive shifting boards down the centres of their holds.

The engine room, traditionally situated amidships in the squarest part of the hull, with a ten foot high shaft tunnel taking up space in the centre of the after holds, could no longer be tolerated. New ships had their diesel engines installed as far aft as they would go leaving the main run of the hull for freight earning cargo. The accommodation, once spread around the midship section of the ship, became one solid square block several decks high on the poop above the engine room.

For various reasons the freight market became over-tonnaged resulting in far too many ships chasing too few cargoes. With the coming of fierce competition every possible economy and expedient came into practice and life at sea changed radically.

The men did not change, they only adapted to the new way of life. Theirs still the long periods away from home and, in the upper ranks at least, the same awesome responsibility.

The sea did not change at all. Still offering its services to those who treat it with respect it remains just as relentless to those who, perhaps for only a moment, relax their alertness. Then it can become just as ruthless as ever, rending apart the greatest vessels built by man.

Chapter 19

Alistair Macquarie shaded his eyes from the morning sun with his hand and gazed intently at the triangle of white on the horizon. Yes, the yacht was coming this way alright, slightly larger than when he had last looked some minutes earlier and on exactly the same bearing. The vessel was certainly the one he was awaiting.

Shifting his position on the rock to obtain more comfort Macquarie ran a finger under the collar of his checked shirt. It was going to be a hot day, no doubt about that. He glanced at his watch, not yet ten o'clock and already it was hotter than any day so far that summer. They had certainly chosen perfect weather for the visit.

How far off was the yacht? Seven, eight miles? About an hour's run in the prevailing light breeze. They should be anchoring off his jetty at about eleven o'clock, just in nice time for a drink or two before lunch.

Macquarie was trying to concentrate on the timing and navigation but his thoughts were not really on the subject, or even on the vessel herself for that matter, his mind kept returning to someone he knew to be on board.

How much had she changed since he last saw her years ago? Not that many years, she would be just as lovely. Pretty as a picture in any form of raiment – Macquarie laughed to himself and touched the bundle of rags he had brought to cushion the rocks on which he sat. No! Not those, the material he was thinking of had been used as paint rags years before – Dressed, beautiful, undraped.....! But he must not remember her like that, particularly now.

Marriage changed women more than men, Macquarie soliloquised. His eye caught the knife-edged crease of his ten slacks and it brought a grin. 'Changed me a bit too for all that.'

Looking over his shoulder to the old cottage he could see but few changes over the years. What alterations had been made blended in with the original building so although the inside had seen many changes, mainly for the better he was forced to admit, outwardly the old place looked very much the same cottage he loved. The main structural alteration was a bathroom added to the northern end of the house, one of the first things his bride had insisted upon in spite of his smiling claim that the original arrangement had suited him admirably.

Some years earlier the house had changed its status from his home to the family's holiday cottage. Reasonably enough his wife did not want to be isolated on the mull all year round, particularly as he was away for considerable lengths of time. Their main residence was near her parents and friends – and incidentally schools and other civilised amenities. Macquarie was happy there but for all that was always glad to get out to the cottage for a few days, or, better still, for weeks on end in the summer.

Macquarie's two boys absolutely loved it, the rocks, the sea, the boat, in fact everything about the place. And because her three 'men' loved it so his wife did too, in spite of the cottage's inconveniences and comparative discomfort. No doubt she would have loved it anyway.

Macquarie stood up and stretched himself. Conceitedly he decided that when they met she would observe little difference in him, a little more grey around the temples perhaps but the rest was the same man she had known. He had not put on any weight since those days, of that he was certain. A quick punch in the stomach served to confirm this. Not exactly a lithe, greyhound figure, more of a bull he thought. Macquarie was a walking man not a sprinter.

He was certain she would not have changed much since their last meeting but he would have to be careful not to get carried away thinking of the old times. Apart from what his own good lady would have to say about it the husband, whom Macquarie had never previously met, was by all accounts the athletic type – and years younger than he.

Again seated on the rock Macquarie felt the warmth of the sun on his hands as they rested on his knees. His eyes focussed on them, yes, she would no doubt notice the difference there. Remembering how she sometimes brushed the bristly hairs on the back of his hands with her tiny finger tips he sighed. That would never happen again even if she so desired.

The doctors had done a magnificent job but so far as his hands were concerned they would sprout no more hair. Otherwise they were as strong and supple as ever and, above all, they had not lost their touch with a sable brush. He was thankful for that.

His hands were always there to remind him of those black days. The loss of the old 'Belisarius', the ship he had sailed on for years, the men who had died and the three who had stayed until the end. He would have been with them if it had not been for that flare, that damned, useless, totally unnecessary bonfire. Not that his presence would have made any difference to the eventual fate of the ship but it might have made him feel a little better over the years.

The hands had taken a long time to heal in spite of the expert attention they had received. They were still in bandages during the period of the official inquiry into the loss of the ship, an ordeal the like of which Macquarie hoped never to have to face again.

The inquiry did not concentrate overmuch on the failure of the generators, the initial mishap which triggered off the chain reaction culminating in the deaths and eventual loss of the ship. The machines were his responsibility however and the praise he received for his efforts in helping to try to save the vessel afterwards did little to leaven the solid weight of the burden on his conscience. It was something he knew he would have to live with until the end of his days.

It was shortly after the inquiry that he at last, long last, returned to his cottage. Even then his hands were far from recovered and he remembered with shame old Robbie MacNab rowing him and his bag across the loch on about the only calm day for weeks, weather which prohibited the use of the boat's sail. Old Robbie who was nearly twice his own age.

It was difficult at first at the cottage, his bandaged hands frustrating everything from log-sawing to buttons, however he was far happier there by himself and away from the fuss of other people.

In the fullness of time Macquarie's hands recovered and he returned to the sea.

Neither Morag or Fiona knew anything of his injuries prior to his rather abrupt return into their lives. The particularly bad handwriting during his convalescence he had 'explained' in one pair of letters as being due to the bad light at the time of writing. Macquarie did not want them to know that the hands which once caressed them were now in such ruin.

At their first reunion Macquarie's future wife was quick to notice his scarred hands and would not be satisfied until she had the whole story from him.

Surprised as she was at the time on discovering that he was the 'famous' sea-scape painter, when she learned that Macquarie had been half way around the world and back and had been injured, nearly killed, on a sinking ship since their last meeting she was utterly dumbfounded. All the time she had imagined him at the cottage painting cloud scenes – or indulging in culinary disasters with his new cooker.

If the damaged hands helped smooth the way of Macquarie's clumsy courting the fire that burnt them may have served some slight purpose after all.

****

Macquarie awoke from his day-dreaming and again cast his gaze out to sea. Judging the yacht to be about half an hour from his jetty he climbed to his feet and walked to the house to collect his family.

On arrival at the cottage he was greeted by his wife's horrified, "Alistair! Whatever have you done to your collar? Your tie is under one ear." She reached up to straighten the offending article and added, "And please run a comb through your hair, it is standing on one end."

"It was your idea I kept vigil on yonder wind-swept rock," protested Macquarie rather dramatically.

"That was only to get you out of the house whilst I finished tidying up."
"I thought you finished yesterday, anyone would think the Queen Mother was visiting."

"I don't want the house in a mess whoever is coming, the place should be spick and span."

In fact, the house was as spick and span as a Scottish housewife could make it. Which was very spick and span indeed.

"It will be the first time she has seen the cottage since…. since I have had charge of it and I want her to have a good impression," the good lady continued.

"She can't have any other, I've never seen the place looking so nice," Macquarie said in all sincerity, "I can't imagine what you are worried about."

"It is <u>you</u> I am worried about," she replied, "If you so much as….."

"I will be the soul of discretion Little Sweetheart. After all I have more to lose than you. From what I hear this Galbraith fellow is twice my size and a decade or two younger."

"Well if you make a pass at her I hope he punches you on the nose," then wistfully, "You have always loved her more than me."

"You know very well that is untrue, I married you to prove it," Macquarie kissed her on the tip of her nose, "Don't ever tell me I don't know how to choose my women – after all she has only produced on daughter, I'm well ahead of the game."

"And that is as far ahead as you are going to get you sex-mad oaf. I'm getting too old to be your brood mare." Appeased she accepted another kiss then pushed away.

"It is ominously quiet, where are those boys now?" Stepping to the window she shouted, "Jamie! Ian! Get away from that rock pool at once and come inside, I haven't time to clean you up again with guests on the doorstep!"

Macquarie had been keeping an eye on the approaching yacht and at this juncture said, "We had better get down to the jetty, she will be anchoring in a few minutes."

After watching the smart ketch drop her anchor in deep water a hundred yards from the jetty Macquarie left his family and climbed into his boat.

Rowing out he had his back to the new arrivals but when within a few yards of the vessel he backed an oar and deftly brought the stern of the boat up to the short teakwood ladder suspended from the yacht's side.

Macquarie lifted his eyes and there she was, lovelier than ever in a smart summer frock, her skirt and hair fluttering in the breeze.

He tore his eyes away and took in the rest of the family, the little girl, the image of her mother, wearing a nautical but very feminine outfit and, towering over them both, a very large man who could only be Robert Galbraith himself.

Brief greeting and introductions were made then Macquarie

returned to the job in hand. It required all his concentration and skill to keep the transom of the boat close to the ladder without actually touching it even though he was assisted to this end by a red-headed youth with a boat hook. Red-head and another boy handling a small cork fender apparently constituted the crew.

In spite of his bulk Galbraith stepped into the boat hardly causing it to rock. Balancing effortlessly on the bottom boards he reached up and lifted his daughter down, seating her in the stern sheets. He then assisted his wife down the few steps of the ladder. Macquarie had not the slightest doubt Galbraith could have transferred his miniature wife into the boat by the same method used with his daughter but dignity had to be preserved.

"I told you you should have worn slacks as you normally do on these occasions," Galbraith whispered as, with both hands gripping the ladder handrails the breeze tried to take control of his wife's skirts. He moved his position slightly to preserve the sight of his favourite legs from the view of the dark eyebrowed man behind him.

As soon as everyone was seated Macquarie bent to the oars and the heavy boat commenced its return journey to the jetty.

"Our 'yachts' hardly bear comparison," grinned Macquarie, "this boat had to be big and heavy as its main function is transporting bricks, timber and suchlike across the loch. I have an outboard for it but that is under repair at the moment – again. I prefer the sail anyway." Quite an admission for an engineer.

"At least it is earning its keep," replied Galbraith, glancing at the deep gouges in the thwarts and gunwales which no amount of sanding and varnishing could disguise. "That thing of mine costs the earth to run," he peered over his shoulder at the vessel which was obviously his pride and joy. "Might have to sell the house to keep her in the family," he added with a mischievous grin to his wife. She wrinkled her nose at him in the manner Macquarie so well remembered before returning her attention once more to her daughter's whispered conversation.

Macquarie warmed to the large man with the sandy hair and wide grin. Even more when Galbraith, who vaguely recollected that one of his fellow directors had once mentioned the names of the artists responsible for his collection of modern paintings and his host's name, he was almost certain, had been among them.

"Ever hear the name Archie Cameron? Associate of mine, has one of your paintings, raves about it. Wait until I tell him I've had lunch with the great man himself!"

One of the reasons for Galbraith's success in the world.

The embarrassed Macquarie made a depreciating remark, then, to himself, 'She has certainly got herself an excellent husband.' And he was glad.

Arriving at the jetty Galbraith helped his wife and daughter onto it where the ladies embraced and greetings were exchanged with cries of "Elizabeth, how you have grown! Quite a grown up young lady now," "My! Who are these two big men?" and the like whilst Macquarie attached the boat to an endless painter and hauled it out clear of the rocks and concrete of the jetty.

"Well it's lovely to see you again – and more beautiful than ever!" Macquarie was rewarded with a cheek presented for a chaste kiss.

"You haven't changed a bit Alistair, married life is obviously doing you the world of good."

A few minutes later Fiona and Morag picked their way carefully along the rough concrete and stones of the jetty and causeway towards the house, each clutching a hand of one of the younger children. Jamie considered himself old enough to walk with the men. The ladies chattered away at the tremendous rate which had always amazed Macquarie, catching up on all the news since they had last met at a wedding or other get-together, functions which Macquarie missed with the regularity familiar to seafarers.

Galbraith, following the ladies with Macquarie, said, "There is not much to choose between them as regards height."

"No, apart from the different coloured hair they could be twins seen from the back," was the reply.

And what attractive backs they are thought both men as the wind moulded the material of the thin dresses to the women's dainty figures. However, this opinion was not voiced.

"That daughter of yours will soon catch up with them if she takes after you at all," commented Macquarie.

"Heaven forbid! Fancy having to marry off a daughter my size," laughed Galbraith, "I sincerely hope she gets no taller than her mother. I prefer my women on the small side – even if it does make me feel like a bull seal at times, if that is the animal I have in mind.

"By the way, I understand you do most of your own construction work around here. Are you responsible for the jetty and all this concrete?" Galbraith indicated the relatively new path along which they were walking.

Macquarie admitted to it.

"Must have been a hell of a job, just as well you have your health and strength. Ref to which I had always imagined you were older, can't imagine how I managed to get that impression."

"How much older?" asked Macquarie.

"About twice. Must have been that I subconsciously thought of all recluse, if you will pardon the term, land-scape painters as being old men with long white beards."

Macquarie pondered this point. Surely the girls did not originally think of him as all that ancient? Galbraith must have received the description of him from one of them, no doubt his wife. He would have to watch himself and not allow people to gain the impression he was older than was actually the case. He certainly still felt reasonably young.

****

Reaching the cottage, the three children dashed inside, the boys anxious to show off their puppy Rob Roy to Elizabeth. Galbraith passed through the porch chatting to his hostess and entered the living room. Following them Macquarie nearly bumped into his other guest, who, shielded from the sight of the others by the wall, spun round and, reaching up to the full extent of her arms, grabbed the surprised Macquarie around the neck and pulled his unresisting head down to kiss him full on the lips. Quickly shifting her arms to around his waist she hugged herself to him. With cheek pressed against his tie she whispered, "The peck on the jetty was for my host, the kiss is for you. Oh it's lovely to see you again Alistair." Another quick hug and she pushed away saying in her normal voice, "That must be the cooker you were expecting to arrive when we were here."

Macquarie, fighting to get his breath back and imagining he was blushing to the roots of his hair again wondered how they did it. Women must be born actresses he decided.

****

The visit passed very pleasantly. Galbraith showed a great deal of interest in everything about the place which pleased Macquarie tremendously as he rarely had visitors to whom he could expound on his favourite subject of the cottage and its surroundings. The boys were in their seventh heaven showing a very appreciative Elizabeth their secret hiding places and local pools and caves. The girl herself was enjoying every minute of having no less than two boys to attend her.

The ladies were more than happy talking sixteen to the dozen about whatever it is women discuss to such great lengths. However, they discreetly never mentioned the last time they had been together at the cottage – not when the men were within earshot. By themselves in the bedroom after lunch repairing their makeup it was a different matter.

The fact that the old bed was still in evidence was remarked upon.

"Actually it is not the original mattress," explained Mrs. Macquarie, "You will remember how some of the springs had gone and how lumpy the old one was?"

"Of course not!" replied her guest throwing up her hands in feigned shock. They both laughed.

"I can't say I recall noticing it at the time either but when we spent our honeymoon here I started taking an interest in things I had seen with different eyes before. Do you know that all the time we were here Alistair's painting stuff was lying under an old sheet in the outhouse? And we had no idea he was the 'famous' 'A. Macquarie, Landscape Painter' until we opened those packets with the pictures on the bus. It is really extraordinary how little we knew about him in those days. It still seems like a dream."

"A very, very lovely dream," whispered her friend. Continuing in more normal tones she added, "Do you remember the time he washed our hair in front of the fire?"

"I definitely do! 'Please try to avoid getting my blouse wet' you said. Silly thing to say to that maniac of a man of mine. It certainly did not get a drop of water on it draped over the back of the sofa. Then I had to submit to the same embarrassing ordeal as he claimed you said he was a sloppy hair washer."

"How mad we must have been. I hope Robert never gets wind of any of those goings on."

****

It was during lunch that Macquarie mentioned the Galbraith's whirlwind courtship of which he had heard.

"Yes it was rather sudden in a way," said Galbraith, "I'd had my eye on the wench for some time….."

"Neglecting to tell me of course," interrupted his wife.

"Well I was seriously thinking of asking her out to dinner or a show sometime when I was not too busy, just to stake my claim as it were. My directorship was due to be finalised at the end of the year as I well knew and directors, as they say of army colonels, <u>must</u> marry. The head office being in London meant my having to live in that part of the world and as none of my family has taken an English wife since Culloden I thought it best to keep up the tradition. Anyway it was high time I settled down so looked round and decided who would be my mate…."

"Oh!" again interrupted his mate, "<u>You</u> decided did you? If I had known that at the time I would have made your path to my door a good deal more difficult."

Galbraith continued his story unabashed.

"However I caught a rumour that some pimply-faced lawyer was…."

"He was not pimply-faced! He was tall, dark and very attentive – and he could dance!"

"Be that as it may the fact that this lawyer fellow was sniffing around rather forced my hand so I phoned to ask her out one evening – and she tried to turn me down!"

"I claimed a prior engagement," corrected his wife, "actually a routine visit to my grandmother. I was waiting for him to talk me out of it when he spoilt it all by saying," Mrs. Galbraith attempted to imitate her husband's deep voice, "'Not with that damned lawyer fellow?'

"That nettled me of course so I said I would go out with whomever I pleased. To which this brute replied, 'You can't go out with that lawyer if he is in hospital.'

"I was rather mystified by this remark as I had only spoken to him on the phone that afternoon.

"He is not in hospital," I said.

"'He damn soon will be,' replies my gentle Romeo, 'I'll be sitting on your doorstep waiting for him if he dares show his nose.'

"What could a girl do with a man like that? To avoid a scene, I had to agree to meet him."

"At least you were courted," said the hostess as she handed Galbraith the tureen of potatoes for the second time, he had a hearty appetite even for a man of his size. "Would you like to hear the story of my romance Robert?"

Although Galbraith was familiar with the story he had no hesitation in declaring he would love to hear it first-hand.

"Well it was just an ordinary quiet Sunday afternoon. I had just washed and dried my hair when I heard a knock on the front door. My father answered it, I could hear his voice and that of another man but could not distinguish their words. After a minute of two I heard Mother's voice too, she sounded rather excited. At first I thought there had been an accident or something, particularly when I heard Dad mount a few stairs and call up asking me to come down as soon as I could. I asked what all the commotion was about and he said he did not know but there was a strange man asking to see me. Of course I asked his name but all Dad could tell me was that it was an 'Alexander Something or other'," She turned to her friend, "You will remember what my father is like for names. 'What does he want?' I called down. I could think of no Alexanders who might wish to speak to me.

"I slipped into a dress and was putting on a pair of shoes when Dad called up again, having apparently asked the stranger my question.

"'I think you had better come down and speak to him,' said Dad in a bewildered tone of voice, 'He says he has come to marry you.'

"Of course I was absolutely agog by this time. As you well know some of our old friends had pretty weird senses of humour but what kind of joke was this?

"By the time I got downstairs the three of them were in the lounge so it was not until I was through the door that I saw who was causing all the fuss. Alistair! Standing in the middle of the hearthrug in a dreadful suit, a bunch of beautiful red roses in his hand and an idiotic grin on his face.

"You could have knocked me down with the proverbial feather. I was absolutely speechless. So far as I knew he was a hundred miles away, in fact I could not imagine him anywhere else but at his old cottage.

"He seemed relieved to see me. I think the folks had been giving him the third degree.

"'Hello,' he says, 'I hope you don't mind my dropping in like this? I was passing this way and thought I would...thought I......'

"Then he faded out completely so to help him out I said, 'You thought you would just drop by and marry me?'

Alistair, who had thus far listened to the discourse in embarrassed silence decided at this point to enlighten the audience with an explanation.

"Actually I did not get to the mainland very often but as I had been to an exhibition in Edinburgh thought I would save a journey by looking her up on the way back. I had rehearsed my arrival speech but had not anticipated having to deal with her parents before we met – I think I must have panicked and got things rather mixed."

Which statement did not help his case at all. His wife was relentless.

"I don't mind admitting that I was embarrassed but Alistair was way ahead of me getting completely tongue-tied and occasionally waving the roses around like a flag until I more or less had to take them from him before they were ruined.

"I had more or less explained to my parents who he was when Mother came to the rescue by saying that no doubt the 'young man' would like a cup of tea and set off for the kitchen, somehow drawing Dad out of the room in her wake."

The account was concluded with Mrs. Macquarie going back on the story to repeat, "'He has come to marry you!' Indeed, he had not even thought to consult me never mind propose! All I had ever received in the way of 'love-letters' was a brief note to say that his new cooker was installed, that he had been experimenting with it and was going to make himself a proper Sunday dinner that weekend. Then a few weeks later another to say that after he had got his Sunday dinner all prepared he had run out of bottled gas."

"Bit of a blow," commented Galbraith to Macquarie sympathetically.

"Oh it was not wasted," came the reply, "I just tossed it all into my porridge pot and boiled it on the fire. It tasted alright."

"Which sort of thing," said his wife, "makes it sufficiently obvious that someone had to come out and look after the dumb brute before he was dragged off to an institution, so here I am."

****

471

The afternoon was spent in complete accord. If Galbraith had any suspicions that the women's original stay had not been quite so short or innocent as he had been led to believe he had sense enough not to impair his extremely happy marriage by asking awkward questions.

In spite of the two ladies' misgivings Macquarie was most discreet, mainly due to the simple expedient of saying as little as possible.

Ironically it was Mrs. Galbraith who came nearest to committing a faux pas.

The guests were being shown around 'the estate' after lunch, the women leading by several yards, when they passed the door of the old stone outhouse. Galbraith saw his wife glance inside and give a quite perceptible start which stopped her in mid-sentence.

"What's up Dear?" he called.

"Oh, nothing," was the immediate response, then, somewhat confused but apparently deciding that a more explicit answer was in order, "I just thought I saw something move."

Galbraith turned to Macquarie, "Have you any animals here?" he asked imagining something in the way of goats or a pet lamb.

"Only the puppy," Macquarie indicated the little dog which was gambolling with the children behind them, "apart from an old ginger cat which occasionally visits us when he can't get enough to eat on the beach but we don't often see him in the summer."

"Must have been a bird or a mouse then," Galbraith muttered just to tidy up that little piece of conversation.

When the men reached the doorway they could see no sign of an animal or anything else likely to move so they promptly lost interest in the subject.

Stepping through the doorway Galbraith noted at the far end of the building a carpenter's bench with various tools lying on it and hanging from nails and spikes driven between the stones of the wall. Lengths of wood of various dimensions lay under the bench and leaned against the wall in one corner. A dismantled outboard motor lay beside the bench. In the centre of the room was Macquarie's easel and other painting paraphernalia which Galbraith was commenting on as the two men left and returned to the sunshine outside.

Galbraith again thought of the mysterious animal and glanced through the doorway but the only objects visible were quite inanimate, a large neat stack of driftwood and a rusty wheelbarrow. Nothing else except a very battered old zinc bath which Macquarie obviously used to tote logs into the house.

****

At the end of the day all four Macquaries sat on rocks near the cottage and watched the yacht, heeling gracefully in the light breeze, making her way towards the north west horizon in continuation of her cruise up the West Coast.

The vessel made an attractive picture in the variated light of the setting sun which caused Macquarie to consider adding her to his next painting. The family camera had taken several photographs of the yacht during the course of the day and he was in no doubt Galbraith would be only too pleased to loan him more at different angles if required.

"Well the afternoon went off very well Dear," he said to his wife.

"Yes it was wonderful seeing them again, really wonderful," The smile changed to a pensive expression, "But I still would not like to trust you alone with her," said Mrs. Macquarie.

Chapter 20

Miss Falkener looked at the lounge clock. At least twenty minutes before they were due, more likely to be half an hour.

She moved to the window and looked across the moonlight flooded valley. How beautiful it was and how peaceful. It seemed so remote from the violence of the outside world. Not many lights in the farms and cottages at this late hour and the reflection of the moon on the still waters of the mere paled these to insignificance.

Miss Falkener smoothed her dress over her hips. It was not a new dress but for all that quite a favourite of hers. Knowing that she looked attractive in it gave her confidence and although comfortable it fitted perfectly. In fact, if it ever felt the slightest bit tight she knew that an immediate return to her diet was indicated. She was quite proud of her figure but at thirty-five it had to be constantly watched.

'It's a pity there is nothing I can do about the shape of my face,' she mused. She considered it too round and although her generous mouth and large eyes were satisfactory her somewhat retroussé nose was a constant source of annoyance to her.

However, few observers would have found much of which to complain.

'Well they have a nice night for their arrival after all that rain earlier today,' she said to herself.

It was not Miss Falkener's usual practice to await hotel guests who arrived at nearly midnight, this task being normally relegated to one of the staff but as she had been working late on accounts decided that an extra hour on duty would be no great sacrifice. And of course, the expected late arrivals were the Careys. Not that there was anything particularly special about them, they had only been guests at the hotel on one previous occasion and that was two years ago. However, they had been most apologetic when they phoned from Kendell, two calls in fact to keep her informed of the progress of the repairs to their broken down car.

She was pleased that one little mystery had been solved, 'Mr. and Mrs. J. Carey' were now 'Captain and Mrs. J. Carey'. On their earlier visit she remembered wondering what his profession was, she had never inquired of course and no information in this regard had been forthcoming during the several short conversations they had had together. She recalled the 'regulars' discussing the Careys shortly after they had left and overheard the words 'shipping' and 'travelled' once when passing through the lounge. And of course, that rather coarse Mr. Grainger, who was as 'commercial' as they come, saying, 'He will need a damn big sample case for that line,' laughing heartily at his own joke before any of his listeners realised what he was talking about.

So he must be captain of a ship. A merchant ship of course, old Colonel Dowerby would have known immediately if he had been connected with Her Majesty's Forces.

She felt a strange affinity to the Careys, as if she had known them before. But this was hardly possible, she herself had spent almost her entire life in the Lake District and they were definitely 'London', that area vaguely delineated in her mind as anywhere within fifty miles of Buckingham Palace. Neither had been to the Lakes prior to their earlier visit as they had actually stated at the time. The feeling was probably only due to the fact that they had said they owned a Jack Russel Terrier similar to her own lately deceased little Cleo.

Now she thought of it it was surprising how many things she remembered about them when people who had stayed much longer and more frequently were soon forgotten. For instance, that chance remark made when they returned breathless just in time for dinner. It had been a glorious sunny day after a week of almost continuous rain and all the walkers had returned to the hotel dry shod for once. Not so Mr. Carey however, he was soaked to the knees. Feeling that some explanation was in order he volunteered the information that he and his wife were having a race, the 'winning post' being represented by the far bank of a beck, or 'stream' as he termed it.

"Of course we would have to pick the only part of the stream where the bank hid the fact that it was too wide to jump at that point. I was in mid-air before I found this out!"

"Luckily I was a few yards behind him," added his wife, "and managed to come to a halt by grabbing hold of a large ash tree at the edge of the water or I would have joined him."

The description would fit any number of places in the vicinity but it was strange they should have mentioned such a spot on the very same day they had spoken of their dog. What was her name now? Something ridiculous. A film star's name? No, of course, 'Miss World', what a name for the poor little animal!

How those two little incidents brought flooding back memories of ten years before. Things she had hoped to cast from her mind long ago but they still returned. Not with the bitterness and tears of the time of course but with a twinge of pain, as if an open wound had healed over leaving the new skin a trifle tight.

If only men realised how easy it was for them to hurt a woman. How a casual remark or gesture, an unfulfilled promise or neglected rendezvous could hurt. Deeply and more sharply than a knife.

It had been such a happy afternoon. A very short time in which to get to know anyone but on which she had built her dreams. That they were just dreams she appreciated at the time, they were liable to dissolve slowly or even to be knocked flat. Either way would have been preferable to what actually did happen. Which was nothing. An absolute blank, a dull, aching void. No explanation, no letter, no message, no word at all, for all the world as if he had never existed except in her own imagination.

He intended to return to her, she knew in her heart he meant to.

476

He was not aware of her address but he knew roughly where she lived so a few inquiries in the neighbourhood should soon have brought him to her door.

As the weeks grew into months after the time she had expected him she tried to think of ways in which he could have been delayed. Trying desperately to think of excuses for him at first but later, when the only reasonable possibility remaining was that he had found someone else, to curse him. However, she was never really whole-hearted about this as it seemed too much out of character.

The only other alternative she could think of was that he was dead. This was too awful to contemplate. Anyway such a dreadful thing did not happen in real life.

If only she knew what had happened. Her orderly nature was affronted by this untidy gap in her past. To most people their lives were like the wakes of ships, a turmoil which soon merged with the sea as the vessels surged forward to new horizons. She considered her own past as a much tidier, more permanent thing, resembling more of a road being built. Not a very exciting road and certainly not a major one but smooth and even for all that.

Except for that one patch ten years ago. As if an area of the surface had been missed by the road gang and although they plodded on laying the asphalt she knew that patch was still there. She felt she had but to look over her shoulder and it would still be visible. A long way off now and growing all the time dimmer in the distance but still definitely there waiting to be covered so that its existence would no longer fret her so she could carry on along her road without looking back.

At this time more than ever she wanted that bare patch of road completed. Less than three months now and she and Alex would be married. Dear, adorable, beloved Alex. Most efficient of doctors, most wonderful of companions and the most clumsy of suitors since.... since...

'Oh God! It is high time that road was completed.'

Miss Falkener brought her mind back to the present. She glanced around the room. It would not be properly cleaned until the staff turned out in the morning but at least it was tidy. The two standard lamps by the fireplace, the only ones lit, cast a soft glow in that part of the room leaving the remainder of it in near darkness. Another log on the fire would brighten it up a bit so she moved towards the log-basket.

The Careys would notice a difference in the place she decided. Much had been done since she took over as manageress three years previously and now the renovations were virtually complete. It had required a considerable amount of tact and persuasion on her part to convince Mrs. Wallace that the outlay was necessary, for the old lady, although officially retired from the actual management of the hotel, still owned it and took a keen proprietary interest.

Much of the old massive furniture had been retained, although the armchairs and settees had been re-covered. The pictures and heavy gilt-framed mirrors remained in their original positions.

'Renovated without being modernised,' Miss Falkener reflected, 'The place still retains its old-world charm.'

She heard the car approaching and returned to the window in time to see its headlights sweep round the curve at the top of the drive and come to a standstill at the front door. A quick glance in a mirror and she proceeded to the door to welcome the late arrivals.

'What a handsome couple they are', thought Miss Falkener as greetings and apologies were attended to in the hall, 'The slim six feet plus of Captain Carey with a face that only just misses being really good looking must set many a female passenger's heart aflutter,' she mused, 'I suppose he does command a passenger liner?' She could not imagine him being in charge of what she understood to be termed a 'tramp ship'.

Mrs. Carey was several inches shorter than her husband with a figure that was the envy of every woman she met. Her light brown, well coiffured hair complemented her hazel eyes. Eyes which seemed to be made for laughter.

'She must have been right in the front row when her nose was issued,' thought miss Falkener enviously. 'Grooming, that's the word I'm looking for. She is always immaculate. On their previous visit even after a day's rambling she would return to the hotel looking as if she had just stepped out of a mannequin parade displaying the latest in casual wear. At that very moment she gave the appearance of having spent the last hour or two in front of her dressing table mirror rather than the whole day in a car.'

Miss Falkener looked forward in pleasurable anticipation to seeing the other clothes Mrs. Carey had brought with her.

The manageress led the Careys into the lounge, the newly renovated room in which she took considerable pride. Mrs. Carey admired the new paintwork and furnishings with interest and sincerity. Her husband contributed appreciative noises including, "I am glad you have not got rid of those hunting prints, I remember admiring them the last time we were here."

Miss Falkener, who had switched on the main lounge lights so her guests could observe the full scope of the room, switched them off again as they walked towards the welcoming fire.

"It is certainly improved by the fresh coat of paint," said Miss Falkener modestly, "though I think we made a mistake with the carpet, it is far too light of a shade. I am just about a nervous wreck by the time the after dinner coffee cups are collected in, it will stain so easily.

"Oh, by the way, I think some congratulations are in order Captain Carey," she emphasised the 'Captain', "Or am I rather late?"

"Almost too early," laughed Carey, "I've only just received my 'brass hat' and it won't be until after this little holiday that 'they' will be finding out if I'm fit to drive."

"I do not think there will be any doubt about that. You know I never thought of you as a seafarer, it is quite a surprise."

"What am I supposed to do, drink rum straight from the bottle and go around singing sea-chanties with a parrot on my shoulder?"

"He does break out into nautical parlance at times," contributed his wife, then turning to Carey, "I'll bet that van driver you 'spoke' to on the way here is still wondering what you meant when you accused him of 'indicating to port and heading starboard'. Some of the other terms you used even I did not understand," she ended demurely.

"Good heavens! Are you still with us?" said Carey, "You can go back to sleep if that is the nicest kind of remark you can make."

"I was nearly asleep too," she replied, "must be the result of all the excitement these last few days."

"Just make yourself comfortable and I will get you something to drink," said Miss Falkener, "No doubt you would like a snack too? It would be no trouble. You must be absolutely shattered after driving all the way from London."

"No please don't bother," replied Mrs. Carey, "we have caused you enough inconvenience as it is and you must have had a long day yourself. We had dinner in Kendell whilst waiting for the car so will just have a few minutes by the fire then go straight to bed. Alright with you James?"

Carey's expression sagged a little. Nothing would have pleased him more than a nice hot cup of coffee. 'Alright for her,' he thought, 'I did all the driving'.

However, before he could speak Miss Falkener came to his rescue.

"Oh please join me in a cup of something hot at least. I usually have a cup of coffee or tea before I retire."

On the strength of this coffee was agreed upon and Miss Falkener proceeded towards the kitchen.

When she was out of earshot Leonora Carey murmured to her husband.

"What a charming woman James. I wonder why she never married?" Then, noting the direction of her husband's eyes as Miss Falkener passed through the door, thought, 'I'll bet that lecherous man of mine is wondering what that pile of red hair would look like loosed over those milk-white shoulders."

Carey jolted back from his day-dream of a snow-bound Swiss mountain hut, a roaring log fire and the ivory-skinned form reclining on a fur rug before it, the cascade of copper tresses doing little to obstruct the view.

He answered his wife in a disinterested enough voice.

"I simply can't imagine. Would you like me to ask her?"

"You dare!" continuing, "What wonderful hair. It is a pity she chooses such an out of date style though."

James Carey was no fool. He leaned over and kissed his wife just under her left ear, whispering as he did so, "She is about four pounds overweight."

Somewhat mollified Leonora returned to her thoughts.

'No doubt he imagines he is in a hotel room with her by now',

Carey had been back in his Swiss hut for some time. He was still way ahead.

"I wonder how old she is?" murmured Leonora almost to herself.

Her husband returned to base.

"Mid-thirties at a guess. Much older than you," Carey said gallantly, even though it only gave his wife two or three years to play with. "Nearly my age probably, much too old for me."

'He tries hard and I love him dearly', she smiled and again lost herself in reverie.

No further conversation ensued prior to Miss Falkener's return to the room with coffee. Very tired, they each found it difficult to stay awake in the comfortable armchairs by the crackling fire.

****

As she busied herself in the kitchen Miss Falkener's thoughts had been of her new guests.

'How happy they are and so obviously still very much in love with one another. Just like a honeymoon couple yet they have been married how long? Seven or eight years did they say on their previous visit? But of course that was two years ago, now they will have been married for about ten. Ten! that number again! If anyone mentions the words 'ten years ago' again tonight I will scream.'

'I must remember to ask about the little dog, particularly as I have remembered the poor little thing's name. 'Miss World' indeed.

'Did they have any special fads or fantasies?' None that she could recall. 'They seemed to enjoy their previous stay, in fact must have done so or they would not have returned.'

Miss Falkener picked up the tray and started walking towards the lounge, little realising what the next few minutes would bring.

She would remember the occasion for as long as she lived.

****

"The weather prospects look good for tomorrow," said the manageress as she placed the tray on the fire-side coffee table.

Ignoring the convenient settee, she pulled up a small upright chair. She would sit with her guests when the occasion was appropriate but she did not allow herself to lounge with them.

Her remark reminded Carey of that previous occasion of a fine day when he literally leaped into a stream.

"The weather is immaterial, I can get very, very wet regardless of what kind of day it is."

Almost asleep Leonora's contribution to the conversation was triggered off by Carey's words 'very, very wet', the term he used when referring to that frightening incident long ago of which she had just been thinking. A coincidence of dramatic consequence.

"Yes, he nearly made a widow of me before he made me an honest woman."

Wondering why her husband had brought up that dreadful subject she spoke flippantly in an effort to head the conversation away. She faltered towards the end of the sentence as she realised her mistake.

'Oh God! What have I done?' she said to herself, 'That is not what he meant at all.'

She would have given anything to have recalled her words but it was too late.

Miss Falkener, concentrating on pouring the coffee, did not notice the faux-pas and said,

"That sounds interesting, what exactly happened?"

Observing his wife's distress Carey felt obliged to answer.

The pause before he spoke was only momentary but long enough for Miss Falkener to sense that something was wrong. What had happened? The previous conversation seemed innocuous enough. She was trying to recall the exact words said when Carey spoke.

"Oh it was something which happened a long time ago, about ten years in fact, the ship I was on at the time unfortunately sank."

'There it is again! Ten years!' Miss Falkener did not scream but gave a start which caused the coffee in the cup she was holding to slop into the saucer.

Captain Carey had spoken lightly, choosing his words with care but Miss Falkener could see that the subject was not one he could treat lightly at all.

Carey had not moved. He still gazed at the fire, his profile remaining at exactly the same angle to her but suddenly he looked years older. Whereas his lips smiled when he spoke again his eyes did not. In them there was not a vestige of a smile.

"She went under rather suddenly and I went with her, only to bob up like a cork a moment or two later. So quickly in fact I didn't have time to see my past life flash before my eyes."

If the last few words were meant to be the punch-line they fell very flat. Carey prayed however that they would mean the end of that particular topic. He hoped the fully alert Leonora would come to his aid but in this he was disappointed, it was Miss Falkener who spoke first and not in a way to turn the unfortunate course of the conversation.

As soon as the sinking ship was mentioned Miss Falkener felt suddenly cold. The shadows in the room seemed to close around the group by the fire. Closer and closer until it appeared to her that only Carey's face was visible. She felt herself becoming increasingly tense as she waited for him to continue. There was something there waiting to be transmitted from the man to her, something important. She did not know what it was except that it was of great moment to her. If only he would say something more, just a few words which would unlock the tension in her breast. After what seemed an eternity of silence she could bear the strain no longer.

"Was there anyone else......" she faltered but Carey guessed what her question would be.

"There were only three of us by then, two of us got away alright but the mate......." For a moment he could not continue.

'For God's sake go on!' Miss Falkener willed of him silently. When the pause had reached breaking point she forced out a few more words.

"His.... his name?"

She felt that she was in a tunnel, a completely dark tunnel and that she had been dragging her feet along it for a long, long time. When Carey stopped in mid-sentence she felt she was close to a door at the end of it, a closed door but chinks of light around the frame defined it certainly a door. If only she could reach out and push it would swing open and all would be light. She was so nearly, nearly there.

"Hi name was Hatch, Gilbert Hatch."

It shocked her to realise his name meant nothing.

'But it must do! It must! It must!' Miss Falkener almost screamed out loud. The coffee cup rattling in the saucer in her hand was of no concern to her and the touch of fingers on her other arm with the vague outline of Mrs. Carey's startled face mouthing words she could not hear meant nothing to her at all.

'Go on! Go on! One more word please!'

She felt she was screaming the words although no sound issued from her lips.

She was touching the door now, leaning her weight on it and it was beginning to swing open.

'Please, please!' she beseeched silently.

Carey, gazing concentratedly at the fire was unaware of the turmoil beside him.

"We used to call him 'Jake', it was a nickname he...."

The cup and saucer went crashing to the floor, coffee splashed the table and settee and made a large pool on the carpet. Only Carey's quick movement prevented Miss Falkener from crashing head-first onto the stone fireplace.

"Good God!" he cried, "She's fainted."

****

It was nearly half an hour after the dramatic incident in the hotel lounge that a white-faced, apologetic, severely shaken Miss Falkener was escorted to her room by the dressing-gowned housekeeper.

James Carey's vague recollection of the geography of the building in his search for assistance fortunately served to lead him to the staff quarters without awakening any of the guests. However, the noise he effected there banging on the doors of broom-cupboard and linen rooms before finding someone had awakened not just one employee but virtually the entire staff. The Careys were therefore eventually taken to their room by one of the maids with the porter-cum-odd job man following with the bags, whilst others collected the cups, mopped up the coffee spilled on the carpet and straightened the furniture. Chattering like starlings in their individual night attire they gave the impression of refugees from an earthquake rather than the smart uniformed people with whom the guests were familiar.

The weary Careys undressed and slipped into bed in silence. They unilaterally decided to put their thoughts in order before opening the discussion on the night's events.

Before either of them spoke a word they were fast asleep.

****

The slight rattle of tea-cups as the maid deposited the tray on the bedside table brought Carey from the depths of sleep. Instantly awake, he glanced at his watch.

"Good Grief! It's nine o'clock, we will miss breakfast."

"Good morning," said the maid hearing his muttered words, "There is no need to hurry, we are holding breakfast for you as you were so late in getting to bed."

Oh, Good Morning," replied Carey, realising he was not alone, "That's fine then. And thanks for the tea."

Only then did he recognise in the neatly groomed maid the woman in dressing gown and curlers who had shown them to their room earlier that morning.

Movement under the bed-clothes beside him indicated that his wife was coming to the surface.

"Good morning Madam," smiled the maid as Leonora's tousled head appeared above the sheets. "I hope you slept well?"

"Wonderfully thanks, and Good Morning to you."

She inquired after Miss Falkener and was assured that that lady was 'quite herself' this morning and had been up and about her duties at her usual hour.

The woman had reached the door when Carey blurted out, "I say, I...."

Leonora's train of though was similar to her husband's now she was fully awake. She continued for him,

"If it is not too rude a question, what is Miss Falkener's first name? I know her initials are 'E' something but....?" She left the question in the air.

"Lots of people wonder that," smiled the maid, "actually it is 'Ellen' but she hates it and uses her second name 'Marion'."

"Thank you," said Leonora as she sank back into the pillows with a sigh.

"Well that settles it then," said Carey as the door closed behind the maid.

"What an extraordinary coincidence," replied his wife, "What do we do now?"

A chilling thought struck Carey.

"Have we still got Jake's envelope? I haven't seen it for years."

"Yes, it is in the wardrobe of the spare room under all those old records and photograph albums. I saw it only a few months ago when I was spring cleaning."

"Good thing we did not dump it, I'd completely forgotten the thing." Then he continued, "Do you know what is in it?"

"Yes, letters of course, or so you told me. Letters to a girl called Marion."

Carey well remembered the occasion, shortly after he brought the envelope home from Falmouth, when he opened it to see what mystery Jake had entrusted to him. Also his surprise and embarrassment when he saw of what the contents consisted. He flipped through the pile of sheets as quickly as he could, reading as little as possible after the shock of the first half page but trying to find an address or other indication as for whom the letters were intended. The girl's name was Marion but that was the only information he could find.

Carey had carefully re-sealed the envelope before pondering the problem. His conclusions were that, a; Any girl deserving of such letters would go to considerable lengths to make contact. Later this idea was discounted as no one made any inquiries at the company's head office or, to the best of his knowledge to anyone who had been on the ship. This left alternative b; The girl was entirely a figment of Hatch's imagination.

Should the latter alternative be the correct one the best thing to do, he decided, was to destroy the letters. However, if the former proved to be the true case he would have to hold on to them until the mysterious 'Marion' disclosed herself. So, as had better men before him, he compromised. He retained the envelope against the chance of it being claimed with the proviso that if the house caught fire it would be the very last thing he would attempt to rescue.

Having arrived at this decision he stowed the envelope with some old books in his flat and more or less forgot about it.

There was then a mad rush to get down to breakfast so the matter was left in abeyance until they were alone.

****

After the meal the Careys walked out onto the paved area in front of the hotel and sat in the morning sunshine on the low wall at its edge. Below them the lawn swept down to the lane among the trees which separated the hotel grounds from the fields and mere beyond.

Carey's thoughts were on the quickest way to get the letters to the hotel.

"Your mother has a key to our place, could you phone her, tell her where the package is and get her to post it here? Express delivery?"

489

"Yes but is it wise James? Is it the right thing to do? Bringing back the past like that. The poor woman has had a severe shock, it would be like…. like resurrecting the dead. Would it not be kinder not to mention the letters and to burn them when we get home?"

"I hadn't thought of it that way. It's an awful responsibility, think how dreadful it would be if somehow or other she found out that we had done that. Seems a bit drastic whatever we do."

Carey pondered for a few moments.

"I'll tell you what. Why don't you tell her I have some letters of Jake's which I think possibly, might have…..there's a vague chance," he floundered on, "of having some connection with her. After all," he continued more confidently, "I don't 'officially' know that they are addressed to a girl called Marion."

Leonora smiled, this was her James

"Although you slid gracefully off the rails at the end of that monologue I think that is basically the best idea." She continued very sweetly. "However the bit I don't buy is that I speak to her. Where would I find you afterwards to make my report? Will you be locked in the bathroom or hiding in the shrubbery? This is, I might remind you James Carey, your idea and your envelope."

After enjoying her husband's entreaties and arguments regarding the feminine touch, etcetera for a few minutes Leonora relented to the extent of agreeing to accompany him for the interview with Miss Falkener. As she had decided from the outset.

They agreed to mention the letters to Miss Falkener when the opportunity offered, but not before they were certain she had got over the shock of the previous night. The letters could always be destroyed if she indicated she did not wish to see them.

On returning to the building however they met the manageress looking for them.

After the appropriate courtesies had been exchanged the Careys were asked to spare a few moments in Miss Falkener's private sitting room. Nothing was said as they passed through the lounge, much to the chagrin of the other residents who had heard but vague and conflicting rumours of a commotion during the night and were straining their ears behind the morning newspapers.

The manageress' private flat was at the back of the building, the view of dale and mere being reserved for the paying guests. Its windows over-looked the outbuildings, once the stables and coach house, which nestled into the grass and bracken covered hillside. Although the sitting room caught little sun, except early in the morning, it was a cheerful room decorated in excellent taste and containing delicate furniture which, if not all exactly antique, was very good reproduction. The round rose-wood table particularly caught Leonora's eye.

'That at least is the real thing,' she decided.

The pale walls displayed several framed water-colours, apparently the work of some local artist, and a few bowls of flowers from the garden added even more colour.

It was a neat, feminine room, aptly depicting the character of its occupant. Any mother would instantly have recognised it as a room in which children rarely strayed.

After asking them to be seated Miss Falkener opened the conversation by again apologising for her extraordinary conduct the previous night and then, in way of explanation, giving a brief account of her meeting with Jake and mention of her disappointment in not hearing from him. Naturally she asked about Jake, particularly of how he met his end and Carey told her as gently as he could. He concluded by saying what had been in his mind ever since the disaster,

"If only I had not gone to the foc'sle head, if only Peter and I had been on the bridge where we had virtually lived for days previously, then there might have been a chance, things might have turned out differently."

"Please, please don't ever reproach yourself," Miss Falkener said in all sincerity, "You could have done no more than you did. Whatever has to be has to be."

She did not say, "In the final analysis Jake would possibly have preferred things to be as they actually happened." Something Carey had often wondered.

Miss Falkener remained outwardly composed throughout the narrative although Leonora could not help wondering how she would have reacted had she been alone. She and Carey decided in their own minds that this was the time to broach the subject of the letters.

Carey concentrated his gaze on a bowl of flowers in the centre of the table composing his opening sentence before turning to Miss Falkener.

"This will no doubt come as a surprise to you, and something of a shock."

Miss Falkener was immediately all attention. 'This man', she thought, 'seems to have an awful lot of my past life buried away in him but what an effort it is to dig it out.' She waited impatiently for him to continue.

Carefully choosing his words Carey resumed speaking.

"What you have told us about your meeting with Jake explains everything. So far as I know he never mentioned your existence to anyone, certainly nobody on the ship."

"If only he had," there was a slight catch in Miss Falkener's voice, "Then at least I would have known. Someone surely would have got some kind of message to me. I only knew him as Jake, I did not even know the name of his ship. When that ship of yours sank I remember reading the names of the people.... Good heavens! Your name must have been one of them, it did not occur to me before."

"Ordinary enough name," said Carey, anxious to get the conversation back onto the subject of letters. "You had no reason to remember it anyway, as you said, the names meant nothing. But to get to the subject of letters."

He stopped, this was rather too abrupt. He was not leading up to the subject at all in the way he had intended.

Carey's pause seemed to indicate to Miss Falkener that his mention of letters was a question she should answer in order to get him speaking again.

"There were no letters. We neither of us knew the other's address so could not write."

'Hell!' said Carey to himself, 'I'm just about to drop another bomb-shell after all my good intentions of breaking this information gently. No good now trying to decide whether or not to disclose the existence of those letters.'

"Jake did write to you." Flatly.

"What? How do you know?" If the ceiling of the room had fallen in just then Miss Falkener would not have noticed it.

"Not long before Jake.... before the ship sank Jake gave me a package to look after. I am certain that his intention at the time was for me to take care of it whilst he was in hospital, where he expected to be for some time after the ship arrived at Falmouth." Carey hesitated for a moment not quite sure how to carry on.

"I investigated the package but could not find an address so thought best just to hang on to it until it was claimed." It sounded rather lame but it was the best he could do.

"Where are….." Miss Falkener controlled herself with an effort. Although it seemed but yesterday all these things happened a long time ago.

"How long did you keep them?" she asked as calmly as she could.

At this point Leonora joined the conversation.

"Would you want them if they still exist?" she asked, "Are you sure it would not be better if they were to be destroyed unseen?"

Miss Falkener slowly sank back in her chair. For a moment or two she composed her thoughts, then,

"Mrs. Carey, I am thirty-five years old and all this happened ten years ago. Even at that time I was hardly an adolescent schoolgirl. I will admit that meeting Jake was quite a dramatic incident in my life which I will no doubt long remember but it is all over and done with now. I am only glad that everything has been cleared up and explained, if only for the sake of Jake's memory. Yes, I would like to have those letters."

****

Miss Falkener usually made her farewells to departing guests in the hall or at the front door. However, when the Carey's holiday came to an end they were honoured with an invitation to her sitting room.

The room as they entered was as they saw it on the previous occasion, nicely feminine and very tidy. With one glaring exception. Unfolding himself from an arm-chair by the fireplace was a tall, gangling individual of some forty summers. The angular frame was draped in an ancient gingerish tweed suit and a pair of brogues which, Leonora guessed, must have been at least a size twelve. The lantern jaw and twinkling pale blue eyes were topped with a shock of untidy hair only a shade less ginger than the suit. A large briar pipe in a ham-like hand seemed almost part of the uniform.

The stranger reached the vertical with rather a clatter having accidently caught the ash-tray on his chair arm knocking it to the floor and at the same time brushing a small side-table with his knee setting the tea-service thereon jingling. Miss Falkener did not flinch which gave the Careys the impression that such near disasters were not new to her.

"Captain and Mrs. Carey," the manageress introduced them, "I would like you to meet Doctor MacKay," adding with a loving glance at the doctor, "My fiancé."

As he shook hands with the doctor Carey could not help but to observe,

"For a holiday this has certainly been one catalogue of surprises."

Miss Falkener offered her guests tea and as this was being consumed the conversation was quite general.

Half an hour later as the Careys were about to leave Doctor MacKay said,

"Captain Carey, if it is not too much to ask, what kind of a chap was my predecessor?" The impish grin directed at Miss Falkener was acknowledged with a frown.

'Here we go again,' thought Carey, 'I'd hoped that particular subject was over and done with.'

He searched his mind for words. How would one describe Hatch? Not a prepossessing character whichever way you looked at him. Bad-tempered, untidy in his person, inclined to blame the world for the misfortunes he brought upon himself. There was little to be said in his favour at all.

Yet this attractive, intelligent woman had apparently loved him so he could hardly put this description into words. What would have happened if the friendship had developed and they had married? Carey could not but think that such a union would have ended in disaster. Nothing in his opinion could have altered Hatch to any extent. She was well out of it.

Hatch had had the same chances, almost anyway, as anyone else making his way at sea, it was his own fault he had never reached command. He had been a misfit, a man who was unable to conform to his environment. Perhaps that was an apt description, a man who did not know how to live?

Carey suddenly became aware of the quietness in the room and of three pairs of eyes watching him. Leonora's face was troubled and concerned, obviously annoyed that this subject had been brought up again. Miss Falkener displayed frank vexation, even a trace of anger. Doctor MacKay's expression was of acute embarrassment, as if he wished he were down a deep hole somewhere on the far side of the county.

'Not that that gets me off the hook' thought Carey, 'Now what was I going to say? Ah, yes, 'A man who did not know how to live''

"He was a man...." The words came out so suddenly they surprised even himself.

"He was a man who knew how to die."

It was not what Carey had meant to say at all but having said it he decided to let it stand.

It was as good an epitaph as any.

~ENDS~

9 STEAMSHIP APPRENTICE

Chapter 1

Reminiscences of this sort seem generally to commence with the words 'the taxi drew up under the overhanging bow of the ship, in which her name was proudly emblazoned'.

Why should I be different?

The taxi drew up under the overhanging bow of the ship. Her name was hardly 'emblazoned' however, in fact it was painted out. Owing to a certain amount of international unpleasantness at the time most vessels were inclined to be a trifle coy at revealing their identities. In fact, at that moment the Japanese were playing havoc in the Pacific, the Germans were romping through Russia and the Battle of the Atlantic was at its height.

By some mental process, the logic of which eludes me after the long passage of time, I decided to leave school and get to sea as soon as possible in case our side suddenly won, causing me to miss all the excitement.

My departure from school, to the mutual satisfaction of both parties, apparently coincided with a government directive which prevented me, (and no doubt a few hundred other like-minded lunatics), from going to sea until I reached the required minimum age. Previously this decision had been a matter of personal choice.

For some months the world passed me by although I utilised the latter part of the time by studying at a nearby Marine School which specialised in preparing boys for a sea-going career. I think the full course was twelve months but after six weeks or so I left to join my first ship. On the authority of a statement by the principal of the establishment I would have departed anyway. He quoted several valid reasons for this culminating in a final one concerning an unfortunate accident occasioned by a booby-trap rigged above a door intended for the discomfiture of fellow students. Who would have dreamed that the first person to enter the room would be the Principal himself?

No doubt I wondered what adventures were in store as I stepped out of the taxi on that cold, sunny November afternoon at Dundee.

My arrival must have been noted as soon a red-headed apprentice, who, appropriately enough, introduced himself as 'Ginger', was assisting me in getting my trunk up the gangway, across cluttered decks and through what appeared to be a maze of alleyways, canvas screens and engine-room gratings to the apprentice's cabin.

As soon as my gear had been dumped in the room Ginger took me along to report to the Chief Officer. The remainder of the afternoon was occupied with a tour of the ship.

Perhaps a brief description of what I observed then and later would not be amiss.

The 'Masirah' was twenty-three years old. According to Ginger, who, I soon established, was blessed with a lively imagination, she would have been scrapped long before if it had not been for the war. In point of fact she outlasted the hostilities by a decade. He also said that the only reason she had survived three years of war was that no self-respecting U-Boat commander would waste a torpedo on her. I did not believe that either.

Built at Glasgow in 1919 and of around seven thousand tons gross she was of about average size for a deep sea ship of her period. Basically she was of the 'three island type' although her 'islands' and hatch layout were by no means conventional. There was a normal raised forecastle then a well deck extending to the bridge containing two hatches, number one forward of the foremast and the main hatchway of number two abaft it. On the raised deck amidships, referred to always as the 'saloon deck', was the bridge structure which also encompassed the accommodation of the master and deck officers, dining saloon and so forth. Directly abaft this was the after hatch of the large number two hold, then number three hatch, the officers' galley, boiler and engine-room casings and engineers and apprentices' accommodation. This extended to a walkway running athwartships overlooking the after well deck. This strip of deck was a social area for off-duty engineers and was known as 'the after end'.

Number four hatch had a well deck of the short 'Death-trap' variety all to itself. When this hatch was not being worked a portable catwalk spanned it to allow easy access between saloon deck and poop.

The long poop accommodated the mainmast, number five hatch, the crew galleys and companion ways to the Indian crew quarters. Right on the stern was the ship's main armament of a 4.7 inch gun and a twelve pounder.

In addition to the life-boats six life-rafts of wood and empty drum construction were fitted on skids at the ship's sides and automatic weapons in tubs were sited on the bridge and boat deck. She had the usual vertical bar stem of her vintage, a cruiser stern and a fair amount of good old-fashioned tumble home. However, her most notable feature was a tremendously high funnel, necessitated by her natural draught coal-fired boilers.

The apprentices' accommodation was exactly what I had expected and a description of such a typical room of the period for embryo officers may be of interest.

The room was situated at the fore end of the engineers' accommodation on the starboard side. It measured about seven feet by eight and was sheathed with white painted tongue and groove boarding. The steel deck was coated with about half an inch of red painted cement- coming up in places – and a well-worn piece of coir matting. No sheathing covered the deckhead so the planks of the boat deck were in full view. Needless to say on such an old ship the deckhead leaked in any kind of weather causing droplets of rusty water to drip from the steel beams and deck bolts. This accounted for the fact that ships' linen and white uniforms of the day were generally well bespattered with brown rust stains.

The doorway, opening into the inboard alleyway, was fitted with a light jalousie door for normal use and a thick teak storm door for bad weather. To pass through the doorway one had to step over the high storm step. There were two small portholes, one on the forward bulkhead and one facing outboard.

The cabin contained four wooden bunks, a pair each on the outboard and after bulkheads, two wardrobes each about a foot wide, a bench with a well-worn cushion and a 'compactum'.

Compactums came in various forms and the latest models prior to the advent of running water on ships were quite attractive pieces of furniture. 'The works' consisted of a square tank of water with a pipe led to a tap above a tip-up washbasin which emptied into a receiving waste water tank below it. The whole thing was contained in a mahogany case with a decorative shelf on top for shaving gear and a mirror. The 'receiver' was emptied by the steward – or 'Boy' as each was termed no matter how ancient he might be – who also filled the storage tank. The frequency of this service and the temperature of the water depended a lot on the officer's seniority. When closed all the plumbing fittings were decorously hidden.

Apart from its being a 'do it yourself' service the apprentices' compactum was rather more elementary than that described above. Its consisted of a wooden box about two feet high with a hinged lid on top which opened to disclose a small round washbasin and a door below to facilitate the removal of the 'receiver'.

The water was poured from a can somewhat resembling a gardener's watering can without the rose, in fact exactly the article used in Victorian houses when the best people bathed in their bedrooms and are still occasionally seen in antique shops. This was filled at the galley tap, our nearest fresh water supply. If one was well in with the cook a scoop or two of hot water from the square tank on the galley range could be added to warm it up a little. The routine was that whoever filled the water-can also emptied the receiver at the same time. Occasionally this latter chore was neglected with somewhat disastrous results.

The water-can was kept handy in front of the compactum, this was both for convenience and the fact that there was no other space on the deck to put it. Unfortunately, this spot was also partly in the doorway so the can was often trodden on at night by people entering the room as the light, if on, was automatically switched off when the door was opened. However, once we got away to sea, the deck was more or less permanently wet what with leaking ports and the sea coming in the doorway so a little extra water made scant difference.

The lighting system was as rudimentary as the plumbing consisting as it did of a naked light bulb in the centre of the deckhead. An electric fan was screwed to the bulkhead and this was supplied with enough flex to reach the light socket. Apprentices were denied the luxury of moving air and light at the same time.

One other article completed the furnishings, a much battered wicker table, no doubt picked up out east when the ship was young.

Apart from the two narrow wardrobes there was nowhere to hang our clothes so they stayed in our various suitcases and trunks, (sea-chests were things of the past), under the bunks. At a later date we did ask a visiting marine superintendent if we could have drawers fitted under the bunks only to be answered with a horrified, "Don't you know there is a war on?"

Other amenities were in keeping. The route to the apprentices' toilet, (there was no bathroom), was out through the cabin door, across the engine-room alleyway, over the boiler-room gratings to the opposite alleyway, through the canvas blackout curtains onto the open deck thence to the toilet at the ship's side. On reaching that room of easement one's troubles were by no means over as, owing to a somewhat unreliable storm valve at the ship's side, in anything like heavy weather one was likely to 'get one's own back' with a vengeance.

It was in these alleyways that I learned my first words of 'Laskari' occasioned by the firemen coming off watch bringing with them a five gallon drum of water from the hotwell for washing purposes. The drum was suspended from a length of wood carried on the shoulders of two men and their warning cry of, "Cabadar – Gurram Pani!", (Watch out, Hot Water!), ensured that anyone else feeling their way in the pitch darkness kept well clear of them. On occasions we used the call ourselves, although hardly justified, to avoid blundering into members of the crew at night.

As the efficient blackout of a ship was essential to her safety all manner of precautions were taken to ensure that no gleam of light betrayed her presence to the enemy. Apart from overlapping blackout curtains at each doorway opening onto the deck a switch at each door automatically switched off the room's light the moment the door started to open and kept it off until the door was again firmly closed. Each porthole was supplied with a 'baffle', a black painted sheet metal contrivance which fitted snuggly into the hole in lieu of the glass. Overlapping plates prevented any light escaping, or, for that matter, much air entering the room. Improved versions incorporated a fine wire mesh as a deterrent to mosquitoes and other creepy-crawlies. A couple of days of normal use transformed this net into a wire reinforced felt board which prevented anything at all passing through.

****

After the inspection of the ship and a quick clean up it was high tea in the saloon then off ashore with the second apprentice and one of the quartermasters. I joined the ship in mid-afternoon and by six o'clock was in the first public house I had ever entered – albeit drinking nothing stronger than ginger ale.

This second apprentice came into my life but briefly. On the second night we were ashore together we were accompanied by one of the quartermasters who was going on leave. Having seen the Q.M. to his train my mate suddenly said, "I think I'll go too", He promptly bought himself a ticket and boarded the train. Either he had decided that sea life was not for him or the torpedoing of his previous ship had shaken him more than he cared to admit.

The bunk allotted to me, and glad I was to climb into it after the long eventful day, was on the outboard bulkhead directly below the porthole. If at the time I thought this would be an advantage, particularly in warm weather, I was soon disillusioned. The port leaked terribly and all the short lengths of timber tucked around and under my mattress could not prevent it from being more or less permanently damp. Another disadvantage of a fore and after bunk I later found was that one was much more likely to be thrown out of it than from an athwartship one when the vessel rolled. And she could certainly roll.

****

For the apprentices the day's work commenced at 7am. Breakfast was at 9am., dinner at 1230 and high tea at 5,30. In the tropics the main meal was in the evening and half an hour later.

Normally we were on daywork in port and watches at sea. There was always plenty for we apprentices to do and it was a poor Chief Officer, in charge of the deck department, who could not keep his apprentices occupied at all times. This worthy, was invariably termed 'The Mate', his immediate juniors being the Second and Third Officers, known usually as the Second and Third Mates. 'The Chief', 'Second', 'Third', 'Fourth' and 'Fifth', (or 'Fiver), with no appendages, referred exclusively to the engineer officers.

Apart from the junior engineers the officers and apprentices took their meals in the saloon. In that dark, mahogany panelled room there was but one table with a three berth settee on the fore side of it, three swivel chairs on the other and a similar chair at each end. The meals were served in two sittings, the senior officers having lunch and dinner at 1pm. and 6pm. and the junior officers, including the apprentices, half an hour earlier.

Breakfast was always the problem, at this meal the seniors ate first, at 8.30. and the juniors at 9am. All very well for the third mate or third radio officer who could just slide into a seat at the table as one became available if the senior officers had decided to linger over a second cup of coffee and a cigarette. Not so the starving apprentices, peeping round the door and trying, by mental telepathy, to will the 'Old Man' and the Mate to quit yapping and go about their business so we could get our noses into the feeding trough.

And an excellent 'trough' it was. All meals were substantial affairs, even breakfast. Although only Sundays and Thursdays were 'bacon and egg' days, (No doubt twice the shore ration at the time), there was on other days devilled kidneys, ling fish with bacon and egg sauce, minced collops and various other almost forgotten delicacies. Always there was toast, potatoes in various modes, rice cakes with syrup, (the 'Turner Morrison' variety were considered the best), cereals and porridge. Kippers and smoked haddock were also frequently on the menu. Ironically our white bread was considered quite a luxury by visitors from ashore who for years had eaten nothing but the wartime standard loaf of greyish brown hue. The reason for this was that only white flour would keep for any length of time on a ship.

The weather had to be pretty extreme before the cooking even faltered.

There was no 'official' eating between the evening meal and breakfast so it is easy to imagine our rumbling stomachs when the captain signalled for yet another cup of coffee. Apart from everything else we were expected to be 'back on deck' sharp at 9.30 no matter how curtailed our meal had been.

The morning after my arrival I was handed over to the second mate who gave me the first job I ever did on the ship. He issued me with two or three Walker's Log rotators, (propeller-like objects, part of the patent log system used to record the distance run at sea), and a tin of grease, instructing me to coat each rotator with a thin film of the stuff. A simple enough task on the face of it but I could not see how it could be accomplished without the risk of getting grease on my hands, I soon found out.

My next job was to paint a barrel – which merits a little explanation.

Ships were destroyed at an alarming rate in both world wars and those sunk in shallow water, particularly in such congested areas as the North Sea, constituted a danger to other vessels navigating there. For obvious reasons it would be of considerable assistance if the position and identity of a wreck could be speedily and readily established which led some tidy-minded person to suggest a simple expedient.

Thus it was that on my first working day I sat on a coil of line on the boat deck with my barrel. One end of the line I was sitting on was attached to the barrel and the other to the ship. I repainted the barrel bright green then, in white paint, carefully filled in the old letters of the words 'Masirah' on one side and 'Wreck' on the other. Somewhat analogous to carving one's own tombstone. Fortunately, it was never required.

Chapter 2

Two days after joining the ship I was sent on a Merchant Navy Anti-Aircraft Gunnery course. The 'theoretical' part was conducted by an old Naval petty officer in a corner of one of the cargo sheds on the quay and the 'practical' at the firing range at Leith. At the latter place I handled fire-arms for the first time in my life. This included firing a burst from a machine gun and several rounds from a shot-gun, (cunningly disguised as a Lewis gun), at clay pigeons. I cannot remember hitting anything with the machine gun, or even what the target was for that matter, but I know for certain that I missed all the clay pigeons- much to my humiliation.

The course lasted for two days and qualified me in the firing, cleaning and oiling of Marlin, Hotchkiss and Lewis machine guns. This constituted a sort of 'O Level' in machine gunnery, the 'A Level' I obtained after a five day course some months later. It was probably the latter which entitled me to an extra sixpence a day – which effectively doubled my salary of fifteen shillings, (75p), a month. In actual fact I nearly did not live to draw any of it as the bus carrying our party to the Leith ranges skidded on an icy road, spun round and had its back torn off on a lamp standard. A few of us were sitting on the bench seat across the back of the vehicle and when things came to a standstill there was nothing behind us but a large hole, both the back of the bus and the back of the seat were lying in the road some distance away. No one was hurt but the top of my uniform cap received a deep cut from a piece of window glass.

Whilst on the subject of remuneration I should mention that when signed on the ship's 'Articles' I also received five pounds a month 'War Rich Bonus'. After two years' service at sea one was entitled to the full amount of ten pounds. I believe tanker men, owing to the additional hazards of their trade, received an extra ten shillings on top of this.

The eventful day concluded with our Dundee bound train – I think it consisted of but a couple of self-propelled carriages – being abandoned in a siding for some hours. There may have been a very good war-time reason for this but most likely the driver thought the train to be empty and had gone home. Someone from the train eventually braved the pitch darkness of the night and raised help.

****

The plots of several sea stories I had read included the cargoes of 'agricultural machinery' which turned out to be rifles and machine guns destined for some revolutionary movement in South America. However, there was no doubt about the cargo the 'Masirah' was loading, it was very military indeed. Guns, vehicles, ammunition and stores for the armed services of every description. Also, just to make things interesting, number one lower hold full of cases of high octane aircraft fuel.

Two holds were partially filled with sand ballast, (I believe there was 1800 tons of it), to 'stiffen' the ship sufficiently for her future movements after discharge. This solid weight in the bottom of the vessel was responsible to a great extent for the prodigious rolling when we got to sea. In fact, it gave the ship a unique roll which I have never since experienced. Normally a ship will roll one way, be it ere so far, then roll back to roughly the same angle the other way in a more or less regular fashion. The 'Masirah' did this most of the time but occasionally at the extremity of the roll she would hang momentarily and then, instead of commencing her return roll, lurch over a further degree or two. Not much but it was this little bit extra which really sent things flying in the saloon and elsewhere.

Loading was eventually completed and the ship left Dundee to proceed 'north about' in convoy for the Clyde.

Shortly before leaving port each vessel had been supplied with a kite balloon as a deterrent to low flying enemy aircraft. As the convoy ran smack into a gale few of the balloons survived for very long. I was told at the time that they cost £85 each which, to my frugal mind, seemed an awful waste.

The weather was clear and sunny, the wind strong and the sea rough. The ship plunged and rolled and spray rattled onto the bridge like hailstones. The bow rose and fell as if flailing the sea with the mine-sweeping 'A Frame' which protruded from it like a double bowsprit. From an observer's point of view, it was most interesting to watch the ship next to ours bucking like a wild horse, often lifting her forefoot clear out of the water before slapping it back again in a cloud of spray. Everything was so new and invigorating I did not know what to turn my attention to next. Goodness knows what kind of a lookout I was keeping! At one stage I was hanging over the bridge wing watching the seas dash down the ship's side, wondering which of the hissing monsters would lap over the edge of the forward well deck and go crashing through the deck cargo, when a voice behind me suddenly said, "Are you alright lad?"

I spun round.

"Fine, thank you sir."

I felt an urge to spread my arms wide and add, "Isn't it wonderful!" but one does not wax poetic to ship's captains.

The 'Old Man' muttered something and moved away. I could not help thinking that he seemed rather disappointed.

Although unaffected by sea-sickness I certainly felt the cold, northern seas in winter being pretty bleak places. I had brought warm clothes with me of course and these had been supplemented by a parcel of 'Merchant Navy Comforts' received on joining the ship but even wearing everything I could get on in the way of woollens did not compensate for the fact that my gabardine raincoat was a poor substitute for a proper heavy weather coat. I well remember longing for the moon to break through the clouds for although this made not the slightest difference to the temperature I sometimes managed to convince myself it felt a little warmer for it. The bridge offered little shelter from the wind and spray and there was certainly no 'wheelhouse watchkeeping' in those days. With the visibility from the wheelhouse greatly curtailed by plastic armour even the master himself stayed on the open bridge.

Before going on watch again that night Ginger advised me to ask to go down to the galley for a cup of tea in mid watch if the third mate neglected to tell me to do so. As nothing had been said by about five minutes past ten o'clock I walked across to the other wing of the bridge and asked the shadowy figure there if I could go down for a cup of tea.

"Tea?" exploded the captain, "Tea? There is nothing in the 'Articles' about tea in the middle of the night!"

My heart sank and, anticipating an entire four hours of cold without a break, decided that in future I would make very certain it was the officer of the watch I addressed on these occasions. However, the captain, having made his point, continued with, "Right Ho Laddie, off you go but mind you are no longer than ten minutes."

Comfort is always comparative and on cold, wet nights it was always a tremendous relief to go down to the warm snugness of the galley for that precious tea-break, (always known as a 'smoke' even by non-smokers), and, at the end of the watch, to crawl into one's bunk no matter how cold or damp it might be.

My watch was the 8 to 12 with the third mate. Also on watch on the bridge was the quartermaster on the wheel, one of the Indian seamen on lookout and a D.E.M.S. gunner. Much of the time at sea, particularly at night, the captain was there as well. When the slabs of plastic armour which covered the wheelhouse are taken into consideration plus a gun tub and oerlikon cannon in each wing, ammunition lockers and ready use flag lockers it will be appreciated that the bridge was quite congested.

One very distinct recollection I have of that first night as the convoy crept up the Scottish coast, eyes straining into the darkness and ears alert for the slightest indication of enemy E-Boats, aircraft or other forms of unpleasantness.

The gunner and I shared the lookout on the port wing of the bridge with the captain and third mate on the other. All was quiet until someone on the ship next to us in the convoy evidently opened a door allowing a momentary gleam of light to escape.

It was not much – but enough.

"Light on the port beam!!" I bawled at the top of my voice.

The effect on the tensed up nerves of those on the bridge, (and possibly the bridges of neighbouring ships), can well be imagined.

A little later, when things had settled down again, the gunner suggested that the correct mode of procedure should be to quietly cross to the other wing of the bridge and report anything I had seen to the officer of the watch.

****

The convoy duly arrived off Gourock and our ship proceeded to the anchorage at what I understood to be 'The Tail of the Bank' to await assembly of the deep sea convoy.

Our stay at the anchorage was enlivened by a strong and sudden gale which caused several ships to drag their anchors resulting in a few collisions and many near misses. However, I missed most of the excitement that night as no-one considered that my presence would have helped much in an emergency.

****

The 'Masirah' left the Clyde in convoy towards the middle of December bound for Algiers. Although, rather surprisingly, we encountered no enemy activity the passage was not without incident.

To confound the enemy the convoy was routed well to the west of the direct course to Gibraltar but even so the general consensus of opinion was that he could have achieved little if he had found us as the weather in the Western Ocean at the time was absolutely diabolical. Even the captain was heard to remark that it was the worst he had ever experienced. This I did not hear until later, at the time I thought the Cape Horn type weather was routine.

Our ship was fortunate, (or well handled?), inasmuch as she suffered little structural damage. In fact, all I recall was that one of the steel booby hatches to the crew accommodation in the poop was carried over the side. For all that there was plenty of discomfort. Very early on a great sea came on board amidships flooding out the starboard engineers' accommodation – which included the apprentices' cabin. I was in my bunk at the time and well remember watching the water pouring over the 18 inch storm step out of the room back Into the alleyway. My new fibre trunk and Ginger's white uniform shoes were never the same again. The effect of that flooding stayed with us for weeks as long after the room had dried out a trickle of water would run out from behind the wood sheathing whenever the ship rolled.

Other vessels were not so lucky. At the time I heard that several ships had actually foundered in that storm but have never had this verified. Certainly in our convoy ship after ship switched on her 'not under command' signal of two vertical red lights and fell away to heave to and ride out the storm as best they could on their own.

"Another couple of ships have left the convoy", reported Ginger as he handed over to me on the bridge at midnight, (I had been on the

12 to 4 watch since leaving the Clyde), his tone implying that the heavy weather was certainly sorting the sheep from the goats.

"Let me know if <u>we</u> put up two red lights", he laughed as he went down to the doubtful comfort of his bunk.

Before my watch was out we had done just that but either by good luck or good management we were still in sight of the commodore's ship when what passed for daylight filtered through in the morning.

The weather eventually eased and the 'convoy' arrived off the Straits of Gibraltar – sixteen ships of the original sixty-odd still with the commodore.

Our escorts as I remember consisted of a frigate and four corvettes, trawler-sized vessels which disappeared in clouds of spray on leaving the shelter of the land and reappeared off the Straits nearly two weeks later. Miserable as our experience had been theirs must have been ten times worse.

When the weather had moderated to a certain extent and the decks were not permanently filled with water the carpenter was able to get a good set of bilge surroundings. 'Chips' dropped his three foot steel rod down each surrounding pipe in turn and hauled it up on its line to check the amount of water in the bilge as indicated on the chalked end of the rod. All was well until he sounded number one hold bilges, Seven inches! He sent the rod whistling down a second time to check. Yes, certainly seven inches – but not water – high octane from the battered and leaking cans! From then on number one bilges were sounded very gingerly – and with a brass rod.

At quiet times attempts were made by the officers to teach us apprentices navigation and other technical accomplishments. Not with any great success at times so far as I was concerned I am afraid. One afternoon I recall out gentlemanly second mate setting his sextant so that I could see the planet Venus on it and getting quite annoyed in his own quiet fashion when I failed to observe it. No one was going to pull my leg to that extent. Seeing 'stars' in the middle of a sunny afternoon indeed! It was not until some time later that I discovered that 'crossing' Venus with the sun was quite a normal way of fixing a ship's position.

Another memory I have of that same officer concerned chart-room scrap paper. To avoid leaving a trail for U-Boats to follow rubbish was only thrown overboard at night. The contents of the chart-room waste paper box were taken a stage further and burnt in the galley fire in case a scrap of paper could contain 'information useful to an enemy'. As the 8 to 12 watch apprentice at the time of this story it was one of my duties to get this done when I came off watch. A simple enough operation in itself, the problem was at midnight, with more pressing things on my mind, such as my bunk for instance, to remember to do it every night.

At two o'clock one cold, raw morning a somewhat bewildered Ginger awakened me out of a deep sleep with the information that the second mate wanted to see me on the bridge. I climbed out of my warm bunk and donning coat and seaboots, (we slept virtually fully clothed in those days), stepped out into the wet and windy weather and followed Ginger to the bridge.

The second mate greeted me on arrival with a very civil,

"Please be good enough to empty the waste-paper box in the galley fire."

I never ever forgot to do that job again.

Other memories I have of those early days include my

introduction to 'Dhobi', the almost universal word for clothes washing. Apparently I stayed clean enough to remain healthy but it must have been touch and go at times. Most people seemed to have little trouble with their laundry but my efforts rarely met with success. Once in desperation I tried using homemade soap-flakes as rubbing with soap in almost stone cold water proved quite ineffective. The flakes were slivers of carbolic soap but in spite of soaking the washing overnight the flakes did not even dissolve so when eventually dry I had to pry little orange-coloured splinters of soap out of my underwear. The actual washing system must have improved by the time I washed my two working shirts. The snag this time was the drying. I had firmly secured them to a line outside our room before going on watch but in coming down four hours later found that although perfectly dry the brisk gale blowing at the time had frayed an inch or two off the shirt tails.

Polishing brass was another thing I was never really good at. There was a considerable amount of brass in the wheelhouse and chartroom of a ship at that time, even the chart drawer handles, (of the 'beer can opener' type), were of brass, all of which had to be brought up to a satisfactory shine – and woe betide the apprentice who left even a trace of 'Brasso' on the chart dividers which could be transferred to a chart! I well remember, after slogging away half the morning on the job, hearing the mate say wearily, "Baxter's usual nice green shine. Do it all again before you go down for your dinner."

We passed through the Straits of Gibraltar at night so I saw little of the legendary Rock on that occasion. Although I stayed on deck a good hour after coming off watch my only reward was the sight of the light on Europa Point.

Our captain was not the sweetest tempered of men and one thing, among many others, which caused him constant annoyance was the commodore's habit of setting the convoy's speed then shortly afterwards reducing the speed of his own ship, and thus the rest of the convoy, in order to allow the slower ships to keep up. They straggled anyway.

The convoy's position had been ascertained at noon one day and the course speed for the afternoon signalled by the commodore in the usual manner.

"Right," said the captain to the second mate, "Six and a half knots. I am going to get my head down for an hour or two. Keep the ship on the revolutions for six and a half knots and do not alter them until I return to the bridge."

The second mate spent much of the afternoon on the signal lamp attempting to pacify an irate commodore and, later in the watch, inquisitive escort vessels when we got among them.

Apparently all was forgiven as, a few days later, (we did not exactly flit from place to place at five or six knots), our ship was appointed to lead our section of the convoy to Algiers as the commodore with the remainder of the ships continued on to Bone further along the coast.

Later in the war, during the Normandy landings, the same captain made the news with another brush with authority. Already frustrated by ships ahead of him being stopped by a Naval Launch in the London River on their return from the beaches he was absolutely furious when his turn came and a young naval officer with a loud hailer had the temerity to call up and ask what stores and fresh water he required when he got to Tilbury.

The answer was a wrathful, "I do not discuss business with ships' chandlers on the high seas!" as he slammed the engine-room telegraph onto 'Full Ahead'.

Shortly before our arrival there we heard that Admiral Darlan had been assassinated and Algiers, starting to settle down after the Allied invasion the previous month, was once more suffering a 'tense situation'. However, we were unaffected by the local politics and berthed in due order on December 26th.

Although I remember a discussion a few days earlier regarding Christmas Day and whether it should be celebrated on the 25th. at sea or on Boxing Day after we berthed I cannot recall, in spite of my apparent preoccupation with food, the final outcome.

As we approached the entrance to Algiers harbour a plane crashed into the sea right ahead of the ship. I was on the after deck at the time and all I eventually saw was a patch of blazing fuel on the water. The tragedy must have been the result of an accident as it was said to have been an allied aircraft.

Chapter 3

The strong warm sunshine and 'Foreign Legion' atmosphere of Algiers was in sharp contrast to the winter drabness wartime England. Being my first foreign port I was of course fascinated by the exotic surroundings. Particularly interesting were the occasional walks some of us participated in through the Old Casbah – made the more enjoyable no doubt by the fact that the area was strictly out of bounds to service personnel.

Although Algiers was naturally short of imported luxuries there seemed to be plenty of local produce available, in fact the export of such items as dates and tangerines must have just about come to a standstill resulting in a glut and prices that even apprentices could afford.

By and large I think I was too young to fully appreciate the delights of Algiers although I had a pleasant enough time there. Reports of such establishments as the 'Sphinx' and 'Black Cat' and an entertainment known colloquially as the 'Exhibish' indicated that they were not suitable diversions for one of my tender years. I have it on good authority that one case-hardened second engineer visited the last named amusement and was so disgusted that he said it put him off women for very nearly twenty minutes.

That first time in Algiers the enemy left us entirely alone so far as I recall although of course every aspect indicated that the war was still very much in progress.

Often I was detailed to run errands ashore, no doubt because my two mates had managed to duck out of them. Once I had to take a message to the agents, who went by the imposing title of 'Worms and Co.', I seem to recall. The mate handed me over to an Army officer connected with the cargo who tossed me a bunch of car keys and pointed out which vehicle I could borrow. To my shame I had to admit that I could not drive – in fact apart from the odd taxi ride I doubt if I had been in a private car more than half a dozen times in my life.

On another occasion I was given the job of taking a sick member of the Indian crew to see an Army doctor. Having arrived at the clinic I found the man spoke no English and as neither the doctor or I could understand Bengali communication was never established with the patient. The M.O. tactfully suggested I took the man back and returned with an interpreter. This however did not become necessary as on arriving back on board the ship I discovered that other arrangements had already been put in hand as I had taken the wrong man to the doctor.

Across the harbour from our berth was the submarine depot ship H.M.S.'Maidstone' so we became quite familiar with the arrivals and departures of her brood of submarines. One I remember arriving with her conning tower very battered and a periscope trailing over her side. However, her 'Jolly Roger' was proudly fluttering over the wreckage so the enemy could not have had everything his own way. The 'Thunderbolt', (ex-'Thetis'), was one of the submarines there and I believe it was from Algiers that she sailed on her last voyage.

Some of us occasionally walked along the breakwater and talked to the submariners. One of our quartermasters was ex-R.N. so 'spoke the lingo'. He once took me on board one of the motor gunboats as he was acquainted with one of her crew.

Another vessel of interest close by was a destroyer, possibly H.M.S.'Oakley'. She had apparently been much damaged by a near miss of sorts as her hull and upperworks were absolutely riddled with small splinter holes. She had no crew on board and I remember how bare and empty were her mess decks when I peered through a porthole. No doubt this was in contrast to the remainder of her machinery crowded hull.

The 'Masirah' made three voyages to Algiers so we became quite familiar with the local naval vessels.

Our cargo was discharged onto the open quay and I was utterly amazed at the amount we had in our holds. The stacks of crates and drums, vehicles and loose cargo seemed sufficient to fill three vessels of our size.

Life was relatively cheap in those days and little fuss was made at the deaths of the two men whilst we were discharging. One was knocked over the side by a sling of cargo into the harbour and failed to re-surface. The other was even more unfortunate. It would appear that one of the Gurkha soldiers guarding the cargo on the quay near the stern of the ship noticed an Arab labourer pilfering cargo from a case near the bow. In a burst of enthusiasm the guard fired at the thief only to have his bullet intercepted by the head of a perfectly innocent workman who stood up suddenly between them.

Apparently in the early days after the invasion of North Africa officers of merchant ships were issued with revolvers for security purposes. The story goes that this practice was stopped when a near catastrophe occurred. Apparently a cadet on one ship noticed a labourer in the ship's hold just about to light up a cigarette whilst sitting on a stow of cases of high octane petrol. Knowing no Arabic with which to admonish the offender the lad did the next best thing and took a shot at the man with his revolver. Fortunately, the bullet hit the man rather than the cargo but it was enough to cause the authorities to reassess their priorities as regards safety.

With our cargo discharged we left Algiers early in January for home. The passage to Newport, Monmouthshire, must have been relatively uneventful as one of my few recollections of it was the use of the deep-sea sounding machine on the run up the Bristol Channel. Having dropped the thirty pound lead and its sounding tube to the bottom we apprentices had the job of winding its few hundred fathoms of piano wire back onto its drum - by hand. The 'Old Man' did not put a great deal of trust in our 'new-fangled' echo-sounder.

The ship paid off on January 22nd. 1943 and as it had been such a short voyage the head office decided that to avoid having to send reliefs to the ship half the officers could go on leave for a week or so and, on their return, the other half. Owing to a slight breakdown of communications all three of us apprentices were sent on leave with the first contingent and were very fortunately forgotten until the recall of the second so we received twice as much leave as anyone else on the ship.

Travelling by rail at night in wartime was an unforgettable experience and I remember arriving home very, very tired and dirty.

******

In the fullness of time I was instructed to re-join the 'Masirah' at Newport.

There had been one or two changes of personnel since I had been away. These included the captain and the third officer but on the whole we were the same crowd.

Although still the junior apprentice my status had altered slightly for the better. I was no longer a contemptable 'first tripper'. Not much of a promotion but it made all the difference to be able to toss into the conversation a casual, 'last trip such-and-such a thing happened' and the like.

Our berth at Newport was No.8 Transit Shed as I remember. It was about 'the first berth on the right' as one came in from the river and a very, very long way from the dock gate. There was a bus service but this was for factory workers only, seafarers had to make their own arrangements.

It seemed to rain most of the time we were at Newport and one memory I have of a very wet evening was going ashore with several people from the ship ostensively to go to a cinema. At least that was my understanding. The party stopped for 'a quick ale' at an establishment named, I believe, 'The Crossed Keys'. Everyone went in except myself as apprentices were expressly forbidden 'to frequent Alehouses and Taverns except on Company's business' as stated on one's indentures and I did not want my career nipped in the bud by a confrontation with the mate in such a place. I have often wondered since what exactly constituted 'frequent' and what 'Company's business' was likely to be conducted in an alehouse. Possibly the owners had in mind the possibility of a squad of sturdy apprentices armed with stout cudgels and leg-irons entering such establishments to round up the crew on sailing day. But that is by the by.

I stood outside the pub in rain and darkness until some kind soul came out to suggest that I joined the party as they had met some friends and intended having another drink. I chose to remain outside but asked the messenger to remind the others that the film programme was due to start shortly.

The touching scene was repeated some time later when my return message contained a certain amount of urgency in as much that if we did not move at once we would miss the big picture.

On the third occasion I reluctantly allowed myself to be drawn into the building as apart from the fact that we had missed the film the chances of the mate dropping in so long after opening time was pretty remote.

I was welcomed warmly enough.

"What will you have?" asked a friendly quartermaster.

"A lemonade please."

"Christ!" hissed a voice in my ear, "keep your voice down if you are going to say things like that. You could get a knife in your back."

I do not think I was convinced of this although the atmosphere certainly lent itself to such a suggestion. A dimly lit room solid with tobacco smoke and bodies, both sea-faring and local. There was even sawdust on the floor.

Translating the remark to mean that lemonade was not available in such a bar, which hardly seemed surprising, I was rather at a loss.

The friendly quartermaster came to my rescue.

"Have a shandy?"

It was the first time I had heard the word but being reluctant to admit my ignorance I took it on trust.

"What do you think of it?" I was asked as I sipped the brew.

"Fine," I replied, adding in all innocence, "but I am certain I can taste lemonade in it."

There was, I suppose, a laugh.

"Try one without the lemonade?"

I did. My very first step on the road to ruin.

It must have been on a subsequent visit to the 'Crossed Keys' that we met 'Jim'. Jim had been a quartermaster on the 'Masirah' some time earlier and was known to 'Blondie', our senior apprentice – who, for his sins, had served all of his time so far on the old ship. Jim was now bosun of the 'Empire Standard' and we gathered, no doubt in whispers, that she would be sailing in our convoy to North Africa.

The military cargo we loaded at Newport included several Bofors anti-aircraft guns and I understand it was the mate's idea to have one of them lashed to the foc'sle head rather than stow them all down a hold.

Beneath the foc'sle head was some pretty spartan spare accommodation. This was occasionally occupied by military personnel in transit – one hesitates to term them 'passengers'. In fact, on my first voyage it was utilised by soldiers on the outward passage but the weather was so vile I can remember seeing them only once. However, on the present occasion the squad of soldiers quartered there happened to be, either by accident or design, ack-ack gunners. Of whom more later.

In due course we left Newport for the Clyde where we joined the ships assembling there.

The convoy left 'The Tail of the Bank' on February 26th. and was soon plugging away into the North Atlantic rollers.

Although I started my first voyage on the 8 to 12 watch I spent most of my stay on the ship on the 12 to 4 watch with the second mate. The mate kept the 4 to 8 watch and the third mate the 8 to 12. This was generally the arrangement on British ships.

The fact that second mates, and, for that matter, third engineers, could spend months on end and years of their lives with never more than four hours sleep at a stretch at sea, (second mates used to get up for breakfast and to take a longitude sight in those days), no doubt impressed their mothers and girlfriends. I read somewhere many years ago that some professor had made a study of sleep and had evolved the theory that the first few hours on going to sleep were by far the most beneficial therefore the best possible arrangement was to sleep for about four hours, find something to occupy oneself with for the next four hours then go back to bed for the second half of the night's repose. I wonder if he ever tried it for any length of time?

Having the middle watch meant that second mates and third engineers had to adjust their sleeping habits to their unsociable hours but for all that they were renowned for being crotchety and difficult to awaken to go on watch at midnight. A story, told to me as true shortly after the war, concerned a third engineer who was notoriously difficult to get on watch. He would stagger down to the engine room night after night invariably complaining that he had not been called.

One dark night the ship was torpedoed and, as she appeared to be sinking, was abandoned. The lifeboats kept together and as soon as it was possible a count of heads was made. Surprisingly only one man was missing, the third engineer.

"Poor old Third," said someone, "however if it is any consolation he probably never knew what happened, the torpedo must have exploded right under his room."

Came the dawn and as the ship was still afloat the lifeboats started rowing back in the hope of reboarding and saving her.

On closing the ship, the survivors were surprised to see a figure wearing nothing but a towel storming up and down the boat deck waving his fist at them.

Soon they could also hear him.

"You bastards! You bastards! You might have called me!"

****

The weather improved as we got further south and on the nice sunny afternoon of March 4th. when we were somewhere west of Portugal the enemy began to take an interest in us. Three Foke-Wulf Condors found the convoy and, after circling around for some time, (no doubt spreading the good word to their friends the while by radio), flew over the convoy in a perfect 'Vic' formation and proceeded to drop bombs on us.

The planes were said to be at about five or six thousand feet and the bombs they dropped must have been fairly large as one landed between us and our next abeam causing an absolute mountain of water and smoke to leap skywards.

The anti-aircraft fire put up by the ships was absolutely tremendous, the puffs of smoke from exploding shells blackening the sky. If it was true that merchant ships' ammunition was set to explode at two thousand feet, (merchant seaman not being expected to spare the time to set fuses even if they could guess the altitude of attacking aircraft), the flak would not have worried the Germans much but they could hardly have helped being very impressed. Our Bofors gun put up a fine performance and was said to have caused one plane to break formation but at that altitude this could only have been wishful thinking.

My action station was cartridge number of the 12 pounder on the poop. My excitement was acute although everyone else seemed to be taking the situation calmly enough.

Orders were shouted above the continuous banging of guns and the occasional whistle and explosion of bombs. The carpenter slammed the first round into the breech with his gauntleted fist, the brass cartridge followed it, the breech clanged shut, the trainer's "On! On! On!" the order to 'Shoot!', the quartermaster's hand slapping the trigger plate and 'Bang!' the first round was on its way.

A split second later the shell exploded, its smoke completely obliterating the distant enemy formation.

"Good shot Dick!" I shouted to the gunner, beside myself with excitement.

A moment later I realised that something was wrong – and whatever it was seemed to have to do with me.

It had! The second cartridge, which I should have passed to the loader, was clasped to my bosom in a bear-hug – completely forgotten in the heat of the moment. From then on I kept my mind on the job in hand.

Having off-loaded the Condors headed for home with, so far as I know, no damage done to either side.

The trio of planes returned in the evening for a repeat performance. Once again they circled the convoy for what appeared to me to be an unnecessarily long time before coming in on their bombing run out of the sun. At least they approached from the west where the sun had just set so far as we at sea level were concerned. Perhaps it was still visible at the aircrafts' altitude and the pilots' thought Its glare would be in our eyes as they attacked? Whatever the intention the result was the same – neither side hit anything.

To this day I have a Bofors cartridge case as a souvenir of the occasion.

****

Two days after the air attacks, in the early afternoon, the 'Fort Battle River' and another vessel were torpedoed in the middle of the convoy. Neither sank or did anything else dramatic whist I was watching them – which was not for long as I was chased over to the other wing of the bridge to keep a lookout from there. I did see something too! About a ship's length off the starboard bow a whale suddenly surfaced – no doubt the poor thing had been frightened out of its wits by the depth-charging which was then going on. In fact, we ourselves had worries on this score as an escort, I think it was one of the old ex-American destroyers, came tearing up between the columns of ships with ferocious looking seaman huddled over rows of lethal-looking depth-charges.

Fortunately, it was not until she was well ahead of the convoy that she started tossing them over the side.

****

The next excitement was off the Algerian coast near Cape Tenez on March 9th.

Off watch I was talking to a couple of quartermasters in their room that evening. The 'boom-clunk', 'boom-clunk' sound of depth charges had been going on so long it had lost its urgency, like a distant thunderstorm.

'Boom-clunk', 'boom-clunk', 'boom-clunk' then, suddenly, 'BOOM-CLANG!' – an entirely different sound. We were on deck in an instant in time to see the 'Empire Standard' on our starboard quarter emerging from a cloud of smoke and spray. A glance astern showed the next ship, the 'Fort Norman', rolling back to starboard after being hit. Our alarm bells were ringing and we were soon on action stations.

My war was getting serious.

The 'Fort Norman' was briefly abandoned and later re-boarded. Although badly damaged she managed to reach Algiers.

The 'Empire Standard' had taken her torpedo in the port side of number 2 hold which caused a hole the size of a double-decker bus. The explosion had blasted her over to starboard and on her return roll to port several vehicles ran out of her tween deck and into the sea. Each time she rolled to port more bren-gun carriers and lorries plopped into the ocean as we could clearly see. A piece of her side plating had landed on her whistle lanyards resulting in the activity to save the ship being carried out to the accompanying deafening scream of the steam whistle.

The stricken vessel hauled away from the convoy and headed for the land several miles away in order to beach – if she got that far.

The 'Fort Norman' had been torpedoed in the starboard side indicating that the U-Boat responsible had been lying athwart the convoy's course waiting for two ships to come into line in order to fire at them with both her bow and stern tubes simultaneously. We decided that if the 'Masirah' had been exactly in station instead of slightly ahead of it as she was, (our old reciprocating engine was difficult to adjust to exact revolutions), we could easily have been one of the targets. One or two people on the ship thought they saw the U-Boat's periscope.

There were no further attacks and we continued on our way at the usual convoy speed of about six knots to arrive off Algiers the following day.

We were pleasantly surprised to find riding at anchor off the port the 'Empire Standard'. It would appear that despite the gaping hole in her side she had steamed to Algiers at nine knots, arriving some time before the remainder of the convoy.

Unhappily I believe neither she nor the 'Fort Norman' ever left Algiers as they were further damaged in air attacks on the port.

Chapter 4

Our stay at Algiers was more or less a repetition of the previous occasion. The ship even occupied much the same berth.

On our first visit there existed a conspicuous column on a hill above the city, a monument commemorating Napoleon I believe. This was said to be used by German aircraft as a marker when they swept in from the desert to drop down over the hills and bomb the port. It was not there on our second voyage having apparently been demolished by the British, no doubt much to their satisfaction and the chagrin of the French.

The ship left Algiers on March 20th and arrived once more in Newport on April 5th. The passage home however was not without incident.

One evening the commodore made a signal to the convoy to make an emergency alteration of course of ninety degrees. This was quite a normal practice when U-Boats were reported to by lying in ambush ahead of the convoy or in order to shake off those shadowing it. However, on this occasion the rumour was that six German 'Marvik' class destroyers were on their way to intercept us. Possibly there was no truth in this but the rumour was certainly original.

I think it was on this passage somewhere west of the Bay of Biscay that one night a U-Boat was attacked by an Escort Group to the east of the convoy. Our ship was vice commodore at the time so we carried a few specialist R.N. ratings. These included at least one radio rating with, something new to me, an early type of radio-telephone.

Fortunately, I was on watch at the time of the incident so was privileged not only to see but to have a running commentary of the battle as it developed just a few miles away. The star shells illuminating the horizon and the sound of exploding depth charges was complemented by the voices of the men actually in the action. 'Codseye' was, I believe, the radio code name of the senior officer.

The U-Boat was brought to the surface and dispatched whilst the lights and flares were still plainly visible.

Apart from these incidents I think the passage was relatively uneventful.

The ship remained in Newport for over three weeks in the course of which I went home on leave for nine days or so. On my return to the vessel, at the same No.8 Transit Shed, I discovered I was to go on a week's gunnery course at Cardiff, starting the very next day.

The following morning I stood by the road at the back of the shed hoping to thumb a lift to the gate on a passing lorry. Needless to say it was raining.

However, my luck was in. The first vehicle to note my plight was a large black Humber saloon. It stopped beside me and the driver leaner across the front seat and asked if I would like a lift to the dock gate. The driver incidentally was a very glamorous Wren in her late twenties. Almost old enough to be my mother.

While passing through the docks the Wren asked if I was going into the town and on being informed that I was on my way to the railway station said she would drop me off there as she was going right past it. I think she guessed I was on my way to a gunnery course and having this confirmed, ('Careless talk' and all that but I did not think that my brushing up on my machine-gun knowledge would affect the progress of the war much one way or another), said she would give me a lift back to the ship as she would be returning to the docks at about the time the train from Cardiff was due to arrive.

The shiny Humber purred to a stop at the station with me thanking the young lady profusely. At that time I was unfamiliar with the mechanisms of motor cars, (I still have trouble with mechanical gadgets), and my efforts to open the door in order to alight met with little success. I think I wound the window up and down a couple of times and locked myself in before I was rescued by the Wren who nipped around the car and opened it for me. A somewhat ruffled Merchant Navy apprentice stepped out on to the pavement – much to the consternation of a hoard of R.N. ratings pouring down the station steps, they apparently having just alighted from a train.

True to her word the Wren was there with her official car when I returned to Newport in the evening. In fact, I was transported to and from the station each day of the gunnery course, which, I believe, lasted four and a half days. I could hardly believe my good fortune and am certain that no one on the ship believed my story.

However, there was an ulterior motive. On my last ride back to the ship the young lady asked me if a certain Mr. ..... was still on the ship and if so to convey to him the message 'that Muriel, (or whatever her name was), was still in town.'

The gunnery course was both interesting and enjoyable. It included such novelties, (to me at least), as the 'Dome', a realistic film arrangement with the student, equipped with a oerlikon gun which fired a beam of light in lieu of shells, trying to hit filmed images of attacking aircraft. There was also a sleeve target towed by an aeroplane to shoot at. One should have been available at Leith on my previous course but the towing plane had been shot down the week before. I wonder who ever volunteered to pilot the aircraft?

We left Newport towards the end of April and proceeded to Milford Haven to join a convoy assembling there.

It had been decreed that on leaving Milford anchorage the ships of the convoy should have a little 'main armament' practice and a target buoy had allocated for this purpose. Each vessel as she passed fired two or three rounds of solid shot at the buoy. The 'Masirah' was towards the tail end of the procession of ships and when our turn came there was no target to shoot at so we fired our rounds at the churned up water of earlier splashes. Apparently a secondary target had not been considered as no one expected a merchant ship to hit the buoy. However, tame as it was the incident still held considerable interest for me.

The 'Masirah's armament had been accumulated during the

course of the war and by the time I sailed on her she had quite a collection of guns.

On each wing of the bridge was a modern 20mm Oerlikon cannon with two more at the after end of the boat deck. On the after end of the bridge structure were two pairs of Marlin machine guns and on the poop a 4.7 inch gun. Forward and above this was the 12 pounder dual purpose gun. On top of the wheelhouse were a few parachute and cable rockets which were fired by lanyard from the wheelhouse. These last were intended for the discomfiture of low flying enemy aircraft. The Bofors gun of the previous voyage had been discharged at Algiers with the rest of the cargo.

The 4.7 was the weapon tested off Milford Haven. It had been manufactured during the First World War and had apparently spent most of its existence in a training establishment as the paint of the yellow band around is barrel was about an eighth of an inch thick. This band had, of course, been painted out with grey paint to match the rest of the gun now it was back on active service. However constant handling and 'stripping down' had obviously worn its several parts. This was more than apparent when the piece was actually fired.

The breech-block of the gun was of the 'interrupted thread' variety, the hinged block being swung into place by a lever which, through a simple mechanism, also turned the block sufficiently to lock it in place. After the gun was fired the lever was swung back thus turning and releasing the breech-block which allowed the empty cartridge case to be ejected and leave the gun ready for the next round.

At least that was the theory. In practice however, with the various parts of our gun being so slack a fit, on firing the sheet of flame from the breech equalled that from the muzzle and the shock of the explosion flung the breech lever back which in turn unlocked the breech allowing the cartridge case to shoot out as a projectile in its own right. Some wit termed the weapon 'semi-automatic'. Needless to say no one stood near this end when the gun was fired. Nobody <u>could</u> stand near the business end as this overhung the ship's side by a good six feet. This was just as well as once or twice the ancient cartridges failed to explode properly resulting in the shell just managing to make it out of the muzzle and plop into the sea. We never had occasion to fire live ammunition, apart from solid practice shot, whilst I was on the ship which was no doubt as well as a dud cartridge and an active high-explosive shell could have proved a lethal combination. For all that the gun was a comfort to us and would no doubt have given a good account of itself had it been needed. On the Milford occasion the only damage it caused was to our own vessel as the blast of the test firing broke every mirror in the crew accommodation in the poop and brought the wood sheathing of the Indian bosun's room down about his ears.

Fire and boat drills were exercised at regular intervals as well as action stations. At this distance in time I cannot remember what my fire station was, no doubt a messenger or in charge of a fire extinguisher. I am certain it was nothing interesting such as handling a fire hose nozzle or I would remember it. However, I do remember that my particular duty on boat stations was to first ensure that the drain plug was in position in the bottom of the boat and then to stand by with an axe in order to cut the boat clear if, at a critical moment, the rope falls or painter jammed. I was also of the impression that I had to defend the boat in the event of the crew panicking and attempting to rush it. Fortunately, my expertise with an axe was never called to test on either count.

****

The 'Masirah' proceeded to Algiers for the third and final time. Although The Battle of the Atlantic reached a climax at about this time we experienced only the usual alarms. The main action was further to the west.

The convoy made an impressive picture as each ship shouldered her way through the seas, slowly, relentlessly, magnificently. From a position near the centre of the front rank of the convoy the rows of ships stretched out over a mile on either side and in any kind of reduced visibility they seemed to reach out for ever, a powerful Allied force which the Axis might damage, might dent but could never, ever stop. If I ever had any doubts of our ultimate success in the conflict they were more than dispelled by those inexorable ships.

On entering the Mediterranean we unpacked and inflated one of our barrage balloons. It turned out to be quite an entertaining afternoon. A combined effort by the gunners and apprentices, supervised by the mate, managed to inflate the balloon on No.4 hatch – after nearly suffocating the junior apprentice in its folds. This lad was a first tripper sent to make up our numbers as 'Blondie' had gone to college to study for his second mate's certificate.

The idea was to allow the balloon to slowly rise until its weight, (if that is the correct term), was taken on its mooring wire which was led from a winch through a lead at the mainmast head. Several men laid hold of the guy ropes attached to the balloon but as soon as it left the deck it took charge and headed towards the heavens. One of the gunners was lifted a good three feet from the hatch before he had the wit to let go. The wire snapped like a thread and the balloon continued its ascent until it burst in the rarefied air thousands of feet above the ship.

"Just square up and that will do," said our philosophical mate.

****

The afternoon of the day before we arrived at Algiers was spent by several vessels taking up new positions in the convoy so that the starboard columns could peel off cleanly for Algiers whilst the remaining ships continued to the eastward.

The leading ships of each of the wing columns were C.A.M. vessels, ordinary merchant ships fitted with a Hurricane fighter on a catapult over the bows. Such vessels were a makeshift defence against enemy aircraft, particularly shadowing planes, until escort carriers became available. As it so happened the vessel on the port wing column, the s.s.'Empire Annie', was destined for Algiers and the other, on the starboard wing, for further along the coast. It was a long manoeuvre for these two vessels to haul out of station, drop astern of the convoy, cross over and then steam up to the head of their respective columns. It was therefore evening before they reached their new positions.

Once again the convoy was off Cape Tenez at sunset – even the weather was similar to that previous occasion when the two ships next to us were torpedoed.

The 'Masirah' was leading ship of the next to starboard column so we had a good view of the C.A.M. ship as she drew abeam of us.

She was just lining up with our ship when she and her next astern were struck by torpedoes.

The blow the 'Empire Annie' sustained was mortal. She caught fire and slowly sank by the stern. Her bow eventually rose vertically in the air and the last we saw was her bow and Hurricane aircraft sliding below the surface of the sea. Even then she left a trace – her barrage balloon slowly descending after her.

There was no further excitement prior to our arrival at Algiers the following morning, May 20th.

After discharging our cargo we bunkered at Algiers. I think this was because the original intention was for the vessel to make the long voyage to the U.S.A. or Canada but in the event this was changed.

In the present age ships bunker with as little fuss and mess as a car at a petrol pump, the fuel itself, unless someone gets his valves mixed, not even being seen. In the days of coal it was an entirely different matter, the ship concerned disappearing in a black cloud of coal dust for a day or more. The dust penetrated everywhere with particularly disastrous results for anyone who had neglected to screw down hard his cabin port or ventilator. Even with everything secured a thin film of dust accumulated on every surface. With no ventilation the heat was terrible in the tropics so anyone who's duties did not keep him on board did his best to spend the day ashore. Most shipmasters would find bunkering day an excellent time to indulge in a very long lunch with the agent.

There were various methods of coaling. For Port Said eastwards the coal was generally brought alongside in barges. Flanks were rigged against the ship's side like so many hanging bookshelves and on these perched men who passed up baskets of coal, one to another, from the barges to the ship's bunker hatches.

Should the coal be more conveniently on a dockside pairs of long heavy planks would be set up from the quay to the ship's deck. A constant stream of men, and often enough women too, with baskets of coal on their heads would pass up a plank from the wharf and, after dumping the basket's contents down the hatch, walk down another plank to exchange the empty for a full basket. Provided the rhythm was not interrupted they could keep it up for hours at a stretch. All very labour-intensive but it filled many a rice bowl.

The usual method adopted in western coal-producing countries was for the coal to arrive at a port in railway wagons. The coal from each wagon was tipped down a chute into the ship. Most of the stuff went down the hatches, the residue being shovelled down from the deck later. On completion the thick black dust was hosed off the ship – with a man wielding a broom keeping the scuppers clear.

At Algiers on the occasion in question the coal was put on board by a large crane equipped with a grab. Owing to the funnel and rigging in the vicinity of the bunker hatches – or the lack of skill on the part of the crane driver – each grab load of coal was loosed in the general direction of the hatches from a height of thirty or forty feet.

The apprentices room being only a few feet from the bunker hatches, it was soon submerged under black diamonds. At the end of the day we had to dig our way to the door.

Whereas bunkering was but an occasional activity the disposal of ashes was not. Steam was the only source of power on the ship so ashes were drawn from the boiler furnaces at frequent intervals.

Large tubs of these ashes were brought up the ash hoist, generally situated in one of the boiler room ventilator shafts, and poured down a large tubular ash-chute into the sea – and often enough over the mate's clean paintwork. As this was impractical in port the ashes were accumulated on deck until they could be dumped at sea. An exception was the last day or two at sea prior to arriving at the Suez Canal when ashes were retained as many a canny chief engineer found that this was one of the few places in the world where they would fetch a price. In other ports the ashes were piled handy to the ash-chute, which, needless to say, was close to the apprentices' room. As this was just outside the galley door its ashes were also dumped there – along with a fair amount of other refuse. After a week of two in port in warm weather the heap became 'high' in more ways than one.

Chapter 5

Just before we left Algiers we experienced an air-raid. At least there were the trappings of one.

The alarm bells rang and we dashed to action stations when a plane arrived over the port. Nothing could be seen in the darkness of the night but its engines could be heard plainly enough.

On the strength of my four and a half gunnery course I was

appointed to a pair of Marlin machine guns situated on top of the bridge structure. In steel helmet and life-jacket I prepared myself to blast the Luftwaffe out of the sky. In retrospect I think I was appointed to these guns as they were generally considered to be of little value so far as destroying enemy aircraft was concerned. In fact, they were thought to be more of a menace to our own side. My information was that they had been designed during the First World War for use by aircraft and were thus small and light with a very rapid rate of fire. Their disadvantages were that they were rather too delicate for use at sea and they could not be conveniently fitted with safety catches. It was also necessary to cock them three times to ensure that a round had arrived 'up the spout' and similarly de-cocked at least the same number of times to make sure no rounds were left in the pipe-line – a precaution sometimes neglected with dire results.

Light guns on merchant ships were normally covered at night to save them from the dew, (in any case firing them at night would do little other than disclose the ship's position), and this sometimes led to a flapping cover triggering off a Marlin. It was rather disconcerting to be treated to a pyrotechnic display in the middle of a dark night in convoy as a machine gun sprayed the air with tracer.

"Ah!" the officer of the watch would say with all the wisdom of experience, "I see that fellow has Marlins too."

Disappointingly on that night I had no opportunity to test my skill. In fact, after a while it was assumed that the plane was 'one of ours' looking for a place to put his wheels down.

If not exactly dangerous the occasion certainly proved picturesque as the balloons of several ships at the anchorage were shot down in flames by trigger-happy Americans. Ours was only punctured and descended onto the water to resemble a dead whale. I believe we were supplied with a replacement before we left the port which we no doubt lost in the first capful of wind at sea as I have no recollection of ever retrieving one to be deflated and stored for future use.

The 'flak' was certainly quite considerable and very colourful. The tracers seemed to curve through the air in slow motion and, on the odd occasion they came close enough, the shells and bullets went 'plop' 'plop' 'plop' as they hit the water – followed by 'bang' 'bang' 'bang' as they crossed the ship. However, our damages and casualties were light. The small anti-aircraft shells and bullets did no damage to the decks and as all the wooden hatch covers were sheathed with steel plates as a defence against incendiary bombs these were only dented although their canvas covers received a few holes.

Our only casualty was one of the Indian seaman who received a few small shell splinters in his rump. According to Ginger, who was of the first aid party, the man suffered his injuries stoically enough at first, it was not until the iodine was applied that he really shrieked.

I think it was on this visit that a ship further along the quay completed discharging and proceeded to the anchorage to await her convoy to America. Some hours later she returned to her berth, which seemed rather odd at the time. As our ship left shortly after she re-berthed I cannot vouch for the truth of the story that not long after she had left her berth it was discovered that the latest word in captured German Tiger tanks, destined for expert examination in the U.K., had disappeared from the quay. Apparently the enterprising crew had literally 'lifted' the 50 odd ton tank with their heavy derrick during the night in the hope of getting a good price for it in the States.

With the fighting in North Africa drawing to a successful conclusion the talk was of the next campaign. This was quite generally known in Algiers to be the invasion of Sicily and it seems extraordinary to me that the enemy were not aware of the fact. There was no mention of defence now, the period of 'holding out' was over and the prevailing mood was to attack and attack again. In fact, I appeared to have gone to sea just as we started winning. Pure coincidence of course.

The convoy left Algiers in due order but ran into thick fog before reaching Gibraltar – a nerve-racking experience for masters and watch-keeping officers. The ships had fog-buoys streamed, contrivances of crossed planks which, when towed through the water, created quite a considerable spray for their size. The principle was that the lookout in the bow kept the buoy of the ship ahead in view and the bridge informed of its whereabouts but often enough he lost track of it and it was next observed alongside the bridge – indicating that the ship ahead was dangerously close. The automatic reaction in such a situation was to stop or drastically slow the ship's engines but what always had to be kept in mind was the fact that four or five ships directly astern were following the same procedure, never mind the remainder of the convoy.

At one stage the second officer sent me down to the forward well deck to find out if the ship next to us was visible underneath the fog but even this close to the waterline I could only just make out the surface of the sea.

Fortunately, although extremely thick, the fog was not widespread and we could soon make out the vague shapes of the ships near us. Ironically enough at night it was the dark shadows in a ship's superstructure which were observed first, long before the light grey hulls could be distinguished. I recall a few frights in this respect at various times when I discovered that what I assumed to be the dim grey shape of the ship abeam at her correct distance turned out to be, in the increasing light of dawn, shadows below her boat deck and the ship much closer than originally thought.

Most of the empty ships carried on to America but some of us anchored at Gibraltar to await the U.K. bound convoy.

The crowded anchorage included the hulls of numerous old sailing vessels ending their days as coal-hulks and also one of our

Company's old ships which had been severely damaged by an Italian limpet mine some months earlier. The explosion did not end her career as she survived many years after the incident, in fact she was the first ship I joined on promotion to chief officer when she was thirty-seven years old.

One of the first jobs on arrival at Gibraltar anchorage was to rig an apron of dangling length of barbed wire right around the ship as a deterrent to enemy swimmers and their infernal machines. Other arrangements for their discomfiture were patrolling launches which dropped small depth-charges at frequent intervals and ships' gunners who took pot-shots with rifles at anything that floated.

Our passage to England passed without serious incident and, after visiting Falmouth briefly, the ship eventually berthed in Birkenhead on June 22nd. 1943.

Shortly after the ship had tied up we apprentices were informed by the assistant Marine Superintendent that, owing among other things, to the shortness of the voyage just completed, we would not be going on leave immediately but would be joining a couple of the new 'Liberty' ships being built in America. He concluded the interview with the words,

"The ships are just waiting for crews in New York so do not take all your deep-sea gear with you as you will only be away for six weeks or so."

It was a long six weeks.

Chapter 6

We three apprentices, along with officers and crews for several 'Liberty' ships, left Liverpool as passengers on the 'Empress of Scotland' on June 24th. for the States and I returned to Liverpool on September 18th. – the following year.

This was no great hardship for me, in fact the voyage proved to be one of the most interesting and enjoyable I have ever made. For other, more responsible people however it was a different story. Some of the senior officers sent out to the two 'Liberties' scheduled to be operated by our Company had been about to join a new vessel then fitting out in Glasgow. The expected six week voyage would have been completed in plenty of time for them to have joined the company ship but in the event she had made a number of voyages before they eventually caught up with her.

The voyage on the liner was an enlightening experience and certainly a change from the mode of progress to which I had become accustomed. To start with the ship sailed independently as her speed of four or five times that of a slow convoy was a considerable safety factor. There was boat drill every day instead of once a week although I am inclined to think that this was mainly in order to get the passengers out of the accommodation for a while to allow the crew to tidy up a little.

The passengers were a very mixed bag, some of the more obvious being RAF personnel bound for training in the States, repatriated 'walking wounded' American service men, Merchant Navy crews for ships being built in North America and a number of German prisoners on their way to P.O.W. camps. There appeared to be very few spare berths on the ship – and there were plenty of berths. Some of the bunks were in tiers four or five high in what had once been first class public rooms and no doubt everywhere else was just as crowded.

For all the crowding I could certainly not complain about the accommodation allotted to me. In peace time it must have been one of the very best state-rooms on the ship. At the risk of being accused of nit-picking I would say however that it might have been even better if I had not been forced to share it with twenty-three other young officers.

The 'Empress of Scotland' arrived in due order at Newport News, Virginia, about midday on July 2nd. having apparently received final instructions at sea in a package lowered from a U.S. Navy airship which hovered overhead.

As soon as the vessel berthed groups of passengers commenced going ashore. The Merchant Navy contingent was about the last to leave the ship, in the early hours of the following morning, after being told to 'stand by to disembark' and then 'stand down' several times during the night. This might have been for some quite legitimate reasons but we decided it was in revenge for the awkwardness of some M.N. ratings who, as passengers for once in their lives, were determined to make the most of the situation. The voice of the long-suffering announcer on the Tanoy, who, after several times instructing all passengers to go to boat stations, adds wearily, "This <u>includes</u> Merchant Navy personnel" remains in my memory.

The first train-load of M.N. officers and seaman left only partly filled as many of the men had slipped through the guard and gone up town for a little light refreshment. The second, ours, was overfilled owing to the return, voluntarily or otherwise, of many of the men who had got adrift. This resulted in some of us, including myself, sleeping on hard seats the first night.

Our train pulled out of Newport News just as dawn was breaking and commenced the long haul to California. So much for the ships' 'waiting in New York'.

The train journey across the American continent was certainly most memorable. It had its bad points but these were far outweighed by the good and I would certainly have liked to make the same trip a second time.

The carriages were fairly old and seemed to suck in soot and smoke but to offset this the bathrooms were spacious and well equipped. The food was quite good but the dining car or cars could only cope with one carriage load of passengers at a time. These cars were attached directly behind the locomotive and the passengers were fed carriage by carriage, starting from the front. We in the last carriage were therefore served quite late, breakfast at about noon, lunch around six and supper at midnight – should any of us still be awake at that hour. One advantage of the last carriage was that one could stroll out onto the little open platform at the end of it to view the scenery and take the air. The train's conductor spent not a little time there and was a most interesting person to converse with.

My memories of the journey are mixed and disjointed. The tree-covered mountains of Virginia, the tremendous railway marshalling yards of Ohio and Illinois and the seemingly endless plains when we reached them. I remember there had been a train crash shortly before our train arrived at one place and rather than clear the line of wreckage a loop line had been laid around the scene of the accident.

The train took us through North Platte, Cheyenne and Laramie and many other places I had read of in 'Western' stories. Our stops for water were frequent but short – however usually long enough for the majority of the passengers to pile out of the train and into the nearest bar. This was generally convenient to hand for as often as not the train stopped in the main street of small towns. In spite of the mad rush to get back on board inevitably a few men were left behind.

There was always plenty of interest to see whether the train was moving or stationary. Cattle on the plains and even a small herd of buffalo. As if to order there was even a real live mounted cowboy at the side of the track waving his hat to the train as it passed. 'Kit Carson's Stagecoach' was exhibited at one of our stops.

Eventually we reached the Rockies. Even with an extra locomotive attached to the train it was a long, slow haul up. As I remember it we passed Lake Tahoe at 11 o'clock one morning and it was still in view, resembling a little silver sixpence, at 4 o'clock that afternoon, thousands of feet below.

From the Rockies it was all downhill, Sacramento was passed and finally we rolled into Oakland, just across the bay from San Francisco. It was 11 o'clock on the morning of July 7th. If July 4th. had been celebrated somewhere in the middle of the U.S.A. I cannot remember noticing it. Perhaps the train staff had decided that it would be tactful to give the occasion a low profile in consideration of the fact that the passengers were 'Limeys'.

On leaving the train we split up to a certain extent, Masters, Chief Engineers and Ratings went on to San Francisco and the remaining officers to a hotel in Oakland. If any of us had any illusions of joining our ships on arrival they were immediately dispelled. The vessel I eventually joined was not even launched until July 21st.

Needless to say the stay in California was thoroughly enjoyable. The warm sunshine, the brightly lit streets, the abundance of everything the heart could desire and, above all, the marvellous hospitality of the people, will always remain among my fondest memories.

We were three glorious weeks in the hotel before we joined our ship. During our stay some of us did a 3 inch gunnery course run by the U.S. Navy on Treasure Island in San Francisco Bay. From our ship designate came Blondie, Ginger and I. The third apprentice from the 'Masirah' had been appointed to the second of the two Liberty ships allotted to our company. Blondie had been at college when he had been recalled and appointed third officer of our ship. As with the rest of us he would 'only be away for six weeks or so' thus could resume his studies without undue interruption on his return. Sadly, this never came about. I still have a photograph of our squad and our large U.S. Navy Petty Officer Instructor to commemorate the occasion.

Whilst we were in Oakland Mussolini was overthrown but there was still two long years of war ahead of us.

Although my pay, plus what seemed to me a very generous 'living allowance', was more than sufficient for my unsophisticated needs many of the others took up temporary employment to augment their incomes. I shared a room with our second mate but saw very little of him as he had obtained a job on the night shift of a biscuit factory. His story was that he was detailed to move a heap of bags of flour from one end of a dimly lit warehouse and dump their contents down a hopper at the other end. At first the task seemed feasible but towards the end of the back-breaking shift it became apparent that the pile would not be finished. However, the foreman was very good about it and told the gasping second mate that he had done very well for a 'green hand'.

After another night or so of relentless endeavour with no greater success the second mate decided that he was attacking the job the wrong way round. By starting at the end of the pile nearest the hopper he was having to walk further each time as the night progressed and as he became more tired. The solution therefore was to start at the back of the pile and thus make shorter and shorter journeys as the shift wore on. This way he thought he might just be able to move the entire heap of bags. To test this theory the following night he trundled his barrow round to the far side of the heap – to find another temporary labourer dumping bags into his pile!

So far as employment was concerned the engineers 'had it made'. The sudden wartime expansion of shipbuilding and other engineering projects in California created an unprecedented demand for the services of anyone with mechanical experience. More than one ship's engineer took advantage of the situation.

One story I heard concerned a chief engineer who, after a week or so's enjoyable idleness, decided to seek employment at the local shipyard. His services were immediately snapped up and he was instructed to report to the foreman in a nearby shed. On entering the shed he asked one of the crowd of men there to point out the foreman. "Oh," said the man, "He is that big Limey over there." It was the chief's own engineer.

Chapter 7

Although I understand the Captain and Chief Officer attended the launching of our new ship the first most of us saw of her was on July 30th. when we went on board to check stores.

A standard Liberty ship she'd been launched as the 'Frank D. Finney' but as she had been allotted to the British under 'Lend-Lease' she was re-named 'Samovar' in keeping with the 'Sam' prefix nomenclature used for these vessels. The other ship managed by our company was named 'Sambridge'. She was completed and sailed before our ship.

We 'officially' joined the 'Samovar' at the Richmond Yard on July 31st. – a mere ten days after her launch – ready to go on trials.

The newness of everything on board was most striking, particularly when compared with the well-worn 'Masirah'. She had numerous advantages over my old ship; Oil fuel, so no more coal dust; running hot and cold water in both cabins and showers and many other unheard of luxuries. The cabins were sheathed in plywood so eliminating the cockroaches which seemed to thrive in the old tongue and groove panelling.

The bunks were particularly comfortable, considerably wider than the standard British bunks they had springs and mattresses nearly a foot thick. Excellent in port but rather difficult to chock oneself into in heavy weather at sea. Each bunk, even the less luxurious ones of the ratings, had its own reading light. I think the third mate's bunk had its light at the after end so he was the only person on board who slept with his feet forward – considered very unlucky at sea.

Once we were all on board – the crew required a little rounding up after so long in port, (among others adrift was I believe the galley boy – discovered washing dishes in Reno), we were kept busy checking and testing equipment, engine and speed trials and, of course, loading our first cargo.

The ship's armament consisted of six 20mm Oerlikon cannon, a 'Pill-Box' rocket launcher which could fire up to twenty 2 inch rockets at a time and a 4 inch dual purpose gun. This latter weapon I remember arriving on a lorry just as we were leaving the fitting out berth. It was re-directed to our next berth, in San Francisco, where it arrived again just as we were moving off the berth. I think it was eventually put on board on the third try. The ship was promised another gun, for the foc'sle head, at a later date.

****

The 'Samovar' sailed out under the Golden Gate Bridge at 10pm. on August 19th. with a full cargo, including cased aircraft on deck, bound for the Middle East via Hobart, Tasmania. The latter was termed the 'A.B.C. Country' by the crew. The initials apparently stood for the 'Apples, Beer and Crumpet', (or something like that). I cannot vouch for the accuracy of this description as it turned out to be another quarter of a century before I actually visited the place, by which time it was very respectable.

One of the first things attended to on clearing the land was to test the ship's armament. A quick squirt with each of the Oerlikons proved they were in order. Testing the 4 inch gun was a rather more complicated procedure.

In order to ensure that the gun was safely bolted to the deck the first few rounds were fired with the gun unmanned. It was loaded in the usual manner although with high explosive shell as we had not been supplied with practice rounds, and trained over the side. The gun crew then vacated the platform and took cover below it. Our gunnery officer, the second mate, had attached a long lanyard to the firing mechanism of the gun and brought the end of this down with him. The ship was rolling heavily at the time so, as the gun was trained to port, the second mate waited until she had reached her maximum roll to starboard when the gun was pointed skyward and tugged the lanyard.

Nothing happened.

Steadying his foothold and taking a fresh grip on the line the second mate tried again.

This time his efforts were rewarded with a double loud bang, the first that of the gun firing and the second of the shell exploding in the water but a few feet from the ship's side as the ship had rolled over to port by that time. Fortunately, no damage was done and the remainder of the test went without incident.

For the first couple of weeks or so of the passage all was peaceful and serene. The weather was good and the ship had no doubt been routed well clear of any area of hostile enemy activity. I heard at the time that we had passed quite close to Tahiti, (though well out of sight of the island), but as we apprentices were on daywork I saw little of the bridge, never mind an actual chart, during this period.

One incident I recall during the early part of the passage was an alarm in the middle of one night.

Without the slightest warning everyone on the ship was awakened by a tremendous bang. The main engine, which had been thumping away in great style, quickly slowed almost to a stop. Shouts from the engine room could be heard, via the ventilators, on the bridge. Further shouts and curses as the engine picked up speed again and was soon on full revolutions. Minutes passed with no explanation emanating from the engine room so the bridge rang down to ask the reason for the commotion. The engineers were at first reluctant to explain but eventually the story emerged. Apparently one of the greasers was rather partial to baked beans and had placed a seven pound tin of this delicacy on some steam pipes to warm up for his supper. Unfortunately, he had neglected the elementary precaution of puncturing the can before heating. Seven pounds of beans is an awful lot of beans and when spread over the gleaming white and light grey paintwork of the brand new engine room the result defies description.

We must have been about equidistant from Tahiti and New Zealand when our peaceful routine was rudely interrupted.

The first I knew that something untoward was happening was when the sound of Morse code blasted from the radio room almost next door to the apprentices' cabin. The muted sound of Morse from the receivers was quite normal but this was different, this was a message being transmitted by our ship which, with the wartime stresses on radio silence, meant something important was in the wind.

The reason for the unusual radio activity was soon known to all on board. A tanker, the 'Trocus' of London, had a fire in her engine room and required assistance. Instructions were received from the New Zealand naval authorities for the 'Samovar' to proceed to the 'Trocus'' position and render what help we could. Later we were told to attempt to tow the disabled ship to New Zealand as, although the fire had been extinguished, the ship was without power.

At 5pm on September 7th. the 'Samovar' turned and proceeded towards the derelict.

The following morning it was a case of all hands breaking out heavy wire, shackles and other equipment and generally preparing to tow.

The 'Trocus' was sighted that afternoon and on arriving close to her our chief officer went across in one of our motor lifeboats to discuss towing arrangements with her master.

On recovering our boat the 'Samovar' spent the night cruising in the vicinity of the broken down vessel.

Early next morning we closed with the tanker who commenced proceedings by firing a rocket line across to us. This was hauled on board along with a heavier line followed by a wire attached to it and eventually the end of the 'Trocus'' heavy 'insurance wire' which was hauled up to our taffrail and shackled to our gear.

Fortunately, the weather remained moderate throughout this operation.

The tow commenced just before noon but did not last very long. Less than an hour after commencement the tanker's wire parted at the eye and we were back to square one. Further back in fact as the derelict had forty-five fathoms of anchor cable, her port anchor and ninety-odd fathoms of wire rope as thick as a man's wrist hanging below her bows to recover. She had to make repairs and raise steam for her windlass before she could haul that lot back on board. This took two days.

On the morning of September 11th. the ships were again connected together and in the early afternoon the tow was recommenced. This time it was eight hours before the wire again parted, close to our ship.

The 'Samovar' cruised in the vicinity of the 'Trocus' as the latter again raised steam enough to recover her anchor cable and towing wire.

Late on the afternoon of the 12th. the tow was re-connected and towing resumed. So far we had been very fortunate with the weather but it was not to last.

With no power for her steering gear the 'Trocus' sheered all over the place as the strength and direction of the wind changed.

The tow continued as steadily as the wildly sheering 'Trocus' would allow on the 13th. and 14th. There was no 15th. as we crossed the

International Date Line.

On the 16th. the weather began to deteriorate and on the 17th. the wind occasionally reached gale force making the two almost unmanageable. Sometimes the tanker was only a couple of points abaft our beam as the two ships climbed and descended the tremendous Southern Ocean swells.

This weather was endured until the 20th. when it became considerably worse, blowing a full gale with sea conditions to match. Although the 'Samovar' was unable to keep any kind of course the main towing wires kept the ships connected even though one of the ancillary wires parted in the late afternoon.

In spite of the weather conditions this wire was replaced the following morning – our Lamptrimmer 'Buster' going over the side in a bosun's chair to make the actual connection. The wind moderated during this day but freshened again during the next two days.

Early in the morning of the 23rd. the bridle wires carried away close astern of the 'Samovar' but fortunately the 10 inch manila 'springs' held the weight until these wires could be renewed, a task which took all of the forenoon.

The tow was resumed just after midday, which was just as well as the weather rapidly deteriorated thereafter, the wind reaching storm force during the morning of the next day. This was the worst weather experienced on the passage and the only time I have seen swell officially logged as 'mountainous' – certainly no exaggeration.

In the early afternoon a number of 40 gallon drums of lubricating oil, originally lashed on the boat deck, accompanied by numerous bags of galley coal, came adrift in the violent rolling. Again it was a case of 'all hands' to get them secured. This was eventually achieved but not before some of the drums had been lost over the side. More would have been lost had not several of them become lodged in one of the lifeboats which were swung out and secured level with the deck at sea.

For a minute or two it was feared that our old bosun had also gone overboard but he turned up in the bottom of the boat under the oil-drums – completely unscathed.

The bosun incidentally had been twice torpedoed and although well over retirement age did not think it right to leave the sea whilst the war continued and he could still be of service.

The weather moderated over the following days allowing us to haul round and continue our journey towards our new destination of Auckland.

On the evening of September 27th. we picked up a pilot in Hauraki Gulf and at 1131 pm slipped the tow south of Flat Rock leaving the 'Trocus' in care of tugs whilst we proceeded to an anchorage.

The tow of 1284 miles was quite a record for a salvage tow at the time – but very soon surpassed I believe. Our average towing speed was 3.70 knots.

We berthed at Auckland early on the morning of the 28th. and began a hectic few days of storing, bunkering and preparing to go to sea once again generally.

After a long, hard arrival day the crew got cleaned up and dashed ashore – only to find that the pubs closed at six o'clock! There was not much else in the way of entertainment either as 'the Yanks had bought the place'.

My simple tastes were more readily satisfied and I thoroughly enjoyed the stay. Unfortunately, the time to relish New Zealand hospitality was all too brief and after less than four days we left for Suez. I recall having to turn down at least two invitations to supper and also having an awful headcold the day we sailed. It was also my birthday.

The 'Samovar' steamed south of Australia and I cannot remember seeing any land between New Zealand and Socotra which we sighted on November 1st. Real sailing ship times and distances!

The ship arrived at Suez on November 9th. where we commenced discharging the cargo we had loaded three months earlier.

Suez was a bustling military port at the time and we were soon discharged. It was before the days of Canal convoys and we must have been fortunate in our timing as we left Suez at 8 am and arrived at Port Said at 5 pm the same day.

Needless to say I found the Canal transit most interesting. Apart from the Canal itself a grandstand view was had of Egyptian scenes, remarkably green fields in places on the west bank where fresh water was available and hardly anything green at all on the opposite bank, the occasional camel and the picturesque local population. There was also considerable military activity and even British nurses sunbathing at Lake Timsah.

After loading at Port Said a part cargo of scrap metal – mainly pieces of military vehicles, bent guns, tank turrets and the like, we sailed in convoy for the U.S.A. on November 17th.

Our armament had been augmented at Port Said by the addition of a pair of 'Floating Aerial Mines'. This apparatus consisted of a rocket which took a long length of piano wire up with it. On reaching its maximum altitude the rocket released a parachute which suspended the wire vertically for a short time. Attached to the lower end of the wire was a can of high explosive. The principle of this weapon was that if released at exactly the right moment in front of a low-flying enemy aircraft its wing would strike the wire, the parachute would pull the wire over the wing until the charge reached it and exploded causing irreparable damage, in the short term, to the aircraft. F.A.M.s were improved versions of earlier types without explosive charges.

The afternoon we left Port Said I was on watch with the second mate. For some reason best known to himself he decided to find out how far the switch for the starboard F.A.M. could be moved before anything happened. He was soon enlightened. With a terrific Bang! and Whoosh! the rocket and its attachments shot several hundred feet into the air and the steel deck at the launching site set down a couple of inches – right above the Captain's head, he having just settled down to his afternoon's siesta.

There had been changes in Port Said as regards apprentices. The homeward bound 'Masirah' was there and the opportunity was taken to transfer Ginger to her as he had finished his time and was ready to start studying for his second mate's certificate. In exchange we received two of the 'Masirah's apprentices, one senior and one junior to me. However, we had not seen the last of Ginger.

The 'Masirah's large funnel comes back into the story here. It would appear that the afore mentioned junior apprentice, directed to join the ship, his first, in Liverpool asked the policeman at the dock gate where she was berthed. The officer directed him and added helpfully, "You can't miss her, she has a tremendous great funnel."

The lad duly arrived on board, found the apprentices' cabin and, as usual, was taken along to report to the officer in charge. That harassed worthy welcomed him on board but mentioned that he had not expected a new apprentice until later in the week. Handed back to his escort the lad spent the remainder of the day looking around the ship and being suitably impressed.

It was not until after breakfast the following day that it was discovered that he was not on the 'Masirah' of the 'tremendous great funnel' but a troopship with an even larger one. The 'Masirah' was tucked under her stern in the next berth.

The captain had been unwell for some time and on passage it became apparent that he required proper medical treatment. After some signalling with the commodore the captain was transferred by our boat to one of the escorts to be landed, I believe, at Bone. Ginger was picked up at the same time to return to us as third mate, the other deck officers being temporarily promoted.

A couple of days after the above incident we passed Algiers and I had completed my first circuit of the globe.

The Battle of the Atlantic must have struck a quiet spell as the convoy steamed slowly towards New York for I can recall no enemy activity on the passage. The weather was our main concern, if we ran into any heavy stuff we would not reach the States before Christmas.

Needless to say the bad weather found us and it rapidly worsened until the night of December 23/24th. when we received a 'real dusting'. The convoy struggled on in a tremendous blizzard. Full navigation lights were ordered but even so those of even the ships closest to us were only glimpsed at infrequent intervals.

In spite of the weather the convoy escaped casualty and duly arrived at New York on the morning of Christmas Day. Many of the ships berthed on arrival but we were not among the fortunate and spent Christmas Day at the anchorage. The vessel was desperately low on vegetables by this time and the main course of our dinner consisted of turkey and rice.

The 'Samovar' berthed in Hoboken early on the morning of December 26th. I find I have a note to the effect that I went ashore that evening with the princely sum of one dollar and sex cents in my pocket. No doubt I would have remembered if it had been a particularly wild evening. However, this was more than made up on New Year's Eve at the Apprentices Club in 76th. Street.

As soon as we had berthed in Hoboken our new captain joined the ship, the officers returned to their original ranks and Ginger went home for his 'ticket'.

It was probably in New York that we heard that our 'sister ship', the 'Sambridge', had been torpedoed and sunk in the Gulf of Aden with some loss of life a few weeks previously.

At San Francisco each member of the crew had been issued with a 'Coastguard Pass'. Although only intended as identification to allow access to our ship, in the confusion of the times and the fact that there were very many concessions to men in uniform, some of us found them very useful in our impecunious state. I recall numerous free rides on the 'Elevated' and 'Subway' on the strength of the little plastic card – even a free trip to the top of the Empire State Building.

The ship loaded for the Mediterranean and on January 22nd. 1944 left New York for Hampton Roads, arriving there the following day.

Whilst in New York a 12 pounder gun had been fitted on the forward gun platform. On leaving the port this weapon was tested unmanned as had the 4 inch gun on leaving San Francisco. Learning by experience the gun was pointed skywards before firing – it was just about flat calm anyway.

The gun fired with its unique ear-splitting 'Crack!' and the shell winged is way into the hazy sky. The mate looked at the captain and the captain looked at the mate before both dived for the chart-room to check whether or not the projectile would land on Staten Island.

After bunkering at Norfolk, Virginia, we joined the convoy assembling in Hampton Roads and sailed from there on February 2nd.

Chapter 8

Again the Atlantic was quiet so far as enemy activity was

concerned although it may have been on this passage that we witnessed a display of air combat – albeit in slow motion.

The convoy had been discovered by a Foke-Wulf Condor which kept us company until our 'air umbrella' – on this occasion a Catalina flying-boat – came to our succour. The resultant dog-fight, if it could be so termed, lasted for some time, each of the unwieldy aircraft attempting to manoeuvre into a position of advantage. Occasional bursts of machine-gun fire could be heard above the drone of the aircrafts' engine and at one stage one or the other jettisoned its bomb or depth-charges. However, there is no dramatic end to this little story, the two planes disappeared into the distance still banging away at one another. It was almost as if the spectacle had been arranged for our entertainment - making it difficult to realise that each plane contained men desperately trying to kill one another.

One night off the North American coast we encountered a terrific thunderstorm. The whole convoy was constantly illuminated by lightening until eventually one tremendous flash left the whole sky lit up with orange light. I thought at first that I had been blinded and was considerably relieved when, after a moment or two's stunned silence, others on the bridge could be seen to start moving about. The light emanated from a great ball of fire whirling in the sky ahead of the convoy. Initially it was thought that a ship had blown up but apparently the cause was entirely natural.

After anchoring in Augusta, Sicily, for a day or so we proceeded to Taranto, our first port of discharge.

It was either on this or the following visit to Augusta that the helmsman left the wheel just as the ship was lining up to enter the harbour between the breakwaters. The mate dashed into the wheelhouse and grabbed the wheel in time to prevent a disaster and we proceeded to the anchorage without further incident. Later the ex-helmsman explained that it was past 'eight bells' and his relief had failed to arrive. At sea when not in convoy it was routine humour for the man at the wheel to remove the wheel from its spindle and literally 'hand it over' to his relief on the wing of the bridge but this was carrying things a little too far. It was not the man's first escapade and eventually the ship 'had to let him go'.

Our deck cargo for Taranto included an 82 ton 'Tanac' tug and several Sherman tanks which were discharged in the stream.

As the ship was not alongside a quay, communications with the shore were carried out by ship's boat. Much to my delight I was appointed coxswain of the motor boat to be used for this purpose. The remainder of the boat's 'crew' consisted of anyone who happened to be in it at any particular time.

There were numerous trips ashore to be made for one reason or another and I very soon got to know the route through the moored ships and net-buoys to and from the landing stage.

On the second evening in Taranto Blondie, the third mate, decided that he would like to make a trip ashore with the boat. Pulling rank on me he steered and worked the engine and I was relegated to 'crew'. We left the ship with a few men off for a run ashore, Blondie in the stern, his fair hair and sheepskin jacket fluttering in the breeze and his gloved hand, (when working gloves were normally only worn on American ships), gripping the tiller. I nursed the boat-hook in the bow as I kept a sharp lookout for buoys and other obstructions in the rapidly gathering dusk.

It was almost pitch dark on the return journey but apart from colliding with a net-boom buoy, fortunately one without anti-boat spikes, we got back to the ship in due order.

Normally the men returning from the shore would lend a hand to lift the boat until it was well clear of the water and any passing traffic. It was not a large boat and half a dozen men tailed on to the rope falls could lift it with ease. I stayed in the boat until the weight was taken on the patent release gear as when slack the block rings were very liable to jump off the hooks.

As soon as the weight was on the falls I nipped up the jacob's ladder to lend a hand with the lifting. However, on my arrival on deck I found that on this occasion the falls had been led to a cargo winch for some reason. A moment later one of the gunners came running from aft shouting, "Has anyone got a torch? I think someone is caught in the winch!"

I dashed down to the after end of number four hatch and stopped the winch but it was too late to do any good.

It was said that Blondie was still alive when we got him clear of the winch but that seems impossible.

We took the boat to a nearby troopship and returned with her doctor but there was nothing he could do.

Blondie was buried at Taranto on March 2nd. and that evening at sunset we left for Brindisi.

****

The ship was a couple of days at Brindisi before carrying on to Bari.

Bari harbour was still littered with the wrecks of ships sunk in an air raid three months earlier. Apparently the defences of the place had been caught napping.

We berthed and discharged without enemy interference although we did have one spectacular evening when the port experienced a thunderstorm.

The whole harbour area was ringed with barrage balloons as a defence against enemy aircraft. They were of the small Naval type which were not fitted with lightning conductors and one after the other was struck by lightning and burst into flames. In spite of obviously frantic winding down of winches within a matter of minutes the port was ringed with a palisade of black smoke columns in lieu of the balloons.

After a few days in Bari we proceeded, via Brindisi and Augusta, to Malta to complete the discharge.

The 'Samovar' entered Valletta harbour at 8 am on March 22nd. and moored alongside the sunken wreck of the 'Talabot', one of only two vessels remaining of a convoy to reach Malta almost exactly two years previously.

The harbour was littered with wrecks and, on going ashore, the bombed out buildings and uncleared debris added grim testimony of the pounding Valletta had received from enemy bombs.

Some amenities were still operational as I can still remember a film I saw there and the name of the bar some of us dropped into on our way back to the ship. Many of the bars seemed to be named after old warships and 'ours' bore the name of the battleship 'Sans Pareil'. Run by an old Maltese couple the establishment was situated in a cave-like masonary arch, probably built into the base of a much larger structure.

A replacement third mate arrived in Malta and quite a character he proved to be. He was nineteen years old and looked about fourteen. His theories and enthusiasms kept us all well entertained for the remainder of the voyage. The tale he told of his adventures coming out to the ship was amusing enough. Apparently he was serving on a ship at Middlesbrough when the call came for him to proceed post-haste to the 'Samovar'. I presume some arrangements had been put in hand by the Company to start him on his way but according to the bold third mate he had to plan his own, quite a daunting prospect in the middle of a war.

As Blondie had died on February 29th. and the 'Samovar' left Malta on April 1st. it left only the month of March for the whole operation. Much of the distance was covered by air, the third mate having to 'thumb a lift' on American transport planes and the like. It was not until he unpacked the sea-bag of clothes he had humped from Middlesbrough to Malta that he discovered that the engineers on his previous ship had stuffed a block of concrete into the bottom of the bag without his knowledge.

It was owing to the courtesy of the Army authorities at Malta that several officers were able to replenish their wardrobes as the 'six week' voyage originally catered for had long since expired. The 'Samovar' was the only ship I served on where some of the officers wore khaki battle-dress. The only requirement I had was footwear and I bought an excellent pair of black shoes for the sum of one pound and fourpence-halfpenny. The receipt is before me as I write.

The Merchant Navy always received a warm welcome from the army, the soldiers could never do enough for us. The Royal Navy at the time I found more reserved, as if trying to give the impression that the sea actually belonged to them, although they would condescend to allow merchant ships to use it without restriction between wars.

****

'Buster', our lamptrimmer, had quite a sense of humour which came to the surface at unexpected times. I remember one occasion when he was busy with palm and needle constructing a canvas 'sleeping bag' to cover the head of our 50 ton derrick and its associated blocks. I was discussing something with him when 'Akki', one of the A.B.s, crossed the hatch on which we were sitting carrying a bucket of something pretty vile in order to toss it over the lee side. In passing he made as if to toss the contents of the bucket over Buster.

The lamptrimmer did not bat an eyelid.

"Akki", he said very quietly, "If you had thrown that stuff and one drop of it had splashed me or this canvas I would have had you straight up to the 'Old Man'. I will skylark with anyone off duty but not during work hours."

"Oh, come off it," replied Akki, "I was only joking."

Then, like a damn fool, he put the bucket down on the hatch.

With the speed of light Buster grabbed the bucket and before he could leap clear Akki received both it and its contents in the back of his neck. His misfortune did not end there as in his efforts to escape he caught his toe under one of the hatch bar bottle screws and limped for weeks afterwards.

Another escapade of Buster's occurred in Valletta harbour. The anti-torpedo net booms were being painted and Buster dangled about eighty feet above the deck applying his brush. Having covered the area he could reach he called down to ordinary seaman Jack to lower him down three or four feet. Jack did this somewhat jerkily causing Buster to look down and observe the O.S. sitting on the hatch reading a comic book. The gantline, on which Buster's bosun's chair and life depended, had been passed once round the drum end of a winch and was being slacked away by the simple expedient of jack lifting his foot off the running end then slapping it back when sufficient line had been payed out.

Buster was not pleased at this somewhat casual arrangement and, among other things, he told Jack to make the gantline properly fast.

"O.K. Buster," replied Jack. He put three or four more turns of the line around the drum end followed by a couple of half hitches. Then he strolled off to the messroom for a cup of coffee.

Now Buster did not take kindly to being left dangling in the air to suit Jack's convenience and took immediate remedial action. A matter of minutes later a startled Jack was confronted by a very wet and angry lamptrimmer who had dived from his bosun's chair into the harbour, swum round to the gangway and reboarded the ship. He hit the water with such force that the American locomotive driver's cap he habitually wore split across the crown and ended up round his neck.

This was not the first altercation between Buster and Jack, or the last, as will be mentioned in due course.

We completed discharging and left Valletta on April 1st. for the U.S.A. passing a beached tanker, the gallant 'Ohio' near the harbour entrance on the way out.

A little adventure befell the ship on the way through the Straits of Gibraltar. It was just getting dark and had been raining as the convoy formed into two columns for the passage through the narrow waters. The manoeuvre had necessitated a little signalling so quite a few flags got wet in the process. As apprentice of the watch I was given the task of hanging them up in the lower wheelhouse to dry. From there I proceeded on a tour of the ship to check that our blackout was in order. Returning along the after deck I encountered the chief engineer who was in an obvious hurry to get aft. He informed me in passing that the steering gear had broken down. A glance around more than confirmed this, ships seemed to be charging at us from all directions and an escort was frantically flashing a signal lamp at us.

I hurried to the bridge and had been there but a few minutes when the chief came up to say that the source of the trouble had been discovered – a bunch of flags had become jammed in the gearing connecting the upper steering wheel to that in the lower wheelhouse.

"Flags!" roared the captain, "Flags!! – where is Baxter?"

The trouble with a smallish ship is that there is nowhere to hide.

****

The ship spent a few days at Casablanca awaiting a convoy and loading a little bulk phosphate, more in the nature of ballast than anything else. We moored with our two anchors forward and the stern made fast to the outer breakwater with lines. Ours was one of a long row of vessels, nearly all Liberty ships. This posed a problem as, particularly at night, the vessels appeared identical. The result was inevitable and one night the mate himself spent several hours on the wrong ship before the French harbour launch returned on its next trip.

'First job' the following morning was to paint a thin white band around the funnel. With this the ship would be identifiable in daylight from a distance for although ships carried their names on boards attached to their bridges these were difficult to discern when passing ahead of a whole row of ships. Soon various other Liberties painted different coloured bands around their funnels. We had started a fashion.

On April 14th. the convoy left Casablanca and after an uneventful passage the 'Samovar' arrived at Baltimore on May 3rd.

When loading our first cargo in California the mate allowed Ginger and I to work on the 12 and 6 arrangement, twelve hours on duty followed six off then six on and twelve off ad infinitum. Thus one of us was always on duty ready for any odd jobs tossed our way by the mate or duty officer and the other completely free to go ashore if he so wished. This was pleasant enough but in Baltimore he went one further. As there was no cargo work for the first few days he said that as long as one of the three of us was on board the other two were free to do as they wished.

We apprentices decided on a rota of twelve hours on and twenty-four off and one of the first ashore from the ship was the junior apprentice. No doubt the other two of us decided to allow him the honour as the 'Old Man' had not then issued any cash in the way of 'subs'.

The captain spent his first evening in port dealing with his accumulated mail. It would appear that among the letters from the head office was a query concerning some detail about the junior apprentice and, on discovering that the lad was ashore, he left word for him to report when he got back on board. Unfortunately, the junior hand decided to waste as little as possible of his twenty-four hour break and crept up the gangway shortly before sunrise hoping that no one saw him. The night watchman not only met him but delivered the captain's message.

Reporting to the captain on returning from the cinema in the late evening whilst that worthy is still at his desk is one thing, waking him out of his first relaxed night's sleep for weeks is quite another.

The upshot of it was that the junior hand had his shore leave stopped. As the original 'one on board' arrangement still stood this meant that the other two of us were permanently off duty. In theory at least, obviously such an idyllic situation could not last for more than a day or so.

****

After a very enjoyable stay at Baltimore we left on May 21st., fully loaded for India.

It was on the passage towards Port Said that we heard on the radio of the 'D-Day' landings in Normandy and also of the mysterious 'pilotless aircraft' the enemy had started to use. These later became better known as 'V1's or 'Flying Bombs'.

With most of the action in the English Channel area our convoy was treated to a relatively quiet passage, in fact the only enemy activity I can recall was not directed at our ships at all. Our convoy was well into the Mediterranean when, around noon one day, two ships in a convoy passing a few miles to the north of us were torpedoed. I am not sure of the exact date of the incident but seem to remember that it was the same day as the BBC announced that the Mediterranean Sea had been entirely cleared of enemy submarines.

One aspect of this attack on the credit side was that a persistent straggler in our convoy, an ancient coal-burning 'Hog island' vessel, suddenly found a new lease of life and was soon apparently trying to overtake the convoy.

We eventually arrived at Port Said and passed through the Canal without due incident.

The passage down the Red Sea was made independent of convoy. I think this is true anyway as one of the few incidents of the time I can remember was a magnificent gunnery practice.

The carpenter and his various assistants had constructed a splendid target consisting of a triangle formed of three long hatch deals which supported three posts with a screen of hessian between them. One of the posts carried a home-made German flag and another a Japanese. The whole contraption looked like a boy scouts' latrine and seemed to shrink in size once it had been launched onto the water.

The four inch and twelve pounder guns each fired a few rounds at the floating target and, by swinging the ship, each of our six oerlikons had a turn at firing a burst at it. Even our 'Pillar Box' launched a couple of rockets in its general direction. According to the people on the bridge with binoculars no one hit the thing but it was all good clean fun.

My action station on the 'Samovar' was the oerlikon gun on the port side of the foremast, my loader being the junior apprentice. Luckily this position was relatively far from the eyes of authority on the bridge and advantage was taken of this fact during the more routine gunnery exercises. Usually a round from the 12 pounder or 4 inch provided a puff of brown smoke in the sky to be used as a target by the automatic weapons. Rather tame stuff for red-blooded apprentices. Our private routine was a quick few rounds towards the puff of smoke then the gun quickly swung and depressed and the remainder of the pan blasted into the sea, the shells ricocheting and exploding in great style among the waves. I always tried to retain a few rounds in order to give my mate a chance of a quick squirt.

Well do I remember gazing over that gun-barrel defying the Luftwaffe and its Japanese equivalent to do their worst. However, in spite of all the wartime secrecy word must have got to them as they never came near me.

No doubt I would not be quite so deaf now if I had not enjoyed gunnery practice so much in those far off days.

Our first port of call in India was Karachi, Karachi happened to be in India at the time. My recollections of our stay there are rather vague as are those of Bombay, our second port of call so I assume I could not have been very impressed by India at first acquaintance.

We fully discharged our cargo at the two ports between early July and early August then proceeded to the anchorage off Bedi Bunder in the Gulf of Kutch.

The land in the vicinity of the anchorage was very flat. At least I assume it was as I never actually saw it. It could not have been very far away though as barges sailed out to us at regular intervals and soon we were loading ground-nuts in bags. Thousands of them. Ten thousand odd tons of them in all.

The stevedore gangs came out in the first barges and camped on board during the vessel's stay – complete with their own fires and cooking arrangements.

No doubt rumours had been flying as regards our next destination but probably it was not until we started loading that we heard that the cargo was destined for the U.K.

Shortly before we left Bedi Bunder I received another alteration in my status which occurred in this way.

Our 'Lampy', Buster, had for some considerable time been at odds with one of the young seaman named Jack. This eventually came to a head in the seaman's' messroom over a pot of tea. The immediate result was that Buster poured the tea over Jack's head. The scalded Jack was rushed, so far as anything could be rushed at such an outpost of Empire, to hospital. From there he was sent to Bombay which he reached just in time to join a homeward bound hospital ship. In the event he was home, no doubt completely recovered from his ordeal, long before the rest of us.

In the longer term this left us one man short of the nine required for watchkeeping duties at sea so Buster, for his sins, was put on watches and I became Lamptrimmer, Acting, Temporary, Unpaid.

Although preparing the gear ready for the men to start work in the morning and squaring up when work was finished for the day meant fairly long hours I thoroughly enjoyed this job. Everyone concerned was extremely helpful and always ready to give me a hand or advice – particularly Buster himself. I think I learned more seamanship from him than everyone else combined. From his blue and white engine-driver's cap to his tatty tennis shoes – worn sockless in all weathers including ice and snow – he was solid seaman. Of course there is a limit to everything, even assistance, and it was on the 'Samovar' that I first heard that delightful expression, "what do you think you are on, your Daddy's yacht?"

The South West Monsoon was at its height in the Arabian Sea so, fully laden as we were, we received quite a dusting. Our lifeboats were 'swung out' in the usual wartime practice and one night one of the two motor lifeboats was whisked away by a particularly heavy sea. At least this is what was assumed to have happened as at dusk the evening before it was snugly in position and the following morning daylight revealed only an empty space where it had been. The noise of wind and sea had prevented anyone even hearing anything unusual during the hours of darkness. The boat was replaced by one without an engine thus bringing the 'Samovar' in line with most merchant ships of the time

– one motor boat per vessel.

The remainder of the voyage proceeded without anything of note occurring. Aden, Suez Canal, Gibraltar and then Falmouth to join a coastal convoy to Liverpool – where it all began.

The 'Samovar' paid off on September 18th. 1944, the same crew, still relatively intact, having departed from the same port on June 24th. the previous year. I had actually left home for the last 'Masirah' voyage in mid-April so had been away for nearly one and a half years.

The marine superintendent who had seen us off on our 'six week' voyage was on the quay to meet us on our arrival in Queens Dock.

Chapter 9

My next ship was the 'Malancha'. I joined her at No.9 Shed, No.9 Dock, Manchester on October 19th. 1944.

The 'Malancha' was far removed from my previous two vessels. The old 'Masirah' with her short voyages and the brand new 'Samovar' with her British crew and worldwide journeying were a world apart from the 'pukka' company ship which had, so far as the exigencies of the war permitted, been run on strictly 'Company' lines.

The Captain was said to have sailed through nearly two world wars without seeing a shot fired in anger and I believe this was to be his last voyage before retirement. He was of the old 'Tin God' school and spoke to only senior officers. I am certain he never spoke to me anyway during the months we were together on the ship. Probably a very nice person when one got to know him. – I never did.

The Chief Officer was of similar mould. An excellent chief officer on all counts apart from the fact that he could never, ever be wrong. An example of this manifested itself early in our acquaintanceship. Whilst steaming down the Manchester Ship Canal we encountered an American Liberty ship passing up. Her crew were struggling with two 'L' shaped booms pointing roughly skyward in the vicinity of her foremast.

"They are her torpedo-net booms," stated the mate with a voice of authority.

"No sir, they are her No.1 derricks, she has obviously tried to get under the first bridge without lowering them." I was happy to put him straight.

The mate was obviously astounded at being corrected by a mere apprentice. He was even more mortified when we closed the vessel and I was proved right. He did not speak to me for the remainder of the watch. It set the tone for our relationship for the rest of the voyage.

The 'Malancha' herself was a particularly handsome vessel even for those days when ships were inclined to look like ships. The drab wartime grey paint did nothing to mar her lovely lines. She had made her debut but a couple of years before the outbreak of hostilities so was in her prime. Turbine driven she had a fair turn of speed and although designed to use either coal or oil fuel I do not think she ever burnt the former.

She was quite up to the minute in most ways although her plumbing was still in the 'compactum' stage – of the most superior type of course – (I might have mentioned the running hot and cold water on my last ship once or twice which would not have helped to endear me to the mate). However, in one respect she was a very long step ahead of most cargo ships of her day, she carried Radar. It was of a very early model and not even termed 'radar' in those days but 'R.D.F.' which I understand to be the initials of 'radio direction finder'. This piece of equipment will be mentioned later.

With the European war now being conducted mainly on land the need for landing craft in that theatre had diminished but there was still a great demand for them in the Far East. It was hardly surprising therefore that literally on top of a full cargo the 'Malancha' had numerous landing craft of various types on her decks and hatches.

These were a nuisance, not so much in themselves but because of their web of wire lashings and bottle-screws festooning the decks. Bad enough to negotiate in daylight they were an absolute ankle-cracking menace at night.

Loaded we passed down the Canal, stopping at Eastham at the seaward end of it to have the top section of our funnel replaced at the sheerlegs there. These ancient sheerlegs were replaced by a handier crane after the war.

The passage to Colombo, via Gibraltar and the Suez Canal, passed without incident so far as enemy activity was concerned.

During the passage through the Mediterranean we ran into some bad weather from ahead. A small escort carrier fairly close on our starboard quarter was recovering her scouting aircraft in the late afternoon when the last of them had much difficulty in landing on the wildly pitching deck. Time and again the pilot tried to land only to abort at the last moment. Darkness was rapidly closing in and no doubt the plane was low on fuel so there was absolutely nowhere else to go. We observers all gave a sigh of relief when the plane eventually got safely down. No doubt our feelings were as nothing compared with the relief the pilot must have felt.

At some time during the outward passage I completed two years of sea service which entitled me to the full £10 a month 'War Risk Bonus', something I had been anticipating with some impatience. At about the same time someone apparently stood up on his hind legs in Parliament and spoke to the affect that he was astonished to learn that merchant seaman had to spend two years at sea on half bonus before they qualified for the full amount. Surely one man's life was as valuable as another's? The anomaly was duly rectified. I was sorely tempted to wipe the smug smile from the face of the junior apprentice.

The 'Malancha' was so thoroughly 'Company' that, harking back to their sailing ship days, she had been provided with a private gunner. Although he had served for many years in the Royal Navy he was employed and paid by the company. Although possibly one of many he was the only man of this denomination I ever came across. All the other gunners I met were D.E.M.S. ratings, either Royal Navy or Maritime Regiment.

Talking of gunners my action station on this ship was loader for one of the bridge oerlikons, (they did not even let me have my own gun!). The man who fired it was an Irishman and we were often on watch together whiling away the time swapping yarns. Most of the conversations were serious enough and although most elude me I always remember one remark of his which has me mystified until this day. We were talking of women, not an unusual subject for seafarers, and how different were their attitudes to ours in many ways.

"You know," said the gunner, "A woman would walk right across a town to buy something a penny cheaper there. A man would not, he would take a taxi."

For the life of me I still don't know if he was being serious.

Referring again to our elementary radar, it was amazing the amount of information the three naval operators could derive from the instrument. In fact, we must have been one of the first merchant ships to use radar-assisted gunnery. This was quite deliberate on gunnery exercises when for surface shooting we used a floating target, similar to the one described for the 'Samovar', modified by the addition of 'radar reflectors' in the form of empty beer cans strung up between the posts. (The cans by the way were of the original 'metal polish' type which some readers may remember). Not only could the radar register the 'echo' of the target but the actual shell splashes as well. Thus the R.D.F. rating shouted the ranges down a voice pipe to the bridge from whence they were telephoned to the gun position on the poop. Again I cannot remember the target ever being hit but it was all good 'high-tech' fun.

The radar/gun system was nearly used in earnest towards the end of the voyage in the Western Mediterranean. It was a cool, damp evening with very low overcast. The gunner and I had just popped the canvas covers over the bridge oerlikons to keep them dry when the R.D.F. rating on watch shouted down that he had an echo approaching from ahead at speed – 'probably an aircraft'. The mate and the gunner leapt to the port gun and I to the starboard but there was not time to uncover and cock the guns before the plane plunged out of the low cloud right ahead of us.

The aircraft's crew were obviously very alert as during the few seconds the machine was in sight it dropped two objects which fell towards us trailing smoke. It was at the time when radio-controlled glider bombs were being used against Allied shipping so anything dropped from a plane was viewed with even more than the normal amount of suspicion.

The plane shot over our ship just clearing the fore topmast, (we were not flying a balloon), and was away before we could get a shot at it. I remember thinking at the time what a pity it was that we had covered the guns but a few minutes earlier otherwise we could have put a lovely row of holes into the machine. It was really just as well that we did not however as it was identified as 'one of ours'. Her crew must have been aware of the convoy however as the two objects dropped were recognition flares.

****

The ship arrived at Colombo in time for Christmas although owing to the congestion of shipping in the harbour we did not commence discharging for several days. The mate tried to persuade the naval authorities in charge of cargo work to at least remove the landing craft so we could get some work done around the decks but this was deemed impossible until after Christmas.

I happened to be in the mate's office when a somewhat harassed naval officer arrived and introduced himself as a port mail officer. Knowing that we had mail for the services he was anxious to have it discharged immediately as there was only just time to have it sorted and delivered before Christmas Day. He said he had a barge and men on their way out to the ship and asked in which hatch it was stowed.

"All of them," was the mate's answer.

This somewhat surprised me as I was of the opinion that all the Colombo mail was in No.4 hatch only. Fortunately, I did not comment on this. Very fortunately.

Within hours a floating crane was alongside and the deck cargo of Landing craft quickly removed.

It so happened that No.4 hatch was the only one of the six with no deck cargo on it. And I was right about the stowage of the mail. An odd coincidence.

It was at Colombo that the 'Malancha' had the dubious honour of being hit by a shell from H.M. Battleship 'Howe'. Although quite a small shell it was quite a large boo-boo on the part of the perpetrator. Apparently the warship's pom-pom guns were being cleaned when one of them was aimed at our ship and the trigger of the 'empty' gun pressed. As has so often been stated, 'it is the empty gun that kills'. However, on this particular occasion there were no casualties and as the anti-aircraft projectile exploded on impact the 'Malancha' suffered no more than a dented shell plate.

Whilst on the subject of guns I would like to mention a pair of Scottish gunners we carried on one ship. I remember them only as 'Big Jock' and 'Wee Jock'. Big Jock hailed from the Hebrides and claimed to have only learned English after he was ten years old. He certainly warranted his sobriquet being very large indeed. He was an Army man,

Maritime Regiment of Artillery, and his shoulder badges earned him many a free pint of beer in American bars when he explained, in what he considered a Russian accent, that the 'R.A.' stood for 'Red Army'. We were all very much allied at the time of course.

Wee Jock was a complete contrast to the fair complexioned Big Jock being dark haired and swarthy. Even the greatly expanded wartime Navy must have been hard pressed to accept that he came up to the minimum requisite height.

The two Jocks were great friends and one of their favourite games ashore was to enter a pub separately pretending to be unacquainted. Wee Jock would deliberately provoke an argument with other customers and when the inevitable fight started Big Jock would come to his assistance. Often enough they had to cut and run for it but both considered the escapades tremendous fun.

As I have drifted away from the 'Malancha' to a certain extent I may as well toss in another irrelevant anecdote.

Early in the war shipowners discovered that when a ship was lost through enemy action no matter how long she took to sink inevitably the chief stewards accounts went with her. This made it extremely difficult for the head office to prove that the ship was not manned entirely by non-smoking tee-totalers. To avoid this happening an unpopular directive was issued to the effect that every effort was to be made to ensure that these documents survived a sinking.

The story goes that one ship, mortally struck in the middle of a dirty night, was duly abandoned and one of the last to leave was the chief steward heroically clasping in his arms a suitcase. A right-minded senior officer snatched the case from him and flung it into the sea with a "No room for luggage in this boat!"

"It wasn't luggage," gasped the chief steward when he managed to get his breath back, "That was the portable radio transmitter."

At about the time the 'Malancha' was in Ceylon paint schemes on R.N. ships seemed to have lent themselves to a fair amount of originality. I remember a Hunt class destroyer with an upside-down 'Rising Sun' design and a fleet aircraft carrier with a full-sized silhouette of a destroyer painted on her side – no doubt intended to confuse enemy submarines.

****

Christmas was celebrated in Colombo in the usual manner with plenty of food and drink.

The New Year, 1945 and expected to be the last one of the war, was seen in in tremendous style with the ships in the harbour setting off rockets and blazing away with their guns in addition to the routine racket of ships' whistles blasting away and each vessel ringing sixteen bells – eight for the old year and eight for the new - on their foc'sle bells. We contributed our full share, (I think the captain was ashore), with the second mate particularly enjoying himself firing off Very cartridges like a demented cowboy. With many of the ships, including our own, carrying explosives and with hatches open it was a wonder there was not a major catastrophe. However, the Gods were kind to us.

In the fullness of time we left Colombo and proceeded to Trincomalee to find that magnificent natural harbour full of naval and merchant shipping.

From Trinco to Calcutta where I particularly remember on this, my introductory visit to this place, twenty-nine hours on duty without a break, much of that time spent mooring in the river, a long process involving, among other things, taking lengths of our anchor chains from forward to the poop in order to moor the ship by chains fore and aft to buoys. Nothing less would prevent the vessel breaking adrift in a River Hooghly bore.

The festive season was still in full swing in Calcutta and I recall regular parties at Princes Hotel, very much European and officers only affairs.

We completed discharging at Calcutta and loaded there, jute and tea mainly, for home.

Owing to the war having swung very much in our favour many British civilians trapped, as it were, in Calcutta since the outbreak of war were desperate to return home. However, with most liners serving as troopships passenger berths were at a premium. The 'Malancha', in common with many other vessels, had additional passenger accommodation fitted, in her case small four berth cabins bolted to the officers' deck above the saloon. All were filled on departure from Calcutta although two passengers left a few days later at Visakhapatnam, (or Vizagapatam as it was then). They were a lady and her son of about five years of age. An archetypical 'Memsahib' she had obviously left the boy's upbringing entirely to her 'ayah' and had absolutely no control over him at all. By Vizag she had had enough and they headed back to Calcutta.

Off the south coast of Ceylon, whilst on passage from Vizagapatam to Aden, we encountered a small aircraft carrier in the early evening. The chief officer and I were on watch and when the carrier flashed the challenge signal on his lamp we replied with the answering letters of the day. The naval ship repeated the challenge and I again sent the reply as the mate hurriedly checked that we had send the correct letters. The third mate arrived on the bridge during the course of this exchange and said to the mate that the warship was apparently waiting for us to send our ship's signal letters. The mate took umbrage at this.

"We don't send our signal letters in wartime!"

"We do if challenged by a warship," replied the third mate.

These two officers did not see eye to eye on many things and the discourse became heated. With the war having been going on for over four years I thought at the time that the answer to this question would have been well known – though I will admit I did not know the answer myself.

At the height of the argument and with the carrier swinging into the wind, no doubt in preparation of sending us something more emphatic than a Morse message, the Captain came on the bridge. He took in the situation at a glance, decided it had nothing to do with him and went down for his dinner.

The argument was settled by the third mate thumping the open volume of the 'Mersigs' signal book in front of the mate's nose. The ship's signal letters were sent, the carrier went about her business and I went down for my dinner several minutes late.

I cannot remember now how many days elapsed before the mate spoke to the third mate again but I know it was quite a few.

Speaking of the third mate reminds me of another little story concerning him and also the second mate. At one stage of the voyage on testing our armament we fired off one of our parachute and cable anti-low flying enemy aircraft rockets, (P.A.C.'s). As was often the case the whole thing wrapped itself around the fore topmast and its associated radio aerials and signal halyards. The third mate went up the mast to cut the tangle free with a pair of pliers and was asked by the second mate to preserve the tin containing the lower parachute as he could find a use for it, (the upper parachute had been torn to shreds). This the third mate did and tossed the can down to the second mate standing on the hatch below. The container was caught neatly but on reading the lettering on it the second mate let out a yell and flung it over the side into the sea. Far from containing a dainty little parachute the canister held eight ounces of T.N.T.

Although in convoy in the Mediterranean we experienced an almost peace time passage before arriving at Gibraltar to join a convoy for home. We were to be commodore ship and I had the honour of escorting the commodore to the captain's cabin when he came on board. Before I left the room the commodore asked the captain if we had plenty of Very light cartridges as his staff were rather short of this commodity. The reply was that we had a full stock as the ship had replenished before leaving the U.K.

The second mate had an additional worry for the remainder of the voyage as he had fired off the entire stock on New Year's Eve. Fortunately, the Very's lights were not required.

We still held our regular gun-drills and on one occasion whilst firing at a rocket parachute several shells from one of the oerlikons rattled down onto the deck instead of winging their way into the distance as designed. Obviously the ammunition was faulty for one reason or another but whoever started the rumour that it was damp owing to its having been salvaged from H.M.S.'Ark Royal' sunk some years earlier?

After an uneventful passage from Gibraltar the 'Malancha' arrived at Avonmouth on March 9th, 1945.

Chapter 10

I signed on my next ship at Glasgow on March 24th.

She was the 'Fort Camosun', a Canadian built emergency construction vessel similar in size to the 'Samovar' but different in many respects from the layout of her accommodation to the fact that she was fuelled by coal rather than oil.

As with many wartime built ships she had been designed with the Western Ocean in view, not extended passages, so it was hardly surprising that she was a trifle short of storage space, particularly that required for food. As she carried a mainly Indian crew the situation was aggravated by the fact that their diet was different to that of the British officers. One particular difficulty was the storage of sufficient Mohamedan killed mutton for a long voyage. This problem was solved by having sheep pens constructed under the after rigging and a number of sheep carried to be despatched as rations as required. Shades of the old-time sailing ships.

The cargo of mainly military stores and equipment was again destined for the Far East – or at least as far east as one could conveniently get without running foul of the Japanese.

We left Glasgow on March 31st. but did not leave the Clyde until April 7th. as we had to await a convoy.

The 'Malancha' was commodore ship to Port Said, apparently her radar helped to make her popular in this role. From Suez ships sailed independently.

Our passage to Gibraltar coincided with what was more or less the final fling of the German U-Boats in that area. The escort vessels of the convoy were in constant touch with a number of them and generally each evening we were admonished by the commodore to 'keep well closed up' during the night as several enemy submarines were known to be closing in on the convoy.

Just as it was getting dark one evening with apparently U-Boats thick on our tail, our main engine broke down. For some hours thereafter we rolled gently in the swell whilst the engine was repaired. As I remember it was a big job concerning the low-pressure cylinder of our triple-expansion engine. Nerve-racking as was the wait on deck it must have been considerably more so in the engine-room well below the water-line. However, in the event we saw nothing of the enemy and in due course rejoined the convoy.

We four apprentices were on 'watch and watch', (four hours on and four hours off), throughout this period of the voyage. One of my colleagues had made one voyage and the other two were first trippers. One of those latter was a tall lad but the other could at most be termed a medium sized type. It was not until the ship had been to sea for some days that it was discovered that the lad, detailed to keep a sharp lookout, could not see over the dodger across the fore end of the bridge.

The 'Fort Camosun' had been built in Vancouver in 1942 and her career, although short, had not been without incident. She had been torpedoed on two separate occasions, the first time shortly after leaving Vancouver on her maiden voyage and the second time off Aden in December the following year on her third voyage. As she was therefore being torpedoed every other voyage on a regular basis we quite expected her to be clobbered again at any time as she was now on voyage number five. However, the expected torpedo did not materialise and the ship eventually ended her days peacefully in a 'knacker's yard'.

The subject of ships being torpedoed was beginning to rankle a bit with me by this time. Nearly everyone one spoke to had been torpedoed at least once. No one of course actually boasted the fact, it just seemed to crop up in conversation now and then, "Old Smithy? We were together on the old 'X.....' when she got the hammer off Madagascar," ... "Lost my gold watch when we were bumped in the Channel"...... that sort of thing. It got to be downright embarrassing – like having to admit that one had never been to bed with a woman.

Apart from occasional alarms we passed into the Mediterranean without incident. With the European war drawing to a close that part of the world was fairly quiet so the mate told the four of us to 'break watches' and to go on daywork the following morning – adding as an afterthought to me, "You will start your second year examination tomorrow morning," So much for 'time off to study'.

As it so happened this was the only yearly examination I sat as an apprentice and communications being what they were I did not receive the results until many months later. The exact wording of the examiner's remarks escape me but the gist of them was that unless I did a bit of studying I had not a snow-ball's chance in Hell of getting my second mate's certificate. This could have been very demoralising if it had not been for the fact that I received the missive just <u>after</u> I had obtained this certificate.

We arrived at Port Said on the night of April 23rd. and, after transiting the Canal, left Suez two days later. Although not in convoy we were not alone. In addition to the landing craft loaded on deck in Glasgow we were now towing two more, of the large 'Landing Craft, Tank' variety.

The ship stopped at Aden on May 2nd. for bunkers, leaving again in the evening. On re-connecting the tows of the landing craft one of them managed to get a wire around her screw but this was soon cleared and we continued our voyage to Bombay.

At this time the radio bulletins were being listened to assiduously although this was considerably hampered by poor reception.

The four of us were painting out our bathroom one morning when the mate stuck his head in the doorway. After inspecting the progress of the work for some minutes he said, in his laconic style, "Do as much as you can this morning and take the afternoon off," then, as if as an afterthought, "We have won the war."

To celebrate the occasion a couple of rounds were fired from our 4 inch gun which brought a signal from the senior officer of our two landing craft of, 'A very enlightening performance.'

All hands were given a couple of cans of beer at the Company's expense – except we apprentices of course as we were not allowed alcohol. We received a couple of bottles of lemonade in lieu – I seem to remember that they were used to extinguish a small fire which had somehow got started in the middle of our cabin table that evening. The gunners and quartermasters had looked after us very well.

Of course the war was still in progress in our theatre of operations so there was no let up on the blackout or other wartime measures.

On the evening of May 11th. we arrived off Bombay with nothing much to report apart from signals from the landing craft to the effect that cracks were appearing in their hulls. However, they were delivered safely so far as our ship was concerned.

After eighteen days, which must have been fairly uneventful as I can remember little of note, we left Bombay for Beira, Mozambique.

****

We apprentices were at a constant state of light-hearted war with the captain and one or two incidents remain in my memory.

Although the mate was our actual task-master the 'Old Man' often shoved his oar in when it came to our upbringing and was inclined to keep a very close eye on our activities.

One hot afternoon the four of us were 'soojeeing' the steel bulkheads of the captain's accommodation. Now afternoons in the tropics were sacred so far as senior officers were concerned, nearly all of whom enjoyed a siesta for an hour or two after lunch. (In passing I might mention a carpenter I once sailed with who went to the extreme of having an hour's kip himself in the afternoon in case any work he did disturbed the mate of 'Old Man'). We were therefore working very, very quietly, being within a few feet of those slumbering exalted beings. In truth I suppose we were hardly working at all.

Suddenly the captain was in our midst, having noiselessly slipped out of his room onto the deck.

Minutes later we were washing paint with considerable gusto. In fact, with much more enthusiasm than the heat of the day justified. It was not a pace we could keep up for long but we were in no doubt that at any moment the Old Man would be paying us a return visit. The problem was solved by placing one of our buckets of water right under the storm-step of the door. About twenty minutes later four very concerned and apologetic apprentices were helping the captain to extricate his foot from the bucket.

A pair of us were once given the task of painting out the captain's bathroom. We knew the 'Old Man' would be on our tails so would have to make a good job of it.

The bathroom deck was tiled but everything else had to be painted, bulkheads, deckhead, door, outside of bath and what appeared to be half of the ship's pipework rendezvousing in that small room.

We cleaned the place before breakfast and commenced painting directly after the meal. Our brushes were worn in and the tins of eau-de-nil paint brand new so we encountered no trouble in this direction. When we finished the job just before dinner that evening even the captain, after a very thorough inspection, could find no fault. We had even painted the side of the bath next to the bulkhead where no brush had been before.

"Right," said the captain before dismissing us, "You can put the second coat on tomorrow."

This job was not anticipated with any degree of pleasure as applying a second coat of paint to a brand new coat of exactly the same colour was simply asking for 'holidays' and runs.

The store-keeper had obviously been got at by the mate before we arrived to collect our equipment the following morning. The paint was old and full of bits of skin and other rubbish – possibly the excuse was that we had been given new stock by mistake the previous day. On the other hand the brushes were brand new, straight from the mate's 'fog-locker', unused and unsoaked so would moult like shaggy black dogs the moment they were applied to the paintwork. Of course all the other brushes were in use by the crew. It was a problem but not insurmountable.

On arrival we placed a can of paint against the bathroom door as a precaution against any sudden appearances of the captain or mate then applied a few streaks of paint to such places as the edge of the door, under the rim of the bath and at the back of one or two pipes where an inspector would most likely test for sticky paint. Then, remembering to make a few 'working noises' now and then, we made ourselves as comfortable as we could and perused the literature we had secreted under our shirts.

We got away with this one.

On another occasion the four of us were given the task of painting out the dining saloon – we seemed to be often involved with interior decorating on that particular ship.

The job was started by painting the intricate parts such as the deckhead with its wiring and pipework and around the ports leaving the expanses of bulkheads to have their paint slapped on last. From a point view of area covered therefore by late afternoon there appeared to be not a great deal done. At least that was the opinion of the captain and mate when they came to inspect our handiwork after their afternoon tea. We were therefore instructed to continue the painting after the evening meal.

We came in for a fair bit of ribbing from the engineers when they saw us turning to after dinner so to put a brave face on it we went back to the saloon over the tops of the bunker hatches in line ahead singing "Heigh Ho! Heigh Ho! it's off to work we go," with the small apprentice bringing up in the rear with his paint pot attached to a stick over his shoulder. However, I do not think the 'Old Man' saw the humour of it when he happened to drift out on deck after his meal.

The painting was resumed just before seven o'clock and I anticipated that when the mate came off watch at eight he would knock us off.

During the war privately owned radios were not taken to sea as they radiated some kind of signal which could be picked up by the enemy. Our 'domestic' radio contact with the outside world was therefore supplied by a set named, as I recall, an 'M.N.100', which was apparently quite safe in this respect. On the 'Fort Camosun' this instrument was located in the dining saloon and had loud speakers led from it to various other parts of the ship such as the engineer's messroom, the captain's dayroom and so forth.

Whilst painting some slight comfort was derived from music on the radio initially but after an hour or so the music programme ended and it was announced that the BBC news or some such was about to begin. This did not suit our scheme of things so I sat down and twiddled the knobs of the set in an attempt to raise more music. It proved a futile pursuit and I was about to acquaint my mates of the fact when I noticed how quiet everything had become. From the corner of my eye I could see one lad slapping paint onto a bulkhead as if his life depended on it and sounds from just outside my range of vision indicated that the other two were similarly employed. The reason was almost self-evident. Sure enough, standing right behind me was a very irate captain.

I finished painting the saloon in the early hours of the morning. You can't win them all.

There must have been a good reason for the ship to visit South Africa but all I can recall of cargo is that we may have loaded some sugar at one port or another and I am far from certain of that. No doubt I had other things on my mind.

The ship arrived at Beira on June 11th. and spent eight days there before proceeding to Durban for the last week in June.

Needless to say we had a glorious time in Durban thoroughly enjoying the South African hospitality. Several of the officers fell in love with local girls, the worst afflicted as I remember being the two junior radio officers – we could get very little sense out of them for the remainder of the voyage.

Before leaving Durban we shifted to the coal berths on the Bluff for bunkers. This proved a very dirty job and in spite of the mate having the whole bridge structure covered with tarpaulins the coal dust penetrated everywhere.

From Durban we went to Cape Town for another few delightful days then we were off for Freetown and home.

I do not recall what justified our Freetown stop although I know we did have a few bags of mail for the place from Cape Town. My main memories of Freetown are of heat, the fact that I was just about crippled by a bunch of boils on my left leg, (my calf still carries the scars), and that I had my wallet stolen – though it is extremely unlikely that it contained any money.

On the lighter side we did get one laugh from, of all things, quinine. Although medicines with patent names were becoming available in the fight against malaria our ship was still supplied with the old-fashioned quinine tablets.

I had been given enough tablets for the four of us and, being familiar with the brutes, warned my mates to ensure that they got them down in one swallow. We left a note for the lad on watch to make sure he took his tablets before turning in. Inevitably someone added a footnote, 'Make sure you chew the tablets up well before swallowing.'

I have been rudely awakened by some pretty awful noises over the years but never by such a blood-curdling shriek as issued from the throat of the lad who chewed quinine.

****

It was odd to observe the ships all lit up at sea as we proceeded northward. Although the Pacific War still raged the European one had been over for months. One of the jobs we apprentices were given was to remove the blackout curtains from alleyways and doors. This resulted in a tremendous improvement in ventilation.

On more than one occasion I have been informed by officers who obtained their early watch-keeping experience during the war that the sudden appearance of navigation lights at the end of hostilities was not always viewed with relief. It would appear that after years of staring into darkness watching out for the vague form of a ship or the whiteness of her bow wave before taking any necessary avoiding action it was rather disconcerting to observe a ship's lights ten miles ahead and enduring a, quote, 'nerve-racking half hour or so before the vessel was safely past.' No doubt they soon got used to it.

****

Home grown fruit was more or less the only type available in Britain during the war although the odd ship did collect a cargo of oranges or the like on her way home from a theatre of conflict. At Gibraltar once we heard that some person of evil intent had secreted a time-bomb in a crate of oranges destined for the U.K. Fortunately the infernal device happened to be stowed in the centre of the hold rather than close to the ship's side as intended and the story goes that pure orange juice was collected in buckets held under the ship's bilge discharge.

Whenever possible ships purchased fruit for their stores abroad and I remember one occasion when ashore at Newport one of my companions taking an orange from his pockets and giving it to a small boy who was playing in the street. One or two of his pals gathered round him but were obviously as baffled as the proud owner as to how the mysterious object should be tackled. When last seen one of the boys was tentatively nibbling the skin.

The lads living near the Manchester Ship Canal were more organised. Whenever a ship passed in from the sea there were shouts of "Throw us an orange mister!" from the gangs of lads running along the banks. Should an orange or other fruit be thrown there was an immediate mad scramble down the steep bank to retrieve it. I have often wondered how many of the boys fell into the canal following this dangerous practice.

Bananas are tricky things to carry at sea, even with the most modern machinery – as many a grey-haired 'banana-boat' chief officer will testify. Without the correctly controlled conditions it is virtually impossible to transport them for more than a few days. Nevertheless, it was attempted by many of our officers at Freetown. Most of them bought a stalk of bananas, (not the apprentices of course, we did not have that kind of money), and each had his own private theory as to how best to preserve them. There were bananas in refrigerators, bananas dangling from awning spars, bananas hanging in engine room ventilators and the shaft tunnel. Officer's cabins and alleyways all contained their quotas of bananas.

For a day or two all was well then one or two bananas became over ripe and were carefully removed and disposed of. Soon others went the same way, singly at first then by the half dozen. More and more became over ripe and it was early estimated that not more than half would reach port. This was shortly modified to a quarter then to 'just a few'.

In the event I believe that none of the fruit survived to reach anyone's home. However, all was not lost, we apprentices became absolutely gorged on ripe bananas.

The 'Fort Camosun' arrived in the Mersey in early August and proceeded up the canal to Manchester.

It was at one of the Manchester Ship Canal locks that a newspaper was passed up to us on 'stations' on the poop from a tug. It made front page news of the fact that the Americans had dropped a bomb on some unheard of Japanese city, a bomb which was a hundred times more powerful than the biggest RAF 'blockbuster'.

'Usual Yankee bull', was the almost unanimous verdict.

The ship paid off at Manchester on August 9th. 1945, the day the second atomic bomb was dropped. Most of the crowd were relieved on arrival but I was retained on board for several days.

The end of the war against Japan was celebrated before I left the ship. Actually I personally did little celebrating as I was left to look after the vessel whilst my elders and betters attended to the social life of things ashore. By the time I did get ashore there was not a drop of beer available in the whole of Manchester, (I did partake of the odd glass by this time).

Eventually I went on leave and after a few days received a letter from the Company to the effect that on going through my record they found that I had served enough 'sea-time' to enable me to sit for my second mate's certificate and what action was I taking?

It would appear that my boy-hood was over and it was high time I started to take a more responsible attitude to life. True enough I suppose as I was nearly nineteen years old.

EPILOGUE

Of all the people I sailed with during the war only a few did I sail with again in later years – although I met quite a number at different times. Most of us initially drifted off to pastures new, some retired, some died. Even the company itself slowly faded from the scene – after more than two hundred years of trading. Ginger left the company after obtaining his second mate's 'ticket' but suddenly and briefly re-entered my life when he boarded my ship as a Singapore pilot more than twenty years later.

As for the ships; I last saw the 'Masirah' in Bidston Dock, Birkenhead, in 1952. She had just undergone something in the way of a refit and I was appointed to her as 'officer in charge' whilst the repairs were completed and bunkers taken – 1700 tons of very dusty coal. Although then thirty-three years old she traded for several more years.

The 'Samovar' I rejoined as third mate shortly after getting my 'ticket' and made two voyages on her before she was sold in May 1947.

Although I never again sailed deep-sea on the 'Malancha' I was relieving on her when she was sold in February 1962 at Birkenhead. Although the new owners were sending her out to Taiwan for scrapping they intended her to pick up a cargo of sugar at Cuba en route. Thus stowage, drafts and fuel and fresh water requirements had to be calculated. I was asked to do this and before leaving the ship was given the clock and barometer from the mate's room as an appreciation. They still operate perfectly after well over fifty years of continuous service.

The 'Fort Camosun' was sold out of the company shortly after the war and I never saw her again.

25.4.1989

'MASIRAH' (Voyages 1 2 + 3)
1942 - 1943

Captain 'Harry' Armstrong (1)   Capt Exley (2+3)
C/O 'Silas' Hosking
2/O Sid Turner
3/O Ian MacClaren (1) 'Plato' Harrison (2+3)
C/E Iliffe (not sure which one)
2/E Brady
3/E Dick Blakey
4/E Rudas
5/E Stevens
C/S Garnet ~ Thomas
?/R/O Tommy Williams ~ Don Butterworth
2/R/O Arthur Oxcum
3/R/O A? Martin
Apprentices: 'Blondie' Greenhaugh, 'Ginger' Watterson
Sam Baxter. ~ then Alan 'Ginger' Watterson,
S. Baxter + one Jones.
Carpenter: Glass
QMs, Matt Miller : S. Parry, Foreman +
'old Rabley' Robinson (Robertson?)
Gunner Dick Williams.

592

<u>SAMOVAR</u> 1943-1944

Capt. Harald Scoins ('Scunsy Bill') + Sid Slade
¹/o Len 'Leo' Jones.
²/o 'Crikey' Mannis ~ Hempsey
³/o G. Greenhaugh ~ Watterson ~ Geof Kenyon
⁴/E 'Andy' Malkie
²/E 'Bud' Taylor
³/E 'Lakri' Wood
⁴/E Bill Connar
⁵/E Bruce.

C/RO: Tommy Williams 2/R/o Ken Bibby 3Ro 'Tiger' Bernard
C/s Jimmy Kehoe
Abbs Watterson, Baxter // Baxter, D. Dodd,
  W. Bailey

ABOUT THE AUTHOR

Born in County Durham in 1926 and growing up in Folkestone, Stanley Baxter, known as Sam, started his career at the young age of 16 with T&J Brocklebank, Liverpool. He continued his career within the company reaching Master in the 1960s.

He left the sea and retired from a subsidiary of The Canadian Pacific at age 58 and enjoyed a long and happy retirement in North Wales with his family.

Printed in Great Britain
by Amazon